LOKANT

CHARLOTTE E. ENGLISH

For Zoltan

GLOSSARY OF TERMS

Arvale: An ancient draykoni name for the realm now known as Glinnery.

Ayrien: An ancient draykoni name for the Lower Realms.

Cayluch: A hearty beverage made from milk, cream, cocoa beans and coffee. Typically enjoyed steaming hot.

Daefly: Insects with small, thin bodies and enormous coloured wings. Feeding on flower nectar, daeflies are instrumental in the pollination process.

Darklands: It is always night in the Darklands provinces of the Seven Realms. During the day, sorcerers use a powerful enchantment called the Night Cloak to block out the light and keep the sun from damaging the eyes of its residents, or the plants brought from the permanently dark Lower Realms.

Day Cloak: A magical enchantment wrought by sorcerers which keeps the Daylands permanently in sunlight (or something like it). This ensures that sun-loving plants and animals native to the Upper Realms may thrive across the Daylands, too.

Daylands: In the Daylands provinces, night never falls. When the sun goes down, sorcerers create an artificial daylight effect called the Day Cloak, less powerful than full sunlight but sufficient to keep light-loving plants and animals content. Daylands realms include Glinnery and Irbel.

Desente bird: A large, dark bird with purple feathers and keen eyesight. Desentes have such enormous wings they can stay aloft for up to eighteen hours without landing.

Drauk: These reptiles are adaptable and can live in

most Daylands environments. They are usually black-scaled, with wickedly sharp claws and long, thin necks and tails.

Draykon: The largest and most fearsome species known to the Seven Realms. Draykons are reptilian, with scaled hide of various colours as well as long tails, claws and vast webbed wings. They are as intelligent as humans and can shape-shift.

Evenglow: Glinnery term for the Day Cloaked hours, when the strong natural sunlight gives way to the more muted light of the enchantment.

Everum: An ancient draykon name for Glour.

Glissenwol: Native to the realm of Glinnery, the glissenwol tree is taller than most other species, with a broad, sturdy trunk and a wide cap instead of branches and leaves.

Glostrel trees: Graceful, slender-branched trees with silvery bark and wide, white leaves. These grow in abundance across Glour, and in some parts of Orstwych and Ullarn.

Irignol trees: Leafless trees with black, frondy bark and very dark brown wood. These form symbiotic relationships with a species of pale silvery-green lichen. They can grow to great heights, and their trunks and branches become ever more contorted with age.

Irilapter: These tiny winged creatures have long, thin bodies covered with fur and comparatively large wings similar to those of a daefly. A typical irilapter will have a long, curled tail and a similarly long, curled proboscis, plus far more riotous colour in its small form than ought to belong to a single creature.

Irtand: Draykon name for the "Middles" or the Seven Realms.

Iskyr: An ancient draykoni word for the place now more commonly called The Upper Realms.

Istore: Named by Llandry Sanfaer, Istore is an indigo-coloured gemstone with a silver shine.

Lokant: A word meaning "Librarian" in an ancient tongue.

Lower Realms: Existing as an adjacent plane to the Seven Realms, the Uppers are so-called because they are believed to be situated somewhere beyond the ground. There is no sun in the Lowers, and as such it is always dark—though there are multiple moons which sometimes change colour. This place is notoriously unstable and difficult to navigate, as the geographical layout and scenery are in a state of constant flux. The Lower Realms may be reached by opening a gate between the two worlds.

Night Cloak: A magical enchantment wrought by sorcerers which cloaks the Darklands in shadow, keeping the sunlight away from the delicate and night-loving plants and animals cultivated by its citizens.

Nivven: The most popular mount across the Seven Realms, the nivven is a tall beast with four long, powerful legs and a graceful stride. Their scaled hides range in colour from pearly grey to dark brown. Nivvens are herbivorous and pacifistic in nature, making them ideal beasts of burden.

Meerel: Tiny woodland beasts with brown fur and long whiskers, noses and tails. They eat fruit and nuts and typically live in nests built of woven grass.

Muumuk: A huge, heavy, slow-moving creature, omnivorous, its hide the colour of polished bronze. Muumuks have poor eyesight but much keener hearing with their enormous ears.

Nara-fruit: A juicy fruit with pink skin and flesh,

grown in Glinnery.

Off-Worlds: A term used to refer to all those worlds (the Upper and Lower Realms) which are not part of the mainland and can only be reached via magical travel.

Orboe: A large beast more than six feet long from nose to tail. Orboes are shaggy-furred, ranging in colour from cream to grey to black, with tiny ears and massive jaws. They walk on all fours and can run at amazing speeds given their size and weight.

Orting: A small mammal with pale grey fur, short ears and a short tail. The orting is a friendly, herbivorous species native to the Upper Realms.

PsiMap: A magical construct useable by Lokants to locate, and subsequently travel to, any part of the world(s).

PsiTravel: A Lokant technology allowing their kind to cross large distances almost instantaneously.

Shortig hound: A small but energetic dog celebrated for its tracking abilities. Shortigs are black-furred, with long ears and large noses. They can be difficult to befriend, but are capable of great loyalty.

Tayn wood: A pale wood from the tayn trees of Irbel. Tayn is the hardest and strongest wood known to the Seven Realms, and as such is popularly used for buildings and machinery.

Upper Realms: Existing as an adjacent plane to the Seven Realms, the Uppers are so-called because they are believed to be situated somewhere behind the sky. Multiple suns shine down on the Upper Realms, ensuring that it is always light. This place is notoriously unstable and difficult to navigate, as the geographical layout and scenery are in a state of constant flux. The Upper Realms may be reached by opening a gate between the two worlds.

Whistworm: A fat worm, native to the Lowers, that climbs the stems of tall plants and feeds off tiny insects. They are an unwholesome yellow in colour and lightly furred.

Whurthag: A fearsome beast from the Lower Realms, long since banned as summoner companions. Whurthags are large, muscular and very aggressive, with night-black hide and vicious claws and teeth. They are adept at stalking prey, their black hide all but invisible in Darklands provinces.

Worvillo: Aggressive pack animals with long legs, shaggy grey or black fur and a sensitive sense of smell. They hunt their prey over long distances, shrieking chilling hunting-calls when in the fever of the chase.

CHAPTER ONE

The moon was barely up when the post carrier arrived, bearing a parcel so large that the driver struggled to lift it. In the graceful, distinctive script of the address, Lady Evastany Glostrum recognised the elegant handwriting of her friend Ynara Sanfaer. She waved the postman inside and signed the paperwork with a smile, though she felt considerably puzzled.

She had recently dispatched a letter to Elder Sanfaer, requesting an urgent meeting. Ynara lived in Glinnery, a Daylands province where darkness never came. Herself a resident of the Darklands, Eva could not comfortably travel to Glinnery; her largely nocturnal eyes could not bear the glare of the sun. As such, she had expected Ynara to come to her.

Instead her friend had sent a parcel. It took Eva some minutes of work with a pair of scissors to open the well-packed box, and then subsequently to work her way through the packaging that shrouded the contents. At length she lifted out a completely unidentifiable contraption made from metal and glass, finding no accompanying letter of explanation along with it.

She turned the thing over in her hands, puzzling. It was bulky, though not particularly large. Two rounded pieces of glass adorned what could be the front; behind them lay several other similarly sized pieces, though their shapes varied. They vaguely resembled spectacles, though of no variant Eva had ever seen before.

That thought sparked off an idea. Hadn't there been reports of new developments in spectacle technology? She had heard of glasses—goggles, really—that could fully protect a Darklander's eyes against the sun. Ynara's husband was a prominent engineer; small wonder if he had been involved in this project.

She tried them on. It took a little adjusting to fit the headgear correctly, but at length the pieces slid into place and the goggles clamped firmly over her eyes, instantly smothering all light.

Eva blinked in the sudden complete darkness. Well, so far so good. They were certainly good at blocking out light. On the other hand, the headset was heavy: already her neck was beginning to hurt. Eva took the thing off with a grimace. Presumably Aysun Sanfaer intended to refine the idea somewhat before it went into production for general distribution.

In other circumstances, the prospect of freely wandering the Daylands would have delighted her. She had seen very little of Glinnery and nothing at all of Irbel. Nothing either of Orlind, though nobody could claim to have visited that distant, untouchable realm. She couldn't even visit Nimdre; it was the only one of the six accessible realms that retained an ordinary day-night cycle, enjoying too many hours of full daylight for the comfort of Darklander vision. As a worldly woman fond of travel, the prospect of seeing the Daylands was attractive.

But the timing was, to say the least, unfavourable. She had returned to her home in Glour City less than a moon ago, and duties and obligations crowded upon her. She had neglected her role as High Summoner for many days while she hunted a criminal with one of the Chief Investigator's men. Her possession of two skilled tracking companions—a shortig hound and a web-winged gwaystrel—had made her instrumental to the task, but she had been hard-pressed to catch up on her duties on her return. And she had had very little time to address some important questions that had been raised on the journey.

But Ynara was worried about her daughter. Only a couple of moons ago, Llandry Sanfaer had accidentally discovered an unusual gemstone which she had named *Istore* after the stars. That stone had captured the attention of thousands of people all the way across the Seven Realms, and eventually it had led to thefts and even murders. Llandry herself had been inevitably caught up in the affair; she had journeyed secretly into Nimdre with a friend of her mother's and there she had disappeared. Eva was one of only two people who knew what had happened to Llandry. If Ynara would not, or could not, come to her, then she must go to Ynara. She owed it to her friend.

Eva's carriage conveyed her only as far as the border

between Glinnery and Glour, a journey of some ten hours. Few carriage-ready roads wound through the dense forests of Glinnery: since the residents held the benefit of wings, they had little use for carriages. Eva disembarked with a sigh: she had never been one to relish the prospect of a long walk.

Luckily for her, the Sanfaers lived in the capital city, Waeverleyne, a mere few hours' walk from the border—though it felt like a much longer trek to Eva's pampered physique, not used to strenuous walking or to the heat of the sun. The beauty of her surroundings occupied her mind for a time as she walked through Glinnery's famed glissenwol woods. Could these shades of blue and green and lavender, so vivid and bright, truly be real? Or were they enhanced by the lenses of the headgear that she wore? She was entranced by the soft blue moss and the fronded purple-leaved ferns, the glitter of dayflies in the air and the fragrances of sun-warmed blossoms.

At least until the discomfort in her feet and legs reminded her of the wearisome toil of the adventure. Recently she'd been obliged to do a lot of walking, pursuing Edwae Geslin overland with her tracker hound. If anything, that only made this episode harder, for she was already tired. She trudged along in a state of intolerable dishevelment, her hair blown out of its pins by the wind and her cotton gown sticking unpleasantly to her skin. When at last she reached Ynara's home she took the opportunity to pause and admire the property... and perhaps to catch her breath and smooth her hair while she was at it.

The Sanfaer home was situated close to the edge of the city. In Glour this position might have indicated a lower status, but what mattered more in

Glinnery was the height of the glissenwol tree in which the dwelling was situated, and the extent of the expansion around the trunk. Ynara's home was magnificent: her family had three storeys spanning from the middle of a vast glissenwol trunk up to the top. Seeking a way in, Eva observed a staircase winding its way up the tree. That made sense, for Ynara's husband Aysun did not have wings like his wife and daughter.

The staircase was blocked, which was not particularly surprising. For some weeks now both the Daylands and the Darklands had been plagued with beasts in unusual numbers, all crossing over from the Upper Realms or the Lowers. Rogue gates leading to these two Off-Worlds had been appearing too regularly, letting all manner of creatures through. The staircase served as easy passage up to the Sanfaer home, but that was no longer desirable when it invited aggressive visitors. For her, though, its deactivation was mightily inconvenient. She sat down in the dark blue moss, tired after her journey, her head bowed under the weight of the curious headset. How should she signal her arrival to Ynara? And how was she to reach the house?

She had not been waiting long before Ynara appeared on the balcony of her home. She was a long way up, but Eva had no difficulty recognising her slender frame and mass of dark hair. She waved and took flight, her dark blue wings rapidly carrying her down to Eva's level.

Her greeting was friendly, though her anxiety showed in her face. 'I'm so grateful to you for coming,' she said warmly. 'I can't leave the house, you see, not for days at a time. In case Llandry comes home. Here.' She walked around the base of her tree, motioning Eva to follow. At the rear, a switch of grey metal was set into the trunk, camouflaged against the glissenwol's smooth bark. Ynara pulled it sharply and a clanking sound began somewhere above. As Eva watched, impressed, a large box descended slowly from the skies. When it reached ground level it stopped, and doors opened smoothly in the front.

'Aysun's latest creation,' Ynara explained, stepping inside. 'They use them all the time in Irbel, but here we only have a few for hauling freight up to the heights. He fitted this when the beasts began surging through.'

'Ingenious,' Eva remarked, watching with interest as Ynara operated another lever. The box lurched slightly as it began to rise, and Eva was obliged to grab hold of a railing that ran around the inside. After that though the ride was remarkably smooth. It stopped adjacent to Ynara's balcony and the doors opened again. Ynara ushered Eva into the house and immediately turned to the windows. She closed shutters and drew curtains from one room to another until the whole building was dark.

'I thought you may wish to take those off once you got here,' said Ynara, indicating the cumbersome spectacles Eva wore. 'They're functional, but not yet conveniently portable.'

'Thank you,' Eva said with real gratitude. She took them off with alacrity, pleased to find that the light levels were comfortable for her eyes. To Ynara, though, it must be pitch darkness.

'Won't this be an inconvenience to you?'

Ynara smiled briefly. 'Not too much. I can still hear you.'

Eva nodded absent-mindedly, then caught herself. 'Of course,' she said, following her friend to the kitchen. Ynara had a light-globe in this room, a silvery ball of soft light which she had set to hover near the stove. Eva shut her eyes until Ynara had finished preparing food, then the light dimmed. Ynara sat opposite, pushing plates of food and drink at her.

Eva sat down, accepting Ynara's offerings gratefully. As she ate, her attention was caught by shadowy movement in the corner of the room. A padded basket rested there and a small grey-furred creature was curled inside. It stretched out its long, thin body, its stubby tail twitching. Then it resumed its slumber.

'That is Llandry's pet,' Ynara said. 'Sigwide was left behind, somehow, when Llandry disappeared. That alone frightens me inordinately: those two have been inseparable since Llan was nine years old. She would never leave him behind deliberately. And he is depressed—he does nothing but sleep. I can't decide whether he merely misses Llan, or whether he knows that she isn't coming back...'

Eva's heart twisted at the look of anguish on her friend's face. She pushed away the food—she could eat later—and searched for a way to begin. On her way to Glinnery she had spent hours rehearsing what she would say to her friend. How could she break such news lightly? Normally comfortably eloquent, Eva found herself at a loss for words.

'In my letter I assured you that Llandry was not injured,' she began. 'That is perfectly true. The last time I saw her she was in good health. But she has been... she has been changed.'

'She's *been* changed?' Ynara echoed. 'By what? Or

who?' She was gripping the table.

Eva sighed. 'I'm just going to tell you everything that happened. From the beginning.' She began, talking slowly and clearly through her experiences of the last few weeks. She spoke of the hunt for the reluctant criminal Edwae Geslin, whose sorcerer friend Tren had been obliged to aid in his capture. When she talked of their journey into the perilous Lower Realms, Ynara said nothing. But when Eva spoke the name "draykon", Ynara blanched.

'Draykon,' she whispered. Eva had expected her to be surprised, but she did not seem to be. Instead she was aghast, electrified.

Eva cast her a quizzical look. 'Have you heard something of it already?' The common belief was that the mythical draykons, beasts with scaled hide and vast wings, were nothing more than legend. But Ynara did not look doubtful. As a member of Glinnery's ruling Council, perhaps she had received reports from Glour.

'I've seen one,' Ynara said with studied calm. 'Or in fact, I have heard one. So I believe. Finish your tale, if you please, and I will tell you mine.'

Eva blinked. 'I... yes. Very well.' She went on, describing the two uncanny sorcerer-summoners she and Tren had encountered. Eva had been brought up to believe that those blessed with magical ability were skilled either as summoners, those with a connection to beast kind, or sorcerers, whose talents included skilled manipulation of light and air. She had never heard of anybody possessing strong talents in both areas; not until now. She and Tren had discovered two apparent dual practitioners—the same two who had stolen and killed for the mysterious Istore stone.

Ynara listened raptly as Eva related how Ana and Griel—both from the Darklands realm of Ullarn, or so Eva suspected—had sought to wake a draykon.

'For the stone that Llandry called *Istore* is not a gem at all, clearly not. She actually discovered the grave of a long-dead draykon. Those stones are draykon bones. You'll have heard the legends.'

Ynara nodded. Many of the stories about draykons were not commonly known anymore; they had disappeared from the realms far too long ago. They were the stuff of long-buried books and obscure theses. Ynara, however, was a sorcerer herself and a highly educated woman. She would know that the draykon was said to be the most powerful creature in the realms, that they were vast, unstoppable beasts. She would also have heard that they were extinct, if they had ever truly existed. Eva herself had been sceptical on that score until recently, but Ynara was speedily convinced. Had she truly heard the draykon?

'I am aware of the end to your tale, though without the details,' said Ynara. 'I can guess that the bones must have been reassembled and the draykon successfully restored to life, though I cannot imagine how. What I do not grasp is how Llandry is involved.'

Eva winced inwardly. Now came the most difficult part of this conversation.

'It's hard to know how to explain this to you when I barely understand it myself,' Eva began. 'But I think you may have seen Llandry more recently than I have.' She recounted the finale to her tale. She and Tren had been in the night-shrouded Lower Realm, but when Eva had been in physical contact with the waking draykon, she'd seen straight through the fabric of the worlds: into the Middle realms where most of humankind lived, and further, all the way into the sun-drenched Uppers. She'd realised that the separations between those realms were far flimsier than was readily supposed. She'd seen Llandry Sanfaer kneeling in the moss of the Upper Realm, sunlight glinting off her deep black hair.

Moments later, Llandry had been pulled bodily through the layers into the Lower Realms. The experience had obviously been painful for her: watching Ynara's quiet daughter screaming in pain had been deeply distressing.

Then she had changed. Her small, winged human body had stretched, expanded and ultimately transformed; when the process was complete, a second, smaller draykon had joined the first. Eva had only been able to watch as they flew into the skies and then, abruptly, vanished.

Silence fell as Eva finished her story. Ynara appeared to be unable to speak at all. At last she managed, 'How is that possible?'

'I don't know,' Eva said honestly.

'Was she—was she changed by those two...?'

'No. It was certainly no part of their plan. If Ana had been able to effect such a transformation, she would have turned herself into a draykon. Her plan was actually to dominate it, to make it her companion. She, and her husband Griel, were obviously as astonished as we were. Personally I do not believe it was effected from outside at all. It had more to do with Llandry herself.'

'You think she did that to *herself*?'

'Not exactly. Not consciously anyway. I think it was inherent within her and brought forward because of her proximity to the other draykon. Otherwise why was she alone metamorphosed? Why not me? Why not Ana?'

Ynara nodded, more out of habit than real understanding as her face revealed a profound confusion. 'Her proximity? But she was in the Uppers, wasn't she? That is a completely different world.'

'I don't think that it is. Our three "worlds" are much closer to each other than we ever realised. They're virtually sharing the same space. I think she felt the draykon waking from the Uppers, and she was drawn to it. And she herself may have inadvertently aided the process by her presence.' Eva shrugged. 'Without speaking to Llandry herself, though, I can't be sure about any of this.'

'Several days ago Aysun and I heard a terrific cry from somewhere overhead,' Ynara said slowly. 'It was like nothing I'd heard before. We ran outside, but there was nothing to be seen. Except for Dev, lying injured outside my house.'

'Dev?'

'I mentioned him to you before, though not by name. He is an old friend of mine. Llandry went with him to Nimdre, though without his knowledge. He says they were attacked, and he was wounded trying to defend Llandry. Since he arrived—or I should say, appeared—he has been raving about beasts the size of houses and being carried here by one of them. I thought he was delirious. But I cannot disbelieve you.' Ynara sighed, her head drooping with tiredness. 'So Llan found Devary and brought him here. Then— what? She vanished again.'

'I don't believe anybody knows where Llandry is now. I'm sorry. I wish I had more information to give you on that point.'

Ynara gripped her hand. 'Don't apologise. You can't know how much I appreciate your coming here to tell me these things. Though I don't deny they are hard to hear. How can I even begin to believe that my daughter is not—not human?'

'Oh, she is,' said Eva. 'She's both.'

Devary Kant was abed in Ynara's house. His wounds were evidently severe, though he suffered no delirium. He glanced only briefly at Eva, then fixed his dull gaze on Ynara as she relayed the news to him.

'That was Llandry?' His words emerged weakly, and when he tried to sit up he gasped and fell back.

'Don't try to move, Dev,' said Ynara wearily. 'Apparently it was, yes. She saved your life, I think.'

Devary said nothing. His gaze had returned to Eva's face, and he frowned slightly.

'Eva Glostrum,' she said. 'From Glour.' It was probably too dark for him to see her clearly, but he continued to try.

She, on the other hand, could see him quite well. Her sharp night eyes filled in strongly defined, Nimdren features, a long, thin nose and Darklands-pale skin. Under normal circumstances his hair must be a fairly light shade of brown, though at present it was splayed out on his pillow, dark with the sweat of fever.

Ynara leaned forward. 'Dev, it seems you were the last person to see the draykon. Llandry, if it was her. Do you remember where she went?'

'There were two beasts. Two draykons, then. I thought they vanished, but I may have been hallucinating.'

'Probably you were not,' Eva put in. 'I have seen them do the same thing. I think they can cross between worlds without needing to open gates.'

'Then my Llandry—if it was my Llandry—could be anywhere. Anywhere in the worlds.' Ynara fell silent, but Eva could hear her unsettled breathing as she struggled to master her emotion.

Devary bestirred himself enough to grip Ynara's hand. 'When I'm well,' he said with difficulty, 'I will find her. I promise it.'

Ynara gave him a stare of disdain. 'My husband will bring her home.'

'Aysun has gone after her?' Eva was surprised at that. She had heard something before of the deep suspicion he held for the Upper Realm.

Ynara nodded. 'Nearly two weeks ago. He said he won't come home until he can bring Llan with him.'

This was poor news. She had counted on Ynara's having her husband's support as she waited for her daughter to come home. Instead, her friend had been alone all this time, and in a state of anxiety about both members of her family.

'I'm sorry, Ynara,' she said with real regret. 'I wish I could stay until Llan returns to you, but I can't.'

Ynara tried a smile. 'I know. I understand. Thank you for coming to me now.'

Eva nodded, unsure of what else to say.

'I'll be here,' said Devary.

'You're the one who lost her!' The words burst from Ynara as if she couldn't hold them back anymore. She swept a hand over her face, dashing away the dampness that glittered on her cheeks.

'I'm sorry,' Devary said, watching helplessly as

Ynara fought to regain her composure. 'I'm sorry.'

Eva stayed as long as she could with Ynara, but she knew it wasn't enough. It took all of her will to leave her friend alone again after a mere day's stay, but she knew she had no choice. She began the walk back to the border with grave reluctance.

Yna's strong, she told herself. *Strong enough for this.*
As long as Llandry comes back.

CHAPTER TWO

Mr. Pitren Warvel—Tren, to his many friends—sat alone and disconsolate in the vast library of Glour City. To be precise, he was sitting in a small reading chamber reserved for those with official access to Glour's hidden store of books: those texts deemed inappropriate for general public borrowing. Fat, musty tomes were stacked in towering piles around his desk, concealing him behind a wall of knowledge. It felt appropriate, for instead of mastering that mountain of academic records and theses, he had been smothered by it.

Sighing, Tren pushed back his chair and turned his head from side to side, trying to loosen the tension in his neck. Two weeks of work, and he, the experienced scholar and able student, had found virtually nothing about the draykons of the past. So little had he uncovered, in fact, that he would be inclined to categorise them as mere legend—if he had not recently seen two such beasts with his own eyes.

The whole experience was intensely dispiriting.

Lady Glostrum herself had arranged access to this collection; it was not something a young sorcerer like himself could expect to receive without patronage. The fact that she had assigned the research to him was proof of her faith in his ability, and he had failed. If there was any relevant information within this hidden library, he couldn't find it.

He plucked absently at the cuffs of his shirt, dissatisfied. His clothes were shabby, his hair unbrushed and he was covered in book dust from head to foot. For two weeks he had barely slept or eaten, aware of the urgency of his task. That dedication having availed him nothing, perhaps it was time to go home and attend to his own comfort. The prospect was a tempting one, but he resisted. He wanted to see Lady Glostrum, and without something to report he felt that he could not impose on her. His pride would not allow it.

She, of course, seemed to have no particular desire to see him. A few weeks had passed since their excursion to the Lowers; three weeks since the draykons had risen and subsequently vanished. He had assisted her in making her reports to Glour's government—she felt that she needed his corroboration in order to be believed, though he doubted it—and that was the last time he had seen her. Since then he had been locked in here moonrise to moonset and he had neither seen nor heard from her. The reflection hurt. Did she remember to think of him, wherever she was? Doubtful. She was a peer of the realm and a member of the government; she had many more important things to think about.

'That's enough,' he muttered, dismissing the negative reflections from his thoughts. He bent his head once more over the book that lay before him, but as he readied his pen for the note-taking he heard the scrape of a key in the door and somebody's footsteps rang on the stone floor. Somebody female, he concluded, and felt a surge of hope.

'Tren?' Eva's voice. He felt a momentary wild happiness which quickly deteriorated into dismay. He had nothing to give her, nothing to show for his efforts. She must undoubtedly conclude that he was useless for the task at hand, just as he had been useless in the Lowers. For an instant he entertained absurd notions of concealing himself from her and somehow making his escape. Shaking his head at his own folly, he stood up, looking over the towers of books behind which he had been sitting.

'Here,' he said, putting on a smile. She crossed quickly to him, offering a warm smile in return which gave him an odd flutter. Belatedly he realised he ought to have addressed her in some more appropriate manner, but it was too late now.

'I admire your dedication,' she offered, stopping in front of his desk. Her gaze flicked quickly over him, no doubt taking in the deplorable state of his appearance. Uncomfortable, he tried to brush down his clothes but only succeeded in spreading more dust over them.

'A perfectly pointless dedication, unfortunately,' he said, trying to speak lightly. 'If draykons were ever a common sight in any of our worlds, there's no real record of it that I can find.'

Her brows lifted. 'Nothing at all?'

'A few children's tales. They lived (always in the past tense) far in the depths of the Off-Worlds, collecting hordes of treasure and sort of randomly breathing fire at things. None of it is particularly credible.'

Eva stood in thought for a moment. 'How curious,' she finally said.

He hesitated, then spoke again. 'Of course, that doesn't mean the information isn't there. I'm sure there must be something. I've probably missed it.'

She shook her head. 'I doubt that. You've been far too thorough.' She smiled at his expression of surprise. 'I've been checking the visitor books whenever I pass through. You've been here for an average of fourteen hours a day, every day, for the last two weeks. Were you aware of that?'

'I've been here for eternity, as far as I can judge,' he said wryly. He couldn't help but be pleased that she had noticed. They had travelled together on the hunt for his friend, Edwae Geslin, and after that she had insisted on accompanying him further—all the way into the Lower Realms in a search for Edwae's killer and erstwhile employer. Had she done it because she cared about him, or because she knew he could not accomplish the task on his own? If the latter (and he suspected it was so), she had been right. Inexperienced as he was, he would have floundered hopelessly in the Lowers without her aid. He might even have perished. The whole endeavour had been directed and largely accomplished by her; his own contribution, he felt, had been minimal. Now he was anxious to make amends.

'I'm sorry to have abandoned you to the job,' she said. 'I might have come in sooner, only I was expecting a visit from you.' Her gaze grew questioning and he coughed, uncomfortable. He had asked her permission to visit her at home, and she had granted it, but her obvious surprise at the request had dismayed him. In the end, he had not had the courage to go.

'I was—well, busy. I wanted to be able to bring you a stack of information to peruse.'

'Admirable focus, but you ought to eat once in a while as well. Somebody once told me that's a good idea.' She smiled and he smiled back, remembering how he'd had to encourage her to eat at the end of their adventures. 'Why don't you dine with me today?' she continued.

'Oh... that's kind of you, but I really couldn't.'

'Please,' she interrupted. 'Don't think I'm taking pity on you. Vale is out of the city this week and I'm terribly lonely.'

He knew that was nonsense. A woman of her popularity could have any number of companions at her disposal whenever she chose. But it was a kindness, and with those beautiful dark blue eyes fixed on him he couldn't possibly refuse.

'Magnificent,' she enthused. 'I'll send the carriage for you. Shall we say an hour before moonset?'

'No!' he said, horrified. 'I mean, thank you but that won't be necessary. I am quite capable of walking.'

She waved a hand dismissively. 'As you wish. But don't be late! I've much to discuss with you.' He watched as she walked to the door and left, taking her perfect figure and her distressingly beautiful face with her. He let out a slow breath, then set about returning all the books to their shelves. If he was to have time to clean himself up properly, he had to hurry.

Tren arrived at Lady Glostrum's mansion promptly

an hour before moonset. In fact he had been at least half an hour early, but he'd walked twice around Fifth Circle before presenting himself at his hostess's door. He wouldn't wish to appear too eager.

He was thoroughly groomed and dressed in his best coat, a dark blue garment that had attracted the praise of more than one of his female acquaintances. Having warred with himself for some time over whether or not to take flowers, he had at length settled on taking a modest bunch of elegant white dusk lilies. He did his best to stifle a flutter of nerves as he rang the bell of the extremely handsome, four-storey house.

He waited, trying to suppress a feeling of inadequacy. He had no business appearing at houses like this; his mother was a shop keeper and his father had been only a minor sorcerer who had worked as a lamp-lighter for most of his life, maintaining the light-globes that lit the streets of their home town of Glaynasser. Tren's powerful talent for sorcery had been a surprise, and they had worked tirelessly to finance his training. Now he was among Glour City's strongest sorcerers, with a well-paid job as an aide to Lord Angstrun, the Chief Sorcerer. But in terms of lineage he was nothing; he had very little real status. And now he was mixing with Glour's highest and finest citizens, a fact which delighted his mother but which troubled him. He was finding it increasingly hard to determine where he belonged.

It certainly wasn't here. He might have left, save that Eva's face rose in his mind, wearing an expression of welcome, and his resolution dissolved. Before he had time to consider the idea further, the door finally opened and Lady Glostrum herself appeared.

'I'm so terribly sorry,' she said, ushering him inside. 'Most of my servants have a few hours off today, but I thought Miriom was in this part of the house. Never mind. Will you have tea?' Her face softened into a surprised smile as he awkwardly presented her with the lilies.

'How kind,' she murmured, putting them up to her nose. 'I wasn't expecting gifts.'

Moments later he found himself seated in a handsome drawing room, sipping tea out of an expensive porcelain cup and trying not to stare at his hostess. He couldn't go so far as to conclude that she had dressed up for his benefit, but she had changed out of her earlier, most practical attire and her gown was now decidedly finer. Her shoulders were largely bare and she appeared to be wearing some kind of waist-defining corset. Her unusual snow-white hair was, as ever, perfectly arranged and her slightly slanted eyes were animated as she talked. In this grand attire she was more alluring than ever.

He began to feel that his coming might have been a mistake.

She was speaking of Lord Vale, Glour's Chief Investigator and her fiance. With an effort of will, he smiled and asked, 'So, when is the wedding to be?'

Her smile faded immediately. 'It has not been possible to set a date. I am too much engaged with business and Eyde also is busy. At present he is following up some leads that have emerged about the Istore thefts that occurred last moon. We are hoping he may uncover something to lead us back to Ana and Griel.'

The subject change was so smoothly done it was

impossible to track backwards from it. Tren resigned himself to a great deal of talk about business and very little conversation about her.

They were halfway through the second course of a magnificent dinner when Eva began to speak of Glinnery. What she said electrified him.

'How can you possibly have been in Glinnery for a few *days?*' He stopped eating to stare at her.

'There are some new technologies emerging from Irbel,' she replied. 'Unfortunately I have already sent the spectacles back to Ynara; I would have liked to show them to you. However, more importantly I learned some few interesting things.' He didn't interrupt as she related her conversations with Ynara and the Elder's guest, Devary Kant.

'I've a new task for you, if you'll accept it,' she said when she'd finished.

'Anything.'

'The books we took from Griel's hall. I had hoped to have time to study them thoroughly myself, but so far that hasn't been the case. I'd like you to take over.'

That caught his attention. When they had searched the hall that had held the draykon skeleton, they had discovered some unusual books that neither had ever heard of before. Tren had carried them away, but it was Eva who had taken them home. He hadn't seen them since. 'With the greatest pleasure,' he said, then winced inwardly. He was instinctively mimicking Eva's smooth, high class speech, which was intolerable. Talking like her would not make him part of her set. 'I'd love to,' he added. 'I've been dying to find out what's in them.'

'Excellent! I've put them in the study. We'll look at them after dinner.'

He nodded, wishing dinner was already over. He felt uncomfortable in this large, grand dining room, and it was hard to enjoy the meal when he was far too reprehensibly preoccupied with watching her eat. She did so with great delicacy and correctness, as if he was somebody of rank, worth impressing. But what really absorbed his attention was the way her full lips closed around the silver fork as she took each piece of food. She caught him watching and he cursed his face as it immediately flushed with embarrassment.

'Are you not hungry?' She gestured at his virtually untouched plate.

'No,' he admitted. 'What I need, I think, is sleep.' Eva immediately rang a bell, and when a neatly-dressed servant appeared she whispered a few words in the girl's ear. The food was swiftly cleared away and Eva rose from the table.

'I'm sorry,' he began. 'I didn't mean you should—'

'I know,' she said briskly. 'I should have realised you'd be tired. Follow me, please. I shan't keep you long.'

She took him into a high-ceilinged room lined with bookshelves. A large desk dominated the centre of the study, its surface strewn with paperwork.

'They're keeping you busy,' he murmured, indicating the papers.

'Horribly,' she said, rolling her eyes. 'The onslaught of rogue gates is slowing at last, but we're still dealing with the volume of beasts that have already come through from the Lowers. Merely cataloguing them is a large task in itself. Already we've found eight previously extinct species wandering the woods of Glour.'

'You have sufficient help, I suppose?' He took a

seat on a brown leather sofa that lived on one side of the room, while Eva went to a locked cupboard opposite. A moment later he jumped up again, yelping at a sudden pain in his fingers.

Eva looked up. 'What? Oh. I'm sorry. Rikbeek has adopted the sofa as his own; I should have remembered to warn you.' She bent over the sofa in question and removed a dark bundle of fur and wings. Tren grimaced. The gwaystrel was a useful beast—it had helped them to find Edwae, though sadly not soon enough to save his friend's life. But the creature was antisocial, to say the least, and its teeth were horribly sharp. He sucked away the blood that leaked out of the small but painful wound on his hand.

Eva threw the gwaystrel into the air, watching with some severity as it flew up and settled near the ceiling. Only after Rikbeek was securely out of the way did she turn back to her cabinet.

'We were talking of help, I think? I've many summoners working at the task, indeed,' she resumed as she searched through a bunch of keys. 'It's not enough, though. It's frustrating to be tied down with these essentially mundane duties when there are more pressing matters to be dealt with. Like the draykons.' She fitted a key into the lock and swung open the doors. 'I'm wondering if I ought to hand the post on to someone else, and concentrate on unravelling our mystery instead.'

Tren blinked. Evastany Glostrum had been High Summoner since he was a child. It was virtually impossible to imagine the city government without her.

Then again, if she were to concentrate on their shared endeavour full time, it could mean he would see her more often.

She began pulling books out of her cupboard and piling them up. Remembering how heavy they were, he went to assist. His fingers brushed the bare skin of her arms as he took the books from her, and he quickly turned back to the sofa. The books made a satisfying pile on the cushions.

'I didn't want to entrust these to the city library,' she said. 'If Angstrun gets his hands on them, we might never see them again.'

He liked that she had said "we". He picked up the topmost book and opened it. This was a series of memoirs written by Andraly Winnier; the title declared her to be a Savant and a Lokant, though he had no idea what that meant. This was the book they had discovered in an isolated tower in the Lower Realms, apparently the home of at least one of the two individuals who had woken the draykon. Tren had been waiting with anticipation to discover why Griel had wanted this book. Handling it with care, for it was very old and fragile, he scanned the first few pages.

Eva settled on the arm of the sofa, reading over his shoulder. She was barely two inches away, close enough for him to feel her warmth and smell the light perfume that she wore. Her breath stirred his hair.

'I think I'll study these at home,' he said abruptly, closing the volume and standing up. 'I really need to get some sleep now, if I may be excused.'

Eva blinked at him in mild surprise. 'You may certainly be excused, but I must oppose the plan to take these books home. It's a matter of security, you see. Griel may be gone, but we have no idea what has become of Ana. If she wishes to recover these books,

I've no doubt she will attempt to do so with all due force. This house is well guarded and protected, more so than yours. I would prefer for you to come here to study them.'

Tren looked at her for a long moment, trying to read the truth of her motives. It was the sort of scheme he might have concocted in order to compel the regular presence of someone he very much wanted to see; could he hope that any such thoughts influenced her?

No. Her expression was friendly but no more than that; she looked upon him with an air of polite solicitude mingled with brisk pragmatism. Her concern was for the books, and for his continued health; not for his proximity.

Studying the books in her house, especially if she herself was present, would be much harder, but her reasoning was impossible to argue with. 'As you wish,' he said finally. She rose with a smile and gave him her hand; finding himself obliged to kiss it, he attempted to do so with an air of easy nonchalance, which he suspected failed completely.

'Thank you for coming,' she said as she withdrew her hand. 'I was disappointed when you did not come before.'

And with that she nodded pleasantly to him and left, leaving him to enjoy the sensations of confused gratification that her words excited.

CHAPTER THREE

Lying in bed in a house not his own, Devary Kant could not help reflecting that the last few weeks had not gone particularly well.

He did not enjoy fighting for its own sake. Indeed, he would rather avoid it and he had always felt that way. But he was, once in a while, called upon to defend himself and so he had dutifully committed many hours of his life to the development of considerable combat ability.

He was also periodically required to defend others. This, he felt, was the more important duty. To fail so completely to defend a woman committed to his care was intolerable; worse when that charge had been Llandry Sanfaer, daughter of his oldest friend. That he himself had been injured almost to the point of death in her defence was no consolation. He should have died rather than allow her to be taken.

But taken she had been, by some means he had been unable to prevent. And whatever had been done to her afterwards was irreversible. World-changing.

Draykon. The word still rang in his thoughts long after he had heard it from Ynara. He connected it with the images in his memory: of the great, winged, ghost-grey beast sailing down out of the skies and carrying him away. At times he concluded he was merely hallucinating again; in moments of greater clarity he was obliged to dismiss this most convenient of excuses. But there was no absorbing *that* piece of information. He had been warned that the furore over Llandry's Istore stone was a greater matter than he realised, but nothing had prepared him for this.

Such reflections were not only unproductive, but outright destructive. Nonetheless, lying as he was immobile and in constant pain, Devary's mind refused to turn on any other topics. It was as he attempted, with the utmost care, to turn himself slightly in his bed that a man appeared out of the air.

The man was tall, looking down on Devary with an imposing air. He wore a slight frown on his too-white face, and his pale hair looked as though it wouldn't dare to drift out of place. His appearance—his strong features and the pale grey colour of his eyes—belonged to no race that Devary had ever met; he couldn't place the man's nationality at all. But he addressed Devary in perfect Nimdren.

Devary might wish he did not know this visitor, but sadly the man was all too familiar.

'Clearly there has been some error,' he said slowly. 'None of your reports have been received by our office. A problem with the postal service, no doubt, or with our messengers, for I am sure you have sent regular reports as usual.' He lifted his brows as he spoke, though his voice never rose above a moderated tone.

Devary said nothing. Seeing that man here, standing with casual impunity in the heart of Ynara Sanfaer's house, was both deeply wrong and deeply disturbing. He had never really expected to escape the pressure of his former employers, but he must have entertained some hopes, for his heart sank with dismay.

'No matter,' the intruder continued. 'Your assignment has changed. There is no further need to maintain surveillance on this house while Llandry Sanfaer is no longer within it. Find her and bring her to us.'

Devary weakly clenched his fists, and shook his head. 'I am no longer your employee. I accept no further assignments.'

The man lifted his brows, surveying Devary's wounds with pointed attention. 'You do not appear to be healing very fast. It would be a shame if you were to suffer a relapse.'

Devary fought down a flutter of panic. 'This family above all others will not be targeted by me. I have won back their trust only recently and I will not betray them again.'

'Your proximity to this family is precisely why you are suited to the task,' the man replied relentlessly. 'Llandry trusts you. When you find her, she will follow you.'

Devary swallowed his pain and fixed his unwelcome visitor with a cold stare. 'Why do you want her?'

'That information is not necessary for you to know.'

'Then my answer stands. I will have no part in this.'

The man said nothing for a moment. Then, 'You're a rational being so I'll make this plain for you. Your injuries are severe. Your recovery will take months; months of lying here, useless and in pain. And you may not recover at all.' He leaned down towards Devary's face, his eyes cold. 'If you accept the assignment, I will ensure that you recover. If you do not, I will ensure the opposite.' He straightened again and shrugged. 'And if you persist in refusing my offer, I will be obliged to send another after Miss Sanfaer. Someone less sympathetic to her.'

Devary closed his eyes. He knew the sort of operatives that would be sent after Llandry if he refused. If she was to be protected, he had no choice but to go after her himself. Once he found her, he would discover a way to hide or defend her.

He opened his eyes. 'Very well,' he said coldly. 'But this is to be my last assignment. I must be allowed to retire.'

'Agreed,' said the man, pleasant now that his purpose was achieved. Devary found his arm seized in an uncompromising grip, and before he was aware of his resented employer's intention his surroundings dissolved into a mess of colour and they were gone, spinning across the worlds to the last place that Devary wished to go.

'Aysun, slow down. You're going too fast.'

The person speaking from behind him was out of breath and just a little bit frantic. Frustrated, Aysun didn't pause to acknowledge his companion's request, but he did slow his pace. A little.

'Thanks,' the voice muttered darkly.

Aysun ignored the words. Strapped to his wrist was his locator; the device was locked onto a ring that his daughter wore, and its function was to guide him to her. As long as he had remained in Glinnery it had displayed nothing at all, and for a time he had feared that Llandry had lost her ring. But then a greater fear had occurred to him: perhaps she had instead gone off-world. Perhaps she was in the perilous Uppers.

Now he himself stood in the light-drenched Upper Realm. The moment he had stepped through the gate, his locator had flashed, and a winking point of light had appeared on the display. The confirmation of his suspicion had both relieved and dismayed Aysun: Llandry was alive and still wearing her ring, so it would be possible to find her. But the longer she remained in the Uppers the harder that task would be, and the greater the danger that she would be injured or killed before he could reach her.

Hence his hurry. His companions, however, felt differently.

Footsteps beat rapidly behind him and then Eyas drew level with him, panting and wearing a scowl on his tanned face.

'If you want me to keep you from being eaten, mauled or gored, we're going to have to work on this arrangement,' his friend said. 'That means I, the trained and experienced summoner, must be in front, in order to ensure that our surroundings are clear of dangers before you advance. If you insist on leading the charge, I can't answer for the consequences.'

'You're too slow,' said Aysun. 'While you dawdle, she's moving further away.'

Eyas threw up his hands. 'Then I don't know why you asked the rest of us to come.'

Aysun glanced over his shoulder. Behind him walked Nyra, a tall and gloriously winged citizen of Glinnery. She was a sorceress and a friend of his wife's. He had needed a sorcerer to open a gate to the Uppers, and he would need one again when it was time to return home. Nyra had insisted on accompanying him in the search for Llandry.

Their other companion, however, was nowhere in sight.

'Where's Rufin?'

Eyas shrugged. 'He circled around us a moment ago and went into the trees. He was loading his gun.'

'Trouble?'

'I'm not sensing anything.'

Aysun nodded. Eyas was a fellow Irbellian expatriate. He had moved to Glinnery years ago to train his summoner abilities—for there was little quality training to be had in Irbel, with its focus locked firmly on engineering—and he was now one of Glinnery's best. Which was why Aysun had chosen him for this expedition. If Eyas's summoner senses found nothing to cause alarm, his word was to be trusted.

But that being the case, why had Rufin left the party, and taken his gun?

A shot rang out off to the left. Aysun immediately altered his direction, heading towards the sound; but he'd no sooner drawn his own hand gun out of its holster than Rufin himself appeared, his weapon slung over his shoulder and a large, dark object dangling from his free hand.

Eyas halted. 'Rufin. Tell me that isn't a desente bird.'

'A what? Here.' Rufin thrust the dead thing at

Eyas, who fumbled it. It fell to the ground, wings splayed.

'It is a desente bird.'

'Nice.' Rufin nudged it with his toe.

'Nicer when it was alive,' Eyas replied. 'And not dangerous, I might add. They're herbivores.'

'And dinner.'

'What?'

'They're also dinner.' Rufin allowed his big body to drop into a cross-legged position on the ground. Deft with his large hands, he began to pluck the bird.

'What? No! These birds are rare, and marvellous. Did you know that a desente can stay aloft for eighteen hours without—'

'Who cares?' interrupted Rufin. 'All I want to know is whether it tastes good.'

'It's dead already, Eyas,' interceded Aysun. 'Let's get it over with and move on.'

Rufin's head came up at that. 'Aysun, old friend. You know about sleeping, I presume.'

'Heard of it.'

'Weren't we planning to do some at some point?'

Aysun shook his head. 'Got to keep moving. Llan needs us.'

He heard Eyas sigh faintly. The summoner was younger than both he and Rufin, but he wasn't as physically robust as the two older men. To his credit, though, he didn't complain.

Nyra, typically, said nothing at all.

As the bird cooked over a hastily assembled campfire, Aysun sat by himself to think. He needed to try to guess where Llandry might be, but that required some understanding of her motives and in that he was entirely stumped. He had always taught his daughter to be wary of the Uppers. He had always feared the possibility that she or his wife might someday suffer the same fate as his father; his father the summoner, who had crossed into the Uppers one day many years ago and never come back. Since then he had lived with the constant fear that his wife or daughter might be killed up there as well.

Llandry must have been in peril when she had gone into the Uppers, that he knew: she would never have done it otherwise. If it had saved her life, he couldn't blame her for it. But why hadn't she returned in the weeks since? What could she possibly be doing? He couldn't shake the thought that she would have returned if she could. Something must have befallen her, but he couldn't imagine what.

For it could be anything in this strange place. Intent as he was on his location device, he had often been oblivious to the scenery through which they passed. But he couldn't entirely ignore the way the landscape changed subtly, minute by minute, until the apparently vast forest of tall-stemmed, wide-capped glissenwol trees that stretched before him faded away and he was striding instead through open hills. There was nothing abrupt about these changes; it appeared as a gradual process, so much so that one hardly noticed it happening.

As he and his companions ate their meal—with less haste than Aysun would have preferred—he could feel the grass steadily lengthening underneath him. That alone was interesting, for an hour previously they had been sitting on deep blue moss. When Eyas noticed the change he grew troubled.

'This may not be a good time or place to sleep after all,' he finally announced.

'Oh?'

Eyas made no immediate reply. He appeared to be listening; whether with his ears or with his summoner senses was unclear. Then he rose and walked slowly around the campfire until he was close to Aysun, and stood staring into the grass. Aysun had seen him in such a posture before; he was working his summoner magic, striving to impose his will on a nearby creature. Aysun stiffened, for if Eyas was so employed it meant that a dangerous animal had moved up on them without his hearing or seeing any sign of it.

At last Eyas moved and took a long breath. Twining around his leg was a snake, its scaled ivory-coloured hide liberally splotched with vivid purple. Nyra hissed and backed away from the fire.

'Don't leave the fire, Nyra,' said Eyas quickly. 'I can sense six more of these within a few feet of us.'

Nyra froze.

Aysun stood and shouldered his pack. 'Best move on, then.'

Standing, Rufin was a couple of inches taller than Aysun. He grinned down at his old friend and unstrapped his shotgun.

'I'll take the lead, shall I?'

A few hours later, Aysun was close to despair. His device was malfunctioning; it had to be. According to the display, Llandry was moving far faster than they were. No matter how quickly he forced his company to move, she continued to draw further away. He knew she could fly fast with her Glinnish wings—she and her mother had often outpaced him on the ground, even when Llandry was a child—but even so, it shouldn't be possible for her to put so much distance between them at such a rate.

A halt was called some hours after they had encountered the snakes. Eyas at last declared it safe to rest, but while the others slept Aysun worked on his location device. He worked relentlessly, ignoring his tiredness, searching for the fault in the machinery that was causing the problems with the display.

But all his efforts only made it worse, for after an hour's work something remarkably strange happened. The point of light that represented Llandry's position abruptly reversed its direction and began to head back towards Aysun's group. He calculated that her position must be more than fifty miles ahead of them, but she closed that distance with impossible speed. Over the space of a mere few minutes, her path traced an arc around them, passing a few miles to the northeast. Then that taunting dot of light veered away once more.

Aysun was an engineer, hailing from the realm of Irbel where talent with machinery was common and highly valued. He was a skilled practitioner of the mechanical arts himself, and had long worked with the outpost of Irbellian engineers based in Glinnery. He was aware of several projects developing vehicles that would move faster than nivven-drawn carriages, but he had never heard of anything that would allow the kind of speed his display was showing. It was unimaginable.

It must be broken, but he could find no fault and as such there was nothing to repair.

Without the reliable help of his locator, how could he ever expect to find Llandry in this fluid place, where nothing stayed the same and no landmark could be relied upon? Despairing, Aysun tossed the device into his pack and turned his back on his companions. He wanted to sleep, but he couldn't; not while Llandry was lost somewhere in the Uppers. He was one of the foremost engineers of Irbel: he had to find the solution.

CHAPTER FOUR

'Who would you recommend as your successor?'

Guardian Islvy Troste regarded Eva with some sadness as she posed the question. Eva's eleven years as High Summoner had just come to an end; Islvy had been at the head of Glour's government for seven of those years, and the two women had often worked together. They had never been close friends, but they had been able to rely on each other.

'Roys Alin,' Eva replied. She hadn't had to think hard for an answer to that question. Roys was no aristocrat, and that must speak against her when it came to government appointments. But she was a summoner whose natural strength almost equalled Eva's own, and had long been Eva's second in command. She was a rational, dedicated woman; she would do well in the role of chief of the realm's summoner practitioners.

The Guardian nodded. 'That's as I expected. I agree with you entirely, and I'll make sure there are no objections from the rest of the Council. Would you prefer to postpone your departure, or is your resignation effective immediately?'

'Immediate,' Eva replied without hesitation. It cost her something to say it, but she ensured that no trace of doubt appeared in her manner. 'There is much to be done regarding the draykon problem, and I have already lost a great deal of time.'

The Guardian frowned slightly. 'That issue has already been passed to the university. Some of their finest scholars are at work on it. Not that I doubt your ability to contribute to the research, but is it indeed so vital that you participate immediately? I don't wish to lose our best High Summoner in a generation unnecessarily.'

Eva permitted herself a small smile. 'They are at work, yes, but you must admit that many of them barely believe me. They think that I spoke of some other large, winged species, perhaps, or that some variety of shock damaged my ability to clearly interpret the events happening around me. I have even heard it said that I was under the influence of some one or other of the hallucinogenic substances that can be harvested in the Lowers. I was, after all, in the company of a youth of twenty-five and everyone knows that all young people are fond of recreational drugs. Few are giving the matter any real attention.'

Islvy smiled rather grimly. 'Is that so? Then they will be addressed on the matter.'

Eva shook her head. 'They cannot be forced to take me seriously, not without any real evidence other than my testimony, and Mr. Warvel's. Even if they could, there is only so far I can help them by describing what I saw. My eyewitness experience is of paramount importance in understanding recent events. At present there are only two of us who can claim that experience.'

'Mr. Warvel has been excused from his duties as Angstrun's aide, I understand?'

'Yes, he is currently working full time on research. It is my intent to join him at once. I do not believe this spell of quiet will last indefinitely; we will see something of these draykons before long, and it would be well to understand the possible consequences of that.'

Eva didn't add her private fears. Llandry's fate had been remarkable, but was it safe to assume that it was isolated only to her? Could there be others across the Seven who might likewise possess the latent potential to metamorphose? If so, it could be extremely important to identify them *before* they transformed for the first time. And Eva feared that those transformations may be triggered by proximity to a fellow draykon, as Llandry's appeared to have been. She needed to answer these questions, fast, before Llandry found her way home.

'Very well,' sighed the Guardian. 'You are already a Fellow of the university, yes?'

'I am. I have never before exploited the privileges of that post, but I will now.'

Islvy nodded. 'I sincerely regret your departure, but I wish you success with your new endeavours.'

Eva rose, recognising that as a dismissal. 'Thank you, Guardian Troste.'

The Guardian dropped her formality for a moment, and smiled with real warmth. 'Take care, Eva.'

Eva smiled back. 'And you, Islvy.'

Eva left the Guardian's office with a heavy heart.

No matter the strength of her motives, it was hard to relinquish a role she had occupied for so long, and which had been the centre of her life for more than a decade. It would be strange to be excluded from the processes of government in the future, no longer summoned to meetings, her contributions and advice no longer sought. But she was beginning a new phase of her life, and the questions at hand were more than enough to excite and inspire her.

And Tren would be waiting for her at home. He had arrived early in the morning, as usual, and when she had left the house he was already deep into his study of Winnier's memoirs. Thinking of this, she quickened her pace.

She arrived home to find an empty box in the hallway of her house. The box was of the sort her tailor, Baynson, packed garments in when they were to be sent to the gentry. Strewn around it were wisps of scented paper.

Eva gave her coat to a servant, then followed the trail of discarded packaging into the study. Tren sat at her desk with several books and notebooks open around him. He was wearing at least three shirts, and several more were being used to pad the spines of the books he was studying.

'That's not what I had in mind when I ordered Baynson's finest,' she observed.

Tren looked up with a grin. 'No? Then what did you have in mind? You owed me two shirts as I recall, but no less than twelve came out of the box.'

'I was just making sure.'

'Making sure of what? Are you planning to ruin

several more of my personal garments?'

Eva grinned. 'It does seem to happen when I'm around.' Tren had ripped up one of his own shirts to bind a hand wound for her, when they had been en route through Orstwych some weeks ago. Later, another shirt had been irrevocably damaged when they both took an unplanned dip in ice-cold salt water. She had promised to replace them, and so she had. She'd even provided an upgrade to the quality. A considerable one.

'This silk is remarkably comfortable to wear, though a little thin,' Tren continued. 'Maybe that's what you had in mind: layers.'

The multiple shirts he wore were in clashing colours. He had a dark red shirt over a leaf-green one, over a beautiful purple colour. Eva chuckled.

'Baynson would have heart failure if he saw you like that. By the way, there are cushions for the books' spines.'

'I know, but if I am to enjoy the luxury of pure silk shirts, why should I deny it to the books? Lulled into a sense of pampered security, they will give up their secrets the more easily.'

'Ah. And how is that working out?'

'Quite well. For example.' Tren leaned forward in his chair and leafed through the book that rested before him. Eva recognised the aged, dark leather of Andraly Winnier's book. 'We—or at least, I— assumed that this book, looking as it does rather terrifically ancient, is the work of a long-dead author. However, there are some entries describing recent events in the Lowers and—this is the good part— they're obviously written in the same handwriting as the oldest entries.' He paged carefully through the book, demonstrating his point, and Eva leaned over the desk to see. She had to agree: the newer script was written in different ink, but the letters were formed in the same manner.

'You're certain the events described are recent? Maybe this isn't the first time that the Lowers have suffered this kind of disruption.'

'Interesting that you asked that. I am certain that these entries are very recent, yes, but there are earlier entries describing the same kinds of things. And these recent chapters refer to that. Here: *The re-emergence of the draykon race has upset the balance of Ayrien, causing serious upheaval of a type previously observed and recorded during the Eterna Conflict.*' "Ayrien" seems to refer to the Lowers, but I've yet to find any more references to an Eterna Conflict.'

'*Ayrien,*' Eva repeated. 'I've never heard that term before, have you?'

'Nope. I'm going back to the City Library tomorrow to look for them both. That's not all, though. Look at this.' Tren turned to approximately the middle of the large tome, revealing the roughly-torn stubs of several missing pages. 'There are a few more torn out throughout the book. No indication as to what they discussed.'

'I wonder if Griel removed them,' Eva mused. 'Though I can't imagine why he might have. It's a pity we didn't get longer to explore the tower; maybe we could have found the missing pages.'

'And who knows what else,' Tren agreed. 'What's making me very curious, though, is the identity of the author. Who is Andraly Winnier? This person appears to have been writing for an impossibly long time.'

'That's not confirmed,' Eva replied. 'Handwriting

can be imitated.'

'True. But why bother?'

Eva shrugged. 'If it's conceivably possible, then it should be considered and investigated.'

Tren grinned up at her. 'You're a curious mixture. In some respects you're a complete rebel, and in others you're a surprisingly conservative woman. Even, dare I say, pedantic.'

'But imagine how dull life would be if everyone was completely predictable. Please, Tren, for the sake of my sanity, take off the extra shirts.'

Tren laughed. 'That's really bothering you, is it?'

'Yes. It's hurting my eyes. I can't consent to stand anywhere near you while you're like that.'

'That is a grave threat,' Tren replied seriously. He disappeared for a moment under a succession of silk shirts as several clashing colours came off. Eva collected the discarded shirts and folded them up, arranging them into perfectly colour-coordinated pairs. At length Tren was down to only one shirt, a perfectly inoffensive blue one.

'Thank you,' she said. 'Now you may proceed.'

'That's everything I had to report.' Tren pulled in his chair and focused on the book again. 'I'll let you know if I find anything else interesting.'

'I'll send Beane in with some refreshment,' she offered.

He shook his head without looking up. 'Thanks, but I don't want to risk getting the books dirty.'

'Very well; then I shall call you for lunch.'

She wanted him to look up and smile again, but he kept his eyes fixed on his book. 'Thank you.'

She nodded, though he didn't see the gesture, and departed.

Later that day, Eva sat in her carriage on the way to the city's sorcery school. The weather was finally warming a little; for once she had no need to bundle herself into her furs, and she went without the stone bottle filled with hot water that usually warmed her feet while she travelled. Outside, the moon was high in the sky and nearly full, casting a strong silver glow across the city of Glour.

She was on her way to see Lord Angstrun, who held the post of the realm's High Sorcerer. His duties within that role were similar to her own, now former duties as High Summoner. He was responsible for maintaining the enchantments that kept the Night Cloak in force across the realm, keeping out the strong sunlight that would cause severe and irreparable damage to the important Lowers-native plants and animals on which Glour society relied. He had a number of assistants in that task, of which Tren had been one until recently. Angstrun was also responsible for overseeing the training of the relatively few citizens of Glour who possessed sorcerous talent. Eva knew from his secretary that he was at the school today, giving a lecture. She was timing her arrival to coincide with the end of his teaching duties.

Her carriage pulled up outside the large, old building that housed the academy, and she was swiftly conducted inside. Angstrun was in his office, still wearing his professor's robes and his customary thunderous expression. He had an imposing demeanour and was obviously afflicted with a flammable temper, but there had been times in years past that Eva had seen him considerably softened.

Unlike many, she had no fear of him.

'Darae. I hope I'm not interrupting.'

Angstrun fixed her with a keen stare. 'I had a feeling I would be seeing you.'

Eva gave him a cool smile. 'You're the expert in these parts. I need your opinion on the matter of dual abilities, such as I discussed before the Council not long ago. Do you recall?'

She expected him to dismiss the idea with his customary bad language, but instead his expression turned thoughtful. 'I've never seen or heard of a person who could manage both sorcery and summoning with any success. I could dredge up some dusty reports of curious happenings in childhood—kids who show some small ability in both directions for a time—but those children always seem to lose the duality as they grow older. By the age of five, in general. After that they develop adult abilities in only one of those two areas.'

'You're very knowledgeable.'

'Your report to the Council was intriguing. I did some research.'

Eva nodded. When she had reported her recent experiences to her colleagues in the government, she had highlighted the fact that the two people responsible for the recent chaos, a pair of Ullarn citizens named Ana and Griel, apparently demonstrated strong skill in both schools of magic. That was previously unheard of: it was common knowledge that magically talented individuals were unable to access both skills. It was so widely accepted, in fact, that Eva had encountered a great deal of scepticism. She was grateful to find that Angstrun at least was willing to take her seriously.

'Has anyone ever conducted a study into this phenomenon? I know that magical training has qualifying children divided into the two groups by the age of eight, and after that they are trained in their given ability. Has anyone ever tried to train a child in both?'

'I found one such study, but it was later discredited. The researchers were accused of manipulating the results. The effect on their careers was highly damaging, and it seems no one has been brave enough to repeat the research.'

Eva shook her head. 'I can't help thinking it strange, than a society so fond of scientific enquiry could have completely failed to pursue this.'

Angstrun shrugged. 'There are many other questions worth pursuing, most of them less potentially damaging to a scholar's credibility. You do realise that addressing this question much further may get you labelled a crank.'

'If so, so be it. There's also the small matter of Ana's disappearing trick. I can't currently imagine how that's possible within either magical tradition, but one mystery at a time.'

He snorted. 'Let me guess. You want me to teach summoning to my sorcery students.' He leaned back in his chair and lifted his heavy black brows at her.

'Yes. And vice versa. I've already cleared it with Roys.'

'Ah yes. Congratulations on your retirement, by the way. Though apparently you aren't planning to spend the next few years living the good life.'

'Quite. I retired because I have more pressing things to do. I take it that the lack of instant objections means you agree to my proposal?'

'It doesn't, but who could possibly refuse you anything?'

Eva thought immediately of Finshay, one of Lord Vale's agents. She had worked with him for a time during the search for Edwae Geslin, and he had made it clear he resented every moment. 'Some certainly could, but I'm delighted to find you aren't one of them.' She rewarded his compliance with a smile, and rose to leave. 'Thank you, Darae. I'd like to be involved with the teaching, if I may.'

'You may. Uh—one moment. Don't leave yet.' He stood up and shrugged off his black professor's robe, clearing his throat. 'When's the wedding?' he inquired, turning to face her.

'We haven't set a date yet.'

'Ah.' He paused. 'Does your engagement mean you're no longer available to...?'

He tailed off, but she understood his meaning. He had been her lover for a time, about ten years ago, and they had occasionally renewed that relationship when it suited them both.

'It doesn't,' she replied. 'I warned Vale that complete monogamy was probably beyond me, and he didn't object.'

Angstrun laughed. 'How like you. Well then, how about dinner? Say tomorrow night?'

Eva paused to consider. Despite what she'd said, she hadn't had any lover besides Vale since her engagement. But Vale had been gone for a week and was due to be absent for at least a week more.

She was about to consent when Tren's face appeared in her mind and she experienced some momentary doubt. For the last few days he had remained at her home until late in the evening, working relentlessly on the books she had given him. She frequently joined him during those hours, working alongside with another book set close to his. There was a companionableness to the arrangement which she enjoyed.

But why should she hesitate? She could forgo Tren's company for one evening. There would be more such nights.

'Dinner would be perfect,' she said. Angstrun nodded, a rare smile smoothing all the severity from his face. He kissed her hand and bowed her out, and she walked slowly back to her carriage alone.

CHAPTER FIVE

'It's been a brilliant jaunt through the Uppers, but if the device has failed there's nothing more to be done.' Rufin sat, legs folded, sharpening a knife that was longer than his forearm. 'Home we go!'

Aysun thought his tone was offensively cheerful under the circumstances. 'I can fix it.'

Rufin's blond brows sailed up. 'You've been trying for days.' He looked up at the sky with its perpetual light. 'Well. Far as I can tell up here. Feels like days.'

'I can fix it.'

Rufin shrugged. 'Right, but make it fast. It's pure luck that we haven't lost anyone yet.'

'And some skill, I like to think.' Eyas lay stretched out in the moss, his head pillowed on his arms. Aysun hoped he wasn't as close to sleep as he looked.

Rufin smirked, polishing the blade of his knife with a rag. 'Some of that, too, but it can't last.'

'The skill or the luck?'

'Certainly the luck. Maybe the skill.'

Aysun said nothing. He couldn't refute the truth of

Rufin's words. Since they had entered the Uppers, they had been attacked three times by creatures well equipped to kill. Rufin and Aysun had shot their way through most of their ammunition, and Eyas's efforts at subduing the frenzied beasts had obviously exhausted him. It would be increasingly difficult for them to hold their own against any further attacks.

'I concur,' came Nyra's voice from somewhere above their heads. Having the advantage of wings to protect her from beasts on the ground, she frequently employed them to lift herself out of danger's path.

'Your opinion doesn't count,' said Rufin cheerfully. 'You're the only one of us not likely to be eaten by an ailigray or gored by a drauk anytime soon.'

Nyra didn't answer. Aysun couldn't even see her, so well hidden was she by the teal-hued leaves of the surrounding trees.

'I cannot leave without Llandry,' said Aysun firmly.

'Right. How are you planning to find her? I love your family, Aysun, but if it's a matter of spending months up here trying not to die while hoping to accidentally bump into your daughter, I can't say I'm up for that.'

'Got to agree,' murmured Eyas. His eyes had fluttered shut again.

Aysun's heart sank. He couldn't ask them to stay under these circumstances; if any of them were injured or killed it would be solely his fault. But nor could he abandon the search.

'All right. Home.'

'Great,' said Rufin. He leapt to his feet, shoving his knife back into its holster. 'Nyra? How about that gate?'

51

Leaves rustled and Nyra appeared, sliding gracefully down from the branches above. She set to work, and within moments a gate hung in the air, shimmering with heat and warping the landscape around it. Looking at it, Aysun shuddered. It had taken all of his courage to step through such a gate before; he wasn't ready to repeat the experience yet.

Eyas was squinting at him suspiciously. 'You are planning to come with us, Ays?'

'Of course,' Aysun replied blandly. Eyas gave him a hard stare, then nodded.

'When the device is fixed, call us. We'll try again.'

'Thanks.' Aysun watched as Rufin stepped through the gate first, disappearing from sight. Eyas went next. Nyra waited, glancing at him enquiringly. He gave a minute shake of his head.

'How will you get home?'

'I'll find a rogue.' Rogue gates opened and closed by themselves, seemingly at random. Recently they had been opening with much greater frequency than normal; this posed a threat to Glinnery's citizens who did not possess any magical aptitude, as they could not see or sense them. Glinnery's sorcerers were working hard to close all of the rogue gates before they could send any unsuspecting civilians through into the adjacent world, but nonetheless Aysun was confident enough that he would be able to find one at need.

And if not, he would worry about that later.

Nyra hesitated. 'Ynara will kill me if I leave you here alone.'

Aysun shrugged. 'The choice is up to you, Nyra. I'm not leaving, but if you stay I can't guarantee that I can protect both of us.'

Nyra heaved a long sigh, then turned back to her gate. Aysun thought she meant to step through, but instead the shimmering in the air faded away and the gate vanished.

'I am our escape route,' said Nyra, turning back to him. 'If we get into trouble that we cannot handle, I will open a gate and we will go through it, immediately and without question. You must promise me.'

Aysun promised readily enough. He was secretly relieved that Nyra had elected to stay.

'The others are going to be furious with you,' Nyra observed.

'Probably. Let's move on.' Aysun shouldered his pack, but Nyra didn't move.

'Rufin was right, Aysun. We need some kind of plan. We can't just wander aimlessly.'

Aysun nodded. 'I'm working off the device. It's got a lot of things wrong, but maybe it has her direction right.'

Nyra looked sceptical, but she didn't object. Aysun strode away into the trees, burying his uncertainty under an aura of confidence. He heard the sound of Nyra's wings beating and then she was aloft, soaring over his head.

'I'll be lookout,' she called as she passed.

Twice that day, Nyra's timely warnings saved him just as he was about to blunder into danger. It was a stark demonstration of how long he would have lasted if Nyra had gone back to Glinnery after all.

When at last they could go no further, Aysun grimly hauled himself up into the branches of the tallest tree he could find. He had no wish to sleep on the ground again, not without Eyas and Rufin to take turns at keeping watch. His sleep was uncomfortable and fitful; after a few hours he gave up and merely sat, watching the colourful landscape of the Uppers changing sluggishly in the sun.

He'd noticed that the changes happened faster when the light was strongest. Not that the light conditions here could ever be termed low, but there were times of the day when the sun shone with particular brilliance. When clouds dimmed the sun and soft rain filled the air, as it now did, the landscape seemed to fall into a half-sleep itself.

A scrap of colour floated past Aysun's vision and he blinked, jolted out of his reverie. With a quick motion, he caught the fluttering thing carefully in his cupped hands and brought it close to his face to examine.

It was a tiny winged creature only a few inches long from the tip of its long snout to the end of its curled tail. Its wings were dusted with jade and rose colours and it had soft, pearly fur covering most of its body. With a shock, Aysun realised he had seen it before. This creature—or one identical to it—had adopted Llandry after it had strayed into the Sanfaer house. It had been attacked by Sigwide, Llandry's pet orting, but she had rescued it and after that it had stayed close to her.

Both Sigwide and the winged survivor had gone with her when she had left her parents' home, choosing to follow Devary in secret. Of the three, only Sigwide had returned to the house. He had assumed that Llandry's other pet had gone with her into the Uppers.

Perhaps it had. Could he really believe that this was Llandry's own pet? Surely there must be more like it. But its markings looked identical to the other one he had seen. Could it be coincidence that this one had flown virtually into his face?

Yes, of course it could. He released the creature, disgusted with himself. He was grasping at straws, so desperate was he to discover some trace of Llandry. He turned his back on it and resolutely put it out of his thoughts. For another brief hour he dozed uncomfortably, covering his eyes with his arm to block out the light.

When he woke again, the winged creature was still with him. It sat a few inches from his nose, its snout testing the air. He felt a slight sting as it jabbed him with the tip of its proboscis, and he realised it was its antics that had woken him.

'What do you want,' he grumbled, pushing himself into a sitting position. The thing took flight immediately and flew a short distance away, then paused expectantly. When he didn't move, it flew back, bumped his face again and then repeated its motion.

If he didn't know better than to think so, he might have said it looked like an invitation.

Nyra dropped down from above, landing lightly on the branch upon which he sat. She used her wings to restore her balance, but he was nearly pitched off onto the floor a long way below.

'Friend of yours?'

He grunted. 'Think not.'

Nyra sat neatly cross-legged and passed him a handful of fruits. 'Looks like it disagrees.'

'It's free to do that if it wishes.' Aysun ate his

meagre breakfast quickly and he and Nyra set off once more. He had gone barely three steps before a scrap of colour soared past his face on jade-dusted wings. After another three steps, the creature passed again, swooping around him in tight circles. After a few more repetitions of this cycle, Aysun stopped, and Nyra landed in front of him.

'It's flying in circles.'

'I noticed.' Aysun started walking again, and immediately a flurry of wings shot past his nose and circled. When he stopped, the creature darted away to his left and paused.

'Huh.' Aysun repeated this process a few more times as Nyra stood and watched. At length she grinned.

'Something odd about that.'

'Reckon so,' Aysun agreed. He hesitated, then told Nyra about the history of Llandry's similar pet.

'Well,' Nyra said when he had finished, '*seeing* another one the same might be a coincidence. But the chances of a different one showing particular interest in you aren't high.'

'Right,' said Aysun. But he still hesitated. He was obviously being encouraged to go left, but according to his device Llandry's trail lay straight ahead of him.

Nyra solved it for him by taking off and veering to the left.

'I'm supposed to be the leader here,' he called up to her. She ignored him. With a sigh, Aysun trudged after her.

As he walked after his unlikely guide, Aysun had the odd sensation that he was covering more ground than he ought to have been. The landscape flowed past him, melting freely and rapidly into new formations. He passed through glissenwol forests that seemed vast, only to meld suddenly into rolling hills and then into boggy marshes and on into leafy woodland. There was a curious buoyancy to his stride, as though his legs stretched themselves and ate twice the regular distance with each step. Occasionally he saw buildings through the trees or away on the horizon, towers and tree houses and once a sprawling mansion. But he was drawn on relentlessly, never given pause to examine the structures that he glimpsed.

He was taken into a narrow pass through a series of mountains that had abruptly shimmered into view moments earlier. Beyond it lay a house built from stacked stone, with mullioned windows and a walled garden visible to the rear. The architecture was wholly Irbellian in style, of the traditional sort popular in his grandfather's day; it looked so familiar that he instinctively stopped to examine it more closely.

A buzz sounded in his ear and he caught himself before he was tempted to waste too much time here. But then his winged friend flew over the gate and made its meandering way through an open window at the front of the house.

A few moments later, the door opened and a grey-haired woman appeared. On seeing him, she clapped her hands together, beaming.

'He's here!' she called. 'And oh my, is this Ynara?' Nyra descended from the skies to stand next to him. Her lips quirked into a grin at that.

'Not a bad thing to be mistaken for Ynara,' she murmured.

'Hm. Doesn't look like her.' The voice was a male

one but Aysun couldn't see who spoke.

'Come out, and say hello.' The grey-headed lady in the doorway stepped aside, ushering someone else through. The man who emerged was stooped, his hair closer to white than grey, but it took Aysun less than two seconds to realise who this was.

'Hello, son,' said his father.

Aysun stared, his mouth set in a grim line. Then, wordlessly, he turned and walked away.

CHAPTER SIX

For a time, Llandry Sanfaer of Waeverleyne had ceased to exist.

For a time, only the draykon lived on, nameless and needing no name. She who was once Llandry had lost sight of herself altogether, forgotten who she truly was in this new shape of hers. The old Llandry had lain imprisoned somewhere in the centre of her heart, while a new Llandry, one proud and vicious and strong, had danced in the skies of the Uppers. She had flown hundreds of miles at impossible speeds, swooped and turned and dived, chased and hunted and fed and sped on once more; testing the power of her form she found it strong, stronger than anything.

Keeping with her, always close, was the larger draykon: the one whose awakening had kindled the draykon fire in her own soul and gifted her with this glorious new destiny. Together they had spanned the world: explored every forest and meadow, traversed every lake and sea, the landscapes below rippling like water and as changeful as the winds as the draykon energies touched them. Exhilarated, fascinated, drunk on power and strength, Llandry had flown on and on—until at last the small part of her heart that remembered her former life had stretched and grown and made itself heard.

Mamma, and Papa. Their faces came to her first, large and vivid in her clouded thoughts. Then she remembered more, her mind flooding with images: Devary Kant and Nimdre; the attack on the edge of the Glinnery forest; her grandfather and Mags his wife; the two pale-haired magical practitioners who had revived her draykon companion; the agony of her first Change. Once these half-faded memories were acknowledged and sought, they could not be stopped; not until Llandry was fully herself again, in mind if not in body.

Then to effect the transformation back to her human shape, so small and feeble and weak in comparison. Finding her way back to her home—or was it her former home?—was surpassingly easy, even once human again. It was the work of the briefest thought to wander between the worlds; a shift in focus was all it took and she could see the three worlds superimposed over one another, each separate and distinct yet irrevocably tangled. Narrowing her focus was all she needed to do, and her next step would carry her into a different series of realms. How simple, then, to go home; and yet how hard, for she herself was not the Llandry her parents had raised, and never would be again.

But go home she must.

She covered most of the distance in the Uppers, tracking her progress across all three worlds at once. When she judged herself near to Waeverleyne, she changed back to her human shape before stepping through into Glinnery itself. Her own, familiar grey wings carried her to her mother's balcony.

No time at all did she have to prepare herself, for Ynara was already standing there, her hand on the door as if she had just that instant thrown it open. Her mother—beautiful and mussed, as always—said nothing for a long moment, merely stared at her daughter. Llandry could not read her expression.

'*Llan,*' she gasped at last, as if drawing in air after long deprivation. Then her arms went around Llandry and she clung to her.

A thud sounded from behind her, and a male voice cursed in a language long dead. Llandry winced as her mother's gaze moved to take in the stranger. He had shifted out of his draykon form as she had, but his human appearance could be alarming.

'Er, Ma... this is Pensould.'

'Pensould,' repeated Ynara faintly.

'My friend,' Llandry added.

Ynara nodded. Reluctantly, she let Llandry go and stood back to survey the newcomer. She surveyed them both, in fact, her gaze lingering longest on her daughter.

'Is it true? I heard that you—you—'

Llandry interrupted, so that her mother wouldn't have to find the words. 'Draykon,' she said with reverence. 'It's true, Ma.'

Ynara's eyes widened and her honey-gold skin paled. Llandry bit her lip, holding her breath as nerves danced within her. How could her mother possibly understand?

'Changed you may be, but you're still our Llan,' Ynara murmured. 'We thought you were lost.'

'I was,' Llandry replied, swallowing a lump that had materialised in her throat. 'I found my way back.'

'This is your sire?' came Pensould's voice. 'Dam?'

'Mother,' Llandry corrected.

Pensould's gaze swept over Ynara critically. The contrast between his pale eyes and his ink-black hair still shocked Llandry a little whenever she looked at him. As did the strikingly blue colour of the veins that showed themselves through his stark white skin. Long hours she may have spent in teaching him to Change, but he hadn't yet fully mastered his human form.

He grabbed Llandry's arm and jerked her backwards, gripping her wrist possessively. 'My mate,' he said to Ynara.

Llandry suffered a surge of annoyance. 'No,' she said to him distinctly. 'I am not. I told you not to say that.'

He shook his head. 'My choice, not yours.'

Ynara's eyes narrowed. She took Llandry's free hand in hers and gently drew her away from Pensould. 'Why don't you both come in?' she said.

Pensould was a true draykon. He had never before taken human shape, and had little understanding of what it meant. Human customs were beyond him, and he had slept through most of human history. It had taken Llandry some days to effect her transformation back into human form, and considerably longer to teach the technique to Pensould. He wasn't particularly taking to it.

Sitting with her mother listening to Pensould speak, both his talents and his shortcomings were equally obvious. He spoke Glinnish haltingly, and he revealed his ignorance of her world with almost every sentence. But that he could speak her tongue at all was remarkable; he remembered every word that he heard and he seemed to have no difficulty understanding their meaning. His progress was slower outside of the Upper Realm, but still he was (she would have said) impossibly quick. It was as though he absorbed the sense of their utterances by some means other than a purely intellectual understanding of the words themselves.

'Soon, you will do that too,' Pensould informed her, interrupting himself.

She blinked. 'What?'

He tapped her head, hard. 'Your senses are dull. Flat. Too human. But I can feel you waking.'

'Waking?'

'Becoming more clever. More draykon.'

Llandry scowled. 'I am human.'

Pensould smiled, a rather frightening expression displaying too many teeth. 'No. Human-shaped outside, draykon inside.'

'I can assure you, Llandry is entirely human. I gave birth to her myself. I detected no sharp teeth, no claws, no unusual proportions.' Ynara kept her voice steady and her eyes on Pensould.

'Wings, though.' He grinned. 'I have seen humans before, long ago. No wings then. Why do you have wings now?'

'I...' Ynara faltered. 'Theories have been made, but no entirely satisfactory explanation has been found.'

Pensould leaned forward suddenly and grasped one of Ynara's wings. He tugged it, ignoring her discomfort, pulling it partially open.

'Not feathers like a bird. Not thin like a daefly.

Webbed, strong. Draykon wings.'

Ynara opened her mouth, but nothing emerged.

'You, Sire-of-Minchu, are maybe half draykon. No, more. But you stay human; you wish it. Minchu—'

'*Mother,*' interrupted Ynara. 'And who is Minchu?'

Llandry's cheeks warmed. 'It appears to mean "mate", Ma.'

Ynara's grey eyes settled on her. Her brows lifted, ever so slightly. Llandry coughed.

'I'm not "minchu".'

'Minchu,' continued Pensould, unfazed, 'she is almost all draykon. I can feel it, not so much here but in Iskyr, she is strong. Draykon heart.'

'Iskyr?' queried Ynara.

'Upper Realms, Ma.'

Ynara was looking increasingly bewildered. 'Llan, please. Slow down. *Who is* Pensould? Where did he come from?'

'How much did Lady Glostrum tell you?'

'Everything she witnessed herself, I believe.'

'Well, Pensould is the draykon that the Ullarn sorcerers resurrected. His were the bones that I found. I know what he means, Ma.' Llandry shifted in her chair, sitting more upright. 'In Iskyr—the Uppers—I could sense his presence. I found his bones, and I *felt* him waking. It's like having several more senses than humans—'

'I used you,' Pensould interrupted. He sounded faintly abashed. 'Your energy. I needed it, to come back. It hurt, yes?'

Llandry frowned at him. 'Hurt? Yes, it hurt. A lot.' She didn't like to remember that experience. As she had felt Pensould's essence roar into life under her hands, she had been struck by incapacitating pain, unable to prevent herself being dragged through the boundaries between the worlds and deposited in the Lower Realms where Pensould in his draykon form was stirring into life.

'I suppose it was you who pulled me through,' Llandry said darkly.

'Yes,' Pensould admitted without remorse. 'You were too far away.'

Ynara groaned, and Llandry looked with quick alarm at her mother. 'Ma? Are you well?'

'Yes,' she replied faintly. 'I'm told my daughter is not a human but a draykon—a creature that, until recently, was not thought to exist at all; I learn that she has become the "minchu" of another draykon and that she has recently been made to suffer extreme pain and discomfort by her self-elected spouse; and after weeks of absence she suddenly reappears and now she sits in my living room, chattering with astonishing comfort about her new form, as if such things were no sort of surprise to her at all. Of course, I am quite well.'

Llandry was silent. It was true that it had taken her precious little time to adjust to her draykon form; instead of feeling uncomfortable in the new shape she felt rather as though her human body was the wrong one. As a draykon she was a different person: no longer shy, afraid, out of step with her own peers, but strong and comfortable in her skin. The experience had been a revelation. She knew in her heart that Pensould spoke the truth, but it was hard to admit such things to her mother.

For now, she elected to change the subject. 'I have more to tell you, Mamma, and Pa as well. Will he be home soon?'

'Your father,' Ynara said slowly, 'is in the Uppers, looking for you.'

Llandry was speechless. She would never have imagined that Aysun, with his lifelong fear of the Uppers so deeply ingrained, might go so far as to go after her.

'How long has he been gone?' She felt a stab of fear as she spoke, imagining the dangers that could have befallen him.

'You returned Dev to us,' Ynara replied. 'He left six days after that.'

Llandry nodded briskly. 'I must find him,' she said, coming to her feet. 'I'll bring him home to you, Ma.'

'How are you going to find him, Llan?' Ynara looked so weary and confused that Llandry's heart sank. She pulled her mother to her feet and caught her in an embrace.

'Same way I found Devary,' she answered. 'Is he... did he recover?'

Ynara hesitated before she replied. 'He did not die.'

Llandry frowned. That answer was cagey and incomplete, but there was no time to pursue it, not while her father wandered Iskyr on a fruitless hunt for her. 'Send him my love,' she said. Pensould frowned at that, but she ignored him. 'I must find Papa at once. We'll return soon.'

'I—Llan, wait—'

Llandry was already running back out to the balcony with Pensould behind her. She jumped and soared, climbing above the glissenwol canopy. Once she was above the level of the trees, she changed. In an instant she was draykon once more, arrowing through the air; in the blink of an eye she flashed through the barrier between the worlds into the Upper Realm of Iskyr.

Aysun had gone no more than three steps before his father's next words froze him where he stood.

'I've seen Llandry.'

Aysun turned. 'What.'

'She was here,' his father repeated. 'Not long ago. Come inside and I'll tell you about it.'

'I'm not coming inside,' Aysun grated. He was almost too angry to speak, but he forced himself to remain calm—at least outwardly. 'Come out and we'll talk about it.'

The old man grumbled at this, but eventually consented to shuffle onto the path before his house. His shoulders were hunched and he leaned heavily on his stick as he walked. He stopped a few feet away from Aysun and regarded his son expressionlessly.

'Where's Llandry?' prompted Aysun.

'She left,' was the cool reply.

'Couldn't you have... you should have...' Fierce anger swallowed Aysun's words and he could only stare at his supposedly long-dead father in pure disbelief.

'I brought her through, and you should thank me for that because she was in danger of her life,' said his father—Rheas—with chilling calm. 'I tried to protect her, but she refused to stay. No doubt she inherited that wilfulness from her parents.'

'You could have sent word.' Aysun forced the words through gritted teeth.

Rheas actually chuckled. 'Where to? It is not as though I have your address.'

'The fault for that is your own.'

'Is it? You stand ready to go to your daughter's aid, but you never came looking for me, did you? Nobody did.'

Aysun could find nothing to say to that. 'Tell me where Llandry went.'

Rheas shrugged. 'She has been caught up in matters far greater than you or I. She could be anywhere.'

'What? What matters?' Aysun took a step forward, his fists clenched. He was shocked to find that, for an instant, he truly wished to hit the old man.

Rheas lifted his chin. 'Llandry will show you herself. We will wait for her here.'

Two days passed and Rheas made no attempt to explain himself. Two days of withering coldness on the old man's part and a stubborn show of indifference on Aysun's. Rheas would not speak of his secret life in the Uppers, and Aysun refused to ask. His father spent most of his time tucked into a rocking chair in the central room of the house; Aysun therefore found it more convenient to wander out of doors, or to sit brooding in the bedchamber allocated to him. Not even Mags, the cheery and good-natured woman who inexplicably consented to live with his father, could draw him out.

He was sitting in this very chamber, sitting and brooding and trying to smother his anger, when a dark shape flew across the sun and cast a shadow over the house. Then came his father's shout, a cry somewhere between triumph, dismay and fury.

'*Come down, son,*' his father cried.

Aysun went instead to the window. Two enormous beasts sailed through the air before him, rapidly drawing closer to the house. One was smaller than the other, its hide ghost-grey and pale. The larger beast wore scales of green-touched blue. They were impossibly big, impossibly winged and clawed. Aysun stared, briefly mesmerised by their grace and vivid colour.

'Aysun!'

He jumped, shook himself. There was emotion of some kind in his father's shouts, which was more than he had shown since Aysun had arrived. He descended to the ground floor, taking his time. Rheas and Mags were both standing at the door, blocking Aysun's view of the outdoors.

'Is this some trick of yours, old man?'

Without turning, Rheas barked a laugh. 'Your suspicion blinds you. If you want your daughter, I suggest you put that aside.'

'Llan? What's this got to do with her?'

Rheas didn't reply. He hobbled slowly out of the door, leaning on Mags' arm. One hand gestured impatiently to Aysun. *Follow me,* it said.

Mystified and annoyed, Aysun followed.

The two beasts had reached the house. As Aysun watched, they spiralled to the ground, one playfully nipping at the other's flanks as they descended. Behind him, Aysun heard Nyra's quick female step approaching, but he couldn't turn his attention to her. The sight of this strange, magnificent, outlandish pair of beasts utterly absorbed him.

'Aysun,' muttered Nyra, coming to a stop next to him. 'What's going on?'

'No idea.'

On the ground, the creatures were ungainly but nonetheless marvellous. Their hides were minutely scaled as though they were covered in a million beads of glass. They were four-legged, with pearly-silver talons and tails of immense length. Their wings reminded Aysun of his wife's in their construction, though these bore considerable differences in size and shape.

He wanted to go closer, despite their size, and examine the flashing trails of silver that outlined each tiny scale. But just as he formulated this wish, the air rippled—in the same way it did when a gate was opened between the realms—and the two beasts vanished.

In their place stood two human figures. They were not yet close, but in one of those figures Aysun could detect a familiar short stature and lithe form, black hair and lofty grey wings...

'Now do you understand?' came Rheas's soft whisper from behind him.

'No,' said Aysun. 'Not at all.'

The two figures didn't seem to notice that they had an audience. They were arguing; as they approached Aysun was able to discern their words.

'... why say you are not Minchu? To your mother, you say that!'

'I'm glad you've consented to use that word at last. I said it because it is not true!'

'But I say that it is true. But why must we speak with our lips and our tongues, Minchu, when we are alone? It is so clumsy.'

'Because you must practice your Glinnish before you meet my father.'

'Father?'

'Sire. We will come upon him any—oh.' Llandry looked up at last and saw Aysun standing before her, flanked by Nyra, Rheas and Mags.

Llandry's face filled immediately with relief. 'Pa! I was afraid you might have been hurt or worse but when I sensed you I felt you were well, only now I'm so glad to be able to see for myself that you are...' She threw her arms around him and continued to babble into his chest, but her words were too muffled to be discerned.

Aysun instinctively tightened his arms around his daughter, though his attention was distracted by her companion. He was a study in contrasts, stark white and deep black, vivid blue. Aysun was alarmed to realise that he viewed both Llandry and her friend with more than just his eyes; he sensed something different about them, a quality that they both shared. He had never noticed such a thing in his daughter before.

'Were those... was that you?' He spoke to Llandry, his voice emerging as a dry croak.

She drew back from him. 'Can you not know? Oh, Papa, this is a terrible surprise for you. I'll tell you everything, I promise. I see that you found Grandpapa?' She released him, and with a sunny smile she danced into the house. Her friend and Mags followed, leaving Aysun and Nyra staring dumbly after them.

'She seems well,' said Nyra.

'Quite,' Aysun agreed feebly. How far changed his daughter now was, Aysun could not imagine; but he was very certain he had never seen her so bright, so happy, and so entirely without the fears and the awkwardness that had plagued her since she was a child.

'Well,' said Rheas. 'Shall we go in?' He hobbled inside without waiting for an answer. Aysun and Nyra had no choice but to follow.

CHAPTER SEVEN

Tren was staring vacantly at the pages of an open book when the woman appeared.

It wasn't that he'd given up, precisely. He had been hard at work since soon after moonrise and it was now long after moonset, but as he had nothing better to do and no company at all, he had every intention of continuing with his reading until he couldn't stay awake anymore.

But some awkward part of his mind had had other ideas, ever since he'd learned that Lady Glostrum was spending the evening with Lord Angstrun instead of studying side-by-side with him as she usually did.

Particularly since he had realised that she wasn't coming home until the next day. What *that* meant did not take a great deal of intellect to decipher. When he had heard light footsteps crossing the floor of the study, his grey misery had lifted with the brief hope that Eva had come back after all.

But when he looked up, he saw a complete stranger.

She wasn't as tall as Eva, but she was larger in every other sense. Her hair was chestnut brown and her complexion was a shade of brown he'd never seen before. She smiled at him and paused before the desk.

'Forgive my intrusion,' she murmured. She had a lilting accent that was pleasing to the ear, though he couldn't place it. 'I wasn't expecting anyone to be here so late.'

Tren stood up and bowed politely. 'I probably shouldn't be.'

'Then that makes two of us, for I shouldn't be here either.'

Tren smiled uncertainly. 'Are you a friend of Lady Glostrum's?'

'I have never met her ladyship. I am looking for some lost property.' The woman shifted her attention to the desk, still scattered with books, and she actually began searching through them. Feeling a flicker of alarm, Tren closed the book he was reading and stacked it up with a few others.

'If you'll grant me your name, I'll tell Lady Glostrum you called. Perhaps she could help you another time?'

'Oh, no, no,' she replied mildly. 'I don't need to be helped. Ah, there it is.' Her hand darted out; she grabbed a book from the middle of Tren's pile and pulled it out. The rest collapsed and slithered to the floor.

'Um—wait, those belong to Lady Glostrum, you can't just—' He quickly began picking up fallen books, stacking them out of her reach.

'This one is mine,' the woman said, leafing through the large book that she held. Then her brow furrowed. 'Hm. Did you remove these?'

Tren realised she was holding Andraly Winnier's memoirs. The torn stubs of the missing pages stuck forlornly out of the centre of the book.

'Certainly not!'

'I see,' she said. 'Thank you.' She turned away and made for the door, but before she reached it her form became suddenly less solid. He could make out the outline of the door before her.

Then she vanished.

For an instant Tren sat frozen with confusion. Then, remembering that the study overlooked the street outside, he jumped out of his chair and hurried to the window. The streets were dark—the Night cloak reigned overhead, blotting out all sunlight—but the lamplighters had done their work diligently, and the streets were well illuminated with silvery-white light globes bobbing gently in the air. He could discern no sign of the chestnut-haired woman.

Tren drifted back to his chair and sat down, suddenly realising how tired he was. He had probably hallucinated the figure out of pure sleep deprivation. But the book was certainly gone...

The prospect of making his lonely way back to his house repelled him; it was a walk of more than twenty minutes and he couldn't face it in his current state. He shuffled to the sofa instead and lay down.

When he woke, he opened his eyes to a vision of smooth white skin and soft, even whiter hair. Lady Glostrum's face, close to his. Her deep blue eyes were fixed on him, bearing a thoughtful expression.

'Oh,' she murmured as he blinked. 'I'm sorry. You seemed deeply asleep.'

'One would think in that case that it would be *more* questionable to stare at me in this way.' He couldn't move without bumping into her, so he stayed where he was.

'I told you not to wait up for me.'

He cocked an eyebrow at her. 'Somebody has to keep an eye on wayward young ladies.'

He expected her to laugh at that, but she frowned and sat back on her heels. He sat up, suddenly feeling awkward. A small black shape fell from his chest and flew off.

'Rikbeek likes you,' Eva said, noticing the direction of his gaze. She didn't move away.

'Lucky me. Does that mean he'll be drinking more of my blood, or less?'

'Probably more.'

His neck itched, right on cue. He slapped the gwaystrel away in irritation.

'Sorry,' Eva said. She didn't sound remotely remorseful. If anything she was trying not to laugh.

'If that monster of yours sucks me dry, I'm holding you responsible.'

'No danger of that. He'd explode if he tried it.'

'It might be worth the sacrifice, in that case.'

She laughed softly. Watching the way her mouth dimpled at the corners, he forgot to speak. The silence stretched.

'Er, so,' he said with a cough. 'How was your dinner? And what time *is* it, anyway?'

She glanced briefly at the uncurtained window. 'Not moonrise yet. And dinner was fine.'

He looked at her, puzzled. She'd obviously stayed the night with Angstrun, yet here she was home before the moon even rose. It was none of his business to ask, of course, but...

'Oh,' he blurted. 'I forgot. Um, one of the books is gone.'

'Gone.' She repeated the word without inflection, gazing at him levelly.

He sighed and rubbed his eyes, still feeling exhausted in spite of his few hours of sleep. 'I hope you are feeling credulous, or I am about to be fired.' He told her about his nocturnal visitor and the woman's curious disappearance, explaining in some detail in hopes of being believed. Her expression didn't change, but he knew his story must be hard to credit.

He finished speaking and she said nothing at all.

'I suppose I'd better go home,' he said at last.

'Must you? I was about to order breakfast.' She stood up and dusted off her skirt. 'Don't worry about the book. Not your fault. But it's interesting. Shall it be eggs?'

'Thank you, I—' He stopped. She was already gone.

Breakfast was a leisurely affair. Suffering from a headache and some degree of eye strain, he was in no hurry to return to the study, and neither did Eva seem to be. Their conversation was restored more or less to normal; his vague feeling of awkwardness faded and by the end of the meal he felt cheered and more like himself. As Eva's servants cleared away the remains of their meal, Eva paused at the dining room door and smiled at him.

'I have the morning free, and I think I shall spend it assisting you. If books are spiriting themselves away, it would be best to take copious notes as soon as possible.'

The prospect of another long day at the desk was suddenly desirable. 'Agreed,' he said, stretching the muscles of his arms and neck as he followed her back to the study.

The desk was empty.

Both stood frozen for some moments in complete astonishment. They had been absent for an hour and a half at best; Tren was certain that all of the books had been on the desk when he had left the room.

'Tren, did you...?'

'I have not moved them.'

She nodded. 'Milyn must have been tidying in here while we were at breakfast. I'll enquire where she put them.'

Tren had a sick feeling that Milyn would know nothing about it. Sure enough, Eva returned to the study looking dismayed.

'All of my staff have sworn that they have touched nothing in here. I do not think they would lie to me, but...' She trailed off, stared at the empty desk. Tren was chilled to see her lost for words; she who normally had an answer for everything.

She shook her head. 'The house will be searched. In the meantime, you spoke of cross-referencing your notes at the city library? Perhaps we should continue there.'

'Of course,' he agreed readily enough. She was taking the event well, he reflected, but just as he formed the thought her elegant shoulders slumped and her face took on an expression of stress. A deep sigh came from her.

'I'm sorry,' he said quickly. 'It's my fault, I should

have guarded them better.'

Her head came up at that. 'Your fault? You've forgotten that it is my doing that the books were here in the first place. I insisted on detaining you at my home instead of the library, because it would be more *secure*. In fact I suppose I was merely being self-indulgent.'

Tren watched her uncertainly. 'No one could blame you for preferring to have them studied here in your own house, under your eye. You couldn't possibly have found time to travel to the city library every time you wanted a report.'

'That was part of it, yes.' She took a breath and looked him in the face. 'There was something else, though, I think. More to do with you.'

'Uhh. Me? What?'

Eva gave him one of her warm, bright smiles, the ones he'd seen her direct at Vale but never before at him. 'I like having you around.'

Tren blinked, trying to decipher her tone. 'Wait, you did that because of me?—I mean, because you— um, no. That can't be true.' He ran a hand through his hair, feeling hopelessly confused. 'I, um, like being around you too. I don't even need to say that I guess because it's obvious, and, um.' Eva was staring blankly at him, her smile gone, and he realised he must sound like an idiot. Adopting what he hoped was his usual friendly smile, he tried again. 'I'm sorry, I'm sleep deprived. What exactly are you saying?'

A tap came at the door.

'Enter,' Eva called, without taking her eyes from his face. The door creaked open and a soft female voice with a broad west city accent spoke.

'Milady, I was wondering if you'd noticed Lord

Vale's carriage has just drawn up.'

Eva blinked as if coming out of a trance, turning to stare at her maid with apparent incomprehension. 'Oh,' she said at last. Then, more firmly, 'Yes. Thank you, Milyn.'

The girl bobbed a curtsey and, flicking a brief glance at Tren, she left.

Eva looked back at him, and in an instant she was all business once more. 'I will be at the library later on. Perhaps I'll see you there?'

'Yes, um. I'll be there.'

With a nod but absolutely without a smile, she was gone.

Tren realised with distant interest that his hands were shaking. Stuffing them into his pockets he ventured out into the hallway, then immediately regretted it. Lord Vale stood near the staircase, his grey hair damp from the rain and his powerful frame swathed in a magnificent great-coat. His arms were around Eva and he held her very close.

'Eva,' Tren heard him say softly, 'I've had enough of waiting. Never mind the grand wedding; we don't need it. Just marry me. This week. Tomorrow, even.'

Tren found that he badly needed some air.

He passed many long hours at the city library, but Eva did not arrive. He found nothing relating to the mysterious Eterna Conflict, and nothing about Ayrien, but that was much as he expected. It was clear by now that this area of research was, for whatever reason, beyond the capacity of the city resources.

Sometime after moonset he abandoned his hope of seeing Eva and went home. There he found a note lying on the floor.

Mr Warvel,

I apologise for my failure to appear at the library today. Vale and I have decided to proceed at once with the wedding. It is another outstanding obligation that I am anxious to remove, that I may focus entirely on our joint venture. We both hope you will attend our modest ceremony at the City Hall on the 12th of this moon.

E. Glostrum.

For a moment he struggled to breathe as a cold, sick feeling settled somewhere in the pit of his stomach. The twelfth was five days away. Five! And the coldness of the address hurt. She'd stopped calling him Mr Warvel some time ago; to resurrect it now placed him at an insurmountable distance from her.

He found a chair and sat down. For some minutes he merely sat and tried to breathe, reading the note over and over again. The twelfth. Five days.

Then, with shaky composure, he sat at his desk and wrote a reply to her ladyship. It was not a particularly long response, but it took him some time to form the words.

He posted the letter at the nearest post box. Lady Glostrum had dispatched hers by the expedited messenger service, but he was in no hurry for her to read his reply.

When he returned home, he drew his sturdy travelling bag out of the depths of his wardrobe and began to pack.

Carefully, experimentally, Devary Kant flexed his left arm. Most of the left side of his body had been badly injured during his fight with the white-haired sorcerer and his inexplicable escort of whurthag beasts, but now he was whole and hale; not even a scar remained as a souvenir of his ordeal. The muscles of his arm responded perfectly. Encouraged, he went through a few experimental blocks and strikes and stretches, slowly at first then with increasing speed as he pulled off each move perfectly.

His body, then, was fully recovered, even if his mind remained perturbed. His superiors obviously didn't trust him, as he had been locked into his recovery room ever since he had been deposited here. Presumably he was to be released and sent on his errand at their pleasure. He would rather do it at his own.

Llandry Sanfaer. He knew from Ynara that she had last been located in the Upper Realms. How long ago that had been he couldn't say; it had been impossible to measure the passage of time in this stark room where the light levels never varied and he never caught a glimpse of the sky. Llandry might be anywhere by now.

Nonetheless, he would follow the only clue that he had. And if he found her, well... he would handle that when it happened.

He collected the few possessions of his that remained in this room. His clothes had been taken shortly after he arrived, but to his relief they had reappeared, laundered and mended, sometime while he slept. His daggers were gone, of course, and that loss pained him, for they were expensive, perfectly balanced weapons that had been designed for him years ago. But no matter. He would acquire another pair.

The matter of escaping from this place would be no small feat. There were no doors or windows in the bare walls. The one time he had caught sight of his captor, the man had appeared apparently out of the air, as he had done at Ynara's house. Devary could not render himself insubstantial, but he was capable of another kind of translocation. Just barely.

Closing his eyes, he reached for the boundary between the worlds. It always took him some time to find the divide, for he was a sorcerer of no particular talent. He was prepared for that, but today the endeavour took still longer than it should have. He searched diligently, visualising the pathways in his mind, but he found nothing.

Puzzled, he took a few slow breaths and then began again. True, he did not absolutely know whether he currently stood in the Daylands or the Darklands or somewhere in the Seven Realms in between. He kept his mind open, casting for any hint of a route into either the Uppers or the Lower Realms. Still, nothing emerged. The spaces between the worlds yawned before his anxious mind, empty and silent.

This he had not anticipated. True, it was a risky prospect to escape through one of the Off-Worlds. Both were perilous, and without his daggers he would be placing himself at risk. But he trusted his erstwhile employers still less than they apparently trusted him, and he found this desperate option preferable to that of awaiting their next appearance.

If it was denied him, he had nothing; no alternative but to sit and wait and hope that they had no worse plans for him than they had already expressed. But how could it fail? Had he somehow lost even his limited sensitivity to the boundaries while he lay ill?

He took a breath to calm himself and began again. This time, he searched not for the familiar shades of possibility that usually hovered just within reach, but for anything that beckoned, however distantly. And at length, he found something.

It was almost nothing at all; merely the barest whisper of a way. It appeared hazy in his mind's eye, as if muffled or shrouded behind something else. Straining, he sought to grasp it before it vanished, but his mind encountered an obstruction.

It felt like he came up against a wall of gauze, fine but infinitely layered. He could sense, increasingly clearly, the opening that lay behind it, but he couldn't reach it. He beat at the bindings in frustration, but only succeeded in giving himself a headache.

He withdrew, and sat upon his narrow bed to think. He could not force his way through, that was clear enough. But if he could make only the smallest hole in its surface, perhaps he could widen that gap until it was possible for him to slip through.

He tried this. It took all of his power of concentration, and at length it was indeed only the very smallest of gaps he created, but it was enough; the boundary was breached. Sweating and gritting his teeth with the effort, he pulled and worried at that gap until he had worked his way through all the layers, and a hole opened wide enough for him to pass through. Then he paused, gasping for air as he explored the possibilities revealed.

Beyond it stretched not just one pathway, but many.

Staggered, he reeled under the onslaught of so many rends in the boundaries of the worlds. They crowded together, kept apart only by some force of energy that Devary couldn't understand. He felt that, without it, they would merge together into an impossible chaos. For a moment he panicked; how could he determine where to go?

But he swiftly found that it was simple. A glance through each gate sent his vision soaring into the world that lay beyond. Some of the paths led into the Seven Realms: he saw a sun-drenched Glinnery landscape and wondered briefly whether it lay near to the city of Waeverleyne. Ynara would have been left without any knowledge of where (or indeed how) he had gone; for a moment he was sorely tempted to go to her and explain. But he pushed the thought aside. Llandry's need was more immediate.

Another gate offered him passage into the Lower Realms, or so it appeared, and he pressed on feeling encouraged, for there must also be a gate into the Uppers.

At last he found just such a gate. He tensed, ready to hurl himself through it, but for an instant he paused. This collection of gates was remarkable; he had neither seen nor heard of anything like it across the Seven. So where was he? He would have dearly liked to remain and explore in the hopes of answering that question; but once again concern for Llandry spurred him onward.

He clutched at the gate and pulled, dragging himself through the hole he had made in the curious shroud. Gritting his teeth against the nausea that such a gate always generated, he stepped through.

The pain hit him halfway. He resisted the temptation to stop, suspended as he was somewhere between wherever he had come from and wherever he was going to. The not knowing added to his sense of disorientation and he had to force his way out of the gate. He fell through at last and dropped to the ground, his body a mass of pain as if the two worlds between them sought to tear him apart.

As soon as he could breathe again, he staggered upright and wrenched the gate closed. Almost immediately the pain receded and the nausea ebbed away.

He stood in a sea of moss, soft and thick and mottled in shades of yellow and green. An enormous sun shone powerfully overhead and he soon began to sweat. A glance at his surroundings revealed nothing on the horizons but empty sky above and hills covered in moss below. There was nothing to suggest a starting point, nowhere he could begin in his search.

Still, at least he had escaped into the Upper Realm. Stretching out the limbs so recently creased with pain, he lifted his chin and set off in pursuit of Ynara's daughter.

CHAPTER EIGHT

Llandry was learning that when two stubborn old men were placed into the same room together, their individual stubbornness not only doubled but increased tenfold. On the topic of any degree of reconciliation, they were both wholly intractable. At last, dejected, Llandry fled their mutual chill of manner and took refuge in the garden behind Rheas's house.

Inevitably, Pensould followed her.

'You see, Minchu,' he said, sitting on the grass at her feet, 'where one has been wronged, one cannot forgive. Your father understands this. Where one has wronged, one cannot likewise forgive. Your grandfather understands this also. Only you and the Mags expect differently.'

'Mags, Pensould, not the Mags. If we think it possible, why shouldn't they?'

'It is because you are female.'

Llandry bristled. 'Don't tell me it is because women are stupid, or inferior, or some such nonsense.'

Pensould bristled as well, in so like a manner that Llandry wondered if he was making fun of her. 'No draykon female is stupid or inferior. You are strong, but you see things differently. And I, too, am different.'

'Oh? In what way are you different? You're a male as well.'

'But I am no ordinary male. I am the special and magnificent type of male which you have never before seen. From me, you should expect marvels.' Pensould gave her a hopeful smile, in which he showed too much of his teeth.

Llandry couldn't help smiling back. 'Are you indeed? How fortunate that I should have met one of those by chance.'

'It is not chance,' said Pensould solemnly. 'It is fate. You are wrong to resist me.'

'Oh? You pursue me because I'm the only female draykon around.'

'Not so.' Pensould looked affronted.

Llandry stood up and flexed her wings. 'Well, anyway. I think it's time to take Papa home.'

Llandry waited with anxiety as Pensould helped Aysun to seat himself on Llandry's back. She had never carried a human before, and this was her father; what if she hurt him?

She hadn't chosen to use a gate because she didn't want to take him straight home, not right away. She'd come to realise how much her father had missed out on during his years of self-imposed exile from the Uppers. It was her home, now; she couldn't imagine leaving it, no matter how much she loved Glinnery and her parents. She wanted her father to see some of its beauty, to feel the magic of the place. She hoped he might then understand her choice.

Once in the air, she circled away from her grandfather's house and began a tour of some of her favourite places in the Uppers. It took some time, for she flew slowly to avoid hurting or losing Aysun. But it was worth it. As they flew over lakes and waterfalls, woods and valleys, mountains and wolds, she felt Aysun's tension relax and his suspicion and fear give way to wonder.

That was victory enough for today. Careful not to overdo it, she headed for home. It was an advantage that, for her, passage through the boundaries was virtually seamless, with none of the nausea and pain that marred the experience of traversing a sorcerer-wrought gate. Nonetheless, Aysun endured it as though it were an ordeal; Llandry could feel his tension return tenfold as he sat between her vast wings.

Ah, well. He would grow used to that soon enough as well.

When they arrived home, a small sea of reporters awaited them.

They were assembled just far enough from the Sanfaer home that Ynara herself probably couldn't see them from the window. Llandry guessed that she had thrown them out, but they, unbelievably, had outright disobeyed the order of an Elder and lingered anyway. As Llandry landed gracefully and let Aysun down from her back, the flashing lights of many image-capture machines went off around her.

And under the onslaught of their curiosity and

their scrutiny, Llandry felt her old nerves crowding upon her for the first time since her transformation. She shifted back to her human form clumsily, too aware of the intrusive gaze of her audience. Pensould however strode up to them in his draykon form, flexing his wings and lifting his chin. He roared for their benefit, then slowly metamorphosed into his still-imperfect human shape, obviously relishing the attention. Grabbing his arm, Llandry dragged him away.

'You're such an exhibitionist,' she muttered as she pulled him towards the elevator.

'Are you displeased? But they are here for a show! I must not disappoint. Why are we walking?'

'Because you... oh.' Previously Pensould had been wingless, like her father, but now she noticed he had sprouted a pair of grey wings like her own.

'I forgot, before.'

'Well, my father must still walk.'

'He must grow some wings as well. I will tell him.' Pensould turned around to do just that, but Llandry grabbed his hand again and pulled him back.

'He can't, Pensould. For us, our human shapes are fixed.'

'Can't? Nonsense. For lesser humans, perhaps, but I can feel plenty of ability in him. Why, he is almost as much draykon as you or I, Minchu, and you too could change this shape of yours if you wished.'

Llandry stopped, electrified by this idea. 'I could?'

Pensould tsked. 'Your education has been lacking. For you, very little is fixed. You must learn this. If you can manipulate the world around you as you choose—and this I have seen you do—then why not yourself also?'

Llandry noticed abruptly that Pensould's colouring had improved immeasurably and his mannerisms were becoming steadily more passable as human. He was perfecting his image very quickly indeed. In fact he was even learning how to make himself quite handsome by human standards.

'That's a horrible idea,' Llandry said at last. 'Imagine if anybody could appear in any way that they liked, changing all the time. You'd never know who was who.'

'Of course you would. I know who you are because you *feel* like my Minchu. It has nothing to do with your face.'

Llandry had no time to reply, for they were at the door. Aysun had still said nothing at all, and when the door opened to reveal Ynara he merely embraced his wife and then disappeared inside. They heard the door to his study close—not loudly, but firmly—and then silence.

Ynara looked at Llandry. 'It didn't go well, I take it.'

'Not particularly well, no.' She paused. 'Although not for the reasons you might think.'

'It's good to have you home, love,' said Ynara later, over cups of Llandry's favourite white alberry and freyshur tea. Sigwide lay curled contentedly in Llandry's lap, having exhausted himself with ecstatic greetings as she arrived. 'I visited your home while you were away,' continued Ynara. 'It's clean and waiting for you.' Her eyes flicked to Pensould, and Llandry read her thoughts clearly enough. Would Llandry's strange new friend be moving in there with her?

Llandry winced inwardly, because her news was worse than that. 'We aren't staying, Ma. At least not yet. See, Pensould believes there are more draykons to be discovered. There are certainly more bones, and if we could find and reconstruct them we could wake up more like him. Like us, I mean. And...' she took a deep breath, for this was the part that truly inspired her. 'He says there may be more like me.'

Ynara took a long breath too; Llandry knew she was trying to control her instinct to object to anything that took Llandry away. 'Like you in what way exactly?' was all that she said.

'Draykons who were born human. I can't be the only one.'

Pensould nodded firmly. 'I can tell, and I will teach you to recognise the draykon energy as well.'

Llandry looked back at her mother, knowing that her eyes were shining with delight at the idea. 'Don't you see, Ma? This has changed my life. If there are others, they have to know what they are.'

'I can see that it has changed you,' Ynara said thoughtfully. She sighed, and for a moment her face was so sad that Llandry's resolve wavered. But she hid the expression behind a smile. 'How do you plan to proceed, love? It's a big world.'

'Pensould says he sensed a draykon grave not long after he woke, so we're going to start at his old resting place. The place where I changed. He'll teach me to seek them out even on the wing. Between us I'm sure we'll find it fast enough.'

'Then what? How did you wake, Pensould?'

Pensould's thick brows knit together. 'Regenerative ability is something all draykons possess. We need the help of a fellow to rebuild body structure, and then a stimulus, and above all a reason to wake.'

'A reason?'

Pensould nodded emphatically. 'Draykons are long-lived and slow to fade, hence we may be re-awakened if we choose. But many do not choose to be drawn out of slumber.'

Llandry frowned as well. 'Why wouldn't you? Nobody wants to die.'

Pensould lifted a brow at her. 'No? If you think about it you will see that this is not true. Imagine that you have been alive for many, many long years and you are very weary. Would you not choose to rest at last?'

The thought made her obscurely sad, but she could see the sense of it. 'Is that what happened with you?'

'Yes. That was a very long time ago, I think. I find that nothing is the same now that I am awake again.'

'Then why did you choose to return?'

Pensould thought for a moment. 'The agent of my recovery was quite insistent. I was drawn halfway out of slumber by sheer irritation.' Llandry remembered the way he had lashed out against the summoner who had awoken him. The white-haired awakener had escaped the punishment, but only because her husband had taken the blow instead. He had not survived Pensould's wrath.

'But that's not all. I could have returned to sleep, but I did not. That is because I sensed you near to me.' Pensould beamed at her, and Llandry's cheeks warmed.

'Oh...'

Ynara cleared her throat. 'When are you two planning to leave?'

'Soon, Ma. I'm sorry. But we'll come back when we can.'

Ynara gave a short sigh. 'Well then, love. We'd better persuade your father to come out of the study.'

Taking leave of her parents was a sad experience. Llandry had lived either with them or close to them for all of her twenty years; they had loved and supported her entirely without condition for those two decades, and it was hard to leave them behind. She also suffered somewhat on seeing her father's obvious distress. It had hurt him badly to learn that his father Rheas had voluntarily deserted his family twenty-odd years ago.

But as Llandry and Pensould flew away—ignoring the flash of image-captures below them—her sense of excitement and possibility swiftly swept away her sorrow. Sigwide had chosen to come with her, and she realised how much she had missed his cheery little consciousness while they'd been separated. He lay nestled between her shoulder blades, his small claws gripping her hide to hold himself in place. She had wondered how he might take to flying with her in this new way, but he seemed entirely untroubled as long as she was near. Nor did her new shape trouble him. She thought of Pensould's words—*it has nothing to do with your face.* Apparently her orting companion also identified her not by her human shape but by some other sense. Was it only humans who relied so heavily on outward appearances?

As Llandry and Pensould crossed into the Uppers,

all her discomfort drained away. She had been attracted to the draykon bone—or Istore, as she had thought of it then—because of the soothing and strengthening effect it had on her. In her draykon form she felt the same effect when in the Upper Realm, only amplified. She couldn't imagine living anywhere but Iskyr, as Pensould termed it.

She followed as Pensould led her with unwavering confidence back to the place where he had once rested, his blue-green scales gleaming in the bright sun. For herself, she barely recognised it; there was nothing to draw her back to the place as for Pensould, and she supposed she had been somewhat distracted the last time she had been here. He circled the location a few times, gliding effortlessly close to the ground.

I sense nothing, he communicated to her at last. She didn't recognise the language he used when he spoke to her this way—if indeed he was using anything that could classify as a language at all. But she always understood what he said.

There was something here, he continued. *I know it. How can it be gone?*

Perhaps you misremembered, she suggested diffidently. *It was a confusing time.*

I was not mistaken. He said it with unanswerable finality.

Llandry hazarded nothing further, merely waited while he made up his mind.

We will go to the west, as we did before. Pensould dipped his wings and soared westwards, and she followed. West indeed they had gone after her startling transformation; west a long way and still west, until they were so deep into the Realm of Iskyr they seemed to have left the human world far behind. Out there, Llandry felt the currents of the world's energy grow stronger, fiercer and more irresistible; for some time she had steeped herself in them, happy to forget what she had once been. Only after the thrill had finally ebbed a little had her buried self-knowledge reasserted itself.

As she flew she wondered, would it happen again? Would she lose herself in the glorious strength of her new form, the energy she held at her beck and call? She was mistress of this world, bending it to her will with increasing ease as she grew more practiced. She and Pensould amused themselves by reforming the lands they flew over, creating tableaus for each other. For him she wrought a set of tiny draykons out of mist, which danced in the air as he passed. For her he reshaped all the flowers to resemble ortings that squeaked greetings as she flew over them. Llandry felt Sigwide's curiosity and delight at the trick, and she had to steady him with her tail to keep him from jumping off her back in his excitement. She could so easily forget herself altogether with such wonders to occupy her.

Then in the midst of her enjoyment came a note of familiarity which tugged at her consciousness. Somewhere below her walked somebody that she knew. She thought immediately of her father, but no—he had been deposited safely in Glinnery and it was impossible that he could have beaten them here. Her grandfather, then? It didn't feel like him. She was not yet so adept as Pensould at identifying people with senses other than her sight, but still she felt fairly sure that it was not Rheas that wandered beneath the trees below.

She thought of ignoring the tug; it might only be that her newly awakened draykon senses, being untrained, were misleading her. But the tug of familiarity nagged at her.

Stop, she called to Pensould. *Wait for me; I'll return.* She circled and flew back at speed, aiming unerringly for the source of the sensation. Immediately she realised she had done this before in exactly this fashion: allowed herself to be drawn by precisely this same beacon. It was Devary who walked below.

It was not long since she had sped to his rescue, newly transformed into her draykon shape. She had felt his pain and fear increasing as she grew closer, and on reaching him she'd found him badly injured and near death. She sensed none of that now. Could it really be Dev, wandering in the Uppers this far west? Surely he still lay at her mother's house, healing far too slowly.

She thought back. Her mother had not said that he was well; she had only said *he did not die*. She had thought it an odd phrase to use at the time, but distracted by her father's danger she had not enquired. In fact, she had not even confirmed that he was still at Ynara's house. Nor had she thought to do so on her second visit.

Guilt hit her in a rush, and she flew faster. Soon she could see him; her draykon heart fluttered with recognition at the sight of that lanky figure and its customary ranging gait, dark hair tied back out of his pale face. He did not have his lyre with him, which was odd, but odder still was his obvious glowing health. Expensive medical care notwithstanding, injuries like his could not possibly have healed less than a moon after the wounds were received.

Wary, she circled in the skies. Perhaps it was an illusion; she could have brought it on herself, the way she still sometimes inadvertently painted the realm of Iskyr to resemble the comforting familiarity of Glinnery. But he looked up, and when he saw her his face and posture registered complete shock. Then he smiled.

'*Llandry,*' he called. His Nimdren accent produced a slight peculiarity in the way he said her name. She had always liked to hear him say it. If he was a figment of her imagination, surely he would not speak? She landed carefully, not too close to him, and waited as he approached.

'Llandry, is that... is that you? Truly?'

With a thought, she shimmered back into her human form.

'Really truly,' she smiled. There was a time when she'd been a little afraid of Devary, with his handsomeness and his charming manner. She was pleased to note that this was no longer the case.

She was less pleased when she realised, with a sudden shock, that if anything he was afraid of *her*. He stared at her looking somewhat wild about the eyes, and he was slow to approach. A sudden lump rose in her throat. Had her parents felt that way too?

'I'm still me,' she said quietly.

He shook his head. 'I don't think you are.'

Her smile trembled, but she forced it to hold. 'Dev. I'm so pleased to see you, and to see you well, but... how? And what are you doing up here?'

'Yes, I—I need to explain some things to you. And I fear it must be done quickly, before we are located.'

Llandry frowned, puzzled. 'Located? By who?'

'My employers. Llan, I was never fully honest with

you and I'm sorry for it. But I feared—I feared you
would reject me if you knew.'

Llandry sensed his anxiety and hurried to calm
him. 'Dev, I doubt anything you can tell me would
have that effect. You're the first real friend I've had,
other than Mamma and Pa.'

'And Sigwide,' he said with a small smile. The
orting lifted his nose in Devary's direction in
acknowledgement, and he chuckled.

'I first met your mother years ago—before you
were born. But it was not an accidental meeting. I was
sent. As a very young man I was recruited by an
agency in Nimdre—based in Draetre, my home
town—to gather information. This organisation was
attached to the university of magic and technology.
You remember our visit? Indren Druaster was one of
my earliest colleagues. The university studied the
history of magic and engineering; our task was to
learn of the newest discoveries and techniques made
by the various scholars and organisations of the Seven
Realms.

'My agency has been troubled in the past by some
of Irbel's technological creations, and they wanted
information about Irbel's recent inventions. But you
must know that infiltrating Irbel itself is extremely
difficult; they keep their developing technologies
under close watch. It was thought that a recent
expatriate may be an easier target: somebody who no
longer lived under Irbel's aura of secrecy might be
more easily persuaded to discuss their work.'

Devary sighed. His face looked worn, even
haggard, and his eyes were anxious as he looked at
her.

'My task was to get close to your mother, if I

could, so that in turn I could become acquainted with your father. He was then, as he is now, a talented engineer; at the time he had only recently left Irbel. To his credit, he never betrayed a word to me about the projects he had been involved with back in Irbel. I learned nothing of use. But your mother found out why I was there, and she... well, she was very angry. As of course she had every right to be. That is why I left Glinnery. We were only recently reconciled, and only then because I was able to swear to her that I had distanced myself from the agency. I was—I am— truly sorry about that betrayal. Your mother's friendship is deeply important to me.'

He paused, awaiting a reaction, but Llandry was unable to give one. Her mind was too busy, putting together all the little things that had puzzled her about Devary. How he hinted at an old quarrel with her parents but would never give her the details. She had overheard him telling Ynara that he had been "sent" to learn more about the Istore; an assignment he had accepted in order to prevent a mysterious "they" from sending someone less sympathetic. And he always carried daggers—which he clearly knew how to use well—even though his ostensible profession as a travelling musician offered no justification for it. It all made a horrible amount of sense.

'The worst part,' Devary continued, and now he sounded as though it was truly hard for him to speak, 'is that my employers will not let me desert my post at the agency. They still have a use for me, and they are able to force me to perform it. My task this time is specifically you, Llan. I don't know what use they have for you but I don't think it can be good. I am telling you this now because you must be warned; you need to take yourself far away, somewhere they can't reach you.'

Llandry remembered to take a breath. Her stomach clenched in fear at his last words; it was not long since she had last been hunted, hounded for the draykon bone that only she knew how to find. But that was over; the bones had all been found and taken. What possible use could she now be to anyone?

'Your employers,' she said at last. 'Who are they? Why would they want me?'

Devary paled. 'I think... I have suspected for some time that the agency is not as it once was. Perhaps it was never as I believed it to be. Some of the people I have lately seen are not... they do not look Nimdren. They speak Nimdren like natives but something about them is not right. I don't know who they are. Now, Llandry, there is nothing more I can do for you. I wish it were not so but they are able to do things no sorcerer can match and I am powerless against them. You, though—as a draykon you may fare better, if you are warned. Now, please, you must keep away from me.'

He started to back away as he said this, as if he intended to put distance between the two of them as quickly as possible. Llandry started to say something to call him back—puzzled and alarmed by his revelations, she had more to ask—but something pulled at her draykon senses and she stopped. She felt the atmosphere warp and bend, a disturbance so subtle she almost missed it. It was not like a sorcerer forcibly pulling open a gate; it felt more like somebody inserting a blade and deftly slicing a neat opening.

A presence came sliding through it, a tall man with pale hair. Was it blonde or even paler than that? His eyes were blue and very direct as they settled first on Devary and then on Llandry.

'Excellent work, Mr Kant. I knew you would not disappoint us.'

CHAPTER NINE

If the child had been better dressed, she could have passed for a miniature version of Eva herself.

The girl was ten years old and her hair was snow-white. She was quietly thoughtful, slightly diffident in manner, and the only one of Angstrun's sorcery students who had shown any ability at summoning.

Lord Angstrun himself stood, toweringly tall and as craggy as a corven, regarding the girl with crossed arms and lowered brow.

'So she's good at control, but otherwise she lacks the full spectrum.'

Eva nodded slowly, speaking to Angstrun in a low tone. 'I've rarely seen a child of this age with so much ability to control a beast, but her communication skills are minimal at best. And her methods are unusual. Most summoners are less... direct. They feel the beast's needs and impressions and behave accordingly. It's manipulative. Susa's approach is pure domination.'

The girl, Susa, looked back at Eva placidly. She

was diffident under Angstrun's heavy stare, but her demeanour hid a surprisingly firm will. When she had turned it on the tiny wood meerel Eva had provided for her, the timid creature had capitulated instantly. Susa had made the little furred beast walk, sit and jump according to her command, and apparently without it costing her much effort at all.

'What I don't understand,' Eva continued, 'is how she came to be sent to your department at all. With manipulation that strong, she should be in summoner training.'

Angstrun shook his head, apparently oblivious to Susa's discomfort. 'Early summoner testing focuses on beast empathy, doesn't it? She failed completely at that. And her sorcery is excellent.'

'True.' Eva was silent for a moment, still thinking. It made little sense for a summoner to be so successful at animal control, but to entirely lack the rest of the skillset. But none of her personal teaching and encouragement had awakened any ability in Susa save her frightening domination.

Eva, however, could detect the meerel's feelings about Susa. Opening her mind to the tiny beast, she sensed none of the fear or resentment she might have expected at the girl's manner of control. On the contrary, the meerel had developed a virtually instant devotion to Susa and refused to be parted from her. Susa's influence over it was practically mesmeric.

'Interesting,' Angstrun murmured, and she could only agree.

'Keep an eye on this one, Angstrun,' she said. 'Get her trained in beast control as well as sorcery. And there might be more like her.' She paused. 'Get all the white-haired children tested.'

He raised his heavy black brows at her. '"All"? There might be as many as three true white-hairs in the whole realm.'

'Then find all three.'

Later, after Susa and her new friend had been dismissed, Eva sat comfortably in Angstrun's chair with her feet up on his personal footstool. Rikbeek lay against her neck, shivering. She was cold, too. Didn't Angstrun use heating? Her gaze rested sightlessly at some spot on the spotless ceiling as she considered.

She was remembering her encounter with the two uncanny sorcerer-summoners in the Lowers. The specific aberrations among their abilities had included a degree of beast control that was normally impossible. Ana was a strong summoner, but still it shouldn't have been feasible for her to reliably control a whurthag taken from the wild. Those creatures— dark as night, fiercely violent and chillingly ice-eyed— had been banned generations ago for their untameable ferociousness.

And as for her husband, Griel, he was a sorcerer. Yet he, too, had manipulated whurthags with ease, especially when he was in the Lowers.

Both had the same rare, natural white hair as Susa. The same colour that Eva herself shared. And she, too, had brought a whurthag under her control when she'd had to. When Griel's pet had threatened Tren, she had protected him by dominating the creature herself.

To her surprise, she had succeeded in bringing it under her control. It was tenuous; she felt that, outside of the magic-enhancing atmosphere of the Lowers—and without a draykon bone to amplify her strength—she would have lost it.

But still. She could do it. And, feeling the fledgling strength of the ten-year-old Susa, she had little doubt that the girl would also be fearsomely strong when she was grown.

Angstrun threw open the door in the middle of her reflections, startling her. She turned a level gaze on him as he crossed the room, stopping in front of her.

'That's my chair.'

'It's mine now. At least for the next few minutes.'

'No it isn't. Get out.'

'No. I'm comfortable. Or I would be if it wasn't so damned cold in here.'

He muttered something and took the chair on the other side of the desk. His desk. 'Right, look. There's only so much I can do with this without securing some extra funding. We're pretty stretched at the moment. Are you making a report about this?'

Eva was silent for a moment. 'No,' she said at last. 'Darae. Think about this for a moment. If I'm right—if Susa's strength and her hair colour—her heritage, let's say—are linked, then we'd be training up a group of people who can take on whurthags with impunity. And we'd be making that public. I don't want a whole group of people like Ana on our hands.'

'Spoken like a true paranoid.'

She smiled briefly. 'Believe me, if you've faced down Griel and a pair of whurthags once, you don't want to do it again. The ban needs to remain untried for the moment. Just keep it quiet for now. Give them whatever testing you can manage without giving them any ideas, and without making it public. Let me know what comes up.' She paused. 'And keep an eye on Susa. I fear that one's already had more training than is good for her.'

Angstrun folded his arms. 'It can't be kept from everyone. Certainly not from Islvy.'

'I'll tell the Guardian,' Eva conceded. 'But privately.'

Angstrun nodded. 'How's Vale got on with finding your friends?'

Eva grimaced. Vale had gone after Ana and Griel personally, but without any success; he was still grumpy about it. 'There was no trace of either of them in Orstwych or Glour, though that wasn't unexpected. He's working on Ullarn's Sorcery and Summoning Schools to share their records.'

Angstrun's lips twitched. Eva could guess his thoughts. Ullarn's magical academies weren't held in high regard elsewhere; like Irbel, Ullarn's focus was predominantly on engineering, and they allocated very few resources to magical improvements. As a result, they usually lacked sufficient sorcerers and summoners to maintain the necessary magical infrastructures; but that didn't bother them at all, as they simply poached promising magical practitioners from the other Darklands realms. That issue was a constant thorn in Angstrun's side.

Eva herself was more annoyed by Ullarn's lack of cooperativeness. They were secretive, suspicious and sometimes outright unfriendly to the other realms, and getting them to assist with anything was usually a difficult task. 'Vale will wear them down,' Eva said confidently. 'He's used to dealing with them.'

Angstrun abruptly leaned forward. 'Speaking of.

You left pretty early the other night.'

"Pretty early" was putting it mildly. Lying in Angstrun's house unable to sleep, Eva had realised she'd made a mistake. It felt wrong, lying there with Angstrun beside her, and suddenly her old friend's house was the last place she wanted to be. She had left well before moonrise, when he was still deeply asleep.

'Sorry,' she said mildly. 'Early start that day.'

Angstrun glowered. 'That's not it, is it? Something tells me I won't be enjoying any more visits from you in the Cloaked hours.'

Eva sighed and sat up. 'I think not, Darae. I'm sorry. I wanted... I *want* to be able to go back to my twenties, when I could do as I pleased in that respect and it didn't matter. But it does matter, now.'

Angstrun looked sad, but he didn't argue. 'You're engaged, for the first time in your life. Things are bound to change.'

Eva didn't reply. It was true that she'd changed; she felt that her life was in the process of altering completely, and she couldn't predict where it would take her.

Because the part that puzzled her the most was *why* she was changing. And the reason she'd felt that sense of wrongness in Angstrun's house hadn't been because of Vale. It had been someone else's face she'd been missing.

Leaving the Academy, Eva had her carriage drop her a few circles away from her house and proceed home without her. She felt in need of a walk. At least, that was the reason she gave herself; underneath that she was oddly reluctant to reach home.

She had not seen Tren for two days. He had left her house immediately after Vale's unlooked-for arrival home, after which she had disgracefully allowed herself to be distracted away from her promise to meet him at the city library. She'd gone there the next day instead but this time it was Tren who had not appeared. He had not turned up at her house as had become his habit of late, nor had he replied to the note she had sent him. His sudden absence and silence affected her more profoundly than she liked to admit, and she feared arriving home to find that, once again, nothing from Tren awaited her.

She hadn't wanted to agree to Vale's pressure to hasten the wedding. But with him standing before her, smothering her with affection and his familiar face lit with hope and love, she hadn't been able to refuse.

But for a sudden, horrible moment, she'd wanted to.

And why? The marriage had been her idea. She felt her approach to the years when her body would lose the ability to create heirs; she felt the social pressure for a woman in her position to marry and have a family; she'd made a rational, clear-headed choice of partner for reasons which were as true now as they'd ever been. Lord Vale was perfect for her. A suitable age, suitable social status, suitable personality. She had never been bothered with notions of whether or not she loved him; she had no faith in the romantic notions that ruled other people. Decisions made for such irrational reasons fell apart later.

Nonetheless, now that she was on the verge of

carrying through her decision, something in her insisted on rebelling. She felt drawn irresistibly in another direction, and much as she tried to reject and repel it, the attraction refused to be suppressed. She had a horrible feeling that her heart, long under her rational and considered control, had betrayed her at last.

But none of that should matter. Particularly when the wholly unsuitable object of her wayward affection was apparently unmoved by it. Tren's manner was almost unwaveringly cheerful, and he bantered with her more in the manner of a comfortable friend than anything else. And when she'd tried to tell him something of her feelings, he had merely blabbered something nonsensical and smiled in his old way and nothing had come of it.

Now he seemed to have forgotten about her entirely. That hurt enough to warn her that she was most definitely in trouble.

Reaching home, she resolved on putting these reflections out of her mind. She had enough to occupy her thoughts, more than enough; the matter of Llandry and the other draykon remained unresolved, and she had a new theory to pursue. She smiled at the servant who came to take her coat as she stepped into the hall, and aimed resolutely for the study.

'This came for you, m'lady,' said Milyn with a curtsey, holding out a folded note. Eva took it with a flutter of trepidation.

'Thank you,' she murmured, taking the note with her into the study.

It was from Tren.

Lady Glostrum,

I have been called away on an urgent matter and will therefore be unable to attend your ceremony on the 12th. I wish you every happiness nonetheless.

At present I am unsure when I will be able to return to Glour. Any urgent correspondence may be left with Mrs Geslin in the meantime.

Yours etc.,

P. Warvel

Eva read this note through three times, her puzzlement only increasing with each perusal. The suddenness of it was peculiar. Only two days ago he had been as involved in their research as she, and apparently as enthusiastic; now he abandoned it entirely, for an unspecified time, on account of an unnamed "emergency"?

He had been on secondment to her for the last few weeks as her research aide, but he was still technically employed by Angstrun. And her own Lord Vale also utilised him from time to time as an investigator of magical infractions. Perhaps one of them had sent him away on his urgent errand? If so, they should have had the courtesy to inform her first.

But maybe they had nothing to do with it. Perhaps she'd simply been too forward, and Tren had responded by taking himself beyond her reach. She was, after all, more than ten years older than he was.

Thirteen, said a traitorous inner voice. Thirteen

years. She would be forty in less than two more years; he wouldn't even reach thirty for another five. She was being absurd. The prospect of committing herself to marriage at long last was making her nervous, that was all, and the result was one of those crises that sometimes affected people in the middle phase of their lives. Perhaps it would pass.

She fervently hoped so, for this uncertainty and doubt did not suit her at all. She straightened her shoulders, dismissing the problem. Sanguine confidence was much more comfortable: she pulled the semblance of it around herself like a well-loved gown and went in search of Vale.

She found him in the conservatory. He was stretched out in her rocking chair, a paper in his hand and the ambient light-globes turned up to their brightest radiance. She blinked a few times as she entered, surprised by the strong light.

'Eyde,' she greeted, bending to kiss his cheek. 'I've a question for you.'

'You were a long time.' Vale pulled her onto his lap, heedless of the fate of his newspaper, and proceeded to kiss her thoroughly. Rikbeek gave a squeak of protest as Vale's embrace squashed his hiding place in the folds of Eva's skirt. She ignored him.

'A question,' she repeated when she could speak again. 'Tren works for you sometimes. Did you send him on an errand lately?'

'How lately?' Vale had that misty smile he often wore when he looked at her.

'As in, the day before yesterday.'

Vale shook his head. 'He was working with you, wasn't he?'

Eva wrinkled her nose, disgruntled. 'He *was*. He's taken himself off somewhere on an "urgent" errand. I was wondering if he'd been seconded away from his secondment.'

'Nothing to do with me,' Vale said. 'But if we're getting back to business, then here. I have something for you.' He rescued the crumpled newspaper and handed it to her. She took one glance at the paper and all thoughts of Vale, Tren and her upcoming wedding flew out of Eva's head.

The front page boasted an enormous picture of a patch of Glinnery forest. The wide caps of glissenwol trees were depicted, and ghosting through the well-lit skies above was a very large beast. The picture had only caught part of the creature, but the general nature of it was obvious. Scaled hide, clawed feet, wings of improbable size...

Skies Darken Over Glinnery

The skies darkened over Glinnery today when two winged reptilian creatures were spotted flying over the city of Waeverleyne. Multiple sightings have been reported, describing the creatures as larger than any other known species. One of the beasts (pictured) was grey in colour and its companion—an even larger animal!—was blue-green. The sightings have caused widespread panic in the Glinnish capital, though there has been no response at all from the Summoner Guild as yet. Do they know more than they're saying about these mysterious monsters?

Eva scanned the rest of the report quickly, her hands beginning to shake. The grey draykon must have been Llandry, but the fact that the other draykon had accompanied her was worrying. She couldn't forget the way it had snapped its fearsome jaws around Griel's robust form, almost breaking the sorcerer in half. And the way it had herded Llandry into the sky and taken her away...

The Summoner Guild in Waeverleyne had of course been notified about the re-emergence of the draykons, though Eva suspected they hadn't taken the tale very seriously. Well, they would now.

She handed the paper back to Vale, working to hide her alarm. 'I wonder if Llandry realises she's causing a panic in her hometown,' was all she said, in her mildest tone.

'The girl should never have appeared in Waeverleyne like that,' Vale grouched.

'I imagine she wanted to see her mother.'

'That could have been accomplished a little more subtly.'

'I doubt she's thinking very rationally at the moment. An experience like hers would be enough to overset the best of us, I think.'

Vale shrugged. 'Well, it's too late now. That report's all over the Seven already. The bulletins are about to broadcast an article on it—a slightly less alarmist format, of course, but there'll be unease. I wouldn't be surprised if you're summoned to Council tomorrow.'

Eva sighed, exasperated. 'I'm not *on* the Council anymore.'

'Yes, but you're still the only person who knows anything about this draykon resurgence. Especially if Warvel has absconded.'

'I already gave the Council everything that I know.'

Vale smiled crookedly at her. 'We can't get along

without your counsel, it seems.'

Eva was not mollified by this. 'It'd better be a brief meeting. I never will have anything more to report on the matter if I'm not given enough time to *find* the information.'

'Oh yes? It's not going well then, I take it.'

'Not swimmingly.' She recounted the progress—or lack thereof—that she and Tren had made, dwelling on the disappearing books and Tren's uninvited visitor. Vale frowned as she reached this part, tightening his grip on her waist.

'Did she hurt you?'

'I wasn't even there.'

'Oh? Where were you?'

'Out. She didn't hurt Tren either, thanks for asking. Apparently all she did was take the book and leave.'

Vale pondered this. 'That is a huge problem for city security.'

'Maybe,' Eva mused. 'It depends what she's after.'

'Books, apparently. I'd better place some wardens in the city library.'

'If there was anything in there she was interested in, Eyde, I imagine it's already gone.' There was a thought. Had she and Tren failed at the library because the relevant books had been removed? If so, why?

Vale shifted in his chair. 'Didn't you say that Ana did the same thing? Vanished like that?'

'I did. That thought occurred to me, too. Tren said the book thief's method looked similar. An instant of translucency before she actually vanished.'

'If we could only get hold of her,' Vale mused. 'Seems the best place to go for answers.'

'Yes, but hard to catch,' Eva replied dryly. 'Any progress with Ullarn?'

'None yet. I'll let you know.'

Eva nodded and moved to stand up. He gripped her harder.

'Eyde, I have work to do.'

'Don't let this distract you again, Eva. Please. You'll be there?'

There meant ready and waiting in a wedding gown at the appointed time, only a few short days away. Eva ignored the tightening sensation in her stomach and gave a smooth reply. 'Of course.'

He smiled at that. A smile sat oddly on his usually grim face, but Eva had always liked to see it. 'Good. Don't work too hard. I want you awake for our wedding.'

Eva slipped off his lap and brushed down her skirts. 'I didn't see anything in the reports to suggest that the draykons hurt anyone. I'm not worried about Llandry, but her companion... have you heard anything?'

'To the best of my knowledge, nothing more untoward happened than the two of them flying over the city. No fire breathing, anyway.'

Eva smiled slightly. The old stories attributed that ability to the draykon race, but she hadn't seen any evidence of it so far. When the blue draykon had attacked Griel, he'd done so with his teeth.

'Good,' she murmured. 'Let's hope they stay peaceful. I dread to think how much damage that thing could do if it really got riled up.'

CHAPTER TEN

For an awful moment Llandry thought that Devary had set her up. The timing was so neat that any other explanation paled in contrast with the horrible idea that Devary had betrayed her. But she could see sincere horror written over his face; more importantly she could *feel* the dismay and guilt radiating from him.

'You weren't asking me to find Llandry,' he said at last, bitterly. 'You were using me as bait.'

'We took the liberty of installing a tracer when we put you back together,' the man admitted comfortably. 'Your loyalties have never been where they ought to be.'

Devary's emotions changed suddenly to anger. 'Where should they have been? With *you*? Who *are* you? You're no countryman of mine. And what do you want with Llandry, that I should help you instead of her?'

The man merely gazed at Devary thoughtfully. 'You were suggested as a candidate for promotion, but I think not. You would go the way of our last partials.'

This speech made no sense to Llandry, and apparently it made little to Devary either. He frowned, radiating confusion.

But the man's attention shifted back to Llandry. 'Don't try to Change,' he said.

She tried it, but his words acted like a binding on her. The part of her that attempted the transformation was relegated to a tiny corner of her mind; the rest obeyed his command with alarming docility. Panic fluttered at the edges of her constrained consciousness. What had he done?

She gathered her will. *Pensould,* she cried. He was far away but at her call she felt him come hurtling towards her.

Minchu?

She tried to answer him but most of her will had gone, taken over by the pale-haired man that stood at her elbow. She felt herself move closer to him, taking his hand. Devary stared at her as if she had gone mad.

It's not me, she tried desperately to tell him, but he couldn't hear her the way Pensould could, and her lips would not speak for her. That discreet gateway opened again and she was pulled into it.

... or only half in, as Devary lunged forward and grabbed her free arm, pulling her back. '*No,*' he said. 'Llan, no! You have to fight.'

She wanted to, but her will slipped away as she grasped at it and she could only stand, immobile, as Devary and his enigmatic employer fought over her.

Then Pensould was upon them. He dropped out of the sky almost on top of them, radiating extreme anger. He plucked the pale-haired man off the ground and lifted him, digging his talons into the man's flesh. Pulled away by Devary, Llandry fell unharmed to the ground. They watched in awe as Pensould carried the man into the skies, moving so fast that his prey had no time to react.

Pensould dropped him.

The man hurtled towards the ground, bleeding and cursing. Llandry felt him slash a hole in the fabric of Iskyr, opening a gateway with none of his former precision. He fell through it and vanished.

Nobody spoke for a long moment. Enraged Pensould, deprived of his prey, circled furiously above, clutching at the air with his wicked claws as though doing so would bring Llandry's attacker back.

Llandry, though, kept her eyes fixed on Devary.

'Tell me you didn't, Dev.' She wanted to trust his word, but the tale he'd told her dampened her faith in him. He was obviously capable of long-term deception if he felt it worthwhile.

'I swear, Llan. I came here to warn you, to help you if I could. I would never have willingly brought him to you.' He stood downtrodden, shoulders slumped, his face a picture of dismay and guilt.

'All right,' she said, still feeling wary. Was it an act? 'He said he "put you back together". Is that how you healed so fast?'

'I suppose so,' Devary replied. 'I was at your mother's house. He appeared... gave me a choice. If I would consent to find you, he would heal my wounds. If I didn't... well, I would be killed, and someone else would be sent after you.'

'That's dramatic. People don't make a habit of

killing their employees, that I know.'

Devary spread his hands. 'This is not a normal contract of employment. I have not been allowed to retire when I chose. I have been threatened more than once, and abducted. And they are displeased with me. I have not cooperated as they feel I should. Do I believe they would kill me? If they thought I was no longer useful, perhaps they would.'

Llandry flexed her left arm, wincing. She had landed on that arm when she fell, and the wrist felt sprained. 'How did you fail to cooperate?' She sent a silent communication to Pensould as Devary formulated his reply. *Pensould, calm down. All is well.*

'I was selected for surveillance on your mother's house—on *you*—because I was already acquainted with the family. But I did not report anything to them.'

Llandry folded her arms and glared at him. 'And you told all this to my mother, but not to me?'

Devary blinked. 'How do you know that I told your mother?'

'Because I was listening. And besides, nobody rational would deceive Mamma for long.'

'You were listening?' Dev looked faintly scandalised.

'You've kept me under a false impression since we were first introduced, so don't try to moralise with me.'

'You knew, then.'

'Knew? Not really. I heard you tell Mamma that you'd been sent by somebody, and I gathered that there was some bad business between the two of you before. But that was it. I never guessed that you... that you would... *spy* on my parents.'

Devary winced. 'That is a harsh construction. I am not a spy, not really. I am merely placed in situations where I might happen to learn things that my employers might find useful.'

Llandry shook her head. 'I can't believe she forgave you for that.'

'Perhaps she has not.'

Llandry grinned. 'You think not? She left you in sole charge of me for actual *days*. '

Devary smiled, a little hesitantly. 'Is that the test? Very well, then. We will assume that your mother is generous enough to overlook my youthful indiscretion in, er, eavesdropping on her family. But you?'

Pensould's rage was finally cooling. Llandry felt him coming up behind her, and a moment later his hand—human now—came to rest on her arm. She gave him a brief smile over her shoulder.

'I just don't understand why you didn't tell me.'

'Because it ruined my relationship with your mother. It took her more than twenty years to forgive me. I did not want you to resent me as well.'

Llandry mulled that over. Devary looked so hang-dog that it was impossible for her to harden her heart against him entirely. She elected to trust her mother's judgement. If she had forgiven him for his earlier betrayal, she must have done so with good reason.

She surprised herself by awarding Devary a hug. 'It's okay. Just don't keep secrets from me anymore. Please.'

Devary returned her embrace a little awkwardly. 'Agreed.'

Hands grabbed Llandry from behind and jerked her out of Devary's arms. She turned to find Pensould alternately glaring at her and casting suspicious looks at Dev. She patted his arm soothingly.

Mine, he told her.

Not yours.

MINE.

Llandry sighed. Pensould alternated between endearingly affectionate and violently possessive with alarming frequency.

Not his anyway. All right?

Pensould relaxed slightly, though he didn't take his eyes off Devary. Dev wisely backed away.

'We need to get away from here,' Llandry said. 'Dev, if you know anything at all about those people you need to tell me. Why do they want me?' She spoke the words calmly but internally she was deeply unsettled. She had undergone similar experiences recently when she was hunted for the draykon bone; now that the bones were no longer under her control she had hoped she would no longer be a target. Apparently she was wrong. She tried desperately to repress the flutter of panic that rose in her at this thought, but to no avail; her breath grew short and her hands began to tingle as anxiety gripped her. And the tonic she usually took to calm herself was back at her mother's house...

Pensould cast her an alarmed look and then wrapped his arms around her. Suddenly she was flooded with cooling, soothing energy, mixed up with Pensould's affection and protectiveness. Her anxiety melted away instantly.

122

'Um. Thank you.' She stared at Pensould, startled. How had he done that?

Pensould kissed her neck. *See, there are advantages to being mine. You are safe.*

Llandry couldn't believe him, not quite. She remembered too well how easily Devary's "employer" had immobilised her. Could he do the same to Pensould?

Devary watched Pensould's actions with an expression of puzzlement. 'I know little about these people, Llandry,' he said after a moment. 'I have met only the man we saw just now, and one other person. I do not know their names. The power they wield is entirely beyond me. And I do not know why they are looking for you.'

Llandry swallowed. 'Where can I go to evade them?'

Devary smiled sadly. 'The first thing you must do is get far away from me.'

'You aren't coming with us?'

He shook his head. 'You heard him, Llan. He has put a tracer on me. I do not know how this thing operates, but it is clear that he was able to find me and travel to me without any difficulty. I must get this "tracer" removed, somehow, and in the meantime we must ensure that I am not again used as bait to get to you.'

Llandry nodded, feeling heavy at heart. 'Where will you go?'

'I don't know. But, listen carefully, they will send others after you. They will be much less sympathetic than me. You must be careful. Now, please, you must leave me before somebody else is able to use my tracer to find you.'

'But—but wait, what will you do? We can't just leave you.'

'I will find my own way home, Llandry, you must trust me. Please, go now.'

He is right. Pensould's voice in her heart gave Llandry no comfort. It hurt to walk away from Devary and leave him alone, deep in the realm of Iskyr without aid, but after another brief embrace she did just that. She took one last glance at him, looking suddenly small and powerless by himself, before she changed into her draykon form and followed Pensould into the sky.

Devary watched as the two draykons ascended into the heavens and began to recede, their forms growing smaller and smaller until they vanished. He stood for a moment, feeling curiously lost. The one thing he most wished to do was to protect Llandry; he owed her that, her and her mother, after failing her so badly before. She had almost been taken because of him. She might have been killed.

But that was the one thing he could no longer do. He had to stay far away from her. How then could he help her?

He thought of the question she'd asked him, her eyes revealing the panic she was trying to suppress. *Why do they want me?*

He felt that he should be able to answer that question. He had not been given any information, but finding information was his job. He was good at it. He had been a successful agent of Draetre's university for more than two decades, and his speciality was uncovering peculiarities in the practice of magics. Sorcery and summoning... and, perhaps, whatever form of magic his employers were using.

The source of it all was the university. He knew it was a small establishment, officially dedicated to the study of magical history. And so they were, but alongside that they studied the more obscure branches of magic, including feats, practices and artifacts that were not understood—in some cases, not even believed in—outside of their faculty. And their methods were not always considered ethical within the academic community.

It was this university that had turned Devary, at a young age, into an agent of discovery. A *spy*, Llandry had called him, and she wasn't entirely wrong. He had always been good at making people like him, getting them to trust him, encouraging them to confide in him, and this he supposed was why he had been recruited.

He had never yet turned his abilities against the university itself. But something about it was wrong. The university's methods had grown steadily more ruthless, ever since his superiors had changed from the likes of Professor Indren Druaster—a woman who could be harsh and ambitious, but never amoral to his knowledge—to the pale-haired man they had narrowly escaped. If they were now turning the force of the faculty against individuals like Llandry, then his scruples meant nothing.

He would find out why they wanted her. He would find out who they were and how they were able to perform feats that were impossible even for the most powerful sorcerers. And he would find a way to extricate Llandry from whatever scheme they had in mind for her.

And the logical place to start must be the university itself.

Having decided on this, he felt much better. Gathering his focus, he began the task of opening a gate back to the ordinary world. He had no idea where in the Seven he would emerge, but he would find his way to Draetre somehow.

CHAPTER ELEVEN

Tren tapped lightly on the door of Mrs Geslin's cramped house. Through the flimsy wood he could hear the squabbling voices of her young daughters and a clattering of metal. He guessed that Mrs Geslin was cooking.

He knocked again, louder. When he still received no response, he tried the door. Finding it unlocked, he ventured inside.

Three young female faces looked up at him in surprise as he entered. He smiled reassuringly.

'It was open,' he explained. 'Hello, Mindra. Larrin, Kaye.'

'Tren!' Mindra came up to him immediately. She was the oldest of the three, almost thirteen, and quite forthright. She took charge of him at once, shutting the door firmly behind him and towing him towards the kitchen.

'Ma's making dinner,' she said. 'You'll stay, of course.'

'Er, if it's all right...'

'Of course it is. Ma always makes enough for you, just in case you turn up.'

Mindra's mother stood at the sink in her tiny kitchen, managing a series of large pans with ease. 'That's right,' she said, smiling at Tren. 'I won't have you starved when you're good enough to come to us.'

'I'm sorry I couldn't come last week,' he apologised.

'Workaholic.' She smiled at him again. Deep lines were graven on her face and her eyes were shadowed with pain, but today she sparkled with life. Tren hadn't seen her in such a good mood since... since before her son, Tren's friend Edwae, was killed.

'Is everything well?'

She put down the pan she was holding and crossed the room to give him a kiss on the cheek. She had always been more affectionate with him than his own mother had ever been. 'Come and eat,' she said. 'I'll tell you all about it.'

As usual, Mindra made sure that Tren sat beside her at the meal. She tended to address a constant flow of conversation to him; very little of it was of much interest but he paid her the courtesy of his attention anyway. Mrs Geslin indulged her daughter for a time, but at last she interrupted.

'Hush now, Mindra. Tren wants to hear about our good fortune.'

'Can I tell him?'

'Let me do it, dear. Tren, you were but a boy when you met Ed's father, but perhaps you remember him?'

'Quite clearly, yes.' Mr Geslin had been a jovial man, the sort who expected good things around every corner. Usually the strength of his belief had seemed to be enough to secure them.

'Well, things have been hard since he passed away, you'll know. To think, if I'd known before about his investments we could've been spared all that.'

Tren blinked. 'His... investments?'

Mrs Geslin beamed at him. 'I never thought of Andrus as one to think of the future overmuch, but turns out I was wrong. He was laying a bit by every year and putting it into one of them schemes that pays interest. We've regular money again, and good money too.'

Tren pondered this. He had to agree: Andrus Geslin hadn't been bothered about planning for the future. He expected such things to take care of themselves. How curious that he'd been making provision all along.

'You've just found out about this?'

Mrs Geslin nodded. 'A letter came, oh, four days ago now. Explained the whole matter, and told me how to collect it. I took that letter to the bank, and sure enough they gave me this moon's money. One hundred osts.'

Tren whistled. A hundred osts was near enough what he earned—or had earned—as a Night Cloak maintenance officer. It was a healthy sum; plenty to provide for the surviving Geslin family.

'That's wonderful,' he said sincerely. 'Though I wonder how it is that it's only just come to light?'

'Oh, the letter said something about misplaced files or whatnot. Here, I'll find it.' She abandoned her half-eaten dinner and bounced out of her chair before Tren could stop her. She was back half a minute later with a sheet of paper in hand.

'There, Pitren Warvel. What do you think of that?'

He scanned it quickly. It was from Ayven and Meerch, the biggest bank in the realm of Orstwych. It announced the transfer of Andrus's previously inactive account into her name and summarised the relevant assets. He was interested to note the nature of the scheme: apparently the late Mr Geslin had been purchasing stock in a local light-globe manufacturing firm, and the profits were tidy indeed. He made a mental note of the company's name: Lawch & Son.

'Wonderful,' he said again, handing the letter back. 'Ah... I actually came to offer you some relief... I mean, now that Ed's money has stopped, and, er...'

Mrs Geslin understood him at once, in spite of his awkward mumbling. She laid a hand over his with a smile. 'You're a good lad, Pitren Warvel. You and Ed are—were—the best men I know. But you needn't worry about us now. We're cared for.'

Tren nodded numbly, swallowing a sudden lump in his throat. Her belated use of the past tense brought home to him Edwae's absence at the table. He had been visiting this house since they were both boys, and he hadn't yet got used to being at the Geslin house without his friend.

'Will you stay here?'

'Oh, I don't know. We're comfortable here, and it's home. But how nice to be able to choose, hm? Perhaps we will move.'

Tren merely nodded. He and Edwae had worked for Lord Angstrun together until Ed had got mixed up in the Istore crisis. It hadn't ended well for him. Coming here always revived Tren's sadness at Ed's fate, and his own guilt at being unable to save him.

Mrs Geslin noticed his distress, for a flicker of pain crossed her own face and she quickly changed the subject. 'What of that lady friend of yours? I've never met such a fine lady in my life. I hope she's been keeping you company, back in Glour City.'

'Something like that. We've been working together on the draykon mystery.'

Mrs Geslin nodded knowledgeably. Tren had already told her the whole story; he felt she deserved to know, even if some those details weren't strictly to be released to the public. 'She might've known she was welcome to come with you. I was a mite snappish when we met before, I'll admit, but she'll overlook that.'

Tren smiled inwardly at the idea that Eva had only stayed away out of politeness. 'I'm sure it's not that. She's getting married tomorrow.' He managed to say it smoothly, without betraying any particular feeling about it.

'Oh?' Mrs Geslin sat back and looked at him appraisingly. 'To who?'

'Lord Vale. He's the chief of Glour's investigative force.'

That statement seemed to remind her of the vast gulf in status between herself and Lady Glostrum, for she dropped her gaze and nodded. Lady Glostrum was not just another of her son's friends; she was a peer in her own right. It was a distinction that Tren had never managed to forget, in spite of the friendly way Eva herself always treated him.

'I just hope she hasn't misled you, my Tren,' Mrs Geslin said finally. 'These white-haired girls...'

She didn't finish the sentence. They both knew that Ed himself had been thoroughly misled by Ana, the white-haired sorceress who had woken the draykon.

Tren shrugged, not liking this turn in the conversation. 'She's happy. Is there somewhere I can sleep tonight? The sofa will be fine. I'd like to be off at moonrise.'

'Of course. Mindra will find you some blankets.' Her eldest girl nodded enthusiastically and was gone in an instant. The other two stopped squabbling and grinned at him in a manner he found mildly unnerving.

'Where are you off to?' Mrs Geslin began clearing plates and he stood to help her.

'Ah, well... it's about the draykon research. When we were in the Lowers, we found some interesting things that I never got chance to look into.'

'Tren Warvel. Never tell me you're going back into the Lowers, and without her ladyship?'

'It's important,' he said defensively.

'So important that it can't wait until after her wedding?'

'Yes.' It sounded lame as he said it.

He followed her as she walked back to the kitchen, a stack of plates in her hands, shaking her head in disapproval. 'I never understood why some young men are so anxious to get themselves into trouble.'

'I won't get into trouble. I know how to manage down there.'

She fixed him with a hard stare. 'All I'm saying, Tren, is if you get yourself killed too I will... Well, I...' she trailed off, looking suddenly so sad and afraid that

Tren almost lost his nerve.

'I'll be all right,' he said, giving her what he hoped was a confident smile. 'And I won't stay long. I'll come right back, I promise, and let you know I'm still alive.'

She nodded, subdued. 'Mind you do. I'll be waiting.'

Leaving the Geslin house early the next morning, Tren didn't proceed immediately with his plan to return to the Lowers. He had another errand to complete first.

He took a public carriage to the other side of the populous town of Westrarc. On the outskirts of the settlement was the premises of Lawch & Son, the light-globe manufactory that Mrs Geslin was now involved with. The establishment proved to be a large one, but it didn't take him long to find the information he needed. Stepping inside the office, he introduced himself to the dapper clerk as a representative of the Glostrum Estate.

The man's face lit up with instant recognition. 'Ah, marvellous! It's some time since we received word from her ladyship.'

'She has had much on her mind of late,' Tren replied. Glancing about the office, he saw several examples of the artistic light-globes that Eva used in her own house. How like her, he thought; if she admired a company's product she would simply buy the company.

'I have the regular reports,' the clerk offered. 'Perhaps you can deliver them directly, Mr Warvel?'

'Ah—no. I have some other business to perform for her ladyship before I am permitted to return to Glour City.'

The man nodded briskly. 'Please convey our continued regards. Her recent investment has allowed us to expand the business considerably. Please also inform her that the new style of globe she suggested has proved very popular. She'll be pleased to know it.'

The clerk's attitude was beginning to prove too oily for Tren's tastes, but he stood his ground. 'I will ensure that she knows. She particularly asked me to check on the progress of her share transfer. I believe Geslin was the name?'

The clerk donned a gleaming pair of spectacles and rustled papers for a few minutes. At length he looked up with a triumphant exclamation.

'Here it is. Geslin, 35th house Ruarch Street? Yes. Those shares were transferred successfully. We are delighted to have her ladyship's friends among our shareholders.'

Tren sighed inwardly, suffering some conflicted feelings. Part of him felt that it ought to have been his responsibility to care for the Geslins; he was practically a member of the family after all, and if he hadn't been able to save Ed, at least he could make up for it by taking over where he had left off.

But he knew that attitude was essentially selfish. Eva had found a simple and direct way of providing for them in the long-term, and she'd done it without mentioning a word to anyone. She had also found a way to protect Mrs Geslin's pride. It was a deeply decent thing to do and also a sensitive one, and he felt a brief pang in reflecting on it.

'Thank you,' he said to the clerk and rose to leave.

'Ah—a moment, Mr Warvel. It occurs to me that her ladyship might enjoy a sample of our newest product. Would you care to see it?'

'I—yes, all right, but I have a great deal more to do this morning.' Tren affected the harried and self-important air of a middle-rank official with surprising ease.

'Of course, of course,' the clerk replied. Moving with bustling speed, he unlocked a cabinet that stood behind his desk and took out a light globe. It was larger than any Tren had seen before, as large as the chandelier that graced Eva's drawing-room. It was encased in a gracefully wrought silver cage; Tren could see at a glance that the globe would throw light onto nearby surfaces in the pattern enforced by the metal.

'Remarkable,' he said honestly.

'That's not all, sir! When activated, this globe will change the colour of the light with every rotation.'

Tren blinked. 'Truly? May I try?'

'Please!' The clerk placed the globe gently on the desk. Tren summoned his sorcery and activated it; the ball rose gently into the air and began to slowly rotate, emitting a soft white light. After about a minute, the light changed to blue.

Tren had seen coloured globes before, but the colours were either embedded into the glass and therefore fixed, or they had to be changed manually by the sorcerer. A colour-changing globe was perfectly possible, as long as a sorcerer was prepared to stand by it and alter the hue of light every few minutes. This globe operated autonomously.

'How does it work? An embedded enchantment of some kind?' Tren made the suggestion knowing it didn't make sense. Embedding enchantments was, again, the province of the sorcerer; Lawch & Son couldn't advertise the properties of the product unless those properties were bound to the globe in some way.

'It's more a matter of science. We had an inventor come in from Ullarn—mighty difficult fellow and the consultancy fees were enormous, but he did a marvellous job, so I'm told. You couldn't ask me to say more than that. I'm an administrative man, not a scientist.'

'Of course,' murmured Tren. 'Fascinating. Has Lady Glostrum seen this yet?'

'Not to my knowledge. Do you think her ladyship would enjoy a sample? It's her money as made it possible, after all.'

'Oh, certainly. Do send one right away. A wedding gift, perhaps.' He paused. 'If you could note that you sent it on my recommendation, I'd be grateful.'

The clerk winked, entirely understanding the apparent attempts of a middle-grade lackey to get ahead. 'I'll do that, sir.'

Tren left the factory feeling thoughtful. He was surprised to hear of the involvement of an Ullarn inventor. It was not common to hear of the Darklands engineers hiring themselves out that way. He had no doubt that the consultancy fees were, indeed, enormous.

What puzzled him most was the mechanics of it. A

new type of glass? How could that possibly work? The colour change reminded him of the way the light changed in the Lower Realm as the moons turned. Instinctively he would have said that this new technology owed something to the world of Ayrien, as he supposed he must now call it. But if there was a link, the probable nature of it escaped him entirely.

He dismissed the problem. He couldn't get side-tracked by new technologies, however interesting they might be; he had a more pressing task.

He was planning to journey south of Westrarc, close to the Ullarn border in fact. When he had travelled that way with Eva some weeks before, they had stepped through a rogue gate into the Lowers—a curious type of gate that remained stable unless it was deliberately closed. Even then, the gate would reopen itself in the same place sometime later.

He had a theory that the gate was not a rogue at all, but placed there and maintained by the sorcerer Griel. He hoped to find it still in place when he arrived, and if it was... going through it would return him to the same vicinity he'd visited with Eva.

In that area had been the tall and highly peculiar tower in which they had found Andraly Winnier's memoirs. They had lost the book, so instead he would go back to the book's source and try his luck there.

And if it got him out of Glour City before Eva wed herself irrevocably to a man she didn't love, all the better.

CHAPTER TWELVE

They had not been long in the air when a wave of excitement swamped Llandry's senses, emanating from Pensould. It was never easy to keep pace with a draykon so much bigger than she was, but by beating her sail-like wings at an unsustainable pace she was able to draw level with him. Glancing down, she saw nothing to explain his enthusiasm.

Pensould? What is it?

He banked abruptly and circled around, gradually descending towards the ground.

Another draykon grave, he replied. *Open your mind, Minchu. You will feel it.*

Open her mind? As instructions went, this was vague to say the least. Llandry wasted a few seconds feeling irritable, but with an inward sigh she put that aside.

She knew how the draykon bone felt. She had sensed it before, but then she had been in human form and on the ground. She had felt it pulse through the earth beneath her feet. Could she feel it from the air?

She cleared her mind with a deep breath and tentatively began to search. She promptly lost her concentration on her flight and descended with unseemly haste towards the ground. A flash of panic froze her body and she failed to right herself. The ground rushed towards her face...

With a grunt of irritation, Pensould darted beneath her and she landed on him instead. They both hit the ground with a sharp impact and she felt a stab of pain from him.

Sorry, sorry.

Pensould's voice in her mind was gruff with exasperation. *You must stop trying to fly like a human. These things? These?* He righted himself, flapping his wings ostentatiously. *They are not arms! You fly as though you are trying to grab the air and pull yourself forward. You must let the currents do the work for you.*

Um, right. Sorry. She stretched out her crumpled legs, mortified. Really, she made a liability of herself. Pensould would do better to leave her behind.

Now, Minchu. I love you still. Pensould nudged her with his nose, sending her a wave of affection that made her instantly feel better.

Until she remembered Sigwide. *Oh no, Sig!*

Pensould's nostrils twitched. *If you will insist on bringing tiny passengers...*

Frantic, she cast out with her summoner senses, looking for the imprint Sigwide's presence made on the world. She knew it better than she knew her own, but she couldn't sense him.

Sigwide! She roared the name with the full power of

her will. To her surprise and alarm, the cry was amplified beyond all reason. She knew the limits of her own, untrained summoner abilities; she should not be able to reach so far, to quest so powerfully for her orting's presence. The depths of her own power frightened her.

A thin, answering cry came from somewhere above. She launched herself into the air, hurling herself in the direction of that call. She discovered Sigwide at last, sitting in the branches of one of the tall, red-leaved trees in this part of Iskyr. He was clinging desperately to the branch as it swayed in the wind, his short grey fur standing on end. His desperation was palpable as she neared him; he screamed again, and to her shock she understood him.

Help.

The word formed clearly in her mind, though she recognised it as an interpretation of his actual utterance. She read his speech in the same way that she understood Pensould when he spoke to her without words.

Help!

Tentatively, she sent a thought back to him. *Coming!*

Carefully, she descended until she hovered near Sigwide's branch. Reaching out with one alarmingly large leg, she delicately closed her claws around Sigwide and snatched him up. The orting screamed with fear and relief as he was borne back to the ground. She released him and immediately transformed back into her human shape so she could pick him up. He nuzzled her face, calming rapidly in her arms.

Siggy?

It was harder to do it outside of her draykon shape. She knew that from Pensould, though it was growing easier the more she practiced. Nonetheless, she caught Sigwide's brief reply.

Food?

She laughed. 'You foolish creature,' she muttered aloud. Try not to fall off again, Siggy.

Yes. No. Food?

If we are finished, perhaps we can proceed?

She was learning that Pensould could be a grouch.

Nearly, she returned. *I don't understand, Pensould. How am I hearing Sigwide?*

She felt his surprise. *You could not before?*

No, though I began to feel his emotions more clearly when I carried one of your bones. And now, when I am draykon-shaped.

Pensould sniffed disapprovingly at the mention of his bones. *The connection ought to be obvious.*

Oh. She thought furiously. *Draykon bone amplifies human magic, doesn't it? That's why people were so interested in it. I was a better summoner than I've ever been when I wore a piece.*

Human magic? There is no such thing. He was arrogantly condescending. *It is draykon magic, pure and simple. As far as I can tell, what you grant the odd name of "summoning" is merely a diluted, weak form of draykon empathetics.*

Llandry blinked. *We've been working draykon magic?*

It can barely be graced with that name in its current form, but yes. I sense nothing about it that is not perfectly compatible with what we are doing.

But we're human.

Are you? You yourself are only a small bit human. You are mostly draykon. Does it not follow that others are mostly human, with a small bit draykon?

You're saying that humans and draykons can breed? Her mind reeled at the thought that somewhere back in time, many generations ago, the draykon and human species had somehow, in some way, been combined, and the draykon traits had bred true ever since.

I cannot say that I have ever tried, he returned. *When I was last awake, humans were magicless creatures and we never thought it worthwhile to try to look like one. But I have an idea.* His mood flashed from pompously didactic to mischievous. *We will both take our human shapes, and then we will mate. If we succeed in producing young, then we will consider the theory confirmed.*

Llandry's face instantly heated, and she buried it in Sigwide's fur. *Um, perhaps another time. Didn't you say something about a draykon grave?*

Ah! Yes. Come. He soared overhead and she rushed to metamorphose. Sigwide was restored to his early travelling position and she felt him grip with his claws.

Good, she told him.

Food? He replied.

She began to think that improved communication with her trouble-seeking orting might have its downsides.

Pensould at last found his draykon grave, but it was not the triumph that she expected. As he circled to the ground ahead of her, she followed with particular care, determined not to repeat her earlier disgrace. But she almost fell out of the air again when she felt his mood change in an instant from excitement to white-hot rage.

What is this drekric?

Pensould used an expression completely outside of Llandry's comprehension, dripping with horror and rage. She made a hasty landing on his left, and instantly she could feel the energy emitted by a cache of draykon bone buried under the moss.

What? Pensould? What is it?

For some time he was too busy thrashing his wings and roaring to answer. Then his voice thundered in her head, making her wince.

Thieves! Bone thieves have been at work, do you not feel it?

Bone thieves? The term made her tremble, for she too had been a bone thief once. She had not known what it was that she was plundering, but still; now that she did, her remorse was undiminished.

That said, her actions had led to the resurrection of Pensould. As had the actions of her apparent enemies, the two white-haired sorcerer-summoners who had reassembled Pensould's skeleton in the Lowers. The thought was an odd one.

Llandry circled around the other draykon, taking care to avoid his thrashing wings. The ground had been partially dug up, the earth exposed by pulling back the grass and moss. The area had later been covered up again to conceal it, but there was no hiding it from Pensould. Focusing on the disturbed area of earth, Llandry began to see what he meant: the energy of the bones was at low ebb, guttering like a fading light-globe. She raked back the loosely thrown moss and trained her sensitive draykon eyes on the tumbled earth, trying to see the damage.

Then she felt stupid. What had Pensould said to her? *You must stop trying to fly like a human.* Perhaps she also stop trying to see like a human.

Closing her eyes to remove that distraction, she instead reached out with some other sense. She couldn't say what it was, precisely, but something shifted in her mind and instead of seeing trees and grass and moss with her eyes, she saw the patterns of energy that those living things created, suspended in her mind's eye view. For a moment she was mesmerised by this new landscape traced in glowing lights.

Turning her attention downwards she saw a skeletal pattern of draykon bone, emitting a faintly pulsing, ghostly silver light. That light was dimming as she watched, the light bleeding away through the rents in the skeleton's structure. Many bones had been removed, and some were damaged. She felt the slumbering draykon's discomfort, spasms of pain wracking its buried consciousness. The realisation made her gasp, sent her out of her trance.

Is that what I did to you?

Pensould didn't answer. He had calmed enough to stop cursing and roaring, though he remained highly incensed. He was stalking in circles, prowling with the graceful menace of a hunter.

Someone approaches.

Startled, Llandry felt a moment's heart-thumping panic. She forced it down disgustedly. She wasn't an undersized and powerless Glinnish girl anymore; she was a powerful draykoness.

144

Who could the intruder be? The most likely answer was that the grave robbers were returning. And if that was the case, Llandry wanted some answers before Pensould ate them.

Pensould. Human shape and hide. Quickly! She was already shifting as she spoke, her body compacting itself back into her small two-legged form.

No! They must be punished.

They will be punished, but not yet. We need to know who they are and what they're doing.

Pensould roared his frustration in her mind, but he didn't utter the cry out loud. She ran to him, grabbing his arm as he took on his other shape, and dragged him out of the clearing. She wormed her way into the centre of a cluster of bushes, dragging Pensould mercilessly behind her.

Careful, I am not as small as you.

Stop talking.

A woman swept into the clearing, head high, her posture and gait arrogant. She was speaking, addressing the stream of men who trailed behind her in lofty, authoritative tones. Llandry was shocked to see that many of the men bore Glinnish wings.

'The bones are delicate, so I expect you to use extreme care. You have one hour to get them out.'

There was something wrong with her head. As the woman came closer Llandry realised she was wearing some kind of mask or headdress that covered most of the top half of her face. The contraption had large lenses that completely hid her eyes.

One of the men spoke up tentatively. 'Couldn't the bones be removed from in the Lowers, ma'am? I thought you said they've a presence in all worlds.'

'Idiot,' she replied. 'Would I do it this way if it were that simple, with this cumbersome monstrosity?' She tapped the headgear that she wore as she spoke. 'The corresponding location in the Lowers has been claimed by a pack of worvilloes. I don't particularly feel like fighting my way through those, do you?' When she turned to address her men, Llandry noticed that her hair was bright white.

'I, um, no ma'am.'

The woman turned away from him. 'Get on with it, please. This stupid hat-thing hurts.'

Her accent was strange. Llandry realised with a start that she had heard it before. She had heard that voice before. The white hair... it was the woman she had met in Draetre, the one who had tried to buy her Istore pendant. Llandry had refused, but soon after that encounter Llandry had found herself the target of attempted robbery and abduction. She had no doubt that this woman had something to do with it.

She relayed this to Pensould silently, her thoughts turning. She had the nagging feeling she had seen the woman again since then, though she couldn't remember where.

I know her, Pensould returned grimly. *She is the thief, the restorer. The irritating buzz in my mind when I slept.*

Yes! That was it. Convulsed with pain and confusion, Llandry had been barely aware of her surroundings when Pensould had awakened and she herself had discovered her draykon form. But distantly she recalled that voice, talking and then later, screaming.

Why didn't you kill her?
I tried. The other one intervened.

146

The other one?

Pensould showed her an image of a tall white-haired man, whurthags at his heels. She did not remember seeing him.

I will kill her now.

No. What if there are others? We must find out where they are taking these bones.

Pensould was not swayed. *They can plunder no more graves if they are dead!*

We need information, not bodies. Do you not wish to know why they are doing this?

Pensould subsided, muttering. Llandry kept a close eye on the white-haired woman, wondering how she intended to effect the transfer of the bones. If she allowed her consciousness to blur, Llandry could detect the warm energy of the realm of Glinnery only a heartbeat away, and the shadowy realm that her people thought of as the Lowers. Moving from one to the other was not a matter of travel at all, not really; she shifted through the worlds with no more than a thought.

But this ability had come with her discovery of her draykon shape. This woman was no draykon; she would have to convey the bones the human way, by opening a gate through to the Seven and then another to the Lowers. The process of crossing gates was always hard on the human body, leading to pain and nausea. She didn't see how this woman was going to accomplish the task quickly.

As her workers set to, the woman began to pace. Llandry realised she was nervous, her body radiating tension. Some minutes passed and Llandry could see no reason for it—until, without warning, another pale-haired figure, a man, appeared beside her. Llandry sucked in her breath. His tall, spare frame and his lined face were instantly recognisable. He was the man who had tried to abduct her not long since. Remembering the way he had seized control of her will, she forced herself to make no sound that could give her away.

His manner was menacing as he turned to the woman. She, however, radiated as much anger as fear and spoke to him with chilling coldness. Their words were lost on Llandry, spoken in an alien tongue; but it was obvious that the man was in charge, that he was angry with the woman, and that she resented everything about their situation.

Llandry could understand that. The man terrified her, too.

Their conversation over, the man glanced at the woman's lackeys, who redoubled their efforts when they noticed his eyes on them. Then, to Llandry's relief, he disappeared.

She frowned. That trick continued to bother her. He gave little warning of his movements, no tell-tale shift in the atmosphere and certainly none of the clumsy rending at the fabric of the worlds that sorcerers were guilty of. It all added to his ability to frighten her. She wouldn't have any way of knowing when he was near.

Pensould shifted beside her, his restlessness unabated. She laid a hand on his arm, uselessly, and resigned herself to an uncomfortable hour. She could feel the pain the men were inflicting on the slumbering draykon throughout, and her resolved frequently wavered, but she stuck to her plan. With considerably greater difficulty, she kept Pensould to it as well.

Llandry puzzled over the matter as she lay on her stomach in the moss with her legs and arms slowly turning numb. This woman had already woken one draykon, and it had availed her nothing; she had merely made an enemy of Pensould. Why would she seek to do it again? And her connection with Llandry's would-be abductor was worrying as well. Pensould had said that Llandry's presence had a great deal to do with his full awakening; was she supposed to have something to do with the repeat performance as well?

At last the men had finished. Llandry flexed her limbs experimentally, aware that she may have to be ready to move at any moment. But before she had prepared herself to emerge, the man appeared again. The workers had laid the bones out onto a large sheet of fabric, carefully placing them in some sort of order. Their careful work didn't seem to interest their employer very much, for he gathered up the fabric and the bones together into a messy bundle.

Pensould, time to move.

Llandry began to worm her way out of the undergrowth that concealed her, taking care not to lose sight of the pale-haired man and woman and their bundle of stolen bones. The female directed her winged workers out of the clearing and they trotted dutifully away. Llandry supposed they must have a gate waiting nearby to take them back to Glinnery.

All right, we—

She stopped in astonishment. The man vanished as he had before, taking the bones with him. To her surprise and dismay, the woman flickered briefly and disappeared in the same manner.

'Oh, no.' She ran to the spot where they had been standing moments before. No clue remained to indicate where they had gone.

'I'm sorry, Pensould. I thought she would leave the same way she came, through a gate or something. Did—did you know she could do that?'

'Apparently the disappearing is not unique to the colourless man.' Pensould's tone was clipped and cold, his posture stiff with indignation.

You should have let me eat her.

Llandry said nothing. She couldn't entirely disagree.

CHAPTER THIRTEEN

Eva arrived home to an empty house. Her footsteps rang sharply on her tiled hall floor, echoing in the silence. Nobody waited to greet her. Nobody except Rikbeek, that is, and he didn't count. Being bitten did not qualify as social interaction. Not when the biter was a gwaystrel, anyway.

Even Milyn had the evening off and had gone out. In her current mood, Eva would have welcomed the sight of Tren sitting at her desk, deep in a book, or even Vale ensconced in the rocking chair in the conservatory. A pang of loneliness hit her, sharp and cutting. *It's as I deserve,* she couldn't help thinking. She had brought it on herself.

True, the day she had had didn't help. She may not be an official member of the Council anymore, but Vale had been right: she'd been summoned to the meetings anyway. It had taken up most of her time for days as the Council and assorted experts, consultants and otherwise interested parties debated the draykon issue with far greater fervour than they ever had before. But to little effect. She had no new information to offer and it was patently obvious that the Council was at a loss. The best they had been able to do in the end was form yet another research team, led by Professor Mayn of the city's university. Eva knew they would meet with little success.

The sight of a large box resting atop her parlour table drew a flicker of interest despite her depressed spirits. The label was stamped with the name Lawch & Son. Excellent: the light-globe manufacturers only sent her unsolicited shipments when they had something wholly new to share with her. And having given them a considerable investment for development a few moons ago, she had hopes that their newest products would be magnificent indeed.

Eva opened the box. Contained within many layers of packaging was a large light-globe, larger than any she'd seen before. It rested inside a patterned metal cage, and as she lifted it out it was already glowing.

Glowing *pink*. The shade was startlingly similar to the pink glow that had suffused Ana's abominable daefly garden in the Lowers.

A letter was tied to the cage with string. She released the globe, letting it drift upwards to hover over her head, and quickly read the letter.

...your representative, Mr Pitren Warvel, encouraged us to offer you this advance sample of our new product...

Eva blinked. *Tren?* What did Tren have to do with Lawch & Son?

She checked the date on the letter. Four days ago... So Tren had been in Westrarc this week.

For a moment she couldn't think how he could

possibly have known about Lawch & Son. It wasn't something she was likely to have mentioned to him in conversation. But then she recalled the words of his message to her. *Any urgent correspondence may be left with Mrs Geslin in the meantime.*

So he had been able to guess where the Geslin family's stroke of good fortune had come from. Eva hoped he wouldn't despise her for it. Why had he put his name to the globe? Was it to tell her that he knew about her actions, and if so was it a gesture of approval? She felt a brief and wholly unfamiliar flicker of nerves at the possibility that he might *not* approve.

These doubts were so uncharacteristic that, for a moment, she hardly recognised herself. She quickly squashed them and turned back to the globe. The matter of Tren's personal opinions could wait: the globe represented a more pressing question. Why had Tren sent this to her? The design was unusual, but besides that there was nothing about the globe that seemed—

It changed colour.

She blinked as the pink faded away and was replaced by a soothing blue glow. She had seen globes that changed colour autonomously, but those operated via mechanics and tinted glass and they required gas and chemicals to function. This was definitely a sorcerer's globe. And it had—presumably—been packed in the box for four days without interference. How could a sorc globe hold a fluctuating enchantment for that long?

She found the letter and perused it again. She'd been distracted by Tren's name on her first reading; now she focused on the rest of the text.

... new type of glass developed with the help of an Ullarni inventor... think there is a clear market for these among high society such as your ladyship's associates... hope that your ladyship might draw attention to the sample ahead of the product's launch next moon...

Eva dropped the letter with an exasperated sigh. That the man could think so much of sales when the functionality was the remarkable thing! Grabbing the globe, she brought it back down to eye level and examined it closely. Most globes were made from clear glass, but this one was not entirely transparent. A glossy sheen covered the surface, and beneath the blue light were hints of other colours.

The metal cage bore a hinge on one side and a clasp on the other. She opened it and took the glass out, running her hands over the surface. It was perfectly smooth, but now that she held the globe in her bare hands she noticed a faint buzz of energy warming her skin. It was an echo of a sensation she had felt before...

Remembering, she almost dropped the globe. She had owned an Istore ring once, until it had been stolen. She had worn such a thing again later, in the Lowers. Those rings had been crafted to allow the stone to rest directly against her skin; wearing them had given her a feeling of strength and vitality and she had later learned that the stone—or draykon bone, as it proved to be—amplified her magical capabilities as long as it remained next to her skin. This glass held a whisper of that same feeling.

Excitement flashed through her. If this globe had really been manufactured using some form of draykon bone, it was exactly the lead she needed.

That there would be more bones to be discovered had seemed beyond doubt, but she had no means of locating them herself. Apparently someone else had been more successful.

Taking a piece of paper from her drawer she sat and began hastily penning a note back to the factory. Then she stopped. No; why should she trust her query to the post? She would go in person. Nothing awaited her in Glour City save another round of futile, frustrating Council meetings, at which she would be questioned, criticised, harangued and blamed by her confused and frightened former colleagues. And it was clear enough that no information of use was to be found in the city itself.

And after she had visited the factory, she would make her way to Mrs Geslin's. Tren had been there only a few days ago; perhaps he might still be.

But her escape from the city was not so simple. A messenger arrived from Glinnery, wearing the uniform of the expedited inter-realm postal service. When he handed her a note bearing the seal of the Council of Elders, Eva guessed immediately that it was from Ynara.

Three pictures fell out when she broke the seal. They were detailed, taken with a top quality image-capture device. She recognised the blue-green scales of the draykon depicted: the draykon that Ana woke had indeed passed over Glinnery recently, though this picture showed considerably more of the beast than the partial shots that had appeared in the papers.

The second picture was of a dark-haired man,

obviously enjoying the attention of the crowd. His eyes were startlingly pale—almost colourless—and he was powerfully built. She didn't recognise him.

... until she saw the third picture. It was slightly blurred, but the subject matter was clear enough. The device had captured the draykon somewhere in between draykon and human form; evidently the two were one and the same.

Here was information to interest her exceedingly. Had the other draykon already known how to shift into human form, or had Llandry taught him? Either way, it was a relief to her to know that the transformation to draykon shape had not been a permanent and irreversible one for Llandry.

I managed to suppress these, Ynara had written. *I thought I had suppressed all of the images, but some have leaked out. I'm sure you'll have seen them by now.*

Llandry has been here twice, bringing her companion with her both times. He calls himself Pensould. For what it's worth, I do not think he poses any threat. He seems to listen to Llandry. But I have asked her to keep me informed, and in turn I will keep you informed.

But you should know that the two of them have gone looking for more of his kind.

Their kind, I should say.

An official communication is on its way to the Glour Council, but that last piece of information is given only to you. I trust you to determine how much to reveal at present. It may be that they will not succeed in waking others.

Eva put the note away with a sigh. She didn't envy Ynara's position: her responsibilities as an Elder were suddenly in direct conflict with her desire to protect her daughter. Now Eva herself faced the same dilemma.

But if Llandry and Pensould were no threat, it did not follow that any new draykons they awoke would be similarly friendly. She penned a reply to Ynara and a fresh note to Guardian Troste. Into the latter she tucked Ynara's pictures. That done, she went in search of Rikbeek.

The gwaystrel was tucked into a corner of the roof in her conservatory. He always chose the spot directly above the heater and hung upside down, wings shut about himself. She knew he did it to keep out the world—Eva included—but she was without mercy this time. She issued a crisp order, embedding it in his petulantly protesting mind, and he came grumbling down to meet her.

'We're going travelling,' she murmured to him. 'I need you to keep me from blundering into any trouble.' Rikbeek bit her thumb by way of agreement, and she tucked him into the folds of her skirt.

She wished briefly that she could take Bartel, her shortig hound, along. The little tracker dog had been a useful companion before, but she had loaned him to one of the handlers at the Investigative Office on Vale's request. He was of greater use where he was.

Too restless to sleep and afraid of further delays, Eva saw no point in waiting until the moon rose. Her carriage rolled out of Glour City in the deep of the night, while the Night Cloak still shrouded the realm.

'I'm sorry, m'lady, I don't know any more details.' Sensing Eva's displeasure, the factory manager was beginning to sweat. Eva fixed him with a stare.

'You must know more than that, Ocherly. The glass was made right here. What did you add to it? How was it manufactured?'

'It was a simple process, m'lady. The powder was mixed in with the sand, then the rest proceeded as normal. Nothing much out of the ordinary and I could replicate it for you at a moment's notice, only there's no more of it on the premises right at present, ma'am. We're in the process of arranging for a new batch to be delivered but it's Ullarn, m'lady, and you know how complicated that can be...' The man babbled on, but Eva cut him off.

'Where in Ullarn are you ordering it from?'

Ocherly almost ran to his desk and snatched a handful of papers from a drawer. He sifted through them until he found the one he wanted. This he presented to her with a placatory smile.

'All above board, ma'am, I assure you.'

The address listed was for a warehouse in Ullarn's capital city, Wirllen. She folded the note and stored it in a pocket of her dress, nodding her approval.

'I'm also going to need the name of the "inventor" you paid to develop this product for you.'

Ocherly's nervousness increased. 'Ah... with all due respect, m'lady, he did insist on absolute anonymity–'

'I don't *care*. Give me the name.'

Ocherly held out his hand for the paper he'd given her and she handed it back. He scribbled briefly and returned it to her.

Iro Byllant.

'You have no additional information about Mr Byllant, I take it?' Eva's voice remained cold and her gaze hard. Ocherly swallowed and shook his head.

'No, m'lady. He was a secretive sort.'

Eva stepped back, relaxing her manner. 'One last question, Ocherly. Did Mr Byllant give his remarkable powder a name?'

'Not that I recall, your ladyship, no. I barely spoke to him myself as it is.'

'Describe him for me.'

'He was a tall fellow, friendly enough to talk to but not somebody you'd want to cross, if you follow me. Your hair colour, ma'am.'

Eva lifted her brows. In her thirty-eight years she'd met perhaps five other people with white hair like her own. If Iro Byllant was another, that now totalled three further adults she had encountered in the last two moons alone. That total was interesting.

'Also...' Ocherly hesitated. 'I couldn't say as how exactly, m'lady, but I got the impression there was something wrong about him. Physically, I mean. He wore a big coat that covered him up well, but he moved oddly. Like some part of him wasn't working right. And he wore gloves the whole time.'

'Thank you, Mr Ocherly,' Eva said. 'You've been a great help.'

'No trouble, ma'am, no trouble at all,' he said, evidently relieved that the questioning was over. 'May I ask as to why you're so anxious to know about Mr Byllant? I hope we haven't done wrong with the new globe.'

'I fear you have,' Eva said frankly. 'If it is as I suspect, it isn't something we want to be mixed up with. But I may be mistaken. In the meantime, don't pour everything you have into this new product. You may find, at the very least, that the supply of this remarkable powder isn't as reliable as you'd like.'

His face fell. 'I have to hope you're wrong, m'lady, but I'll bear your words in mind.'

Eva gave him a severe look. 'Do that, Mr Ocherly. I'll be in touch when I know more.'

Eva left the factory with her thoughts in a whirl. If more draykon bone had been discovered, she would have expected to hear of more draykons re-emerging; either that or a trade in the bones themselves, sold intact to sorcerers and summoners seeking augmented abilities. Llandry's jewellery trade had proved that there was a great deal of money to be made in that area. That somebody could be using it to develop technologies that were essentially domestic and unimportant was unfathomable.

But the fact that the powder had gone unnamed was significant. Judging the bones to be dangerous, the governments of the Seven Realms had recently taken to confiscating all examples of the stuff; any trade in whole bones was now essentially illegal. But if not for Eva's connection to this particular factory, the new light globes would probably have avoided the government's notice altogether. How many other businesses had been sold similar products in the last moon?

And if it was draykon bone—and she had little doubt on that score—where was Iro Byllant getting his supply? How could he possibly gain enough of it to guarantee repeat orders to businesses like Lawch & Son? These questions, she realised, would only be answered by a journey to Ullarn itself, and that prospect made her shudder.

It wasn't only that Ullarn was a closed society given to suspicion and an offensive sense of superiority over the other realms. The terrain was also perilous, a fact that the Ullarni saw as an asset. They weren't quick to assist travellers. How could she enter the realm and find Iro Byllant without assistance?

A few ideas occurred to her. She had status, riches and—most importantly—connections. It could be done. But she didn't want to do it alone. She needed help. And that meant finding Tren.

'He was here about four days ago, your ladyship, that's the truth,' said Mrs Geslin, sitting comfortably in her parlour with the pinnacle of Glour society seated opposite her. 'I'm surprised he didn't tell you himself what he was planning to do.'

Something in the woman's tone warned Eva that she wouldn't like Tren's plans. 'I expect he didn't want to bother me,' she replied smoothly. 'I've been much occupied with government meetings of late, unfortunately.'

Mrs Geslin wasn't convinced. 'Seems it's an important matter to leave unmentioned. It's not like my Tren to be inconsiderate and forget to tell these things to folks as care about him.'

Eva winced inwardly. That comment hurt. 'I certainly care about Tren's whereabouts and welfare, Mrs Geslin. I've been concerned about him since I received his note. In it he only said that he had an urgent errand to attend to. His departure was, I admit, unexpected.'

Mrs Geslin shifted in her chair. 'I don't know what to tell you,' she said. 'If Tren didn't tell you himself, mayhap he didn't wish for you to know.'

Eva was growing nervous now, but she hid it behind her usual unflappable manner. 'I collect that he's doing something of which I would disapprove. Is that right?'

Mrs Geslin sagged suddenly, her face revealing her tiredness. 'Seems there's nothing as can keep our boys safe,' she murmured. 'Not when they're determined to get themselves into difficult situations. He told me about your research, Lady Glostrum. He said it was no use wasting any more time in the city; that you weren't finding anything. Not when those books you found are gone.'

Eva had a sudden premonition. 'He didn't... he went looking for the books, didn't he?'

'He said maybe the books were taken back to where they was found. Or if not, maybe there's more as can be uncovered there, if a man were to be determined enough to go looking.'

'*Determined enough?*' Eva repeated, her voice rising. Her heart sank like a rock, then began to beat hard with fear. She knew without asking that Tren had gone back to the enigmatic tower they'd found, a building stranded in the middle of the Lowers that appeared and disappeared with the changing of the moon. He may have to find—and fight—his way through many Changes before he reached the tower, and then what? They knew almost nothing about it. It had been deserted when they had been there before, but it might not be this time.

She found her voice at last. 'How could he have gone alone?' To her dismay, her mask of smoothness had abandoned her; her voice betrayed her feelings.

Mrs Geslin nodded with some private satisfaction. 'It's clear there's more to all this than I'm aware of, your ladyship, and I can't answer that question. But believe me, if I'd known he was going without your knowledge I'd have made sure you were informed.'

That explained the slight chill in Mrs Geslin's manner when Eva had first arrived. She had thought that Eva had consented to Tren's expedition, willingly leaving him without help or support. The thought was a mortifying one.

'He didn't take anyone else along?'

Mrs Geslin shook her head. 'He said you'd disapprove of him sharing all your findings with random folk, and he wasn't sure who he could trust. He wasn't sure who *you* would trust. He was confident he could manage alone.'

Of course he was. She could believe that all too well of cheerful, sanguine-tempered Tren. He would expect good and hope for better. She rose decisively.

'Then there is no time to be wasted. I apologise for the brevity of my visit, Mrs Geslin, though I'm sure you understand.'

'You take some care, Lady Glostrum. I've a notion you're the last person Tren would want to see hurt on his account.'

It was the work of a moment to guess where Tren

had gone. He would retrace their steps, following the route that had taken them to the tower the last time. He of course could open a gate if he arrived to find the old one had gone; she would simply have to hope that it remained open. Luckily, this time she was not tracking anyone; she would not have to travel all the way on foot. Directing her coachman to convey her to the nearest possible road, Eva sat back to wait, most impatiently, for the beginning of her next journey into the Lowers.

CHAPTER FOURTEEN

Devary Kant slipped into the grounds of Draetre's University of Magic at such an early hour that the sun had not yet risen. After days of travel and only a few hours of sleep, he was tired, but he felt he had little time to waste.

He entered the building with the casual air of a regular visitor—as indeed he had been, once. He wanted to check the library's catalogue; he knew first hand that the university held some unusual texts, because he had helped to build that collection, and not always by entirely above-board methods. But first he had to talk to someone.

He wasn't surprised to find that Professor Indren Druaster was already in her office. She was notoriously dedicated—obsessive, even—and she was always the first person to arrive and the last to leave. Devary wondered sometimes what she did at the university during the lonely hours of the early morning and late night. He knocked on her door and entered.

She looked up with an air of annoyance, but that expression quickly changed to surprise on seeing him.

'Devary, what a pleasure.'

'Professor.' He crossed to her desk, picked up one of her hands and kissed it. As he had hoped, her manner warmed immediately. She had always liked those little gestures. He smiled and took a seat without waiting for an invitation.

'Devary, dear, I can't tell you how glad I am to see you well.' She paused, studying him with narrowed eyes. 'You *are* recovered, I suppose?'

'Oh, quite. Thank you.' He watched her closely, looking for anything unusual in her manner.

'Ah... good. I had heard that your injuries were severe. I'm relieved to see that report was in error.'

Devary didn't answer. He and Indren had been colleagues and friends for years, but lately he didn't know who at the university he could trust. He had no intention of telling her any more than was necessary for his immediate purposes.

'So, how is that nice little girl you brought with you last time?'

Interesting. Was there a reason she had brought up the topic of Llandry so quickly, or was it a coincidence? 'She is fine, as far as I know.'

Indren made a soft clucking noise of disapproval. 'Poor girl, what a mess she got herself into. Why did you bring her along, anyway?'

'That is not important. Indren, I need to know if you talked to anyone about Llandry.'

The teasing manner she often adopted with him faded into a cool stare. 'With "anyone"? You know I am obliged to report all of the university's doings to my superiors.'

Devary sighed inwardly. 'And who are those people?'

'You know them as well as I do.'

'No. I don't believe I do. I think that you endangered Llandry by speaking of her to your bosses.'

If he expected surprise from her, he was disappointed. What did surprise *him*, however, was a trace of fear in her eyes.

'This... isn't a good place to discuss these things, Dev.'

He shrugged. 'There's nowhere I can go that I won't be watched, so I'm unconcerned.'

She paled. 'You've been tracered?'

Another shock of surprise. 'Tracered. Yes. So I am told.'

'You've been promoted, then.' She smiled slightly. 'In which case you're in a position to tell *me* more.'

He blinked. Llandry's attacker had spoken of his being considered for promotion at one time... 'Promoted? I don't think so. But I don't know what you're talking about, Indren.'

She shook her head. 'If you've been tracered, it amounts to the same thing.'

'What?'

Indren stood up. 'Walk with me.' The sun was beginning to rise outside, lightening the grounds to a dull grey. Devary followed Indren out of the building and onto the well-kept grass around the university premises.

'Why are you asking me these questions, Dev?' she

began once they were clear of the building.

He related to her the latest attempt to capture Llandry, and how it had ended. He sensed a palpable tension from her when he described the man who had almost taken her.

'I don't know what you did to attract his attention, but you're in trouble,' she said when he had finished.

'Who? Who is he?'

'I don't know much about him,' she said after a moment's pause. 'He's known as Krays. He's not often seen; I think he's a higher-up, doesn't usually dirty his hands with the grunt work. If he's after Llandry in person, then she is in more trouble than ever.'

Divining from this that Indren knew nothing about Krays's purpose in seeking Llandry, Devary's heart sank. He asked her anyway.

'He is not the type to share his motivations,' she said wryly. 'But...' she hesitated. 'Understand, I am not supposed to share this information. You did not get it from me.'

He promised.

'I saw him once, last moon. He came into the office late at night, ordered me to drop all of my current lines of enquiry and take up a new research. Genealogy.'

'...genealogy?'

'I know.' She smirked. 'Not our usual area of expertise. He said he wanted the lineage of all the most powerful magical practitioners traced back as far as possible. Then broadened, to identify any individuals with similar genealogy but who aren't trained. Did I understand that Llandry's an untrained summoner?'

Devary nodded warily. 'A strong one, I think.'

Indren sighed. 'Before you ask me, no, I don't know what all of this is intended to discover. But it seems to me that what we're really looking for is people with similar lineage to Llandry. A lot of powerful sorcerers or summoners in their family trees. We're finding mostly summoners in Glinnery and Irbel and more sorcerers in the Darklands, generally speaking, but of course there's some crossover. And there are more untrained people with the potential to be significant than you might think.'

Devary nodded. He could follow the logic, as far as it went; the sorcerer and summoner training schools would have full records for all of their students, but people like Llandry who had never attended an academy would have passed unnoticed. And it had long been known, or at least suspected, that magical ability was largely hereditary.

He was silent for a few moments as his mind clicked through the possibilities. 'They're looking for people with similar abilities as Llandry,' he concluded. 'But there are many summoners across the Seven, so it isn't her strength as a summoner that's significant about her.'

Indren finished the thought for him. 'Llandry is the only known practitioner who can metamorphose into draykon form. This is staggering to the magical community; until a moon or so ago we weren't even sure that draykons had ever existed, not in the way they were represented in legend. So questions were asked. Is it something all summoners have the potential to do? But Llandry is untrained. The likelihood of her spontaneously discovering that on her own seems small, and we would have expected to see some level of shape-shifting occurring elsewhere before now. So it must be something unique to Llandry that grants her that ability.'

'But it might not be unique, merely very rare.'

She nodded. 'It was suggested that there may be some form of mutation in her biology that allows for it. That makes me concerned for Llandry. If what you say is true, that Krays himself is after her, then the consequences of capture will be severe.'

Devary frowned. 'A mutation? But what of the other draykon?'

'Precisely. We currently have *two* live draykons on our hands: one is Llandry, and the other, as I understand it, is the creature whose bones were spread over the Seven and subsequently reunited and restored. I heard a whisper that somebody from this department was involved in that, but I haven't been able to confirm it.'

To hear Indren talking like an agent was disconcerting. She had never been part of that side of the faculty; people like Devary brought the information to her, and she analysed it. Things had clearly changed.

'It has been posited that Llandry may have effectively created the form herself out of her own imagination, based on the old stories. But the existence of the second draykon refutes this notion. What we appear to have here is a so far inexplicable link between an ancient, extinct species and a human girl of twenty.'

'That is another question,' Devary remarked. 'I

have never previously heard of an extinct species being resurrected, not until the last couple of moons. Then suddenly we were seeing it happening repeatedly.'

Indren nodded enthusiastically. 'Yes. There have been a lot of reports—most confirmed—of previously extinct species coming through the rogue gates from Lowers and Uppers both. We might have been mistaken in some cases; perhaps they were merely rare, not extinct. But it seems unlikely that this explanation applies to all of them: some fifteen species at least. And for them to appear all at once? It has not been accomplished by any known ability. However...' She stopped walking, her eyes travelling up Devary's form to his face. 'I've never heard of a man, near death, being well enough to travel alone less than a moon later either.'

Devary took her hand. 'Indren, we've been friends for years. Can I trust you?'

'I won't willingly betray you to Krays, if that is what you're asking.' She was affronted at the idea, but Devary ignored that.

'Krays healed me. He took me somewhere, I don't know where, but some deathly silent place where I didn't see a soul except him, once. I don't know what happened. I woke up, whole and healthy.' He told her about his escape from Krays's unknown infirmary.

'You *escaped* from Krays.' Indren's voice was heavy with disbelief.

'No,' he said quietly. 'I think not, in the end. He was using me as bait; he guessed I would go straight to Llandry, or that she would come to me. I imagine I was permitted to escape.'

Indren pondered that. 'Dev, you should know something about Krays. We've never been ordered to study the draykon bone or Llandry's transformation; all of our resources have been diverted into the genealogy project. I get the impression that Krays knows exactly what is going on, and that suggests that Llandry's peculiarities have more to do with her genealogy than anything else.'

Devary nodded. 'Are there others?'

'Like Krays? Yes. I don't usually deal with him. There's a woman too, or there was; she hasn't been seen in a while. I knew her as Ana. She was usually the person who gave me my orders for the department.'

That name struck a chord somewhere in Devary's memory. Ynara had spoken of a woman with that name; she was the white-haired summoner who had brought back the draykon. Could it be the same person?

'Describe her?'

'She's a white-hair. Like Krays, only more colour about her. Arrogant manner.'

Devary couldn't help smiling inwardly at this. He knew that many people found Indren herself insufferably superior. 'Thank you, Indren,' he said seriously. 'I appreciate it. And please, don't share anything with Krays that you don't have to. Llandry's safety may depend on it—and others, if your project is successful.'

Indren bit her lip. 'I fear it must be, in time. I don't like it, but what can I do? You can't say no to Krays.'

No; one couldn't refuse Krays anything. 'Just drag it out as long as you can. And, *if* you can without endangering yourself, get word to me about anything else you discover. I'll keep you informed as well.'

'Oh? What is it that you're up to next? If you're tracered you won't get far.'

'Tracered. What exactly do you mean by that? And what did you mean by "promoted"? The way you said it, it didn't sound like a good thing.'

She gave a bitter little laugh. 'It isn't. I'm a promoted official. I was thrilled until I realised that I'd become fiercely entangled with the likes of Krays. Suddenly I couldn't avoid the white-hairs; they always found me, wherever I was. They would appear without notice at any time. Eventually I learned about the tracers. It's a device of some kind, embedded somewhere in the body. I don't know any more about it than that, but once you're tracered you're marked forever. I suppose it's a compliment, in a twisted way. They must have found me useful.'

Devary was silent. He knew why he was useful: he was a direct link to Llandry. This tracer device must have been installed while he lay unconscious in Krays's world.

'There's no way to remove it?'

'Not that I've ever heard about. I don't even know where it is.' She looked down at her own body as she spoke, as if hoping to spot it.

Devary resisted the impulse to mimic her gesture. His skin crawled at the notion that his own body harboured a little traitor that reported his whereabouts to his enemy.

'To answer your earlier question,' he said instead, 'I've got to find a way to help Llan. I need to know who Ana and Krays are—more importantly, *what* they are. And I need to know why they want Llandry.'

Indren was about to reply, but her mouth closed as they rounded a corner and almost bumped into another walker. An elderly man was strolling placidly across the grass, his hands clasped behind his back. He nodded politely to Indren and Devary and smiled. His pale blue eyes were friendly.

'Morning,' he said in a gentle tone. Devary tipped his hat in response, but Indren made no reply at all.

'It's time to get back to my desk,' she said to Devary. She grabbed his arm and hustled him inside, leaving the old man alone in the garden.

Later, Devary stood in the middle of one of the university's smallest research libraries, grateful to find it empty and silent.

I can show you my research notes, Indren had said. *Or rather I can tell you where to find them for yourself. You'll have to be quick, and very careful.*

Following her instructions, he stood in the centre of the room and turned his body towards the north corner. The sorcerer-warded door was supposed to be somewhere here, with a five-hundred-year-old map of the Seven Realms covering part of the adjacent wall. Finding the map, Devary paused, scanning for any sign of a portal.

There was none. The wall beneath the map was featureless and unremarkable, with no sign of any mechanism. It was a good illusion.

Devary followed Indren's instructions, placing his fingers just under the aged and wrinkled paper of the map and running them downwards. His first attempt found nothing, but on the second he detected a notch in the smoothness. Feeling his way carefully, he slipped the key into the tiny keyhole and turned it. The door opened under his hands, though he couldn't see it: the wall remained apparently intact. Steeling himself, he walked through, closing and locking the hidden door again behind himself.

The chamber beyond the door was larger than he might have expected. It was empty, but several desks stood ready to accommodate researchers. The bookcases lining the walls were all locked, but Indren had provided him with another key for that purpose. He located the one she had described to him and opened it up.

Inside was the bulk of her genealogy research. It was Llandry's records he was most interested in, and it took him several long minutes to find them in the stacks of papers. He found that Indren had been drawing a chart, beginning with Llandry's name at the top and the names of her parents underneath. The tree was already complex, covering several sheets of paper with the details of Llandry's ancestors. Most of the names were highlighted in blue or purple: Indren had explained that blue indicated a summoner and purple denoted a sorcerer. Llandry was descended from an enormous number of summoners, it was clear, with more than a few sorcerers in her family tree as well. No wonder she had so much raw summoning ability.

How common was it to have so many practitioners in the family? He wondered how many of the current day's most powerful sorcs and summoners could boast such an impressive pedigree.

But did it relate to her draykon shape shifting? If so, how? There were many very powerful practitioners across the realms who had not discovered any such latent ability as Llandry's. Sheer force of power couldn't be the answer.

Indren's findings stopped eight generations back on the Glinnery side of Llandry's family and four generations back on the Irbellian side. She'd told him that the research was incomplete; she had agents digging for more information from within Glinnery and Irbel, but it took time. She had promised to keep him informed, and he hoped she would.

He noticed one name on the tree that was heavily starred: Orillin Vanse, apparently a distant cousin of Llandry's. He shared many common ancestors with her, and where the trees diverged Orillin's showed similar characteristics. His parents were both Glinnish and both summoners, and he had a sorcerer grandfather.

Intrigued, Devary searched through Indren's papers and found a separate file on Orillin. The boy was currently nineteen years old, and enrolled as a student at the Summoner Academy of Waeverleyne. Indren had written notes in her own hand: *Model student. Year's most powerful.*

Looking at Vanse's profile, Devary felt a sense of foreboding. The boy had so much in common with Llandry, he would certainly attract Krays's notice as soon as Indren submitted her report. The boy had to be protected, but he had no time to divert back to Glinnery himself.

A gentle voice interrupted Devary's reverie. 'Good morning again, young man.'

The elderly gentleman they had passed in the gardens stood a few feet away. Devary started, astonished. He hadn't heard the door open, and Indren hadn't behaved as if she knew this man. Did someone else keep keys to Indren's private library?

'Morning,' he said warily, straightening up. He hadn't been addressed as "young man" in many years, but compared to this man perhaps he was indeed. The newcomer looked at least eighty, though his age didn't appear to hinder his mobility at all. He sat easily at one of the desks, though his gaze didn't move from Devary's face.

'Can I help with something?' The man smiled again as he said it, though the expression didn't make Devary feel any more at ease.

'Ah... I don't know. Who are you, if you don't mind my asking? I wasn't expecting to meet anyone here.'

'Just a fellow scholar,' the man replied. 'My name is Limbane.' The man stood up and bowed. 'Whom do I have the honour of addressing?'

His courtesy was charming in spite of Devary's unease. 'Devary Kant,' he replied with an answering bow. 'A colleague of Professor Druaster.'

'I see.' Limbane looked at him for a moment, his eyes narrowing. 'I am quite familiar with this library,' he offered. 'Perhaps I could assist you with your research.'

'I'm finding my way around, thank you,' Devary demurred. Limbane may seem friendly, but he hadn't given his last name and he hadn't explained what he was doing there.

'You're one of Krays's, aren't you?' Limbane sat

down again and rested his aged hands on the desktop.

Devary's wariness increased. 'You know Krays?'

'Better than I'd like to,' Limbane replied dryly. 'Tell me, are you a willing assistant or a coerced one?'

'Um... I haven't been working with him for very long,' Devary stalled. He wasn't sure how much he could say to this man. Was he an associate of Krays's?

'Coerced,' Limbane concluded. 'I disagree with his style, personally. People work poorly under coercion. It's a clumsy way to accomplish anything useful.' His smile was back. 'That's apart from its being morally questionable, of course.'

Devary stared.

'I do not number Krays among my colleagues,' Limbane said. 'To my relief. You may set your mind at rest on that score: I am not here for him.'

'Then why are you here?'

'I came to meet the young man who is championing the cause of that most interesting young lady, Llandry Sanfaer.'

'You know Llandry?'

'I know of her. We have not yet been introduced. But when I asked myself the question of where to find that elusive young person, I came to the same conclusion as Krays has apparently done.'

'I don't know where she is,' Devary said quickly.

Limbane nodded. 'Good, I do approve of loyalty. You need not fear, however; I do not wish to capture or hurt your young friend. On the contrary, she is in grave need of assistance and it is time she was offered some.'

Devary shook his head, backing away. 'How can I trust your word? As far as I'm concerned, anybody connected to Krays is dangerous. Besides, I speak the truth: I do not know where she is. I made sure that I would not.'

Limbane's pale blue gaze sharpened. 'Ah,' he said after a moment. 'A tracer.'

'What do you know of the tracers?'

'It is certainly an inconvenient device to be carting about,' said Limbane cheerfully. 'I may be able to help you as well, young man, but not yet. Miss Sanfaer's need is currently the greater.' He stood up slowly, though with no apparent sign of discomfort. 'We'll meet again, Mr Kant.' He bowed, turned and walked to the door. But before he reached it, he vanished.

Exactly the way Krays had done.

Devary sat down at the desk and put his face in his hands. More vanishing people, more cryptic hints, not nearly enough clear facts. He wished that, just for a little while, life would make sense again.

CHAPTER FIFTEEN

Tren got as far as the third Change before he ran into trouble.

His journey had begun well enough, if one discounted the customary pain and nausea associated with crossing the boundaries between the worlds. He'd stepped into the Lowers to find a yellow moon in the sky and an essentially benevolent, if hot, panorama of gold-tipped grasses grazed upon by an array of herbivores. He'd found a rock to climb up—the highest point he could find in the otherwise flat landscape—and searched the horizon, but no spindly tower rose in the distance. So he'd sat down on the rock to wait.

As if his weight gave it more substance than it might otherwise have enjoyed, Tren's rock remained stationary as another Change passed. He stayed where he was as the moon's light darkened to deep green and a dense evergreen forest took the place of the savannah. When the tower had been visible before, the reigning landscape had been an undulating whistworm meadow clustered with floral bushes, and Tren was hoping that the light would change to the purple he remembered quite quickly. So he waited on.

But the third Change rolled around; the evergreen forest shimmered and vanished, and instead of the gentle meadow he was hoping for came a dull grey light and a rocky landscape.

And barely twenty feet from where he sat roamed a muumuk.

His first thought was a kind of gratitude that no muumuks had yet wandered into the Seven Realms through the unstable rogue gates. The creature was easily three times as tall at the shoulder as he was, its body so large and heavy that the ground shook when it moved. Its hide was a dull bronze colour, its eyes buried under folds of loose skin. This led to a lack of precision with its vision that boded ill for anything that managed to get under its enormous feet—and the muumuk tended to be willing to eat anything that it happened across.

And of course it was lumbering its way directly towards him.

He slid off the rock, trying to be quiet. Its vision might not be spectacular, but he had no idea whether its senses of smell and hearing were any better. Would it follow him? He opted to hide rather than run and tucked himself against the side of his rock that was furthest away from the muumuk. Drawing his sorcerous Cloak around himself, he prayed that sufficient shadow covered the ground here to allow him to blend in.

Slowly, far too slowly for his liking, the muumuk lumbered past his hiding place and away. He held his posture for some minutes more, wondering as he did so about the mysterious Changes in this world. When the light altered and this landscape faded, what happened to the creatures that populated its surface? Where did those enormous muumuk beasts go? And why was he himself not carried with them? As far as he knew, no one had yet produced a satisfactory answer to that question. It was one of the many mysteries of the Off-Worlds.

He stood up at last, shrugging a dusting of mud off his coat. The Changes were still coming fast in the Lower World of Ayrien; he'd waited barely an hour between each one so far, so as near as he could judge he had perhaps half an hour before the next. He had nowhere to go, and in fact he had no wish to go far, or he may take himself out of sight of the tower once it did finally emerge. So he sat down again with his back to his faithful rock, and waited.

But before he'd been seated many minutes his attention was caught by an odd flicker of movement ahead of him. He tensed, fighting the temptation to stand in order to see better. If it was another dangerous beast, he didn't want to draw attention to himself.

But it didn't look like one. The movements of the tiny figure more resembled the smooth two-legged gait of a fellow human. He watched intently as the figure grew steadily closer.

Certainly a human, and a female one he guessed. Fortunately he was still Cloaked; if she looked his way she would see nothing but a dark patch of shadow at the base of a tall rock. He waited, hoping she would come close enough for him to see her face; but after travelling towards him for a time she veered away to the right and slowly vanished again. All he could determine about her was that her hair appeared to be brownish.

For a moment he considered following her. It was rare to encounter other humans down here. Was she a herbalist, here to harvest the unique plants of Ayrien? Part of a summoner exploration party? Or was she connected in some way to the mystery he and Eva pursued?

But while his real errand remained uncompleted, could he afford to chase after this lone figure on the mere hope that she was relevant in some way? He paused a moment in indecision, and as he did so the grey light drained away and a purple radiance bathed the ground instead. Tren stood up, all thought of the mysterious woman forgotten. As he watched, the rocky terrain pulsed and vanished; in its place emerged the soft hills and meadow grass he'd been hoping for. Whistworms emerged from their burrows and began crawling up the stalks, hoping to reach the fragrant blossoms that crowded the low-growing bushes. After a brief check for threats—he didn't know for sure that the muumuks wouldn't still be wandering this new environment—Tren climbed his rock again and stood tall, shading his eyes against the silvery light of the larger, constant moon that shone perpetually overhead.

For a heart-pounding instant he thought that the tower was gone. Therein lay the potential for disaster; it hadn't occurred to him that the building might not re-emerge with the meadow, and what would he do if it did not? He had no possible means of determining where it had gone.

But no: his observation was merely hindered by a touch of mist that clung to the cool ground. He spotted the indistinct image of a tall, thin structure some way off and his heart leapt. Jumping down from his rock, he aimed for it at a run.

When he arrived at the base of the tower, his heart beating hard with exertion and his shirt sticking to his skin, he discovered another problem. He'd forgotten that the peculiar building had no door or other discernible means of entry. What had Eva done last time? She had caused the stone itself to form a ladder by some method that remained somewhat unclear to him.

Running his fingers over the stonework didn't help. He felt nothing but cold stone, fixed and immutable. Mustering his will, he tried again, pushing harder at the blocks. Eventually, tiresomely slowly, the stone softened the barest bit under his hands and the tip of one finger sank slightly into the rock...

'Can I help you with something?'

The voice, female and waspish, cut through the silence like a whip and Tren jumped back, staring around for the source. Leaning out of the window near the top of the tower was the woman he'd seen earlier, her chestnut-brown hair loose around her face.

After a moment's scrutiny, he recognised her as the same woman who had wandered into Eva's study and taken Andraly Winnier's memoirs.

'Um,' he stammered. 'I might have knocked, if you had a door.'

She narrowed her eyes at him. 'You're the book

184

thief.'

'What? *You're* the book thief.'

'I can't steal what was mine in the first place.'

'That was your book?'

'By virtue of the fact that I wrote it. Have you come to steal it again?'

She wrote it? Tren thought that through. 'Then you're Andraly Winnier?'

'Yes,' she snapped.

'You were friendlier before.'

'I didn't have a runt of a human male sticking his fingers in my stonework at the time.'

'Runt?' Tren pulled himself up to his full, six-foot - and-a-bit height.

'All right, you're a beanpole, but in *years,* boy, you might as well be about three. What do you want?'

Tren sighed. What was it with imperious older women casting aspersions on his age? He was twenty-five, not twelve.

'I was wondering what became of the book,' he replied. 'And I had some hopes of reading the parts that I didn't get to study before.'

She considered him for a long moment, her face unreadable. 'You've some nerve,' she said at last.

He spread his hands apologetically. 'The matter's urgent.'

'Oh? What matter?'

He considered for a moment before he spoke. 'The matter of Llandry Sanfaer and her draykon friend,' he said, hazarding everything.

Her eyes narrowed again. 'You're a friend of Llandry Sanfaer?'

'Er. Sort of. I mean, we've met, though I don't

think she was in any condition to remember me at the time.'

Andraly Winnier made a sound of disgust and disappeared from the window.

'Hey, I—wait—' She was gone. Tren subsided, cursing inwardly. He looked around, seeking some other way to reach the distant window, but then the stonework crunched oddly and a line snaked its way through the blocks, forming a door. It opened to reveal Andraly standing on its other side, glaring at him.

'Hurry up,' she said.

He hurried.

'I thought this tower belonged to someone else,' he said a little later, sitting uncomfortably in Andraly's workroom at the top of the building. She sat easily in a rocking chair on the other side of the room, keeping her pale eyes fixed on him. He'd had no luck guessing her age or anything about her. Her face was neither young nor wrinkled; her eyes gave nothing away.

'Oh? Upon whom did you obligingly bestow ownership of my home?'

He winced. 'Look, I know the circumstances of my arrival weren't ideal, but I didn't mean any harm. Could we drop the acidity?'

She smirked. 'You were planning to break in.'

'I didn't know it was your house! I thought it belonged to an Ullarni sorcerer I've reason to dislike.'

Her eyes opened a little wider at that. 'Ullarni? Why would you think that?'

'Because it's practically on the doorstep of a

recurring rogue gate that opens into Orstwych, right on the Ullarn border. I followed the sorc down here and I thought that this must be something to do with him. Especially when we found an Istore ring in here.' He flicked a hand at the floor not far from his chair, pointing out where the object had lain.

'We?' Andraly prompted.

'I was with Lady Evastany Glostrum at the time.'

Her face cleared. 'Ah. That's interesting.'

'Is it?'

She shifted in her chair. 'Were you also the person who turned all my belongings upside down?'

It was fair to note that the place was a lot tidier than it had been last time he'd visited. 'Um, no. It was a mess when we got here.'

Andraly rolled her eyes. 'I really need to work on my security. That ring wasn't mine, by the way. I've never had such a thing in here. I suppose my *first* uninvited guest made himself at home here—I found a number of objects that didn't belong to me—and then my *second* intruder stole from both of us.'

Tren sighed. Her repeated use of words like "stealing" and "intruder" and "thief" was making him nervous. 'Look. Griel killed one of my friends. He was also responsible for the death of one of Lady Glostrum's friends. We felt we had reason to do as necessary to catch up with him.'

'Griel?' Her brows lifted.

'The sorc.'

'Hmm. A bad character to get tangled up with. Poor judgement.'

Tren sat forward, electrified. 'Oh? What do you know about him? We've hardly been able to find out anything.'

She shook her head. 'Nor would you; his kind tend to be well camouflaged. Well, I suppose I must forgive you for your thievery, even though I *did* have to travel an awfully long way to get my book back.'

'That's true. How did you know where to find it?'

She gave him a withering look. 'There are ways, book thief. I'm not foolish enough to leave my life's work lying around without any means of tracking it should it happen to wander off.'

Tren was silenced.

Andraly resettled herself, crossing her legs. 'So. About Llandry Sanfaer. How are you mixed up in her business?'

'I don't know about that,' Tren said. 'It's my turn to ask some questions. Who are you? If you wrote those memoirs—all of them—why do they span such an impossibly long period of time? And what's your interest in Llandry?'

She smiled. 'That's asking far too much. Pick one.'

He shook his head. 'All or nothing.'

'You do realise I have you at a disadvantage, yes? You're locked in *my* tower without obvious means of escape.'

Tren shrugged. 'If you were really inclined to take exception to me, you could've kept me out in the first place.'

'Fine. Tell me your story first, then we'll talk about mine.'

'You'd better keep that promise.'

She arched a brow. 'Or what?'

'Or... I'll unalphabetise all your books.'

Her eyes flicked to her perfectly ordered collection

of tomes, then back to Tren's face.

'Start talking. Begin by telling me your name.'

Tren complied.

It took some time to relate the entire tale to Andraly. He began as far back as he could, with the emergence of Llandry's Istore jewellery wares at the Glour Market and the subsequent uproar it had caused. Andraly nodded impatiently through most of this, suggesting that she knew that part of the story already, but she didn't interrupt him until he began to relate the part he and Eva had taken in the tale. Then she frequently questioned him, picking minute details to verify or clarify, and his pace of narration slowed dramatically.

But when he talked of the circumstances of Llandry's first metamorphosis, she listened with rapt attention. Her eyes were faraway, as though she were adding his information to her existing store of knowledge. When he had finished the questions started up again, and he answered them until his throat was sore from talking.

At length she sat back, staring at the ceiling for some time.

'I can see we should have talked to one of you before,' she commented at last. 'Though we were unaware that anyone else had been closely involved in the business save Griel and his wife.'

'So you do know them.'

'Something like that.'

Andraly stared at Tren for so long that he began to feel uncomfortable.

'It's your turn to start talking,' he reminded her after a while.

'Not here,' she said, standing abruptly. 'I think I'll take you somewhere more secure.'

Tren stood too, feeling uncertain. 'Er. That sounds great, but where are we going?'

She grinned wickedly. 'I really think my colleagues would like to meet you.' Her fingers fastened around his wrist with a fiercely strong grip, making him gasp with sudden pain. Before he had time to raise any further objections, her image wavered and she blinked out of existence.

And he, helpless, was dragged along with her.

CHAPTER SIXTEEN

Pensould was still angry.

He had been flying at an enraged speed for so long that Llandry felt ready to drop, but he showed no signs of slowing. And he wouldn't speak to her.

Pensould, please. I'm sorry.

No response. Llandry wasn't sure he had even heard her. He had blocked her out completely, intent on his crazed search. Ever since he had learned of the extinction of the draykon race, he had grown steadily more urgent in his quest to bring them back to the worlds; now, having seen, and failed to halt, the fate of a fellow draykon—its bones exhumed and scattered—he was unstoppable.

Pensould...

His voice roared in her mind. *Do not distract me now!*

Tired, saddened and angry, Llandry at last rebelled. She was not bound to Pensould; if he no longer wanted her, she was more than happy to go her own way. She slowed her pace and began to circle downwards, her exhausted wings screaming for rest. Pensould's huge blue-scaled form gradually disappeared into the distance.

She came to rest on the ground and stayed, motionless, for some time. She felt as if it would never again be possible to launch her sizeable draykon form into the sky. How Pensould found the stamina was beyond her.

It wasn't that she didn't understand his rage, though the duration of it alarmed her. She too suffered enormous discomfort—and guilt—at what they had witnessed. What rankled the most was that they had arrived too late; had they reached the grave sooner, they might have been able to prevent the initial plundering of the beast's bones. The skeleton could have been restored instead of broken up and taken away. How many other draykon graves remained undiscovered? And how many more had already been stripped bare?

She understood his urgency. It was only that she, still a fledgling draykon, lacked the physical strength to keep up with Pensould. And she did wish he wouldn't be so very angry with her.

A gust of air buffeted her and Pensould dropped from the sky. His head snaked out, his teeth snapping dangerously close to her hide.

When I said "do not distract me" I did not mean you were free to leave!

Llandry fluffed her wings in a shrug.

What are you doing? Get off the ground!

Resting.

There is no time for rest!

Then do not fly so fast! She bared her teeth at him. *I*

am not coming with you.

His only response to that was a roar. She hunched her shoulders against his fury, her body shaking.

And that is why! she screamed at him when he'd finished. *I am not owned by you! You may not abuse me, roar at me and wear me out and then expect me to remain with you.*

He put his face close to hers and bared his long teeth. *We will rest,* he said finally. *For a little while.* He bumped her neck with his nose. Recognising the gesture as an apology, albeit a poor one, Llandry sighed. When Pensould curled up his large body and tucked his head under one wing, she arranged her smaller body against his and hid her eyes. He was maddening; his pleasant moods were beguiling, but his rages were truly frightening. Would his fits of anger subside once his quest was achieved? She would give him the chance to prove himself more pleasant than otherwise; but she couldn't allow him to control her.

Having made this resolution, she fell asleep.

When they went on again, Pensould set a more sustainable pace. His anger had dissipated while he slept, and his mood now was more subdued, even dejected, though his drive remained undiminished. They hunted. Llandry had not yet grown used to the draykon style of dining; raw meat was no substitute at all for her mother's cooking, but she was hungry enough to eat anything. Pensould gobbled his food, barely giving her enough time to finish her meal before he drove them on again. She didn't know where he was going, but she didn't trouble to ask.

At last his onward flight stopped and he hurtled downwards so fast that she feared he would drive himself nose-first into the ground. But he landed, successfully if ungracefully.

Here, he told her. *Here!*

He was right. A grave lay beneath the soil, a web of draykon bones pulsing faintly with energy. Scanning the area, she found no holes in the pattern. To all appearances, this skeleton was complete.

They had travelled so far into the realm of Iskyr that Llandry recognised nothing. Gone were the glissenwol trees of her homeland; they were far beyond those parts of the realm that corresponded geographically with Glinnery. She and Pensould stood within a wide plain, carpeted in feathery silvered grass. Two suns shone in skies stained a deeper shade of purple than the lavender she often saw. A tiny scaled creature ran over one of her feet, its long tail lashing with fright when her head moved. Sigwide bounced down from his station between her shoulders and ran after it.

Fun, he observed. She left him to it. Pensould was aloft again, circling the plain with powerful strokes of his sweeping wings.

No intruders, he reported to her. *We go to work.* He settled near to her again and turned his attention to the sleeping draykon that rested beneath their feet. Llandry did the same.

At first she sensed nothing but the faintest pulse of energy flowing through the bones. It was enough; some trace of life remained in this somnolent beast. It was a spark that could be fanned back into a roaring blaze.

But she had to go much deeper before she felt a flicker of consciousness. Some peripheral trace of awareness remained as well, not really awareness but something that had the potential to be. Pensould began calling to it, plucking and nudging at this whisper of consciousness, trying to draw it out. She joined her efforts to his, celebrating as gradually, slowly, she began to sense echoes of the beast's mind.

Pensould began pouring his own energy into the sleeping draykon, turning its faint life force into a steady flow. Llandry felt its mind snap open. It recognised their efforts, understood and consented in what they were trying to do. And it—she—was ferocious in her desire to awaken.

That was when the pain began. It gripped Llandry's body, relentless, the same pain she had felt when Pensould had awakened near to her. Now she understood what was happening: the draykon was drawing away her life force, channelling it into its own regeneration. Beneath her feet, bones were disappearing under muscle, under scaled hide; a renewed body was being formed from the vitality of Llandry's own.

It hurt worse even than it had last time. At first she couldn't understand this; she shared this burden with Pensould, so how could the pain be so *shattering*? But then she remembered. Pensould's regeneration had already been largely complete when she had arrived; this draykon was rebuilding herself entirely.

She gritted her teeth, trying not to scream. She failed. The scream emerged as an animal roar, her voice joining Pensould's, though she heard as much elation as pain in his cry. An extreme pulse of energy set the earth shuddering; it cracked under her feet, the earth loosening itself, preparing to expunge the beast that fought to escape.

The ground erupted and the draykon rose, shrieking. She was larger than Llandry, her hide wine-red traced with black. The pain eased now as the draykon separated herself from the tangled life forces of Llandry and Pensould. Llandry crouched, panting, waiting for the trembling in her limbs to stop.

Thank you, the new draykon said, her mind-voice crisp. *How long have I been under?*

I am unsure, Wing-Friend, but that the years number in the thousands I have no doubt.

Llandry felt the draykon's shock. *What? That cannot be.* Her tone became suspicious. *I do not recognise you, either of you. Are you of Eterna's people?*

I do not know that word.

Nor I, Llandry added weakly, wishing she had Pensould's ability to recover.

The war! The draykon shrieked the word, her voice rising to a pitch that beat painfully in Llandry's brain. *Is it over, then? Is it won? Why was I not returned sooner?*

Llandry felt that Pensould was as puzzled as she. *What war?*

The human war! The war Eterna swore to win, and we swore to support her until death. And so I did. The words were spoken with a ferocity that chilled Llandry to the core. This was not what she had expected.

Wing-Friend, Pensould said at last. *Things are not as they were when you and I last flew. If there was war, it occurred after the day when I went into the Long Rest. And if the war was with humans as you say, then it appears that that war was lost by our kind.*

Llandry waited, tense, as Pensould explained the nature of the new world—a world that, until recently, had not seen draykons in many generations. When Pensould came to relate the circumstances of Llandry's own transformation, the new draykon's mood changed from disbelieving dismay to anger.

Half-breed? Abomination! How could such a thing come to pass?

That is not known, Pensould said, his tone placating. *However it happened, it was not of Llandry's making. And it is to her that we owe our renewed existence.*

The red draykon circled Llandry, her hostility still strong. She lashed out with her teeth, landing a deep bite on Llandry's shoulder. Screaming with pain and surprise and anger, Llandry fought back, sinking teeth and claws deeply into the other draykon's flesh.

Enough! Pensould beat the red draykon back, forcing her aside with sheer size and muscle. She hissed at him, but at length she subsided.

There remains a greater enemy, she conceded. She looked Llandry over appraisingly. *If this one is in truth a human, she will know their ways well. She can teach us their weaknesses.*

Llandry backed away, alarmed. *I will do no such thing. Why should you wish to revive a long-dead war? What is your complaint with humans?*

Everything! Your loyalties are misplaced, fledgling, if you think to defend them. Do you think them the victims? The war was begun by them, and they did not stop until they had taken precious Arvale.

This word was unfamiliar. She was about to say so when a picture formed in her mind, placed there by the newly-awakened draykon. With a gasp, she recognised Glinnery.

And then they took Everum. Next came an image of a forest Llandry recognised as Glour.

When they began to look to Iskyr and Ayrien—when they PRESUMED to impinge on our sacred spaces—we swore to destroy them all. ETERNA SWORE IT!

Pensould was trying to soothe her, bathing her with the gentlest of healing energies. *Wing-Friend—*

MY NAME IS ISAND, she yelled. *AND I AM NOT YOUR WING-FRIEND.*

Isand. Calm yourself. Pensould kept his voice cool but a note of menace lurked beneath. *You cannot revive this war. We are too few: there are but the three of us at present.*

At present, Isand repeated. *We will wake others! We will find Eterna herself! Arvale and Everum must be taken back! If you will not help me, I will do it alone.* She bared her teeth. *And deal with you later.*

Isand did not wait for a response to this. She launched herself into the air and with several powerful beats of her wings, she was gone.

No! Unthinking, Llandry threw herself into the sky after her. She had barely begun her pursuit before Pensould was on her, driving her back to the ground.

Minchu, what are you doing?

What does it look like? I'm going after her!

To do what?

To stop her! She's going to attack Glinnery!

Pensould bit her, not hard but enough to bring her up short. *How are you going to stop her?*

Llandry flailed, raging. *You're going to help me and somehow we'll persuade her to give up the idea.* She knew as she spoke that it was hopeless. Fury like Isand's could not simply be explained or persuaded away.

We will think of something, but for now you must leave her alone. She is not going to attack Arvale now; she is going to wake more draykon-kind.

More like her. Llandry hung her head, despairing.

Perhaps. Perhaps also more like you and me.

Llandry curled herself up, trying to hide from the world and the problem she now faced. Her rage and fear cooled quickly; anger did not suit her. She fell to thinking instead.

Pensould?

He twitched. *Yes.*

Why weren't you upset about it? About Glinnery. Arvale, I mean. Wouldn't it have been draykon territory when you lived?

Pensould didn't reply immediately. She felt his sadness as he thought her question through.

Much changes over time, he said at last. *I was sad at the fate of Arvale—of draykon-kind as a whole—but I accepted it as the result of many long years passing. I had no way of knowing that it had once been taken by force.*

I find it so hard to believe, she returned. *My people are not warmongers. How could our ancestors have been so different?*

Pensould nuzzled her affectionately. *Things change, Minchu. It can't be prevented.*

Somebody heaved a sigh. The sound— undoubtedly a human utterance—came from behind Llandry.

'What a mess,' said a regretful male voice. She jumped to her feet and spun, bristling. An elderly man was standing on the edge of the crater that had once held Isand. His pale blue eyes wandered from Llandry to Pensould.

'Miss Sanfaer?' he asked, his gaze coming to rest on her. 'I admit these are not the circumstances under which I had hoped to meet you, but I am nonetheless delighted to make your acquaintance.'

Who is this? Pensould's voice in her thoughts was sharp.

Not somebody I recognise.

The man smiled encouragingly. 'Perhaps if you put your human shape back on, we could talk. I take it I am too late to prevent your waking another draykon?'

Llandry studied him. He did not seem threatening, but his appearance troubled her. How had she failed to sense his approach? Nor had Pensould apparently noticed anything. He had appeared as abruptly and as noiselessly as the man who had tried to take her. That thought made her shiver.

She hesitated, then allowed her body to reform into her human shape. The process still felt odd to her; almost as if her bones and muscles and skin melted and then moulded themselves into the new shape. It was unpleasant. She blinked her human eyes at the man and took a few steps backwards.

'Who are you?'

'My name is Limbane,' he said with a bow.

'Limbane? What is your first name?'

'Just call me Limbane. May I address you as Llandry, or do you prefer Miss Sanfaer?'

'Until I understand who you are and what you want, I am unconcerned with what you call me.'

Limbane nodded. 'I've been looking for you for some time, but you mustn't let that alarm you. I have nothing to do with the man who tried to abduct you. His name is Krays, by the way.'

Llandry started. 'How do you know about him?'

'Because I have spoken to your friend Mr Kant.'

Fear gripped her at that name. 'Did you hurt him? Is he all right?'

'Of course I didn't hurt him. I met him in a library at Draetre. We had a perfectly civilised conversation. I would like to have the same with you, but I must suggest we hold it elsewhere. You've created a disturbance here that I could feel a long way off; and if I could feel it then I imagine Krays will soon be along as well.'

She shuddered at that prospect. 'Is that how you found me?'

'Yes. Pulling a draykon out of the ground tends to create some waves. I imagine even your friends in Glinnery will feel the effects.'

'I don't understand.'

'You do, I think. You saw the effects of last moon's events. When the draykon bones began to be disturbed, all the worlds felt it. All the beasts felt it. I imagine we'll be seeing more of those pesky rogue gates making a nuisance of themselves, and a lot of confused beasts wandering between the worlds. I might suggest you refrain from waking any more draykons at present.'

'I don't—' she began, but then she stopped. Another figure blinked into existence, one with white hair, a colourless face and a cold expression.

'Limbane,' said Krays, without an ounce of warmth.

'Ah, Krays. I had a feeling we would be seeing

you.' He eyed the younger man with no sign either of surprise or trepidation. He turned back to Llandry.

'I would urge you and your companion to consider my offer fairly urgently,' he said.

The presence of Krays decided her. *Pensould, come with me.*

He bristled with suspicion. *Are you sure?*

No. But I'm going to trust him.

Pensould replied only with a snarl of annoyance, but he rapidly adopted his human shape.

'Excellent,' Limbane said. He took Llandry's arm in one hand and gripped Pensould's wrist with the other. With a cool nod to Krays, he disappeared. Llandry had just time enough to grab Sigwide before she was whirled away.

CHAPTER SEVENTEEN

When Eva arrived at the tower in the Lowers, it had the unpromising air of abandonment about it. Not a whisper of sound or movement reached her as she walked around the base of the narrow building. Her heart thumped oddly with suppressed anxiety at the thought that Tren might not be here after all.

It still hadn't developed a discernible door, so she took the other route. Her practiced fingers sank easily into the stone; working it like clay, she moulded the first few rungs of a ladder in the side of the stonework. To a strong magical practitioner like herself, it was a simple matter to reform parts of the realm of Ayrien according to her needs, though it was only recently that she had begun to learn how far it was possible to take the technique.

Urgency lent her speed, and she was up the side of the tower and through the window at the top within a matter of minutes. Inside she found the round chamber that she'd visited before, only it didn't look the same. Someone had tidied up. She wondered who; had Ana been back here?

That prospect made her wary in spite of the silence. Finding a door partially hidden behind a curtain, she eased it open and listened for a moment. Nothing. She stepped softly down the stone stairs that wound down into the depths of the tower. Finding another door halfway down, she went through it.

Light-globes flared into life as soon as she stepped into the room. The sudden flash made her blink, and for a few moments she couldn't see. She stood still until her sight cleared. The presence of the charged globes suggested that somebody still used the tower, and she didn't want to blunder into Ana.

The room proved to be empty. It appeared to be a reading chamber, and for a single occupant. A lone wing-backed chair was placed before a cold, dark hearth. Rugs covered the floor to ward off the chill, and bookcases lined the walls. Eva gave them a cursory perusal, but no titles caught her eye as significant.

She returned to the staircase and descended another storey. The next chamber down was some kind of laboratory. Eva lingered here rather longer, examining the instruments that sat atop the high counters. She recognised tools for magnification among them, but most were beyond her comprehension.

The stairs went on and on, descending further than seemed possible given the apparent height of the building. Eva was standing with her hand on the doorknob of the next room down when she caught the sound of slow footsteps coming towards her. She froze, her heart picking up speed. The stairwell was bare of hiding places; her only option was to conceal herself in the room ahead and hope to remain undiscovered.

But then a voice began speaking and she realised that her presence was already known.

'It's only recently that I have taken the trouble of installing wards in this building. I never needed to before, because your kind tend to be shy about wandering about down here and the Others never took much interest in Ayrien. But here again, more of you.' The voice was female, low in tone and authoritative. And unmistakeably annoyed. It was certainly not Ana's voice.

'Then again, you're a bit more elusive than some of the others. Harder to pinpoint your location. And that's unusual.'

Eva turned to face the stairs. The woman's legs appeared and then the rest of her, not quickly for she apparently did not think it worth hurrying her pace. She was wearing trousers, Eva was interested to note; not absolutely unheard of but certainly uncommon in Orstwych and Glour. She had abundant chestnut hair and an ageless face. Her expression was annoyed, but when she saw Eva it changed to something closer to shock.

'Ah,' she said after a moment. 'That explains it.'

Eva blinked. 'What?'

'Lokant heritage,' the woman replied with a speculative smile. 'Trained, it would appear, which must mean you're one of Theirs.' She circled Eva, her posture full of menace. Her fingers closed around

Eva's wrist in a harsh grip.

'Lokant,' Eva said, keeping her voice steady. 'I've seen that word before, though I don't know what it means.' She tried to withdraw her arm, but the woman's grip only tightened further.

'Is that a denial?'

'Of what?' Eva retorted. 'I don't know who you mean by "they", if that's what you are asking.'

The woman's eyes narrowed. 'You've *seen* the word, you say. Where?'

'Here. In a book. Or on it, actually.'

The woman's face registered sudden comprehension. 'You wouldn't be Lady Glostrum, by chance?'

'I am.' Eva yanked her arm, sharply, and the hand that gripped it fell away.

'Still more interesting,' said the other woman, then she smiled. 'Your pardon for my rudeness then, your ladyship. How curious that Pitren did not speak more of you.'

'Tren?' Eva advanced on the woman, elated and alarmed by turns. 'You've seen him? Where is he? Have you taken him somewhere? Who *are* you anyway?'

'My name is Andraly Winnier,' she replied, her eyes sparkling with some emotion that looked offensively like amusement.

'Ahh,' said Eva slowly. 'That makes sense.'

'Yes, I have taken your friend somewhere, but no, he isn't hurt. Worry not; you'll be coming along too.'

Eva stiffened. 'To where?'

'You'll find out. It would be useless trying to explain.'

Eva surveyed Andraly warily. 'I suppose I'm to have a choice in the matter?'

'You want to see Tren, you're coming along. I can promise to leave limbs, organs and ocular devices intact.'

Eva felt a headache coming on. Too many questions, too many mysteries. What did she even know about Andraly Winnier? Precious little, save that the woman knew far more about the realm of Ayrien than seemed possible. And if her memoirs were to be believed, she was unnaturally long-lived. What in the world did she mean by "Lokant" anyway?

None of that mattered, however. If Andraly knew Tren's whereabouts then Eva would make no objection to being taken to him. Which was lucky, because without waiting for an answer Andraly grabbed Eva's wrist again and pulled. With a brief rush of dizziness, Eva found herself elsewhere.

'Wait here,' Andraly said, and vanished. Dizzy and numb, Eva could only obey.

She stood alone in the centre of a bare, empty room. The chamber was truly gigantic. The ceiling was so far above her, Eva could only barely discern that it was domed. The round walls stretched and stretched, probably covering a distance of a mile all the way around. The decoration was curious: the plain, pale walls were covered in lines, vertical and horizontal, marked starkly in black. Clearing her disorientation with a shake of her head, Eva began to cross the room for a closer look. It took her some time to reach the wall.

On doing so, she realised that the horizontal lines were in fact letters. Words, written so small that it was difficult to read them. And the wall was not covered in plaster or paper as she might have expected. The material resembled the interactive bulletin boards back in Glour, if anything: smooth and flat and pale, with a faint shimmer of possibility. As Eva stared at individual phrases the words enlarged themselves for her benefit until she could read them.

They were names. She stepped back, startled. There must be hundreds of thousands of them scribed around the walls of this room. And the floor. And probably the ceiling. Spidery ladders crawled up the walls, set on rails and wheels to allow access even to the data scribed near the top. A cursory survey revealed that the arrangement was a family tree of some kind, vast and impossibly exhaustive. She moved slowly around the room, scanning the names that appeared on this mesmerisingly complex tree.

Then she heard a door swing open behind her—though she hadn't seen any exits set into the walls—and she spun around.

Tren felt apprehensive as he stepped into the chart room. Eva was indeed there, as Andraly had said. She turned, stared at him in shock. She looked tired and unusually dishevelled; her hair was coming loose from its elegant braids and her clothes were disordered. Her face registered such infinite relief on seeing him that his heart sank under the weight of sudden guilt.

But in an instant she metamorphosed into a vision of pure anger.

'Tren! You foolish, ignorant, impossible, utterly *absurd and unbearable piece of stupidity*! What could possibly *possess* you to go jaunting off to the Lowers without me?' She advanced on him as she spoke, her hands spread as though she would like to fasten them around his throat. He backed off, clearing his throat nervously.

'It's so good to see a friendly face.'

'Tell me you took somebody with you. *Someone*. If it couldn't have been me, tell me you at least took another summoner with you. Or a guard. *Something.*'

There wasn't a favourable answer to give to that, so he didn't attempt one.

'*Idiot,*' she spat. 'Of course you didn't. Arrogant, stupid bloody youth. You think you're immortal! You think it couldn't possibly happen to you!'

'*Hey,*' he said, getting rattled now. 'You did exactly the same thing when you were younger.'

'Yes! I was a raging idiot too, just like you. You know why I stopped wandering merrily through the Lowers by myself? *Because I almost died.*'

'Ah...' He swallowed, stuffing his hands into his pockets in a defensive gesture he'd had since childhood. He couldn't understand why she was so toweringly angry. Maybe it was time to change the subject. 'How... why are you here?'

She raked him with a withering look. 'I came looking for you, of course.'

'Um...' That silenced him for a moment. It hadn't occurred to him that she might come after him. 'Ah... I hope you brought someone with you.'

It was a feeble attempt at a joke, and it didn't go down well. She looked ready to strike him.

'You could have died!'

'But I didn't.'

'That's just luck. Promise you don't do it again, Tren.'

'I can't promise that!'

'Why not?' She stood right in front of him now. She had to look up into his face, but not by very much. She was a tall woman. The expression of fury in her eyes hadn't diminished.

'Because—because I can't know that I won't ever need to do it again.'

She regarded him silently for a few moments. He steeled himself for a renewed barrage of anger from her, but it didn't come. Instead she spoke softly.

'Why did you go without me, Tren?'

'You were busy with... with weddings, and suchlike...'

'Nonsense.'

'So it appeared.'

'You couldn't have waited until I was finished?'

'It was important!'

Her eyes narrowed. Then she gave a deep, exasperated sigh. To his complete surprise, she put her arms around him and pulled him close.

'You're a fool,' she said.

'Probably,' he agreed. He hesitantly hugged her back, feeling awkward. She'd never shown him any real sign of affection before.

Dishevelled she may be, but she still smelt delicious.

'So,' she said at last, releasing him. 'Are you going to tell me what in the world is going on here?'

'Oh... yes. I'm to take you to the others. Um, I was

probably supposed to fill you in a bit first.' He grinned sheepishly.

She arched a brow. 'You are disgracefully behindhand.'

'Hey. I was distracted. Somebody was busy lambasting me.'

'Well, get on with it now.'

'No time now. They'll be wondering where we are.' He offered her his arm with exquisite courtesy. 'If you'll attend me, Lady Vale.' It felt strange and unpleasant, calling her that, but he got the word out creditably.

She took his arm. 'I'm not Lady Vale, Tren.'

He frowned. Keeping her own name was an unusual decision, but this was Eva. She frequently rewrote the rules. 'Pardon my error, Lady Glostrum.'

She looked at him for a moment, but said nothing. With an uncertain smile, he led her out of the chart room.

A group was awaiting them in Limbane's reading room. Llandry and Pensould were there along with Limbane and Andraly. Tren felt Eva's surprise at beholding this curious assembly.

'Llandry? What?'

For her part, Llandry was obviously delighted and awed in approximately equal measures. If she had been shy with him, it was nothing compared to her manner on addressing Eva. She managed to stammer out a greeting, smiling with obvious pleasure but blushing all the same. The more awkward Llandry was, the more protective her companion became.

Tren was amused to see Pensould glare at Eva and bare his teeth slightly as he drew Llandry towards him.

'Pensould, isn't it? I'm not going to harm her.'

Llandry's face betrayed some of the surprise that Tren felt himself. She knew the other draykon already? How Eva managed to keep one step ahead of everyone never ceased to amaze him.

'Your mother has been in touch,' she said dryly in answer to Llandry's unspoken query. 'The two of you caused a stir in the interrealm press.'

Pensould beamed with pride, but Llandry looked crestfallen.

'I—we—I didn't mean for that to happen,' she said.

Eva patted her shoulder. 'Your mother managed to suppress most of it. She's a resourceful woman.' She looked enquiringly at Limbane, who so far hadn't said a word.

'Ah, yes,' said Tren, stepping in. 'Lady Glostrum, this is Limbane, um, just Limbane. And you've met Ms Winnier?'

Eva made her courtesies with exquisite manners. As she did so, Andraly leaned towards Limbane and spoke one word in an undertone. 'Unclaimed.'

Limbane's eyebrows rose.

Eva's eyes flicked from Andraly to Limbane and back again, betraying her uncertainty. Then she smiled, her virtually unshakeable self-possession back in place.

'Would somebody be so kind as to tell me what in the world is going on?' She looked straight at him. 'Tren? Who are these people?'

'Librarians,' he said.

'What.'

'It's what the word "Lokant" means. Please, sit down,' he begged as she continued to hover in the centre of the room. 'Limbane will explain.'

'Again,' muttered Limbane under his breath.

Tren watched Eva closely as she took a seat. Her eyes were thoughtful, her mind obviously busy putting the pieces of this mystery together. He knew it wouldn't take her long.

She looked at Andraly. 'Ms Winnier. Is that your natural hair colour?'

Limbane laughed. 'Oh, Krays made a mistake in letting you alone.'

Andraly was grinning too. With a few quick, deft movements she loosened the wig she wore and pulled it off. Underneath that her hair was pure white.

'I'd have dyed it, but the colour just won't take.'

Eva was silent for a moment. 'Then—that means—'

Limbane smiled briefly. 'Why don't I start at the beginning?'

'All right,' said Eva faintly. Tren wished she'd placed herself a little closer to him; somehow she had ended up on the opposite side of Limbane's comfortable room. He sighed inwardly and resigned himself to watching her reaction from a distance.

'Lokant. As Mr Warvel has already informed you, it does indeed mean "librarian", in our tongue—a language that has never been spoken in your world. And before you ask, *this* is the Library. You are sitting in it.

'I'm afraid our race predates the human one by a

long way. I won't say how long; the human mind isn't equipped to comprehend the full stretch of time. Usually we keep to ourselves. We study the different worlds, document their workings and contents and add those records to the Library. There is more knowledge here than any of you could possibly imagine. Andraly, for example, is based long-term in Ayrien, supplementing our thin records there.

'But others of our race are more meddlesome. We have learned—far too late, I fear—that the Sulayn Phay organisation returned to this world some time ago. They have been creating considerable mischief and all of you are bound up in it.'

Limbane's gaze settled on Pensould. 'Some of you have been creating additional complications all by yourselves.' Llandry looked dejected, but Pensould was completely unruffled by Limbane's disapproval.

Eva spoke up. 'So the other organisation—Sulayn Phay?—are you saying they are responsible for the draykon crisis?'

'No,' Limbane replied after a moment. 'Indirectly perhaps, but I doubt that they intended to return the draykon race to this cluster of worlds.'

'Why not?'

Limbane smiled thinly. 'That is a story for another time.'

'There's a great deal you aren't telling us,' Eva said.

'Of course,' Limbane admitted comfortably. 'All in good time, my dear.'

Eva made a small sound of annoyance. 'Ana and Griel. Are they part of this organisation?'

'Something like that,' replied Limbane. 'If we wander back in time a number of generations—we won't say how many—we come to a time when some of us entertained ourselves by mixing with the human societies. We called it "study", and it was, but it went much further than that for some. I don't think any of us expected that the two races would be able to successfully breed, not until it happened. The likes of Ana and Griel are the descendants of those kinds of unions. Not Lokants, but retaining some of our traits. The hair colour always breeds true, for some reason, along with a few of our abilities.'

'The vanishing,' Eva said, nodding. Her face, always pale, was very white now. 'That means that I—'

'You are part Lokant, yes. In fact, you are descended from one of my very favourite colleagues. She'll love to meet you. Perhaps later.'

Eva was silenced. She stared at Limbane with her dark eyes very wide.

'But I... I cannot...'

'That's just because you haven't been trained,' Limbane said, guessing her query. 'Ana and Griel were adopted by Krays, it appears, and put to work at some nefarious project or other. Why he didn't tap you as a recruit is something of a mystery.'

'Krays?'

Tren felt obscurely relieved to find that Eva didn't know everything after all.

'Krays. Formerly a Librarian, now part of the Sulayn Phay group. He seems to be heading up whatever project is going on here. Making use of the partials was inspired, it has to be said.'

'Partials?'

'Part-blood Lokants.'

'So you don't know what they're up to?'

Limbane shook his head. 'I tried asking him, but he didn't want to talk to me for some reason. That is why we require assistance.'

Eva sat back, her drawn face speaking of the headache she was probably suffering. 'Oh?'

Limbane steepled his fingers and looked at the ceiling. 'We know that Krays is after Miss Sanfaer, for some reason unknown to her. We know that he has put Ana to work collecting draykon bone from the realm of Iskyr, possibly from Ayrien also. We know that Sulayn Phay had something to do with the re-emergence of the draykon race, though it may not be the outcome they had intended. What does all of this add up to?'

Tren had a question. 'Limbane. How could such a thing happen by accident?'

Limbane cast him an amused glance. 'Oh, it was no accident I'm sure. Not exactly. I suspect that Krays has encountered some insubordination among his recruits. If Ana is collecting draykon bone now, we may tentatively assume that she was doing so before, on Krays's orders. But she and her husband diverted the bones to their own purpose. What I am more interested in is what Krays wants them for.'

To his surprise, Llandry spoke up. 'So - so we are... a mistake?'

'I'll get to that, Miss Sanfaer,' Limbane said in a gentler voice. 'But no. You yourself are no mistake; the timing is merely not as we had intended.'

Eva blinked at that. 'We? What did you have to do with the draykon affair?'

'A lot, in fact. But I believe we have had

revelations enough for the present. I encourage you all to partake of the Library's facilities; take as long as you need, time is currently ignoring us. Lady Glostrum, Ms Winnier took you to the chart room for a reason. I believe you may find it interesting to peruse more closely.' He looked at Llandry again. 'You too, Miss Sanfaer.'

'What about me?' Tren asked.

Limbane grinned. 'I imagine that you, Mr Warvel, will be happy enough to place yourself at her ladyship's disposal.'

With that, the old gentleman stood up, smiling. 'All right, off you go. I have some other matters to attend to. We will reconvene at some point fairly soon, and before you ask, yes, I will answer more questions at that time. Now, go.'

CHAPTER EIGHTEEN

Ynara knew the Vanse family a little. Sayfer Vanse was a strong summoner, his wife only a little less so. Orillin, as expected, followed in his parents' footsteps and had been enrolled in Summoner School at a young age. He was already shaping up to be one of his generation's stars.

But that didn't explain why he was attracting the attention of an obscure university faculty as far away as the realm of Nimdre. Dev's brief missive wasn't exactly clear. Being Dev, it hadn't occurred to him to explain how or why he'd left her house, where he'd gone to, or what he was doing now. His scrawled mess of a note merely babbled about some connection between Orillin and Llandry, saying that they shared a great many ancestors. *Something to do with Llan's draykon shift?* he had written. Ynara sighed a little. "Something"? Dev ought to be better at conveying information; he'd certainly had enough practice at it.

She could make some inferences herself. If Llandry's metamorphosis was a product of her ancestry in some way, then Orillin himself may have similar potential. She couldn't guess why Dev's university was especially interested in the possibility, but she could guess that it probably did not mean good news for Orillin.

There was a final note of warning in Dev's missive that unsettled her.

Get him out of Glinnery.

When she showed the note to Aysun, he looked grim.

'If this boy is anything like our Llan, he has a world of trouble on the way.'

Ynara couldn't disagree with that. 'Dev meant for us to do something about it,' she replied. 'I wish he'd been more explicit; it's hard to protect someone from a virtually undefined threat.'

Aysun shrugged. 'It doesn't matter. We know what Llan went through—what she's still going through.'

'We couldn't protect her.'

Aysun smiled grimly. 'Because she's a headstrong girl, like her mother. What we can do for this boy is get him out of here before somebody comes looking for him.'

'And take him where exactly? Hiding didn't work too well for Llan, as I recall.'

'I have an idea.'

Aysun's workshop was a cluttered mess. This was unusual, but Ynara didn't say anything. She watched as her husband searched frantically through the piles of objects, picking up and discarding sundry bits and pieces. At length he found what he was looking for. He attached a small piece of metal to a box that he held in his hands, tinkering with the mechanics for some minutes. Then he placed it down on the high surface of his workbench. The box emitted a crackling sound for several seconds, then the noise cleared.

Aysun pressed a button. 'Rufin. Rufin.'

Nothing happened. He tried again, repeating the name several more times. Then, to Ynara's amazement, another voice came out of the box.

'Ays? What the bloody hell? You made it work, you raging genius.'

'No time for that, Ruf. Get Eyas and get here, by tomorrow.'

'You going to ditch us again like last time?'

'No. Stop wasting time. You're not here by noon tomorrow, we're going without you.'

'Ah—where are we going?'

'You'll find out tomorrow.' Aysun switched off the box and the noises faded. Ynara looked at him for a long moment.

'You,' she said at last, 'never cease to amaze me.'

Aysun grinned like a schoolboy.

Orillin was in class when Ynara arrived at the school. As an Elder of the Realm, it was no trouble for her to gain access to his lecture. She had only to say a few things about "extreme importance" and "complete urgency" and she was ushered straight in.

Orillin was a bright young man with a shock of

messy blond hair. He looked at Ynara with a mixture of interest and puzzlement as she was shown in.

'I'm afraid I need to borrow Mr Vanse,' Ynara said, addressing the tutor.

The tutor, a middle-aged Glinnish woman with a cheerful demeanour, looked at Orillin in amazement. 'Oh! Is there some problem?'

'Hopefully not, Ms Pelne.'

Orillin stood up slowly, his red face showing that he was conscious of the stares of his classmates. He left the room with her without looking back.

'Ah... I'm not in trouble of some kind, am I?'

Ynara shook her head. 'Truthfully, Mr Vanse, I hardly know. But possibly. Quite possibly, yes.'

That silenced the boy. He followed her outside, palpably nervous.

'Elder. Do my parents know about this?'

'You'll see your parents in a few minutes, Mr Vanse.' Ynara spread her wings and jumped. Orillin followed her into the air. To her relief, he asked no further questions as they flew to Ynara's home; the pace she set was extremely fast, but he didn't complain.

Aysun had collected the elder Vanses while Ynara extracted Orillin from his lessons. When she arrived, he gave a tiny, almost imperceptible shake of his head. She understood. He'd questioned the Vanses and discovered nothing; if there was anything unusual about their son, they knew nothing about it.

Orillin smiled nervously at his parents as he entered the Sanfaer living room. They stood up, looking at Ynara anxiously.

'Elder Sanfaer, what is this about?'

In answer, Ynara simply handed them Devary's note. 'This came from an agent stationed in Nimdre,' she explained. It wasn't too far from the truth.

The Vanses read rapidly. When they'd finished, they both looked up at Ynara with identical expressions of alarm.

'Ori is in danger? From who?'

'The precise identity of the enemy is not known,' Ynara replied steadily. 'But our Llandry has encountered considerable trouble since she discovered the cursed draykon bone. If her enemy is also Orillin's, then he must be removed from Glinnery with all haste. We propose to take charge of his safety. He will be taken to some relatives of ours; we do not anticipate that anyone will guess to look for him there.'

'Where exactly?' Orillin's mother looked the way Ynara had often felt lately: alarmed, confused, and oppressed by a degree of fear she only felt when her child was threatened. She felt a stab of deep sympathy for the woman.

'Irbel,' Ynara said. 'As you know, my husband hails from there. Is there some story you can tell to explain Orillin's absence for a time?'

'Um.' Orillin's mother faltered, looking at her son with terrified amazement. 'We can say he is ill, perhaps.'

'He's in a specialist infirmary in Glour,' Ynara decided. 'Don't say which one.'

Mrs Vanse nodded, but her husband was not satisfied. 'I mean no disrespect, Elder Sanfaer, but can you protect our son? The two of you alone? Shouldn't he be placed under government guard?'

Aysun spoke up at that. 'A government guard did nothing for Llandry. Your son needs to be placed somewhere he can't be found. And we won't be alone.' He crossed the room in two strides and opened the far door. On the other side stood Rufin, cleaning his gun. He beamed and bowed extravagantly.

'We'll have help,' said Aysun.

Sayfer Vanse frowned. 'Where *is* your daughter?'

'Somewhere safe,' Ynara said firmly. She only wished she felt as sure of that as she sounded. As was too often the case of late, she really had no idea where Llandry was now.

Orillin himself asked considerably fewer questions than his parents. He was scared and it showed, in spite of his efforts to be cheerful. He stayed close to Ynara, watching the insouciant Rufin with a mixture of awe and dread.

'Time's wasting,' said Aysun gruffly. 'Let's go.'

Mrs Vanse clung to her son for a long time. After a while Aysun looked ready to separate them, but Ynara held him back. She understood the shock the Vanses were suffering; in some ways Orillin's danger would be hardest on them. They had the unenviable task of doing nothing, only waiting for Orillin to come home.

At last Mrs Vanse released Orillin. She and her husband left quickly.

'Your parents packed some of your things,' said Ynara to Orillin gently. 'Are you ready to go?'

He didn't say anything, just nodded. Ynara gave him a smile, squeezing his hand briefly. This boy was as brave as her Llandry.

They left the house on foot, on account of their wingless comrades. The boy walked along in silence for some time, his mind obviously busy. Ynara took up a station on his left, keeping him company without pressing him to talk. He would have enough to worry about soon; she left him his peace, for a brief space.

After perhaps an hour, he roused himself from his reverie and looked at her. 'Elder Sanfaer? How long will I have to be away? You see, my exams are coming up and I'm due to graduate soon.'

'I'm sorry about that, Orillin. I'll make sure you're given the chance to make up the lost time later. I really don't know how long you'll be away.'

The boy sighed a little and nodded. 'Ah, Elder?'

'Yes.'

'I don't understand any of this. You say I'm related to your family in some way?'

'You and my Llandry are distant cousins, yes.'

'Why does that put me in danger?'

Ynara debated briefly about how much to tell him. She didn't want to scare the boy, but he deserved to know why he had been suddenly pulled out of his comfortable life by a family he barely knew.

So she told him everything. About the draykon bone, about Llandry's transformation, and about Pensould. When she had finished, poor Orillin's eyes were very wide and he swallowed nervously.

'If anybody but you had told me such things, Elder Sanfaer, I'd say they were crazy. But those news reports... was that Llandry?'

'The grey was Llandry, yes.'

'And you think I may be able to do that too?' A note of excitement crept in and when he looked at her his eyes were shining.

'I don't know, Orillin, but it's possible.'

'I'd like to meet Llandry. Just to meet her, I mean in a sociable way, but also maybe she could—maybe she could teach me things.'

Ynara sighed. She didn't have to ask what "things" he meant.

'I want to see her too. Perhaps we will, soon.' She signalled to Aysun and he drew level with her.

'We're far enough along the Irbel road,' she murmured to him. 'Shall we move it along?'

Aysun nodded and turned off the road, heading into the trees. When they were well hidden from view, he smiled at his wife.

'Go ahead.'

Ynara looked at him for a second, trying to gauge his state of mind. For many years he'd hated it when she worked sorcery in his presence. She couldn't tell if he truly felt differently about it now; his face was, as ever, impassive.

Needs must, she thought. She closed her eyes for a moment, letting her mind slip into the working-trance. It had been a long time, but she had forgotten nothing. In an instant the paths to the Upper Realm were within her reach. A swift, sharp tug was all that was required, and a gate blossomed in the air before her. She inhaled, enjoying the heady fragrance of flowers and honey that drifted through.

'After you, Ruf. Eyas.' She watched as Aysun's friends stepped through first.

'Aren't we going to Irbel?' Orillin's excitement had faded; his fear was back as he hovered on the edge of the gate.

'Irbel isn't far enough away,' said Aysun. 'Don't be afraid. You'll be safe.'

Orillin swallowed, nodded, then he too passed through.

Brave boy, Ynara thought.

Aysun turned to her. 'You sure about this?'

She nodded. 'I want to. Are *you* sure about this?'

'No choice, really.' He kissed her briefly, then placed a gentle hand on her lower back, guiding her to the gate. Taking a deep breath, she allowed herself to be drawn into the portal.

It was the first time in a decade that she'd used an expletive, let alone several of them in quick succession.

'Why... the bloody hell... does it have to be so painful,' grated Rufin. Ynara agreed with him entirely, setting her teeth while her body tried to expel every piece of food she'd ever eaten in her life.

'Won't last,' she gasped. Poor Orillin's face had passed through stark white and progressed to pale green. She went to him, holding his head while he vomited.

'You'll be all right in a moment,' she murmured.

He managed a weak smile. 'It's training. I've made the crossing too many times lately. Wears you down, I suppose.'

'Of course.'

Eyas was lying on his back in the grass. 'Every time I do this, I think—this time—I'm definitely going to die.'

'Rubbish.' Aysun was white with tension under his

tan, but otherwise he was remarkably unaffected. Ynara knew him well enough to guess that he simply refused to display his discomfort. She patted his arm lightly and he flashed her a brief smile.

'Better get on,' he said. 'Sooner we reach my father's house, the better.'

'How do you know where to find him?' Ynara asked the question in an undertone. Aysun responded with a humourless smile.

'I don't. But he has a habit of finding me.'

Aysun was right, for soon after their arrival in the Uppers there came a whirring of wings and a flash of colour and Llandry's erstwhile companion appeared. At least, it looked like the same creature. Ynara raised a questioning brow at her husband and he nodded confirmation.

'Follow that,' he said curtly. Orillin watched the creature's progress with an expression of puzzlement on his youthful face.

'Irilapter?' he asked. 'Odd. Its mind doesn't feel the way I'd expect.'

'It has a passenger,' Aysun replied, though he refused to explain further.

Rufin took the lead, flanked by Eyas and—at his own insistence—Orillin.

'I can be useful in this,' he'd protested when Ynara had tried to shepherd him behind the others. Watching him take his position at Rufin's left, she suffered some misgivings. He was under their protection, and it was *her* job to keep him safe. But she ruthlessly suppressed her doubts. She'd tried to protect Llandry by hiding her from all danger, but all she'd achieved by it was frustrating Llan to the point that she'd run away. The consequences of that had been severe. The last thing they could afford to do was push Orillin's youthful pride to breaking point.

Aysun kept his wife close, stationing them both behind Orillin. Ynara had to be content with that, merely praying that they wouldn't encounter anything excessively dangerous before they reached Aysun's father's house.

She sneaked a glance at her husband. She had been surprised when he'd suggested taking Orillin to his father. He'd returned not long ago swearing never to have anything to do with the man again. But she couldn't deny that the plan was the best option they had; up here, Orillin would be well hidden.

And she was curious to meet the infamous Rheas Irfan.

'Trouble yonder,' said Orillin suddenly. Ynara noticed Eyas cast him a sharp look.

'You sure, lad?'

At Orillin's nod, Eyas whistled. 'You've a better range than mine, then. What's the danger?'

'Orboe,' he replied.

Ynara didn't recognise the name, but the word rattled Eyas. He turned back quickly.

'I'd like to suggest you travel on the wing for a while,' he said to her. Feeling her arm squeezed, Ynara glanced over at Aysun.

'Go on, love,' he said.

She obeyed, but reluctantly. She flew low, keeping Orillin and Aysun in clear sight.

Until her attention was distracted by a blur of

movement up ahead. She flew higher, rigidly controlling the pulse of dread that threatened to freeze her limbs.

Apparently an orboe was a creature more than six feet long from nose to stubby tail and covered in shaggy grey fur. It walked on all fours, its horrifyingly powerful body heavily built. Its eyes and ears were tiny, but its jaws were massive. Ynara had no trouble imagining the size of its teeth.

It would be only a few minutes before it would see—or smell—Ynara's group.

She dived back towards the ground. 'Aysun,' she gasped. 'We cannot handle this creature. We need to get out of here.'

'Don't worry,' Orillin said over his shoulder. He smiled, looking remarkably at ease. 'I can deal with it.'

Eyas was shaking his head. 'Ynara may have a point,' he said. 'Facing down an orboe is not—'

'It's fine,' Orillin interrupted. 'I've done it before.'

'What? Don't be an idiot, you can't just—'

He was interrupted by a shattering roar and the orboe came on, crashing through the yellow-tipped bushes that covered the ground ahead. Swearing again—her vocabulary of expletives had rarely been so well exercised—Ynara returned to the air, watching anxiously as Rufin levelled his shotgun at the beast and Eyas prepared to attempt mastery over it.

To her horror, Orillin walked freely towards it. He was actually holding out his hand, as though he expected to make friends. She wanted to cry out, but the words froze in her throat.

The orboe slowed its charge, shaking its head as

though confused. After another moment it stopped before Orillin and then—to her complete amazement—it butted its head against the boy's chest, hard enough to knock him to the ground. Ynara felt another spasm of alarm, but the boy was actually laughing.

'Want to keep him?' he called merrily. 'His name is Graaf.'

Eyas was staring at the boy in flabbergasted silence.

'What... in the Lowers... was that?' he said at last.

'Weirdest thing I've ever seen,' said Rufin, shouldering his gun again.

Orillin grinned a little apologetically. 'I've always been good with the bigger animals.'

'*Good?*' Eyas almost shrieked the word. 'That's not even possible!'

Ynara swooped down to land next to Aysun. 'I wonder if Llan would've been like that.'

If she'd been summoner trained. She didn't add those words; she didn't want it to seem like an accusation.

Aysun merely grunted.

The orboe was now accepting chunks of fruit from Orillin's hands.

'Wait,' she said. 'It's a herbivore?'

'Omnivore,' he corrected, petting the creature's massive shaggy head. 'But he doesn't think of any of you as food anymore.'

Anymore? She shuddered and decided not to ask.

When the company travelled onwards again, they did so with Graaf ambling along at Orillin's heels like an overgrown dog.

Rheas and Aysun were so alike in face and manner that Ynara felt a foreboding chill.

Please, don't let Aysun turn into his father when he reaches that age.

They sat glaring at each other with identical expressions of stubborn dislike.

'Led us into an orboe,' Aysun said accusingly.

'That was my fault, was it?'

'We were following your lead.'

'Didn't mean you didn't have to look out for yourselves. I'm not a nanny.'

'Don't require a nanny. Just some basic concern for our welfare.'

'If you think I'm careless, why did you bring the boy?'

'He's not safe in the Seven.'

Rheas snorted. 'According to you, he's not safe up here with me either.'

'You planning to take proper care of him? Because if you wanted to make up for your earlier neglect, here's your chance.'

That older, grey-headed version of her husband scowled at his son. 'He'll be all right with me,' he said grudgingly. 'Not that he seems to need much protecting.'

Ynara glanced outside, where Orillin was still playing with Graaf. 'That's true enough.'

Rheas's cold blue eyes turned on her. He'd shown her distant politeness but nothing more; she'd responded with an icy coolness of manner that was barely civil. Let him work for his forgiveness.

'You staying?'

It didn't sound anything like an invitation. 'No,'

231

she returned. 'Much as I'd love to accept your generous offer, I've duties to attend to.'

Rheas didn't reply, only turned his stare back on his son. 'You?'

Aysun nodded. 'Rufin and Eyas too. The boy needs a proper guard, until this is over.'

Rheas accepted this news with extremely ill grace. 'You wouldn't think peace and quiet would be so much to ask for,' he said petulantly.

Aysun shrugged with complete indifference. 'Please yourself. Anything happens to that boy while you're napping, though, and I'll kill you myself.' She'd rarely seen him looking so grim.

'Seconded,' she added in her iciest tone.

Rheas chuckled. 'You two are as warm as twin blocks of ice.'

Ynara stood up. 'Time for me to get back,' she said to Aysun. He jumped up instantly and followed her into the hallway. She didn't bother to say goodbye to Rheas.

'Keep this with you.' Aysun produced a small metal box from somewhere and tucked it into her hand. It was the device he'd used to talk to Rufin. 'You remember how to work it?'

She nodded. The process hadn't looked complicated.

'It'll make a sound if I'm trying to contact you on it. I don't know if it will work between the Uppers and Glinnery, but we'll try it. All right?'

She kissed him. 'How would I manage without you?'

He gave her the boyish grin that still made her heart flutter, even after so many years. 'No idea.'

CHAPTER NINETEEN

Devary opened the note hastily, almost tearing it in his anxiety to know the contents. It was addressed in Ynara's hand; he couldn't remember the last time she had written to him.

To his disappointment, the note was very brief.

He is safe.

He sighed in frustration, rubbing at his tired eyes. It was good to know that she had got Orillin away safely, but the extreme brevity of the communication was frustrating. Was she well? Had she forgiven him for losing Llandry—at all? Even the faintest note of warmth and support would have lifted his spirits enormously.

No matter. He would have to manage without her approval. He burned the paper, then stood up. He had an appointment to keep.

Indren had put him in touch with one of the faculty's longest-serving members. Ern Greyson proved to be in his sixties, a man as grey as his name and with an uncompromising frankness of manner. He surveyed Devary with suspicion as the younger man sat down opposite his table in one of Draetre's smaller eating houses.

'I'd better tell you right now,' Devary began immediately. 'I'm tracered. We'd better make this quick.'

Greyson's eyes sharpened. 'Tracered means Krays's boy. You expect me to trust you?'

'Yes,' Dev said bluntly. 'I'm not promoted, just a minor information agent.'

'Then why the tracer.'

'Have you heard the name Llandry Sanfaer?'

'Huh,' Greyson spat. 'That name's coming up an awful lot lately.'

'I'm a friend of her mother's,' Devary said quickly. 'I was tracered because Krays is trying to find her and he knew she would find *me*. I need to know what's being said about her.'

'Word is she's draykon-kind,' Greyson countered. 'That true?'

'Word travels fast. Does that mean something to you?'

Greyson drained the contents of his earthenware mug in one enormous gulp, then set it down. Devary grew irritated at his leisurely manner, but he made himself sit patiently waiting for the answer.

'It means something to Krays,' Greyson said at last. 'Which means something to me.'

Devary waited for more. Indren had told him that Greyson had no love for Krays, but unlike Indren he obviously didn't fear the man either. He had been steadily collecting information about the new masters of the faculty for the last few years.

'Couple of moons back,' Greyson continued, 'masters issued a general order. All promoted agents—white-hairs, most of them—were sent to Glinnery to investigate Llandry Sanfaer's enigmatic Istore stone. They came back with several examples of the stuff, and to a man they were raving about it. Full of stories about its magical properties and what have you. Soon as Krays got his hands on a piece he was obsessed with it. Diverted all faculty resources onto it on the spot. And I heard that he had his two pet agents on the case.'

'Who were they?'

'Woman, a white-hair. Calls herself Ana. Her husband too, also a white-hair.'

Ana again. This corresponded with what Indren had told him about the faculty's new bosses. And he had used the same term to describe her.

'Why do you call them white-hairs?'

'Because Krays's type always are. Him and his colleagues and their most trusted agents. Only, I got the feeling Ana and her hubby aren't so trusted nowadays.'

'Because?'

'Used to be in and out of the faculty all the time. Haven't seen either of them in a while, and Krays is grooming some new favourites. Whatever they did with that stone, it wasn't what Krays ordered.'

Devary turned that information over for a moment. 'You know what it is they did?'

Greyson shot him a look. 'Krays's top agents disappear. Next thing I hear, Krays is acting like they never existed and there are draykons on the scene. Can't be a coincidence.'

Devary nodded. 'She and her husband, Griel, took those stones—draykon bones—and resurrected the beast. You're saying that wasn't Krays's intention?'

'I'm pretty sure not.' Greyson was looking at him with increased respect. 'How do you know all that?'

'I've talked with an eye witness.' His source was more complicated than that, in fact; he'd heard Lady Glostrum's account from Ynara. But it amounted to the same thing.

'Nice,' Greyson approved. Then he frowned. 'You sure Griel was the name?'

'Pretty sure, yes.'

'Haven't heard it. But then I saw less of that one. Didn't mix with the rest of us as the lady did.' His face as he said it suggested that the lady's interactions with the faculty agents hadn't been pleasant.

'Greyson,' said Devary seriously. 'If Krays wasn't looking to wake up a draykon, what *was* he doing with those bones?'

The older man was silent for a minute. 'I don't know,' he said at last, 'but I got a few leads I can share. What're you looking to do with them?'

'Krays is after Llandry,' Devary replied. 'And possibly others like her. I'm set to find out why, and then—somehow—I have to stop him.'

Greyson's lips twitched. 'Large task you've set yourself there.'

'I know,' Dev said heavily.

'Indren couldn't help you with that?'

'She knows nothing of it. Which makes me think Krays knew what the stone was immediately; if not, it would have been Indren's job to study it. The only piece she ever saw, though, came from me.'

Greyson nodded slowly. 'Ullarn,' he said cryptically. 'Lot of the bones were shipping out to there. Reckon that's where the imperious Ana hails from also, maybe her husband too. Can't tell you more than that, I'm afraid. I never was posted out that way.'

Ullarn. That was it? Ullarn was the largest of the Darklands realms and certainly the most mysterious. If that was all he had to go on, he was very much out of luck.

'Thank you,' he said anyway. Greyson had been useful, even if he couldn't answer every question Devary had.

'How are you going to pursue this with a tracer on you? You can't just go to Ullarn.'

And that was the other problem. 'Maybe there's more I can do here,' he said. 'There has to be something around here to tell me what Krays is up to.'

'I find anything, I'll let you know.'

Devary shook the older man's hand. 'Thanks.'

Five days passed and Devary heard nothing from Greyson. He spent that period of time combing Indren's library and the more public collections at the faculty building. The most interesting find was a tumbled stack of research notes without a title or any indication of the author, but what caught Devary's attention was the repeated use of the word "Istore".

When he showed them to Indren, she merely

nodded. 'Those are the records from my brief research project on that stone you brought me. I wanted to pursue it further, even after you took back the pendant, but Krays cancelled it.'

'Did he? Why?' Sifting through the papers, he found three pages of scrawled notes on the so-called stone's magical properties. It enhanced summoning ability, amplified sorcerous talents and imparted a sense of well-being even to those humans without a shred of magical talent.

'He said it was a waste of time. Like I told you, I don't think it was ever a mystery to him.'

An unpleasant thought occurred to Devary's habitually suspicious mind. 'Indren. Greyson told me that Krays's two favourite agents were sent to take the draykon bone. That would've been well before I arrived here with the pendant—and Llandry. Did you know about that?' He remembered her manner when he'd turned up with that stone. She had been enthused about the project—and, apparently, shocked when Llandry was attacked over it. Had she been acting a part? He now recalled that visiting that restaurant had been her idea; it sickened him to think that she might have colluded with Krays to get Llandry away from her guards.

If she had, then she was still acting a part now.

'No!' Indren blurted. 'I swear, I knew nothing about it at the time save what I heard in the papers. And I had precious little time even to read the news during those weeks. Whatever Krays and his friends were doing at that time, I wasn't involved in it. Not until later.'

Her face was white with alarm and she stared at

him with such horror that he was inclined to believe her. Indren was one of those women who was rarely discomposed, and it took a lot to shake her.

'When were you involved?'

'Only recently, truly. This genealogy project is the first assignment I've been given that has any direct relationship to the draykon bone.'

Devary sighed. It was becoming harder than ever to choose allies that he could trust.

'You wouldn't lie, Ren, would you?' They had been closer friends, once, before Indren had been promoted so far above him and he had been sent across the Seven. Ren was the name he used to have for her. He hoped it would encourage her to be sincere.

'I lie, Dev. All the time, these days—I have to. But I wouldn't lie to you. Please believe me.' She caught his hand in a pleading gesture.

He frowned, letting out a long sigh. Life had truly become impossibly complicated of late—dating precisely from his return to the Sanfaer home in Glinnery.

Though if he could turn back and undo that action, he still wouldn't.

He summoned a smile for Indren, watched her face relax in relief. 'What of Greyson? Where did you find him?'

She gave a crooked smile. 'The white-hairs aren't popular within the faculty. Last year some of the agents formed a co-operative to share information. The ultimate goal, I suppose, is to be rid of them, though I don't see how that is to be achieved. Greyson is their leader.'

'Oh?' He looked narrowly at her. 'Are you a member?'

'I joined.' She paused. 'Recently.'

He looked a question; she fixed her gaze on the floor.

'When I was given the genealogy project, I realised... it wasn't hard to guess who was behind Llandry's attempted abduction. I felt awful. I might not have known beforehand but it was me who took the two of you to that restaurant. I had been serving Krays's purpose without even realising it. And I was so full of myself.' She raised her eyes at last. 'I was awful to her, wasn't I?'

He shrugged one shoulder slightly. 'I don't think I noticed if you were.'

She rolled her eyes and gave a quick laugh. 'How like you. Yes, I was perfectly horrid to her. I can scarcely remember why, only... I hadn't seen you in so long, and then for you to arrive with...'

She trailed off, then shook her head with an air of finality. 'No matter. I joined soon after that. I have no love for Krays's methods or his agenda, and I am tired of being manipulated by him and his friends.'

He smiled. 'You're a better woman than I thought, Ren.'

'Thanks.' She spoke the word in a flat tone, and he realised the statement hadn't emerged as he'd intended.

He hastily changed the subject. 'Ah, so, Greyson. He's trustworthy then?'

Indren shrugged. 'You know as well as I do that it's hard to be sure. But if we can't trust Greyson, we can't trust anyone. He has my confidence, if that helps at all.'

'Thank you, Ren.' He picked up her hand and kissed it lightly, smiling his thanks. A light appeared in her eyes for an instant, then faded.

'Anything for you, Dev,' she said lightly.

A few days later, Devary was walking through Draetre's eventide market when he felt a light touch on his arm. Thinking of pickpockets, he was instantly on his guard. Checking his pockets, he found his money whole and untouched—and a scrap of paper.

Astendre Wharf 17.

He knew that area, though not well. It was near the river that marked the city's south-eastern boundary. The area was mostly occupied by tradesmen's storage buildings.

He stopped and looked about himself, knowing it was already too late. Nobody waited to see if he found the message. He saw nothing but crowds of shoppers moving briskly from stall to stall. Puzzled, he folded the paper and tucked it back into his pocket.

'That's Greyson's writing,' Indren confirmed later.

'You two have been writing to each other, have you?'

Her cheeks flushed slightly and she spoke with infinite dignity. 'He has communicated with me on occasion.'

'Always by letter?'

'Don't forget the tracers,' she reminded him tartly.

'It's unwise to keep too many meetings with the same agents. It arouses suspicion.'

He grinned at her. 'You've been spending a lot of time with me. Is that not then a risk?'

'That is different.'

'Is it? How?'

She ignored the question. 'Are you going?'

He frowned, smoothing the paper in his fingers. 'Do you know what this is?'

'I've never heard of it before. That doesn't mean much, you understand. I'm viewed in some circles as a higher-up but I'm not given access to much.'

'I must investigate,' he decided.

'Dev, those tracers aren't to be just ignored. If he looks for you while you're there, I don't know what will happen to you but it won't be good.'

'Do not be worried about me,' he smiled.

She snorted. 'Someday, Mr Kant, that abominable overconfidence will get you killed. I am coming with you.'

His smile faded. 'Two tracered agents in the same—very secret—building? Will that not merely double the chances of our *both* being caught?'

She glared at him. 'Two of us can cover the area faster, meaning we can be out again sooner.'

'Flawed logic.'

She was adamant, immoveable and would not be argued down.

In the end, he simply left without telling her.

The seventeenth building on Astendre Wharf was tall, narrow and squashed haphazardly between two much larger warehouses. No windows adorned the front, so he couldn't immediately tell whether the building was occupied.

He paused to check the position of his weapons. He had given up carrying them for a time; having learnt about the tracer, he'd felt such hopelessness about his situation that he'd lost faith in his ability to control his own fate. But he shouldn't have allowed those events to affect him that way. His daggers, sometimes so repulsive to his essentially pacifistic nature, now imparted a feeling of confidence that he hadn't felt in some time.

He jogged down the street, darted through the first alley he found and circled around to the back of the buildings. He had opted to go at night in the hopes of finding the area deserted, and so far he was in luck.

The darkness, though, was a problem. Heavy clouds covered the sky, hiding the light of the moon, and this part of Draetre wasn't worth the trouble of lighting at night. It took him a few minutes to find his way to the rear door of building number seventeen.

It was, as he expected, firmly locked. Far from feeling discouraged, he felt a thrill of anticipation. Something important was here; no sense in using locks otherwise.

He hadn't picked a lock in at least a year, but the skill hadn't faded. He had it open inside a minute. He entered, moving with soft, silent steps into the building.

The interior was so dark he could see nothing at all. With an inward curse, he fished a small, portable light-globe from the pack he carried. He had no wish to draw attention to his presence, but he could investigate nothing without light. He activated it with a swift thought, dampening its radiance down to a gentle flicker of white light. It was just enough to illuminate his surroundings, but it wouldn't carry far. Or so he hoped.

His heart sank on finding himself standing in nothing but a cramped and empty antechamber. Ahead of him loomed another door, bigger and no doubt much more securely locked. He released the globe, guiding it to hover a few inches above his head, and set to work.

Half an hour later, tense and sweating, Devary finally found his way through the maddening door. No less than three locks secured the portal, two of which were operated by codes rather than keys. More evidence that something here was not intended for general access.

The building was bigger than it had appeared from the outside. A long hall stretched before him, and he guessed that three more storeys of similar size rose above. The room in which he stood was furnished with benches set at regular intervals, each spacious and, he guessed, well-lit when they were in use. The exterior looked ramshackle, but the interior had the polished air of a professional setup.

All of the benches bore clusters of objects. Devary bent over the first, drawing his light-globe down close to the surface. It didn't avail him much; he recognised nothing in the complex structures of metal and glass that he saw.

But he did recognise the smooth indigo substance that was securely clamped into place in the centre of the contraption. Opaque and glowing faintly silver under his light, it was undoubtedly draykon bone.

Moving as fast as he dared, he checked the other benches. The constructs varied widely but all bore a piece of draykon bone locked into place somewhere in the convoluted machinery. He received the impression that the bones were integral to the workings of each one; could they be powering the devices in some way?

If only he had a better knowledge of engineering. He had no chance of understanding the workings of these horrifically complicated objects, so he didn't waste time trying. He climbed instead up to the next floor, and the next. Each held the same layout and contents, though on the third storey he received a shock.

Happening to glance down, he discovered that the floor beneath his feet was virtually transparent.

He jumped back with a soft cry, then silenced himself with a swift inner curse. Fool. He may be able to see straight down into the floor below, but the strange, clear substance was obviously firm enough to hold his weight securely.

He climbed steadily up more long flights of stairs, noting that each storey bore the same transparent floors and ceilings. Reaching the top floor, he found that the roof was also clear and obviously well-tended, for he saw no dirt obscuring the clarity of the glass-like cover.

Light, he realised, would pass straight through those clear expanses and stream uninhibited all the way to the bottom of the building. In which case, light must be as important a component in those curious technologies as the draykon bone. That made sense, as far as it went: many of the Daylands technologies used sunlight as a power source. But then, why build a workshop in Nimdre rather than one of the Daylands realms, where there was always good light?

Perhaps some of them were intended to function without light as well, in which case Nimdre was the only option for development and testing. It was the only one of the Seven Realms that experienced both conditions in equal measure.

He passed silently between the benches that lined the walls of this room, pausing to examine each machine. The appearance of these differed somewhat from the ones on the lower storeys. He was hard pressed to define precisely how, but that some of the parts eerily resembled human limbs was difficult to ignore. He shuddered, staring at a device that looked like some kind of robotic arm...

A faint noise startled him, sent him backing away from the machine and searching for a hiding place. He had spent too much time here, distracted by the puzzle of the peculiar machines that surrounded him. If Krays found him here—

A cold voice interrupted his thoughts. 'I'd invite you to participate, but it is clear that you cannot be trusted.'

Krays. His heart leapt into frenzied activity and he began to run, tearing for the stairs.

His flight was useless. Krays caught him up easily and grabbed him in a ferociously painful grip. He didn't say anything else, merely stared at Devary with complete coldness.

An instant later, Devary found himself back in

prison, in a room similar to the tiny cubicle that he had woken in after his recovery. The same narrow bed dominated the cramped space, the same small sink and chamber pot the only other items present.

Krays said nothing more. He released Devary, dropping him to the floor. Then he vanished.

Frantic, Devary picked himself up and searched the room. One door, a massive thing that he knew would be unbreakable, its lock unpickable. No window, no weaknesses or openings in floor, walls or ceiling. No way out.

Heart pounding, he sought with his mind for the mode of escape that had saved him last time. As he feared, it was gone. The area was shrouded in an enchantment that muffled everything he tried to do and obscured any means of outward travel. He could not break through, no matter how violently he hurled himself against the misty walls in his mind.

At length he was obliged to give up. He collapsed on the bed, spent and in despair.

He was stuck, thoroughly so, and this time he had no doubt that there would be no escape.

CHAPTER TWENTY

Time passed strangely in this strangest of places. In point of fact, time didn't pass at all, or so Limbane claimed. Llandry didn't know how to believe or understand him on that point.

Nor, indeed, on any other topic on which he'd spoken since she had been brought here.

It didn't help that he frequently spoke in enigmatic riddles and refused to explain himself. Lady Glostrum was right: he was keeping a great deal of information from them, for reasons she did not know and did not trust.

But it didn't matter whether or not she trusted him, or the equally reticent Andraly. Her thorough exploration of the "Library" had merely revealed more of it; more and more and more rooms and halls and corridors and silent people intent on alarmingly big books, and never any hint of an exit.

She couldn't even tell where in the worlds this Library was. Neither could Pensould.

The four of them—Tren and Lady Glostrum as well—had taken to congregating in the chart room. It was a peculiar place, so packed with information that it made her dizzy just looking at it. But the group attempt to decipher the puzzle themselves, instead of waiting for Limbane to explain it, kept her occupied.

It kept her wayward mind from imagining red-scaled Isand descending on Glinnery with an army of draykons behind, intent on taking back Arvale.

All in good time, Miss Sanfaer. That was all Limbane had said when she had questioned him about it.

I need to go home! Glinnery must be warned!

All in good time, Miss Sanfaer.

So she waited, anxiously and with poor grace. She tried to slide between the worlds the way she did so easily in her draykon form, but on passing the walls that enclosed this strange place she encountered nothing.

Simply nothing, as if the place really did exist entirely in isolation from everything—even time.

That had shaken her badly.

How she wished to be on the wing in Iskyr again, strong and proud and sure of her place in the world. Too rapidly was she turning back into the person she'd been until only a moon ago: insecure, unsure, full of doubts and anxieties and prone to the distressing attacks of panic that she'd hoped never to feel again. Pensould's presence could not wholly soothe her, for he was as uncertain and confused as she; he had little calming influence to share. Only Sigwide could comfort her. Loyal as ever, her orting refused to be parted from her. The warmth of his small body and the softness of his fur under her hands kept her stable, more or less, his chattering distracting and amusing her.

Cold, he often said, and she would wrap him in her cloak and hold him close until he stopped shivering.

Food, he would say next, and she'd share the bowls of nuts she begged from the Library kitchen.

Thanks. She was trying to teach him manners, and some of it was finally starting to take. For a while she had waited for him to communicate in more detail, hoping that it was her lack of ability that kept his impressions brief and simple. But he stayed the same. Loyal though he was, perhaps intellect wasn't his strongest attribute.

It didn't matter. She loved him anyway.

She was sitting in the middle of the chart room one day—not that days could be counted anymore—when Tren approached. Pensould, against whom she was resting, tensed with the usual suspicion he felt whenever anybody approached Llandry—especially anybody male. Placing a hand on his arm to soothe him, she mustered a smile for Lady Eva's friend.

And privately she agreed with Pensould in wishing him away. He was a stranger and a confident, good-looking one at that. That combination was painful to her frayed nerves.

He had obviously taken her measure, for he approached her with a kind of gentle, essentially patronising carefulness that she often experienced from good-natured strangers.

'Miss Sanfaer,' he began.

'Llandry.'

'Llandry. I've found something that may interest you.'

She stood up with some reluctance and followed him, all the way across the vast chamber to a stretch of the wall that looked the same as any other. It had been Tren who had discovered how to activate the weird enchantments that operated the wall's writings. The text had been plain black when she had first entered this room, but now the walls glowed with colour. What the significance of the different shades was had not yet been determined.

Most of the writing on this part of the wall was blue, with splashes of purple.

Tren gestured to the nearest ladder. 'Up about halfway. Take some care, it's wobbly.'

Warily, she climbed. Pensould stood at the bottom holding the base of the ladder, though her diminutive, too-thin frame did little to affect its stability.

'That's about right,' said Tren after a while. 'Do you see it?'

'Do I see what?'

'Keep reading, right about eye level there.'

Llandry let her eyes run over the neatly-scribed names. None of it meant anything to her, and she turned to cast Tren a puzzled look.

'Keep reading,' he said, smiling encouragement.

She obeyed, having little else to do after all.

Ayla Sanfaer.

Sanfaer? She read on, faster now, her thoughts suddenly buzzing. *Eron Sanfaer, Octovan Sanfaer, Liritia Sanfaer.*

Ynara Sanfaer.

Llandry Sanfaer.

She blanched, staring at her own name on that impossible wall. Most of the Sanfaers' names were written in blue or purple, though predominantly blue. Hers shone blue, purple and gold by turns.

Bright, bright gold that dazzled her eyes.

'What does it mean?' she asked, her voice shaking.

'I don't know,' Tren admitted as she climbed slowly down. 'Have you seen any other names in gold?'

She shook her head.

'Eva said the same thing. It's something to consider, isn't it?'

He was too cheerful, given their predicament. It was impossible that he didn't chafe under the confinement as did she and Pensould. It was impossible that he didn't feel frustrated at the too-small nuggets of information that Limbane fed them, and the vast deal more that he withheld. But he was one of those people whose cheerfulness somehow never wavered.

She hated those people on principle. They made her feel wholly inadequate.

'Thank you for showing me,' she said with stiff politeness. He nodded, his eyes quizzical as she turned away from him.

It was Lady Glostrum who discovered the next gold-touched name, some immeasurable time later. In fact she found several in the same section of wall, though they were not linked by any obvious relationship to one another.

'There is some time scheme here, some kind of chronology,' she murmured, mostly to herself. 'But I cannot understand it.'

This new crop of gold names was situated a long way around the room from Llandry's own. Interestingly, none of them had family names. Further, in this part of the room many of the names remained plain black, displaying no colours at all.

Llandry studied them carefully, though without much effect. Each gold name was connected to a plain black name. Springing from these groups were more black names, and an occasional blue or purple one. As the chart progressed, the colours became more common and each name was in two parts: given name and family name.

Pensould, she said silently. *Can you make anything of this?*

Pensould had long given up on ladders. He spent a lot of time in his draykon form, the room being quite large enough to accommodate him. Now he flew to her side, hovering with a skill that impressed her.

I cannot read human letters. You must describe to me what you see.

She hadn't realised that before. Gracious, no wonder he was so bored.

Can't you learn, the same way you learned to speak my mother's language?

Perhaps, if you will teach me.

I think we have time, she replied with a little laugh. She relayed to him everything that she saw, watching as his keen eyes swept the wall where she pointed.

What is being displayed?

Family relationships. See, here is my name. My mother's name, and my father's. The names of their parents, and so on.

Is there a link between your name and the other gold

names?

Llandry stared round the room, noting the distance between her own name and the section where Lady Glostrum still stood.

Pensould, it could take weeks to track backwards from my name, all the way around to here.

Well, we appear to have time. His tone was disgruntled, for which she didn't blame him. It didn't suit him at all to sit and wait.

True, she admitted. At least she could teach Pensould his letters while she worked.

Long before Llandry completed this lengthy task, she discovered something else.

Evastany Glostrum, marked on the wall in blue. But as Llandry watched, it melded into pale whitish-silver and back to blue.

Eva greeted the discovery with irritation. 'Gold names, silver names,' she muttered. 'What is this, some kind of test?'

Her ladyship's composure was crumbling further as time passed. Llandry found it unnerving to watch the woman's unflappable demeanour steadily erode away. She could see that it affected Tren, too, for he moved towards her with the air of a person anxious to comfort. But she scowled at him so fiercely that he backed away.

Llandry sighed and turned her back on them. The atmosphere in this curious puzzle of a prison was deteriorating further the longer Limbane and Andraly absented themselves.

'The silver must denote Lokants,' Lady Glostrum

said after a while, in a steadier manner. 'If we could find Ana or Griel, or Krays, we could confirm that theory.'

Llandry thought fast. 'If that's true, then perhaps—perhaps the gold means—'

'Allow me to assist,' came Limbane's voice. 'Not that you aren't doing splendidly on your own.' She whirled to find the white-haired old gentleman standing at Lady Glostrum's elbow. He smiled pleasantly and pointed up at the dome.

'My name is up there,' he said. 'Near the top. We coloured it in silver. Andraly's—also silver—is a little further down. Yours is a weaker hue, my dear, because while you have a great deal of Lokant in you, your unusual make-up consists of some other heritage as well. Notably draykon, and a little human.' He looked at Llandry. 'Gold, as I think you were about to infer, denotes draykoni. Miss Sanfaer, we estimate that you are approximately ninety percent draykoni, with only minimal human heritage. That has happened because most of your ancestors are descended directly from draykoni. You may imagine that this is a rare occurrence.'

Llandry found nothing to say.

Limbane pointed without hesitation to another part of the room. 'Mr Warvel's name you will discover over there. Perhaps seventy percent draykoni heritage. Mostly from the Everum tribes, which usually results in sorcerous talent. And with your strong heritage, Warvel, that means a lot of it.'

'Wait—what—'

Limbane ignored Tren's stuttering and turned on Pensould. 'Master Pensould is not on this chart, because his blood has never been mixed with another's and he has no descendants. Nor were his parents ever recorded on this chart, because he predates our system.'

Llandry felt Pensould's flash of pride at the idea.

'Have I now answered most of your questions?'

'No!' Eva said. She stood glaring at Limbane with her elegant hands clenched into fists and her mouth set. 'Questions and more questions you've raised and only partial answers offered. The most important question I wish to put to you is *why are you keeping us here?*'

Limbane patted her arm. 'You were supposed to be resting, your ladyship, that was the plan. Though I apologise if I have left you here for longer than I intended. I am used to the workings of the Library, I suppose, and that tends to eradicate any real sense of urgency after a while.'

'*Resting?*' Eva spat.

'Resting,' Limbane repeated, with offensive affability. 'There is much to be done and you will be needing your strength.'

'Ah—*what*, exactly, are we to be doing?' That was Tren, hands stuffed in his pockets as usual and watching Limbane with a befuddled air.

Limbane began to appear annoyed. 'That is not a constructive question, Mr Warvel. We have another Eterna Conflict brewing, thanks to the efforts of our draykon friends here; Krays is up to something and I usually dislike anything Krays is up to; and I fear he has altogether lost his grip on some of his trained partials, and that means rogue Lokants, and—'

'What,' said Eva with studied calm, 'is the Eterna

Conflict?'

'That has been discussed,' replied Limbane, a dangerous edge to his tone.

'No. It hasn't. After you explain *that*, you might also be kind enough to inform *me* of who, or what, I am.'

'And me,' Tren put in.

'And how is it that I could be draykoni and never know it?' added Llandry.

Only Pensould had nothing to say, choosing only to bare his teeth at Limbane.

Limbane inhaled sharply, his expression turning testy. 'If I am to have to repeat myself *every* time I see you I imagine it would be more efficient to find assistance elsewhere.'

'Now, Limbane.' Andraly appeared beside him. 'You know how you forget things. I imagine you've left a few gaps in our new friends' knowledge.'

'I feel certain that we discussed the matter of Lokant heritage and the Eterna Conflict,' Limbane replied stubbornly.

Eva shook her head. 'You abandoned that story halfway through.'

'Very well,' he sighed. 'Conduct them to my room if you please, Andraly.' He vanished.

Andraly grinned at them. 'He's old,' she said. 'He gets forgetful. And crabby. Follow me, please.'

Llandry found Pensould's hand and gripped it hard as Andraly led them out of the chart room and through a muddling series of corridors, staircases and chambers until at last they arrived once again in Limbane's quarters. He was already seated in the most comfortable chair, sipping at a glass full of dark liquid.

Andraly offered her some of the same; tasting it, she found that it was sweet and alcoholic. The effect it had was calming, much the same as the tonic she had used to take.

Andraly winked at her.

'Beginning at the beginning, then,' said Limbane after they were all settled. 'A long time ago, draykoni were relatively numerous. They arranged themselves largely into two tribes: one lived mostly in Iskyr, what you call the Upper Realm these days, though some of their kind took up residence in the connected world of Arvale. Now called Glinnery.'

'That is not the beginning, Limbane,' said Andraly.

He smiled at her. 'Don't interrupt, Andra, please.'

She sat back with a chuckle.

'The other,' continued Limbane, 'preferred the realm of Ayrien—the Lowers—and its Middle World counterpart, Everum or, these days, Glour. Humans never set foot in Iskyr or Ayrien in those days; indeed they were unable to. They had little notion that such worlds even existed. They lived mostly in those areas you now call Irbel, Orstwych, Ullarn, Nimdre and Orlind.'

'Orlind?' Eva repeated the word sharply. Limbane shot her a dark look.

'Interruptions are, as I said, unwelcome.'

'My apologies.'

He nodded. 'You are all aware of the properties of draykon bone. Humankind, ever ingenious, discovered its properties once before, a long time ago. They learned that by wearing or imbibing the bones, hide, claws or teeth of draykoni they were able to access some diluted form of the special abilities that came easily to draykoni but never to humankind. You may imagine the result of that discovery.'

Llandry shuddered. Covetousness over the draykon bone had led to thefts and murders in recent times, and Ana had even tried to turn a live draykon to her will. If that knowledge spread across the Seven, she could indeed imagine the scale of the conflict.

'You may think that draykoni had some insuperable advantages over humankind, particularly in those days. They were the superior in size and strength by many times, and they had their magics. But now humans were learning to harness some of those abilities, and the more draykoni they killed and dissected, the more they learned. Soon they were able to follow the draykoni even to Iskyr and Ayrien.

'Furthermore, draykoni have never been quick to breed. It is the major flaw in their design. Birthing is difficult for them and young draykoni often die before they reach adulthood. When I said they were "relatively numerous" I meant that their numbers were still far below those of their enemy. And humans had their own advantages: they had the ingenious brains to imagine better, cleverer ways to win and they had the bodies—in particular, the hands—to bring them about. In time, they won the conflict—in spite of the efforts of a draykon known as Eterna, after whom that war was eventually named.

'Eventually the draykoni were almost entirely destroyed. Barely twenty remained, and they seemed intent on throwing themselves at their foes until none were left. A certain stubborn pride and a fondness for revenge might be considered psychological flaws with that species.' He glanced at Pensould as he said it, whose face indeed displayed a fierce anger at Limbane's tale. Llandry stroked his arm, trying to soothe him, though her own heart was sorely oppressed by what she heard.

'We did not wish to see the draykoni driven to extinction,' Limbane continued. 'So we intervened. We persuaded most of the survivors to abandon their plans for revenge—and no, that was not easily done—in favour of the race's survival. For you see, draykoni can be hard to kill; their consciousness is almost impossible to entirely extinguish and they may, if they choose, restore their bodies to health when they wish to wake. But it requires the assistance of another draykon. If the species was not to die out, some had to survive, somewhere.'

'You taught them to shape shift,' Llandry said, awed.

Limbane nodded his approval. 'Very quick, Miss Sanfaer. Yes, that is what we did. Taking human shape, they were thoroughly camouflaged. They identified suitable communities of humans, generally choosing those who had not participated in the war against the draykoni. They blended in easily enough, and some of them even married in time. To our satisfaction, they also had young. We had never been able to determine how far the camouflage stretched; we learned then that the shape taken was not merely a shell but that the whole biology of the creature was changed.

'It wasn't long before the effects of those unions began to be seen. In Arvale—Glinnery—where the Iskyr draykoni had settled, some children were born with wings. Of course they were cast out as mutants at first, but as it became more common it became also more accepted. In time it was the wingless who were considered "different", and they began to leave the realm, leaving it to the winged. The people of Glinnery also began to show some talent at beast empathetics, a talent that had once belonged to draykonkind alone. They had found their way back to Iskyr by then, and they used these new abilities to befriend animals from the Off-Worlds and bring them home. Thus they termed the skill "summoning".

'As for the Ayrien tribes, they settled mostly in Glour, and one or two in Orstwych. There were some winged children born, though for various reasons it did not take in that realm as it had in Glinnery. These peoples inherited a different set of draykoni magic, specifically manipulation of light and shadow and the outward appearance of things. Sorcery, as it is now called.

'It remains something of a mystery as to why the draykoni magics divided in this way. We wondered whether, in time, some individuals might combine the two again, though that has not usually happened. We have taken great pains since then to engineer virtually pure draykoni bloodlines, to ensure that someday there would be the chance of revival. Should we wish to encourage that.'

Silence followed Limbane's long speech when he finally stopped talking. He sipped at his drink, oblivious, apparently reminiscing. Andraly, on the other hand, watched the group closely. Llandry felt the woman's eyes on her, though she refused to meet her gaze.

So the other gold names on the chart—the ones

without family names—were those first draykoni shape shifters. And she herself was the eventual product. The word *engineered* stayed with her, chafing at her. She disliked the implication that the relationships chosen by her ancestors had been, in some way, chosen for them.

For a moment she thought of asking Limbane what exactly he meant by *engineered,* but she decided against it. At the moment, she just didn't want to know.

'But,' she said. 'You said that Krays didn't intend to bring back the draykoni. And you certainly didn't plan it. Why not? And why did it happen anyway?'

'We've discussed the possibility many times,' Limbane replied. 'I suppose for one, we weren't sure that we could. Additionally, we feared that we would merely begin another human-draykoni war. And that fear seems to have been well-founded. So we bided our time.'

'That's why you took our books,' Tren said suddenly. 'That *was* you, wasn't it? And you've probably been at it for a while. No wonder I couldn't find anything in the libraries.'

'Mhm,' Limbane said. 'A boring and repetitive task. It's amazing how some bright-eyed idiot is always stumbling over sensitive information. It was safer for humankind in general to forget about all of this.' He shifted in his chair. 'As for Krays, he has no scientific interest in these questions and no reason to love draykonkind, nor to wish for their return. But at one time he did take a great deal of *scientific* interest in the draykon bones. If he has involved himself, and it is clear that he has, then it is the bones and the hide and the teeth he is after. But I do not know why.

'We learned recently that his organisation has been making use of the inhabitants of this Cluster to further their aims. A sensible enough plan, as his organisation has always been small. And it was inspired to seek out the Lokant descendants, though training them may have been less intelligent. It appears one or two of them have taken his training and turned it to entirely different purposes. How the one known as Ana learned about the draykoni, I don't know, nor how she conceived of the idea—and the means—to restore one of them. But the damage is done there.'

Pensould bristled at that. '*Damage?* I must thank you, I suppose, for your interference or there would have been no Minchu to assist my own return and that of my kind. But do not speak of it in that negative way.'

Limbane regarded him without expression. 'For you, Pensould, it is a good thing. That I understand. For Miss Sanfaer also, I believe. But you must see that other draykoni are not as tolerant as you. You have already returned one who was killed, I believe, in the conflict and who was neither resurrected nor her body discovered and plundered. To her, humankind will always be the enemy and she has already begun her ill-considered but nonetheless fervent revenge mission. For this Cluster, that is indeed a negative occurrence.'

'Cluster?' Tren's query was diffidently spoken; most of his attention was on Eva, who as yet had only stared stonily at Limbane and said nothing.

'Cluster of worlds,' Limbane explained. 'Very few

worlds exist in isolation. This cluster consists of Iskyr, Ayrien and Irtand; what you fancifully and erroneously think of as the Upper, the Lower and the Middle. In fact there is no physical hierarchy of that kind. Clustered worlds inhabit essentially the same space, existing more as one central world—in this case Irtand—and one or more echoes of it. This Cluster is particularly nicely balanced, I must say. Two mirror images of Irtand, one reflecting the lights and the other the darks. Beautiful stuff.' A note of enthusiasm crept into his tone and his eyes lit up at the concept.

'Er, right,' said Tren, staring at him with bemused amazement written across his features.

'Never mind,' Limbane sighed.

'You've glossed over the Lokants in all of this,' Eva said, breaking her silence at last. 'I could ask you where you come from, but your last comments suggest that the answer would mean nothing to me. So, instead: what am I, and what is our part in this?'

'You, my dear, may be thought of as something of a throwback to your ancestors. Some of the Lokant children have the white hair and little else; others inherit a great deal of the unusual make-up of their forebears. Ana is one such, I suspect, if she does indeed "vanish" as you say. I suspect you will also prove a strong partial. Tell me, are you that type of person who enjoys unshakeable popularity? Never have any trouble persuading people to your cause? Very, very good at summoning?'

'All of those things,' Tren put in, when Eva merely glared at him.

'Naturally. Draykoni magics spring from their very

close bond with this Cluster of worlds; they manipulate it and its native inhabitants with ease because they are essentially woven of the same fabric. Lokants, on the other hand, are entirely other, and cerebral beings at that. Our talents lie in areas such as relocation of ourselves, other beings, or objects, and—er—shall we call it charisma? If you are a strong Lokant then you possess a strong will, and it is the easiest thing in the world to impose it on others. You have tapped into that without realising, I do believe, and profited considerably by it.'

Lady Glostrum stared at him in growing horror. 'I met a little girl recently—white-haired—who was chillingly good at domination over beast kind. She wasn't using Summoning; it was something else. Are you saying that I also employ such skill? And—and over *people* as well?'

'Exactly,' Limbane enthused. 'Though in your case you are also a summoner derived from draykoni, so the methods you use in your profession are mixed. But as far as people are concerned, yes. If you want somebody to like you, then they are pretty sure to like you because you will it. Your mind is a great deal stronger than almost everyone you meet.'

Eva looked sick, and Llandry had no trouble understanding why. She knew what Limbane meant, too. Whenever she met Lady Glostrum, she received an impression of awe-inspiring grandeur that inclined her to worship the woman. Thinking about it now, she could think of no direct, rational reason for that reaction, the woman's beauty and stateliness notwithstanding. Her ladyship presumably wished to have that effect on people, and so she did.

She also didn't envy Limbane his current position. Everybody was angry with him except her. Pensould was still livid; Eva looked ready to kill him; even Tren's habitually cheerful demeanour had vanished and he looked like he wanted to hit something.

'That isn't fair,' Tren burst out. 'If you're suggesting that Eva's popularity isn't real, that is not true. She is loved because she's good-hearted and intelligent, dedicated and beautiful; not because—not because—'

'Peace, Mr Warvel. I'm sure that in some cases that is quite true. Nonetheless, I have spoken the truth also.'

He stopped talking, perhaps expecting more questions, complaints or objections. There was only shocked silence.

'Am I correct in thinking that you all require a little time alone to absorb my tales?'

Llandry glanced Eva again. Her ladyship had stopped looking angry and horrified; now she looked stricken, which was much worse.

And Pensould was still raging, though thankfully he was doing it silently.

'Yes, sir, thank you,' she said quickly. She needed some time to get Pensould's violent emotions back under control. And her own, come to think of it.

'Wait,' said Eva, straightening in her chair. Llandry watched, amazed, as she visibly composed herself, all signs of distress disappearing under her usual air of calm. 'You've spoken more than once about our assisting you. Tell us what you wish.'

'Excellent. You will make a terrific partial, Lady Glostrum. You mentioned that you had found a lead

266

of some kind in the matter of the draykon bone, is that correct?'

Eva nodded. 'Some of it is being leaked to a business in Orstwych. It may be coming from another group entirely—I don't suppose Krays can guarantee control over all draykon bone in the realms—but it is worth investigating. I have a name in Ullarn.'

Limbane beamed. 'Excellent. Then you must follow that lead, your ladyship, and Mr Warvel will assist you. Miss Sanfaer and Pensould will do as they have wished all along: that is to return to Glinnery and see about preparing the realm for a draykon attack, should one occur. They will also endeavour to avert said attack, if they find the means.'

'Couldn't you just *persuade* the draykoni not to attack?' Eva's tone was sarcastic.

'Draykoni design includes a degree of imperviousness to those techniques,' Limbane said with a shrug. 'Or perhaps it is merely their cursed stubbornness. I said that it was terrifically hard to hold them back the last time; I did mean it. Llandry and Pensould will likely be much more successful in this, and much more quickly.'

'But Krays had no trouble with me,' Llandry admitted. 'He immobilised me, took over my will. If Pensould hadn't been there I wouldn't have been able to resist him.'

Limbane gave her a genuinely kind smile. 'Don't trouble yourself over that, Miss Sanfaer. You were human at the time, I imagine?'

She nodded.

'And you are yet new to your draykon heritage. You still think and operate largely as a human does, but you are learning. You will grow stronger in time.'

Llandry swallowed and nodded. 'I'm happy to do as you suggest, sir, to the best of my ability, but what of Krays? He'll come after me again, and I'm not strong enough yet.'

'Ah yes, that's another point. It's possible that Krays's intention is to use you to locate more draykon graves. He will soon discover that you are not the only person who can assist him with this, and his attention may turn away from you. In case I am wrong, I will be sending Andraly with you, and another Lokant.'

Llandry's heart hammered. 'You speak of more hereditary draykoni?'

'I can think of two potential ones,' he said. 'Before you ask, yes, sooner or later they too will be in danger from Krays. I don't believe he knows of their existence yet, as Sulayn Phay were not involved in our draykoni project. But I've no doubt he will discover them one way or another. While the rest of you are off averting disaster in Glinnery and tracking down Krays's operation, I will be locating our other two hereditaries.' He paused. 'Or rather, I will be delegating someone else to do it.'

Andraly laughed aloud at that. 'So I'm to visit Arvale? It's been some time since I set foot in the Daylands. Delightful prospect.'

Limbane rolled his eyes. 'I'm glad someone is happy.'

CHAPTER TWENTY-ONE

Limbane was having a singularly unsuccessful day.

It started with the matter of Mr Devary Kant. Opening this world's PsiMap in his mind, Limbane travelled to the small college in Draetre where he had met Mr Kant not long ago. He had a task for the man, and it was therefore highly inconvenient to find him missing.

Not just absent, but missing. He was not at the university. He was not at home. Nobody had seem him in days.

He was interested to note that some of the staff, notably a female professor he'd met before, seemed to be well aware that Mr Kant's disappearance meant bad news.

Krays, he thought. He wished briefly that he'd thought to record the unique pattern of the agent's tracer when he had seen him before. But it was too late to think about that now.

He could have used Mr Kant's help in finding the

two hereditary draykoni—after all, it was more his line of work than Limbane's—but he did not feel disposed to launch an invasion on Sulayn Phay territory on account of one man. Perhaps later.

He moved on.

Arvale. It had been some time since his last visit, possibly as much as a century. The place was busier than he recalled; the pace of population growth did take him by surprise sometimes. But it had lost little of its beauty. He made for the summoner school near the outskirts of Waeverleyne.

It took him nearly twenty minutes to find the administrative office. He might have a Lokant's PsiTravel technology at his use but he never had been any good at ground level navigation.

But when he spoke the name of Orillin Vanse to the secretary, the response was not promising.

'Mr Vanse—yes—ah—I've a feeling you may be out of luck there, sir, but I'll enquire.' She was gone before he could ask what she meant. He took a seat, composing himself to wait with much impatience.

'I'm afraid the boy was taken ill last week, sir,' she said a little later, strutting back into the office on heels that clicked against the tiled floor.

'Taken ill,' he repeated.

'Yes, sir. He's expected to be confined to the sanatorium for some weeks.'

'Which sanatorium?'

'I don't have that information, sir. Is there anything else I can help you with?'

He left the office in a black mood. That a boy of nineteen years should suddenly fall so violently ill as to require weeks of quarantine and care was highly doubtful.

Krays again.

He visited the boy's parents. That they knew something was obvious; they were both tight-lipped and unhelpful, though they dutifully repeated the same tale that the secretary had given him. They were obviously afraid of something.

Krays had that effect on people.

Not for the first time, he regretted the impossibility of working backwards through time. His Library hovered on the edges of the time flow, barely touched by it. He could stay in there for years, and when he left the premises and returned to the regular time stream he would find that little time had passed beyond its borders. His body didn't age as long as he stayed in the Library. These things were useful, but there were frustrating limits to the technology. Lokants had worked for centuries on the problem of moving themselves about in time, but to no avail. He couldn't jump back to last week and extract Orillin before Krays could reach him.

And curses to that.

On, then, to Glour, trying not to wish he'd listened to Andraly years ago and tracered all the hereditary draykoni. Another female, this next one, older than Llandry Sanfaer by more than fifteen years. He knew that much about her; he knew her name, Avane Desandry; he knew she was a sorcerer.

He knew absolutely nothing else.

Cursing the ineptitude of agents who got themselves hauled off by Krays, Limbane began the tiresome process of tracking down one human (sort of) in the middle of several hundred thousand of the creatures.

The Library really did go on forever.

Or so Eva was convinced. She had spent what felt like an entire day wandering the halls, drifting through library after library, and they never ended. The Lokants probably did have books on absolutely everything somewhere in this building.

What interested her particularly was the quantity of books that obviously had nothing to do with her world, or Cluster as Limbane had said. The prospect of other worlds out beyond the confines of her own was an inspiring one.

Or it would have been were she not feeling so essentially self-absorbed. For Limbane's revelations had shaken her to the core. He had spent some time training the Lokant side of her, teaching her in particular the ability that he called translocation. It required some manner of implant, which she now wore buried somewhere in her body, and continued with a great deal of rigorous mental training as he taught her to access and use the PsiMap. She didn't mind the work. Learning these skills would make her more effective in the ongoing struggle against Krays's enigmatic projects, and besides, the training kept her mind busy, preventing her from brooding.

Now Limbane had left the Library, leaving her training in hiatus. He'd said he couldn't spare another Lokant to finish the training just now, and awarded her a short holiday to recover her focus and spirits before the next lesson.

She had spent it wandering the corridors of the

Library, feeling confused and so very low in spirits that she hardly knew what to do with herself. She was thinking back over the years of her life, reliving every relationship she'd had with every friend, every colleague, every lover. She thought of the students who'd worshipped her, the tutors whose favourite she'd always been, the colleagues who'd deferred to her, the shopkeepers who saved the best products for her and charged her lower prices.

It wasn't fair to say she had never encountered opposition. There were certainly forces stronger than her Lokant mind. Hatred, resentment and envy were stronger; she'd encountered those before. She had taken on the prejudices of others and failed to overcome them. She was not an unstoppable force by any means.

But nonetheless she enjoyed a far greater level of social success than was common. Her summoner ability too: she was one of the strongest ever recorded in Glour, that she knew, but now both of these defining characteristics were called into question.

How much of her success was down to her own efforts, her own personality and her own determination? And how much of it was due to her essentially *cheating* with her Lokant magics? Could she trust the sincerity of any friendship? Had any of her romantic relationships had any true substance? And could she truly call herself a summoner, let alone a former High Summoner, when her ability was unfairly augmented by her Lokant heritage?

She had no answers to these questions and she knew she never would. It would never again be possible to trust in anybody's affection for her, because she would never be able to measure how much of it was real and how much was imposed. Limbane assured her that she would learn to control her mind; she would no longer employ those abilities across the board and without intent or knowledge. But that wasn't enough to reassure her. She knew she wouldn't trust herself again.

Given the nature of these reflections, she was not pleased when the door to her sanctuary creaked open and Tren wandered in, hands in his pockets and a tentative smile on his face.

'Found you,' he said lightly.

'So you have.' She returned her gaze to the books in front of her, studying them with a show of absorption. Most of the titles were in languages she couldn't read, but she didn't see why that should be any obstacle to her studying them instead of talking to Tren.

'I was looking for you,' he persevered.

'Why?'

'Um, I was worried about you.'

'I'm fine, Tren, just been busy training with Limbane.'

'Uh huh.' His tone was profoundly sceptical. 'Ever since Limbane's little lecture you've been looking like somebody died.'

In a way, she thought, somebody did. Evastany Glostrum as she'd known herself had died. She didn't know how to live with her new self.

'I'm fine,' she repeated. 'It's just that the revelations have come thick and fast lately and I'm trying to keep up. This place, the Lokants, hereditary draykoni and now my heritage... I need a bit of time to think about everything. That's all.'

'That's true enough. I'm reeling a little myself.' Tren wandered the room for a few minutes, jingling something in one of his pockets. The insistent sound disrupted Eva's concentration and she scowled in annoyance.

'You know,' Tren said at last, 'if you're thinking you just manipulated everybody into liking you, you're wrong.'

'What?'

'That's what you're thinking, isn't it? I'd be thinking the same thing in your position. But you're wrong. That can't be the whole story. There are too many good reasons to admire you.'

En Diraja o Mahj read the spine of the book directly before her eyes. She repeatedly gravitated back to it because, unlike the rest on this shelf, she could at least decipher the letters. The characters on the rest were incomprehensible, written in an alphabet she'd never seen before.

'I've no doubt Vale would agree with me,' Tren continued, annoyingly persistent. 'He knows you well. He knows *you*, not just the persona you put on for the world. He married you because he loves you, and that's an emotion that's far too complex to be imposed from outside. You could encourage people to admire you, worship you, make them infatuated with you, that's probably true. But to force real love on someone? Real friendship? I think those things are beyond your ability.'

Limbane had said something similar, but it hadn't soothed her in her present mood. It still didn't now.

'I'm not married,' she said, suddenly feeling more

tired than annoyed.

'What?'

'Vale didn't marry me. We ended our engagement. It was probably lucky for him.'

That statement was met with complete silence. She turned to look at him at last, her irritation returning. 'What? I told you that before.'

His brows went up. 'Er. I'm *fairly* sure you haven't mentioned it, no.'

She spluttered. 'I recall *with perfect clarity* my saying to you "I'm still Lady Glostrum, Tren." And you have been calling me that ever since, so I believe you must remember it too.'

'That's not exactly perfectly clear communication, is it? I thought you meant you'd opted to keep your own name after marriage. It seemed like a perfectly rational decision to make in your situation so I didn't enquire further.'

'Why in the world would I do that?'

He held up his hands. 'All right, never mind that. You're not married. I get it. But everything I said still stands.'

'Does it? How do you know Vale didn't shake off my manipulative influence and change his mind? Cast me off?'

'Impossible.' He said it with total confidence.

'I could tell you that's what happened.' She lifted her chin, looked him straight in the eye.

'You'd be lying.'

'All right, I'd be lying. I ended it. But I maintain that you can't possibly know what you're talking about.'

'Um. Can I ask why you ended it?'

'No,' she snapped.

'All right,' he said mildly.

She maintained a mulish silence for some moments more. Then she let out a long sigh.

'I'm being terribly petulant, aren't I.'

He grinned. 'A little bit.'

'It's just that I feel like I've lost all certainty. How can I possibly *know,* ever again, that I have real friends? I'm glad I ended the engagement; how could I be married, when I'd be eternally wondering whether my husband married me voluntarily or because I in some way forced him into it? It's rearranged my whole future.'

'I can only repeat everything I said before. You may have doubts, but I don't.'

'You're just being stubborn.'

'One should exercise one's talents,' he replied gravely.

She smiled in spite of herself. 'I suppose you're good for me, wretch. You keep me from taking myself too seriously.'

'That's a bad habit.'

'Right,' she said, taking a deep breath and straightening her spine. 'Enough moping; there's work to be done.' She couldn't just believe Tren's words, but he was right to pull her out of her poor mood. She would deal with that issue again later.

Something passed swiftly behind Tren's eyes and he moved to block her path. 'Wait.'

She looked up, puzzled. His tone had lost all its notes of levity, settling into something more serious than she was used to hearing from him.

'I wasn't really speaking on Vale's behalf,' he said

in a rush. 'I was speaking for myself.'

She tried to think back over everything he'd said in the last twenty minutes or so. 'What? When?'

'I know you.' His hands jangled in his pockets more agitatedly than ever, and she realised that he was extremely nervous.

'Probably you do, yes. What's the relevance?'

'I've seen you in good moods and bad. I've seen you in control and completely at a loss. I've seen you upset and grieving, and I've seen you happy and confident. Now I've seen you suffering something wholly unknown to you before: self-doubt. Lack of confidence. I *know* you. And I like what I see.' He paused, cleared his throat uncomfortably. 'I love what I see.'

Eva could only stare at him, stupefied. 'That's a lot of words. My head's spinning and I can barely understand what you're saying. Can you just keep it simple please?'

'Simple. Okay. I love you.'

'Um.' She blinked. 'Well, that's straightforward enough. Mhm.' For an instant her heart swelled with happiness and something like relief.

Then it all drained away.

'Oh, Tren, don't you see. That just makes everything *worse*. '

He blinked, shocked. 'What? How can it possibly...?'

'Don't you realise how *absurd* that sounds?'

Now he looked hurt. 'Absurd? I don't understand.'

'Consider the disparity. I'm more than ten years older than you. We come from completely different backgrounds, move in different circles—we don't even have anything in common, Tren! Nothing! You can't possibly have an honest affection for me. It's infatuation if anything, and that's probably just because you've spent enough time with me to be thoroughly manipulated.' To her embarrassment she felt tears prickling behind her eyes.

'You'd better keep away from me for a while, and maybe it will pass.'

He muttered something that sounded like a curse. 'I don't—I can't—I don't even—I mean, you can't seriously...' His face registered pain, and her heart twisted with guilt. 'Ah, fuck,' he said softly. 'It was exactly the wrong time to tell you that, wasn't it?'

Thinking of escape, Eva turned away, but Tren grabbed her arm.

'Look, I can prove it. You think you've imposed some perfect image of yourself on me? You think I can't see the truth about you? I know you too well. I know the good things about you, and the bad. Did you encourage me to see your conceit? Your vanity? Your irritating need to be right? Your inability to fail gracefully? Those things weren't part of your plan, were they? But if I could see *those* things in you, then how can I be wrong about the good? I've long since stopped seeing the *perfection* that you project for the world in general.'

Conceit. Vanity. Failure. Those words hurt.

'Thank you for that. Is this how you talk to all the girls?'

'No. Just you.'

'Lucky me. Anything else to add?'

'Yes. Those are your weaknesses. Want to know about your strengths? You're more truly good-hearted than I'd ever expected from an aristocrat. You're much smarter than me, and almost everyone else too. You're funny and witty, you care about things and you're capable of love, even though you try to deny it. You're strong-willed and determined and hard-working. And you're beautiful, more so every year. You shouldn't think that people are only drawn to you because you're a partial. All those qualities are as obvious to others as they are to me.' He was gripping both of her arms hard enough to hurt, his face uncomfortably close to hers. 'Come on, believe me. It's not like you to wallow in self-pity. You're too rational for that.'

'Please let go of my arms.'

He didn't. 'Is that it? Nothing else to say?'

She struggled until he let her go. Her arms hurt; she massaged the pain away, looking at him helplessly. Was he right? How could she possibly tell?

'Could you just leave me alone for a while?' She turned her back on him, shutting out the look of pain on his face. She crossed to the door quickly before she could change her mind, and left him alone in the library.

Realising Eva's intent, Tren made to stop her as she brushed past him, but he was too late. She was gone.

Idiot, he cursed himself. Eva could be difficult occasionally; he knew that, and he ought to have handled her with greater care when she was in such a delicate frame of mind. Stupid, to burden her with that when she already had so much else to come to terms with. And he'd made such a royal mess of it all.

He hoped he hadn't ruined his chances completely. A flash of panic lanced through him at that prospect, and he shuddered. One mistake and he might have fucked everything up forever.

'If she doesn't want it, I'll take it.' Andraly stood in the doorway, wearing an inviting expression. She wandered into the room, stopping far too close to him. 'Though I have to say, you aren't great at sweet-talking a girl.'

'Huh. What?'

'You heard me.' She smiled up at him.

'I thought you were angry with me.'

She frowned in annoyance. 'Why would you think that?'

'You were quite vocal about it when you found me standing outside your tower.'

'Oh, that,' she shrugged. 'I wasn't really *that* unhappy to find a good-looking boy on my doorstep, trying to get in.'

He backed away several paces. 'Look, apparently you heard some of our conversation so you'll understand if I don't take you up on your, er, offer.'

Andraly chuckled. 'How about if I change the offer?' She slid her chestnut wig from her head, exposing white hair bound into braids. Each one of these was quickly unbraided until her hair hung loose.

'Now, watch closely,' she commanded.

'Er, I really need to—'

'Watch!'

Unfortunate that she was standing between him and the door. He glowered at her, his temper wearing thin.

His irritation turned to shock as her features

blurred and altered, becoming more delicate and refined. Her eyes grew in size and changed colour; her body lost some of its voluptuous curves and became slimmer and a little taller.

After a few seconds, Eva stood before him. Eva exactly as he knew her, down to the tiny half-dimple that appeared in one cheek when she smiled.

'What the—' He backed away, stumbling over furniture as she followed him around the library.

'Impressive, isn't it? Are you sure you won't change your mind?'

'That's a sorc trick,' he gasped. 'How did you...?'

She wrinkled Eva's elegant nose. 'Illusions are sorcerer territory, yes, but this level of sophistication is rare. That, as you must know, is because you would have to build all the personal details yourself. Nobody really knows another that well. But that is not what I am doing.

'This, dear boy, is pure Lokant. It's a mental trick, see. I encourage your own mind to tell you that it's Eva that you're seeing. It's completely convincing to you because it's built from your own impressions.' She kept coming on relentlessly, closing the gap between them. Tren found himself with his back to the wall, his exit cut off by the approaching Eva—lookalike.

She grabbed his hand and applied it to her torso. 'It even *feels* convincing. See how easy it is to deceive oneself?'

Tren tried to pull back his hand but she was scarily strong. 'Let *go,* ' he said angrily. 'I don't care how much you can make yourself look like her, you are *not* Eva.'

Andraly stepped back at last, wearing an expression of disgust that he'd never seen on Eva's face before. 'A tendency towards monogamy is one of the less interesting traits of your world's inhabitants.' Her face and body returned to their usual patterns and she stood aside. 'Go and be miserable then, if you'd prefer.'

He went.

CHAPTER TWENTY-TWO

At two years old, Lyerd Desandry was still a little unsteady on his feet. Avane picked him up as he tumbled, yet again. She had stopped expecting to hear screams and cries from him when he fell and struck his knees on the hard ground. Other people's children might be given to histrionics, but not her son. He was giggling as she set him on his feet again.

'You're getting better,' she smiled. 'Once more around and then we'd better go home. All right?'

They were standing on the edge of the Virun Park, the largest piece of public ground in the town of Glaynasser. This area was designed to appeal to children: it had swings and a box full of sand, and plenty of space to run about in. Lyerd embarked on his final run around the little grassy square, his short legs pumping hard as he tried to outdo himself. He completed his circuit without mishap and collapsed into his mother's arms, giggling.

'Tired,' he said, holding up his arms.

Avane picked him up, groaning at the weight. He was getting too big to be carried, but she could never resist him when he smiled like that.

Turning to leave, she froze. Standing only a few feet away was a stranger, a man, watching her and her son. He looked quite old with his white hair and lined skin. His eyes were weirdly colourless. He nodded to her as she caught his eye.

'A fine young man,' he said.

'Thank you,' she replied, eyeing him doubtfully.

'May I walk with you?'

She shifted Lyerd onto her hip, gathering her bag with her free hand. 'I suppose so.' She wanted to say no but she couldn't think of a polite way to refuse his request.

'Does he take after his mother?'

'Er, sorry? In what way?'

'You are a sorcerer, I think.'

She shot him a surprised glance. 'How do you know that?'

'One can tell these things, sometimes. It is the truth, however?'

'Well, yes.'

'Good, good. But are you the sorcerer that I need?'

This man was making her nervous with his strange talk. 'I'd better hurry home,' she said in an apologetic tone. 'Lyerd is about ready for his nap.'

'His name is Lyerd, hm? An old-fashioned name.'

'It was my grandfather's,' she said involuntarily, then wondered what had made her say it.

'Ah! Then you would be Avane.'

'How—how do you know my name?'

'I knew your grandfather,' the man replied

smoothly. 'I'd like you to help me with something, Avane.'

'I'm afraid I've no time. My work at the school keeps me very busy and Lyerd needs so much attention.'

The man stepped in front of her, cutting her off. He looked at her gravely; despite the lack of smile or welcoming expression she felt drawn to trust him.

'For a friend of your grandfather's you would find the time, I'm sure.'

'Um, all right,' she said reluctantly. 'What do you need of me?'

'I just need you to come with me for a while. I'll tell you more soon.'

Her doubts returned full force. 'Where are we going? Is it far?'

'Quite far, yes. Worry not: I will see that you are returned at the proper time.' He gripped her wrist and she began to feel afraid again.

Now he smiled, but it wasn't a reassuring expression. 'You see? It's always so much easier when people don't make a *fuss.* '

Avane's fear grew and she began to struggle, trying to pull back the hand that he still held in a fierce grip. He was fearsomely strong for a man of his apparent age, his fingers digging hard into her skin.

'Let *go*,' she cried.

'I wasn't really *asking* for your compliance. It would be nicer if you'd come along quietly, but if I have to drag you, I will.'

'*Who are you?* '

'My name is Krays.' He tugged and Avane felt a falling sensation. With a cry of fear she hugged her son closer, closing her eyes as the world dissolved around her.

Ynara shut off the voice box with a soft sigh. These strange, distant conversations with her husband were inadequate compared to having him in the house, but it was so much better than nothing that she always ended them with reluctance. How long would he remain away from her this time? Increasingly she resented the duties as Elder that kept her from following her family.

He had nothing but good things to report. Orillin was thriving in the Uppers; he'd taken instantly to the world, and now behaved as if he'd always lived there. She smiled a little sadly at the thought. It had been the same with Llandry: ever a little off-kilter in this world, she'd found her place Above.

Every day she hoped Aysun would have something of Llandry to convey to her. Every day she was disappointed. He hadn't seen her; he didn't know where she was. He could speak only of Orillin, Eyas and Rufin, all bored and amusing themselves in increasingly questionable ways. Of his father, Aysun refused to speak at all. Apparently it hadn't helped for him to spend time in his father's house. The feud raged on.

This had been an early morning conversation. The sun had only just taken over from the Light Cloak that kept the darkness away. Gathering her coat and bag, Ynara left her home and set off for the Council Halls. She had a long day of meetings ahead of her.

Laylan Westry was already there when Ynara arrived. She greeted the older lady with affection. Laylan was the Sorcerer-in-Charge in the realm of Glinnery, responsible for maintaining the Light Cloak and for overseeing the sorcery schools. She had served in that role for longer even than Ynara had served on the elected panel of governors; the two were close friends.

'Morning, Layla.' She left a brief kiss on the other woman's cheek. 'All's well with the Cloak?'

'No problems. Any news of that fine daughter of yours?'

'Not yet,' Ynara replied, managing a smile. 'Aysun's taking care of it.'

'She's a good girl. Stronger than she looks, I'd say,' Layla smiled. 'Like her mother.'

'I don't know. She's changed so much recently, I hardly know who or what she is anymore.'

Laylan regarded her with a frown. 'She is still your Llandry, whatever else has happened to her.'

Ynara mustered another smile, but this one felt weak. 'I hope so. I've a feeling that I won't be seeing much of her at all from now on, though. It's a harsh change. Not long ago I saw her every day.'

Laylan patted her arm. 'That's being a parent for you. Wait 'till you have grandchildren. I'm afraid it only gets worse.'

That was an alarming thought. Ynara's mind jumped immediately to Pensould and his stubbornly unorthodox appearance. Would he be Llandry's spouse? He was certainly determined to claim her. What would their children be like?

Would they be human? On any level at all?

288

Not liking this image of herself as grandmother to a litter of draykonets, Ynara changed the subject.

'What do you think of Ullarn's new trade proposal? It's likely to be the biggest topic on this week's agenda.'

Laylan opened her mouth to reply, but she was cut off by a violent shriek from outside.

'What the—' Ynara knew that sound. She had heard it once before: when Llandry-as-draykon had deposited Devary, wounded and dying, outside her door. Was this Llandry coming back?

But if so, why would she come to the Council Halls? And why scream that way?

Ynara ran to the window. Seeing nothing, she crossed to the door, threw it open and stepped into the air, her wings catching the breeze to hold her aloft.

Nothing: the skies were empty.

Then, streaking into her line of sight, a draykon. Not Llandry, and not Pensould either. This beast's scales were wine-red, her wings tipped with black. Judging from the creature's screaming, whirling descent, this was not a friendly visit.

Behind the red draykon came two others in swift succession. One was big, bigger even than Pensould, its vast body deep purple in colour. The second was the smallest of the three, its hide stark white. Together they circled above the centre of Waeverleyne, screaming in concert. Those raucous voices were full of rage, so much anger. Ynara felt a shiver of horror run over her skin and fear set her heart hammering.

Panic was erupting around her as Waeverleyne's

citizens left their homes and offices to find the source of the noise. The draykons played to the attention, roaring and diving at the gathering crowds, snapping their heavy jaws. They hadn't actually attacked yet, but their intent was clear.

Laylan Westry was beside her, her lined face pale and wan as she watched the invaders.

'Layla,' said Ynara, 'Get away from here. Fetch the army. Now, please.'

'They're already here,' Laylan replied.

Not exactly true. A company of armed patrol guards, not army recruits, was taking to the air, gripping drawn weapons. They wore the uniform of the Council Guard, a fact which turned Ynara's heart over anew. They really weren't soldiers; their role was as much ceremonial as martial.

Seeing the unit's approach, the draykons paused in their antics and instead formed a whirling circle around the cluster of guards, taunting them with claws and teeth. The winged human figures, perhaps eight in total, were dwarfed against those three gigantic beasts.

'That is disaster in the making,' Ynara said. 'They must be called back!'

Too late. As one the draykons ceased their game and struck in earnest. Eight tiny winged figures fell under the onslaught of snapping jaws and lashing claws and tails, falling swiftly to earth.

Ynara's hands flew to her mouth.

'Layla,' she murmured, pulling herself together. 'Get the army. First though, give me your cloak.'

Laylan raised her brows but she asked no questions. She removed her cream-coloured cloak, bundled it up and tossed it to Ynara.

'What are you doing?'

Ynara didn't answer. The garment wasn't exactly white, but it would do.

Supposing, of course, that draykons understood a symbol of parley. She would just have to chance it.

'Yna...' Laylan spoke the word in a tone of gravest foreboding.

'Please, Layla, just get word to the army. Don't worry about me.'

With a final, fearful glance at Ynara, Laylan obeyed.

Ynara stepped to the door and jumped into the air. She held the cloak in both arms, letting it stream out in the wind. Her approach caught the eye of the red draykon and it flew to meet her. It was impossible to judge its intent; was she to be parleyed with or eaten?

Ynara flew on anyway.

When she reached the red draykon she stopped, keeping her flag of parley clearly visible. She hesitated. She had assumed that the creatures could communicate with her, because Llandry and Pensould could. Now she recalled that they had not actually done so when they wore their draykon shapes. How was she to hold a conversation with this beast?

The draykon solved the problem for her.

A parley?

The word reverberated in her mind, crashingly loud and layered with rage and indignation.

There can be no cause to parley, for there is nothing to be discussed.

'Not so.' The other two draykons flew up to flank the red one and renewed fear gripped Ynara's heart, but she forced herself to speak with steady firmness anyway. 'Why do you attack our city? We have not harmed your kind.'

Not recently perhaps.

'I don't know what you're speaking of.'

It's easy to forget the wrongs done to others, isn't it? Your race destroyed mine, human.

'If so, that must have been a long time ago. The current generation cannot be held responsible for the offences of our ancestors.'

It can and it will! The draykon's anger flared in Ynara's brain and pain gripped her head. She felt a trickle of warm blood on her upper lip; her nose had begun to bleed.

'What do you aim to achieve by this attack? Perhaps an agreement could be reached—'

I want revenge! Nothing less!

Ynara's heart sank. Revenge was a goal with which she couldn't argue. A thirst for revenge was unappeasable, a thirst that could only be slaked through carnage.

'Please, there must be some way to make amends without—'

You intrigue me, human. The draykon's mind-speech changed suddenly from anger to curiosity. *I sense something of the draykon about you. Why do you wear that shape?*

Disconcerted, Ynara couldn't immediately find her tongue. 'I don't know what you mean,' she replied. 'I am human.'

Then yours is a double betrayal and you shall be among the first to fall. The anger was back, and it was aimed at her with deadly force.

Ynara released the cloak, folded her wings and dropped, just as the draykon struck. She was too late, or too slow; the beast barrelled into her, its enormous body hitting hers with staggering force. Pain blossomed throughout her bruised body and with a shriek of agony she fell, hitting the ground hard.

This second impact jolted her broken body further, but she could only voice the barest whimper of protest. She lay in the deep moss staring at the sky, barely aware of her fading consciousness.

As she slipped into blackness she thought she saw a flicker in the skies, streaks of blue-green and ghostly grey darting across the heavens. A scream of intense fury split the air, rending her ears with shock and rage. Then consciousness faded altogether and she knew no more.

Llandry was in draykon-shape and on the wing, Pensould flying at her side. The towering caps of Waeverleyne's glissenwol dwellings had just appeared on the horizon when the first screams reached her ears.

Draykon cries, unmistakeably.

We're too late!

She beat her tired wings harder, forcing herself to triple her speed.

Peace, Minchu, it may not be as you fear.

She ignored Pensould's counsel, all her thoughts bent on her mother and father. She cursed herself, cursed Limbane and Pensould, cursed everything. Limbane had sworn that time as she knew it was not passing while she had been cooped up in the Library, but how could that be true? If so then Isand had reached Waeverleyne with impossible speed.

Remembering the other draykon's boundless anger, though, perhaps it was not impossible. She was driven by the sort of fury Llandry had never known. She should have anticipated that, spared no effort herself to reach her mother before Isand had time to enact her plan of revenge.

As she arrived in the skies over Waeverleyne with Pensould hard behind her, all other thoughts faded. She saw Isand, flanked by two draykons Llandry had never seen before. She took in the crowds of panicking Glinnish citizens filling the ground and the air, some fighting to escape the city and others, stupidly, watching the conflict.

Then she saw the lone human figure that hovered in the air before Isand's massive jaws. Slender and frail she looked in contrast, her black hair blown loose by the wind, her dark blue wings beating fast to hold her aloft.

Llandry would know her mother anywhere.

Ynara was holding a length of rippling white fabric. The sight sent her heart plummeting; she could have told her mother that parley would not work on Isand.

Then yours is a double betrayal and you shall be among the first to fall.

The words were Isand's, spoken at a volume to cause Llandry a small whimper of pain. She screamed a warning, screamed again as Isand struck her mother to earth. Watching Ynara plummet to the ground, Llandry shrieked with uncontrollable fury.

Ah, now she understood how Isand felt.

Pensould's voice joined hers in a shattering roar. He flew to the attack, but Llandry angled down, down to the ground. She was human again in seconds, changing so fast that she couldn't walk properly on her human legs. She staggered to her mother's side and dropped down beside her.

'Mamma! Ma, speak to me.'

No use; Ynara lay unconscious, blood covering the lower part of her face and bruises everywhere on her honey-coloured skin. She didn't wake.

Sigwide lay in the moss where he'd fallen from Llandry's back. She felt a twinge of pain from him as he staggered onto his feet.

Ouch, he grumbled.

She scooped him up, hugging him close as several human figures ran towards her. One woman dropped to her knees on Ynara's other side, ripping open some kind of bag.

'I'm from the infirmary,' she gasped, breathless from the run. 'I'll take care of her. I need you to move away, miss.'

Llandry felt like clinging to her mother, all her adult rationality wiped away in the wake of pure fear and anxiety. She forced it down, nodding.

She couldn't help to heal her mother, but she could avenge her injury. Finding the ball of anger still coiled inside her, she cultivated it into a blaze of fury.

Stay with Ma, she said to Sigwide, placing him near Ynara's feet. She didn't wait for his agreement. Backing away, she flashed back into her draykon shape, ignoring the gasps of shock and fear from the assembled crowds. In seconds she was back in the air, arrowing towards Isand.

295

Pensould was in the midst of the three draykons, hard pressed but holding his own. Llandry felt another stab of guilt; in her anxiety for her mother she'd left Pensould to fend for himself against three draykons.

Well, now she would even the odds.

Tensing herself for impact, she hurled herself into the fray, letting her body collide with Isand's at maximum speed. The red draykon bellowed and dropped, but she wasn't incapacitated for long; her head came up, her jaws fastening on Llandry's hide. Her teeth pierced the skin and Llandry shrieked with pain.

Minchu, get out of the fight!

What a time for Pensould to get protective. *Don't be absurd,* she replied. *Take care of the other two. Isand is mine.*

She turned on the wine-hued draykon, absolutely intent on killing her for the attack on her mother. She bit and clawed ferociously, heedless of her own safety, uncaring as long as she took Isand down with her. Claws raked fire across her side; she bellowed and turned, darting in and around Isand's guard to snap at her neck. Her smaller size gave her the advantage of speed and agility; her teeth connected, sinking deeply into the red beast's flesh. She ripped her jaws free, revelling in the other draykon's bellow of pain and the flow of fresh blood as she circled away and back.

Why fight us? Isand's speech was laced with pain, a fact which gave Llandry considerable satisfaction. *We are the same.*

We are not the same! Llandry screamed the words at her. *These are MY people!*

Your people? The question was heavy with confusion. *That cannot be.*

But it is so. And the woman you may have killed is my mother. For that, I WILL kill you.

Your mother? Such a thing is not possible. She is human; you are draykoni. Isand's jaws snapped at Llandry's flanks again, but half-heartedly. *I do not wish to fight fellows. Cease your defence of these worthless creatures.*

Llandry attacked again, raking her claws across Isand's red hide. *I will not!*

Isand shook her great head and roared. Then she began to retreat, her blood streaming away to the ground.

We retreat! she bellowed. The other two draykoni paused in their harassment of Pensould; Llandry felt their confusion and resistance to Isand's order. But they obeyed it.

As they fell into line behind Isand, Llandry launched herself in pursuit.

MINCHU! The name was roared so loudly that Llandry felt her brain might explode. *Cease your pursuit! NOW!*

Llandry flew on.

Pensould's massive weight slammed into her from above, knocking her off balance. He kept on her, herding her to the ground, using his superior size to cut off her escape. Fighting him every inch of the way, she was nonetheless forced to earth.

Pensould snapped his heavy jaws near her face, growling. *You will not DARE to kill yourself in pursuit of revenge! That is for the likes of Isand. Your family needs you alive. I need you alive. Stop it now!*

Llandry drooped, her rage dissipating under the

weight of Pensould's disapproval. He was right, of course. She had lost her temper, something she never remembered doing before.

And once you are calm, Pensould said more gently, *there may be something we can do for your mother.* His nose nudged gently at her flank; she was surprised to feel a flash of pain there. *And these must be tended to also.*

For the first time she noticed that his own hide was striped with wounds and dotted with abrasions.

I'm sorry, Pensould. I got carried away.

She felt him sigh, a whistling of breath through tired lungs. *Well. Let us see what's become of your parent.*

Parent, singular. She realised that she hadn't seen her father. He ought to have been by her mother's side; he would have been, if he were here.

Where, then, was Papa?

When Llandry took her human shape again, she was alarmed to find bloody wounds decorating her arms and torso and bruises shading her skin. It hurt to breathe, and one of her legs felt horribly weak. Pensould was in little better shape. He wrapped her in a brief hug, soothing her fears with a rush of affection.

I would tend to these first, but I fear we may need all of our energy for your mother.

She nodded and pulled away from him. They were in the infirmary, waiting to be taken to Ynara. At first the medics had refused them admittance: Ynara's condition was too severe for visitors, they said. They had spoken to Llandry stiffly, keeping their distance from her.

With a start, she realised they were afraid of her.

This was a curious reversal. All her life it was she who had been afraid of other people, cursedly, irrationally afraid. To find herself in the stronger position gave her a brief feeling of power.

She had used that rush of confidence to press her point. The nurses, their fear of her weakening their resolve, had given in.

'Please come with me, Miss Sanfaer.' A medic appeared in the far doorway, clad in coveralls and with her hair tightly bound back. She said nothing further as the two of them followed her upstairs and through the halls to a private room.

Ynara lay in a narrow bed, white-faced and unmoving. Her chest still rose and fell, but her breathing was shallow and irregular. Llandry couldn't see any obvious wounds on her, nothing but bruises and cuts.

'The injuries are internal,' said one of the attendant medics. Three of them were in the room, monitoring Ynara's condition and keeping her comfortable. 'She is bleeding somewhere inside, but I can't tell where from. If the bleeding doesn't stop soon, there will be nothing to be done for her.'

Llandry's heart twisted and her breath stopped. Her strong, confident, untouchable mother was dying. And she was dying because of something Llandry and Pensould had done. *They* had woken Isand. *They* had gone ahead with the plan in ignorance, knowing nothing of the forces they would unleash. It should never have been undertaken.

Pensould?

He nodded and moved to the other side of

Ynara's bed, standing opposite to Llandry.

We will do our best, though I can promise you nothing.

It would have to do. Llandry took a shaky breath and nodded.

Tell me what to do.

Limbane's plan held one or two flaws, Andraly thought as she watched the two draykons fly in to join the conflict. In his usual hazy way, Limbane had dropped the two of them on the borders of Glinnery, either forgetting to ascertain where Llandry's mother lived or simply not caring.

He had also forgotten to tell Andraly when they departed. She and her fellow Lokant Jace had been left to catch up. Of course, the two draykons had been long gone by the time they had emerged from the Library, and so she and Jace had simply gone ahead to Waeverleyne to await the arrival of Llandry and Pensould.

Their advantage in timing gave them ample opportunity to observe the arrival of the other three draykoni.

'I'd say we're too late,' Jace muttered as the red draykon laid into a unit of guards.

'Warning unnecessary,' Andraly agreed. She watched dispassionately as a foolhardy Glinnish woman attempted parley.

'That's doomed to failure.'

'Stupidest thing I've seen in a long time,' Jace nodded.

The attempt at parley ended as she had foreseen. The Glinnish woman's frail form toppled to earth, and the red draykon turned its attention back to the population of Waeverleyne.

That was when Llandry and Pensould arrived.

'Oh, beautiful timing,' Jace said with approval.

'Couldn't have been better.' Though she wasn't sure what these two could do against three draykoni, all of them bigger than Llandry.

In the end, she was pleasantly surprised.

'What a demon,' said Jace. He actually sounded slightly awed.

Having watched the small grey draykon drive the enraged red beast away, Andraly had to agree. The girl was so feeble in person, a cringing, shy thing without spirit of any kind. Apparently she had hidden depths.

The attacking draykoni flew away and the show was over. Andraly stretched her limbs and rolled her shoulders, stiff from staring into the sky for so long.

'I'd better tell Limbane,' she said.

'Right.'

And back to the Library she went.

CHAPTER TWENTY-THREE

If there was one thing Eva particularly detested in life, it was being a failure. At anything, for any reason. Tren was certainly right about that.

She hadn't had much experience of it, perhaps that was why. So when Limbane pronounced her an inept healer and refused to teach her any more, she had been irritated, disbelieving and uncomfortably awash with self-doubt.

'Never mind,' said Limbane with offensive good cheer. 'You mastered mental control over both animals and intelligent species before you ever came here, and your performance with the PsiMap is creditable. With a bit more practice, you'll be very good at self-camouflage; your performance as Andraly was almost good enough to fool me.' He patted her arm in a grandfatherly gesture, which only irritated her more. 'No partial ever has a full spectrum of abilities. There had to be something you couldn't do.'

'Did there really,' she said through gritted teeth.

He chuckled. 'If you'd like to prove me wrong, you're welcome to try, but don't waste too much time on it. Regenerating flesh is not your strong point.'

Limbane declared her training over soon after that, and disappeared on his mysterious errands. Llandry and Pensould had already gone, followed by Andraly and the other Lokant, Jace. Eva hadn't found a reason to like him much, so far; he was laconic and unfriendly, his grey eyes lacking warmth. Perhaps she wouldn't see him again.

That left herself and Tren unattended and unescorted. She no longer needed the help of a full Lokant to get around. She could translocate herself and others without assistance. It was an empowering thought: *almost* enough to make up for her lack of mastery over regeneration.

Tren had stayed away from her since their conversation in the library. She didn't regret it. She certainly refused to admit that she missed him. The boy *should* stay away from her; it would give him some time to shake off her influence over him.

For she still doubted not that his blurted confession of affection had more to do with her Lokant heritage than any sincere depth of feeling. The gulf between them was too enormous for any other explanation to hold water. And it had come out of nowhere, this declaration. She had seen no sign of special interest from him before. Awful thought: perhaps he had been knowingly insincere, trying to make her feel better.

That was a still more humbling notion, one she tried to shake off. She really couldn't take any more belittling reflections.

A small but persistent part of her heart insisted on hoping she was wrong about Tren. With the utmost ruthlessness, she squashed it.

When she finally went in search of him, she adopted a brisk, business-like air designed to keep him at a distance.

'Are you ready to depart?'

'Perfectly.' He opened his door wider to reveal a packed bag waiting just inside.

'Excellent. I'm going to need to make some kind of physical contact in order to transport us both. I apologise.' She reached out and carefully locked her fingers around his wrist.

He smiled, but it was a sad smile. 'No apology necessary. I promise not to be scandalised.' He collected his bag with his free hand, then straightened. 'Where is it exactly that we're going?'

She didn't answer for a moment. Her mind was already busy, reaching for the PsiMap as Limbane had taught her. It opened in her mind's eye and she could see their Cluster, three worlds nestled around each other. She searched through, turning them about until she found the spot she sought.

'Ullarn,' she replied. 'Specifically, Wirllen.'

'Straight for Wirllen? Is that a good idea?'

'Trust me.' Selecting the precise location she wanted, she focused her will on translocation. Energy flashed through her and her body weight dropped away, fading to nothing. The process of preparing to translocate was bizarre and still unsettling; it had never felt that way when she had been merely a passenger.

But then it was over and she was elsewhere.

'Freaky.' Tren tried to pull back his arm, but she still held his wrist in a fierce grip, afraid of losing him somewhere on the way. She forced her fingers apart and he immediately began massaging his wrist.

'Did you just call me a freak?'

'Er, no, certainly not, never.'

'Sorry about the, er.' She made a vague gesture at his arm.

'No problem. There's still blood in it, somewhere.'

'Let's get on with it,' she said. Then, under her breath, 'I really don't like Ullarn.'

'It can't be as bad as they say. Surely.'

'No, really it can.' She wasn't looking at him as she spoke: her eyes were busy scanning their surroundings, checking whether she had brought them to the right place.

Shame that all alleyways looked the same.

'So, where are we?' Tren asked.

'*Hopefully,* we are in a secluded alley off Wirllen's city square.'

'Great! And what are we doing here?'

'The first thing we're going to do is buy a carriage.'

'A carriage.'

'And better clothes. For you as well, I'm afraid. You're now my factotum.'

'Er. Yes, your ladyship.' Tren stooped his broad shoulders and arranged his features into a servile expression.

'Stop that. You can be normal.'

'I enjoy theatrics. I was an amateur thespian once, did I ever tell you that?'

305

Eva made her way to the mouth of the alley and he fell in beside her, one leg dragging with each step.

'What's that about? Are you hurt?'

'I'm a factotum with a wooden leg. That's because I used to be a pirate on the high seas before—'

'Tren,' she said, allowing an intense weariness to creep into her tone.

'All right,' he sighed, straightening. 'But it'll be a lot less fun this way.'

'Must everything be fun?'

'I am allergic to boredom.'

'Then I shall try not to bore you.' Pausing at the entrance to Wirllen's city square, she glanced out. They had arrived at a quiet time of day, or strictly of night. The moon was low on the horizon, almost ready to set.

Beside her, Tren gave an extravagant bow. 'That, my lady, you have never yet managed to do.'

'I hope you'll still be saying that in a couple of days. Come on.'

The salesman grossly overcharged for the carriage, of course. Eva paid the asking price without hesitation, earning herself an incredulous smile and a great deal of extra attention she didn't want.

'No, thank you, I've already arranged for the horses. I do not require new upholstery. The existing curtains are perfectly adequate. Oh, all right. Add an extra hot brick. In fact, make that two.'

Tren leaned in slightly. 'It's late spring.'

'So?'

'So it's nearly summer.'

Eva graced that observation with a flat stare.

'Er.' Tren stepped back. 'Forget I mentioned it.'

'It'll get cold later. When that happens, you don't get to share.'

The outfitters was next on the agenda. It pained Eva to settle for ready-made clothes, she who was used to custom tailored attire. She swallowed her revulsion and submitted to the fittings patiently. These were, after all desperate times; desperate measures must be gone through.

Tren objected to the suit she picked out for him.

'I look like a clerk.' He turned in front of the tailor's full-length mirror, eyeing his drably grey-clad self with distaste.

'That's more or less what you are, for the next few days.'

'But... *the cuffs.*' He plucked at the neat, completely unadorned snow-white cotton with so much dejection she couldn't help but laugh.

'You'll live.' She gave him a soothing pat on the back.

'How do you know? I might suffer death by sartorial disappointment.'

'I defy you to die over a jacket.'

He folded his arms. 'I want my silk shirt back.'

'No factotum wears silk shirts, Tren. Please be serious.'

His expression became mulish. 'I am serious.'

'Fine,' she said with a sigh. 'I keep my factotum remarkably well dressed. Just the shirt, mind!'

'It's all right,' Tren said, shrugging off the jacket with relief. 'People will just assume that we're sleeping together.'

Eva couldn't find a response to that.

Ready-made clothes or not, it felt good to be in silk and velvet again. Reclining on the purple upholstery of her new, temporary carriage and listening to the clip-clop of four horses' hooves outside, Eva felt like herself again.

Or her old self. It was hard to be sure who she was these days.

Tren sat opposite, his fine silk shirt largely hidden by the drab grey jacket he wore. She'd asked a maid at the inn they had chosen to do something with his hair. The girl had tried, but in her defence it was a difficult task. Tren's dark hair, quite long by this time (for he resolutely forgot to have it tended to) was tied back into a tail, but much of it escaped around his face.

'So, where *are* we going?'

'You'll find out when we get there. Which will be in about five minutes.'

Tren rolled his eyes. 'You're mysterious just for the fun of it. It amuses you far more than might be considered normal.'

She grinned at that. 'It's my prerogative to be enigmatic.'

'I suppose it will have to be, for nothing can cure you of the habit.' He shivered a little. It was late now, the moon had set and the Night Cloak had taken over. Lights shone softly in the rigidly laid-out streets, failing to make the unimaginative architecture look pretty. A brisk wind sent draughts whistling through her carriage, regardless of the upholstery and the curtains.

'Are you sure you won't share one of those bricks?'

'No.' Eva kept a firm grip on the stone hot water bottle that rested at her side; the other one was hidden under her skirts, warming her feet. 'I warned you. You mocked me before; now you must pay the price!'

'Yours is a vengeful nature, O Revered Employer.'

'You didn't have to come along. I told you I don't need you for this part.'

'I can't let you wander off alone. *Especially* when I have no idea where you're going.' He shivered again and wrapped his arms around himself.

'Never mind. It will be warm in Brun's house.'

'Brun?'

Eva ignored that question. They were already pulling up outside of a large house, as plain and unlovely as the rest of the city, though she knew it to be an expensive property in Ullarn. Tren stepped out as soon as the carriage came to a stop, politely handing her down after him.

'Thank you,' she murmured, smoothing down her skirts. 'How do I look?'

'Er.' Tren stared. 'Is that a real question?'

'Of course it's a real question. I have a reputation to uphold here.'

'Um. You... you look more beautiful than ever.'

The teasing tone she expected from him was absent. He was looking at her with a hint of awe and a great deal of regret.

She suddenly realised that bringing him here had probably been a huge mistake. She should have asked Limbane to find him something else to do.

A sigh escaped her. 'Let's go in.'

She stepped up to the great door and rang the bell, listening as it resounded through the house. Footsteps soon approached and the door was opened by an immaculately uniformed woman.

'Is Ambassador Recender at home, please?'

'Whom shall I say is asking?'

Eva gave her name. The woman's eyes widened.

'I'm sure he'll wish to see you, my lady. Please come in.' She stepped back, opening the door wider. Eva stepped briskly inside, adopting her haughty noblewoman's air.

'I'll tell the ambassador that you're here.' The woman's eyes flicked to Tren, but she didn't say anything further. She dropped a curtsey and disappeared up the stairs.

'*Ambassador Recender?*' Tren's whisper held a strangled note.

'What of it?'

'We just walked into the personal home of *Ambassador Recender?* Are you crazy?'

'I know exactly what I'm doing.'

He snorted. 'You couldn't have warned me about this?'

'No, because I knew you would react in exactly this way. Now you have no choice but to go along with it. You *are* going along with it, aren't you?'

Tren's only response was a despairing groan.

'Hey,' she reminded him. 'You were the one who insisted on coming.'

'I might not have if I'd been suitably informed.'

She lifted a brow at him. 'Really?'

'Fine, fine, you win. I still would've insisted on

coming.'

The ambassador's servant returned. 'He'll see you, my lady.'

Eva beamed at the woman. 'Of course he will.'

The ambassador was in his drawing-room. He wore a fabulous silk dressing-gown and matching slippers, his gleaming brown hair perfectly arranged. His black eyes watched Eva's progress across his drawing-room floor with interest.

'My lady. An unexpected pleasure.'

He spoke in Ullarni. Eva replied in kind, with a silent apology to Tren. 'I was passing, my lord, and thought to pay you a visit.'

'Passing?' He grinned. 'One does, I suppose, "happen" to pass Wirllen once in a while.'

'Frequently.' She returned his grin, allowing hers to become mischievous.

'Who's the passenger?' Recender jerked his chin at Tren.

'My factotum. I drag the poor boy everywhere, but he's so useful.'

'Another of your thralls.' Recender's lips twitched.

'A willing one, my lord Recender.'

He stood abruptly. 'You'll stay the night with me, of course. I suppose I can find somewhere to stow your boy.' He crossed to the door, opened it slightly and snapped his fingers. A maid appeared almost at once, dropping a hasty curtsey.

'Have a room prepared. Nothing too grand.' He dropped his voice to a low murmur and gave some further directions which Eva couldn't hear. Then he closed the door again and returned to her with a smile.

Eva didn't realise his intention until it was too late to avoid it. His arms went around her and he pulled her close, trapping her in a long kiss. She heard Tren shift uncomfortably somewhere behind her.

'My departure from your fine city was too precipitate last time,' said Recender. 'I regret that, for our friendship was terminated at an inopportune moment.'

'Then let it be renewed now. Though I fear I may only stay a brief time myself. Business, of course.'

'Ah,' he said regretfully. 'Then we will make the most of it.'

He was every bit as handsome as she remembered. Awarding him a smile, she said, 'That we shall. Oh, Brun? We're going to need clearance to stay for a few days. You know how testy the authorities can be. Make up something plausible, hm?'

'Naturally.' He began kissing her neck.

'For my factotum as well. Don't forget, please.'

'Anything you like,' he replied. 'Later.'

Eva waited until she had Recender in a state of perfect satisfaction before she presented her next request.

'I've a small problem, Brun, with which I was hoping to enlist your help.'

He stopped in the process of kissing her arm, casting her a wry smile. 'I should have expected that your ladyship would not visit without a reason.'

'We all do as we must. You're usually the first

person to say that.'

He sighed. 'Fortunately for you I, too, am a willing thrall. What may I help you with?'

For an instant Eva felt a crawling sensation of disgust with herself. *In thrall.* He had no idea how true that observation was. And now she manipulated him deliberately, turning the force of her will on him as well as her charm.

It was disgusting, but she did it willingly.

We all do as we must, indeed.

She turned her smile back on. 'I have a few names on my list. Difficult people, hard to find. I've reason to think they are all Ullarni citizens.'

Brun Recender marred his handsome face with a frown. 'I cannot assist you in pursuing Ullarni citizens, Eva. You must realise that.'

'Brun, I swear. This is nothing to do with politics. It holds no bearing on the relationship between Ullarn and Glour. It is more a personal matter.'

He looked at her silently, obviously troubled. 'Powerful I may be, but if it became known that I have helped you in such a way I could lose a great deal. You understand that as well, I hope.'

'I do. I will not be revealing your assistance, and my visit here is not known.'

'And your "factotum"? What of him?'

'I trust him as I do my own self.'

'Do you indeed. And he is what to you?'

She pulled out of his embrace. 'That is hardly a relevant question.'

'Forgive me. I am sadly prone to jealousy. I realise I will always have competition; I seek to establish how much.'

Eva steeled herself to say the words. 'He is nothing to me. An employee, nothing more.'

He shook his head, a dangerous glint appearing in his eyes. 'That, I think, is a lie. Such care you showed for his comfort. And he was displeased to see you with me.'

Eva's heart fluttered oddly. She suppressed the feeling, keeping her features smooth of expression. 'His feelings are his own business.'

He gave a soft laugh at that. 'So ruthless, my lady. I love you for it. Very well, I will help you as I can. You will give me the names and I will enquire. Discreetly. It may take a few days.'

'I must leave in two.'

'Must? Or are determined to?'

'Some of both,' she admitted.

Tracking Tren down the following day was no easy task. When she finally found him, he had the hollow-eyed appearance of a man who hadn't slept. She inspected him with some concern.

'Are you sick? What ails you?'

'Nothing physical.' Tren backed away from her scrutiny without looking at her.

'I'm going in search of Mr Iro Byllant. Are you well enough to come, or would you prefer to go back to the inn?'

'Are we going on this search alone?'

'As in, without the ambassador? Yes. Of course.'

'Then I'll come.'

She felt a rush of relief, though she was careful not to show it. 'Right away, then.'

Tren was uncharacteristically silent in the carriage. They were heading for Wynn Street and the warehouse that Ocherly of Lawch & Son had named for her. It was situated on the outer edge of the South District, so the journey took some time as they inched through the traffic. Tren rode for half an hour without looking at her, directing his attention out of the window instead.

Eva remembered Brun's words. *He was displeased to see you with me.*

It wasn't long since he'd talked to her of love. The ambassador's worship of her was, she knew, a product more of manipulation than anything else. He was indeed, as he termed it, a thrall. In his case her guilt was minimal; he was the type to use and drop people as he saw fit. It wouldn't hurt him to undergo some of the same treatment.

Tren, though, was different. Always different. She now had sufficient control over her Lokant side to withdraw what Limbane called her "charisma" in his presence, but it was too late. She wished she'd learned of it before, when there might still have been time to avoid enthralling Tren. His affection for her might be largely imposed, but apparently it still hurt.

'Tren?'

He reluctantly turned his face to her.

'There were reasons why I wanted you to stay behind last night.'

'So I imagine.' He turned back to the window.

The conversation seemed to be over with that, but a moment later he spoke again.

'An old paramour, I suppose?'

'I suppose so. Yes.'

'How many of those have there been?'

She shrugged. 'I don't count.'

He turned cold eyes on her. 'Do you have any affection for them or is it all practicality?'

She pondered that. 'Would it make it worse or better if I did?'

'Worse,' he said promptly. 'No, better. I don't know.'

'I don't really have any affection for Recender. He's not that type of man. But we understand each other.'

Tren snorted. 'I'm sure.'

She welcomed the flash of irritation that burned away her guilt. 'You're telling me you've never bedded anyone without feeling affection for them?'

'That's different.'

'How can it possibly be different?'

'I wasn't using them for anything!'

'You were using them for your own entertainment. They were using you for the same. Just now I'm using Brun to advance our cause; his contacts will get the job done much faster than we could alone. He in turn uses me to amuse himself for a day or two. Is it different?'

Tren looked bewildered. 'I'm just surprised.'

'I thought you said you *knew* me. Everything about me.'

'I thought I did.' He turned away from her and in this gesture she recognised rejection.

Well, she thought. *That solves that problem.*

She turned her face to the traffic as well, resolutely swallowing the lump that rose in her throat.

The warehouse had an unpromising air of abandonment about it. Eva checked the address for the third time, her hopes sinking. Wynn Street, Wirllen South. Number eight. Windowless and boarded up it might be, but this was indeed the right building.

Tren had pulled himself together as they left the carriage. He was back to his normal self, or something near it. It was a fragile facade, but one she was grateful for. They had work to do.

'What's the plan?' Tren stood looking up at the roughly boarded windows doubtfully.

'Search it. In a moment.' She nudged Rikbeek with her thoughts, instructing him to check for threats.

He didn't move.

Rikbeek. Budge.

His miniscule brain registered stubborn refusal. He was cocooned somewhere in her skirts, determined to be asleep.

'Sorry,' she said aloud. 'Not an option.' Finding his small, dark-furred body, she plucked him off the fabric and tossed him into the air. His wings opened just in time to catch himself and he flew off, blazing indignation.

'Don't tell me there's insubordination in the ranks?' Tren had watched the exchange with a grin on his face.

Eva snorted in reply. 'Always.'

They waited for the few minutes it took for her gwaystrel to make a circuit of the building. He didn't detect any other humans nearby.

'Okay. We can go.' Eva walked around the building until she found a door that didn't have planks nailed over it. It was locked, of course.

Tren pushed her gently out of the way, and bowed. 'Allow me.'

She stood back, puzzled. Tren had never mentioned a talent for picking locks.

Apparently he scorned such delicacy. Instead he simply ran at the door and kicked the hell out of it. It took him a few tries before the door fell in.

She walked past him as he stood, breathing hard and looking slightly dazed.

'Feel better?'

'Much,' he panted.

'Excellent.'

The interior was in full darkness. Tren produced a tiny light-globe from somewhere and activated it. It was the portable type that resourceful people hung on their belts or kept in their handbags; Eva was glad to find that Tren was one such practical-minded soul as she hadn't thought of it herself.

She was less impressed when she saw the feeble glow it emitted.

'Well,' she said. 'You made an awful lot of noise back there so we'd better be quick. Try not to crash into anything.'

'Ma'am.' Tren found his way back to the door, taking the globe with him. She waited, trying not to feel unnerved by the darkness. It was almost absolute; even her night eyes could barely see anything.

The sound of a lever being pulled broke the silence, and a light came on in the ceiling far above.

'Lights still work,' Tren observed redundantly.

The building really was empty. It didn't even have furniture. The large expanse of bare floor stretched before them, devoid of clues.

'Fake address?'

She sighed in annoyance. 'Must be. Curse it, I really hoped for something here. Brun had better deliver.'

She turned to leave, but Tren stopped, dropping into a crouch on the hard floor. He ran his hands over the cold stone, then rubbed his fingers together.

'What have you found?' She crossed to him and crouched down beside him.

'Hold out your hand.' She did so and he sprinkled dust into her palm.

'Dust.'

'Look more closely.' He sent the tiny light-globe to hover directly over her palm.

Eva gasped as indigo lights shone from her skin. 'Dusted draykon bone?'

Tren nodded. 'I reckon so. That globe at Lawch & Son? I bet that's how they made it. Mixed this with the glass formula.'

'Hmm. I wonder how they discovered that.'

'And what else they've discovered.'

An interesting thought. The Seven Realms could be flooded with small technologies like the light-globe, things that were unlikely to reach the attention of the authorities. And if they did, Mr Byllant had an old, long-abandoned address to cover his tracks.

Whoever Byllant was, he must be making a fortune at this venture.

'He *has* to be linked to Krays,' Eva said. 'How else could he be getting quantities of draykon bone?'

'But why would Krays be gathering draykon bone just to spread it around like this? Can someone like him care about money? Why would he need it?'

'I don't know,' she admitted.

'We shouldn't get fixed on that theory. There's nothing here to link any of this to Krays.'

'True.' She thought back over all the information they'd gained. She had nothing but a name and this address, and no way to access any of Ullarn's bureaucratic records to find out the rest. She would have to trust Brun for that.

And she had nothing else. Nothing on Byllant, nothing on Ana and Griel. She didn't even have last names for the latter two.

'Brun had better deliver,' she said again. If he didn't find something for them to go on, they had hit a dead end.

CHAPTER TWENTY-FOUR

Aysun dropped his voice-box back onto the desk with a grunt of irritation. Three days he had been trying to reach her, and his wife hadn't accepted the call.

She had forgotten to carry it around with her, he supposed. It lay somewhere in the house, out of hearing so she never knew when he was trying to get through. Or the box was broken. That was a possibility.

Or perhaps she had actively decided not to answer. She was avoiding him for some reason. His irritation grew greater at the mere thought.

All of these conclusions he drew and steadfastly clung to in favour of the notion that something had gone wrong. He was of a protective nature, and frequently over the years he'd been gripped with fear when his wife had been late or absent and he'd become convinced that some catastrophe had befallen her.

She'd laughed at him for it. Every time.

He gave the call one last try, listening sadly as it beeped on without Ynara's beloved voice cutting in. At last he set the voice box aside and left the room, sore at heart.

Through the window he could see Orillin in the garden with Graaf. The orboe had never left, sticking to the tousle-headed boy with endearing stubbornness. If you could call it endearing. The creature was as enormous as ever and looked just as unfriendly to Aysun's eye. He still had to restrain himself from rushing to the boy's aid when his slight form disappeared under Graaf's huge, shaggy body. But always the maddening boy emerged unscathed, laughing his irrepressible laugh, tumbling on with the orboe as if he hadn't a care in the world.

He would lose that carefree nature as he grew older. When he had a daughter out in the worlds somewhere alone, and a wife who refused to answer his calls, he would know about cares.

Aysun grouched his way back to the main room of Rheas's house. He collected a mug of beer for himself, refusing to acknowledge the grey-haired man in the rocking chair. But when he turned to leave, he only made it halfway across the room before Rheas spoke.

'No answer again, I take it.'

'What do you know of it?' He glowered heavily at his abominable parent, fiercely glad to have a target for his irritation.

'Were you planning to do something about it, or will you settle for stamping about my house all day?'

'Like what?' Aysun demanded. 'I'm stuck here for the present, playing nurse-maid to that child out there.'

Rheas smirked. 'I could do that without your help.'

'Ynara asked it of me.'

Rheas shook his head. 'You're a pushover.'

Aysun's fists clenched. 'Shut up, old man. You forfeited your right to criticise my doings long ago.'

Rheas shrugged. 'I was going to suggest a solution, but if that's the way you feel about it I'll stay out of it.'

'Oh, for the love of...' Aysun massaged his temples. Never was anybody cursed with such an irritating, reprehensible, aggravating excuse for a sire. 'Fine, make your suggestion.'

Rheas's eyes glinted. 'It means accessing those summoner abilities you've been busy denying, my boy. Still interested?'

Aysun took a long breath. 'All right. Yes.'

'Good. You haven't forgotten Prink, I'm sure.'

Prink? Aysun didn't recognise the name, but he did recognise the colourful bundle of fur and wings that zipped past his nose.

'Odd name.'

'Your daughter's choice, not mine. Prink will take you as a passenger for a short time, if you're good and don't snap at him.'

Aysun frowned harder than ever. 'A passenger? You're talking nonsense.'

'If I am, it's remarkably effective nonsense. I've kept a close eye on our Llandry for years by this very method. And before you object, I'm the reason she survived that fight. I got her out, and that was due to the help of Prink here sticking to your girl like a burr. Still want to argue?'

Aysun shook his head, mute.

'Right. You're going to have to do something pretty uncharacteristic for you. You're going to have to forget yourself. For the next hour, you and Prink are the same. Now reach out to him. Not with your eyes or your ears; use those summoner senses you pretend you don't have.'

This came hard. Used to brutal denial of this traitorous, dangerous part of himself, Aysun struggled with the command to open himself to it.

In the end, though, it wasn't that hard. The very strength of his summoner nature was part of the fear. It rested just below the surface of his conscious mind, always threatening to break free of his ruthless control. No matter how hard he tried to be an ordinary engineer, magicless and safe, he had never managed it.

He felt Prink's mind like the touch of a feather on his skin. The little beast was enjoying the sensation of air across its wings, welcoming the room's draughts like caresses.

'Good,' Rheas approved. 'We don't have time to muck about with this so I'm going to help you out. All right?'

Aysun didn't have time to reply before a mental blow struck him. He reeled in confusion as his befuddled mind divided between defending itself, fighting back and understanding what had happened.

Juicy.

The thought flitted across his own mind, but he knew it wasn't his. Then he tasted something crunchy in his mouth—his mouth that remained, he was certain, empty—and a hot, sharp liquid ran over his tongue. He crunched the insect down, swallowing it with satisfaction. His wings beat frantically multiple times per second, but he didn't need to concentrate on that; they took care of their own rhythm.

And alongside all this he was still Aysun, a tall human with two arms and two legs and a deeply confused brain.

'Talk to me,' came Rheas's voice. Looking his way, Aysun saw him through Prink's eyes: enormous, hairy in the wrong places and imposing. But, oddly enough, the irilapter felt a pulse of affection for the man.

'Hello?' Aysun's lips formed the word clearly; for a moment he'd been afraid he wouldn't be able to manage speech anymore.

'Good. Getting the hang of it?'

'Mhm.' Aysun's attention was only half on the conversation. The rest of his brain experienced Prink's world with fascination.

He was almost jolted out of Prink's consciousness when Rheas opened his mouth and bellowed a single word. '*MAGS!*'

'Yes, dear.' The little woman's answering cry came merrily down the stairs and she herself soon followed.

'Gate,' Rheas barked. 'Quickly.' He pointed at Prink.

'Right,' said Mags placidly. She worked fast. Almost immediately a gate opened right in front of Prink's long proboscis and, with a small cry of indignation, the irilapter was sucked into it.

Aysun tumbled along, his soul protesting vehemently as the two parts of his mind were spread across two worlds. He was Aysun, standing in Rheas's parlour before the fire, and he was also Prink, tumbling out of control through the Sanfaer house in Waeverleyne.

If Prink didn't get control of himself soon, they were going to crash into a wall.

Use those bloody wings! he roared.

Shout less. Prink arrested his headlong flight inches before the far wall of Aysun's kitchen. He banked sharply and flew back into the middle of the room, his mind ablaze with indignation.

'Sorry,' Aysun said. He wasn't sure whether his physical lips moved as he said it; was he speaking the words aloud, or only to Prink? No way to tell.

He forgot Prink when he noticed the state of the kitchen. The first thing Prink's surprisingly impressive vision centred on was a stack of washing-up lying next to the beautiful big, stone sink he had built for Ynara. The woman was obsessive about leaving the kitchen tidy when she went to bed, but those dishes looked as though they'd been there for longer than a few hours.

He nudged Prink to make a circuit of the room, noting that the surfaces were gathering dust—something else Ynara hated. A cup rested on the table, full of an unidentifiable liquid that was covered in a layer of mould.

They made a tour of the rest of the house, and what he saw heightened his anxiety beyond anything he'd known since Llandry was carried home, her small body a mess of blood. Everywhere were signs that Ynara hadn't been home in a while. He knew her habits so well, he couldn't believe that she'd simply become sloppy in the time since he'd left.

Something big had to have happened. Something

bad, to have kept her away from her home for days at a time, without warning him first and without taking his voice box device with her.

Back to the portal, he told Prink. The irilapter dithered, attracted by some passing fragrance. Merciless, he used his anger to drive the creature on, back to the kitchen, through the gate that still hovered in the air.

Back in Rheas's house, he wrenched his consciousness free of Prink's, ignoring the flash of pain that sliced through his skull. He crossed to the chair in which Rheas still sat, his fists instinctively clenching. He felt like striking the old man.

'What was that about?'

Rheas had the cheek to offer him an innocent look in response. 'What?'

'That was completely unnecessary. I could have gone through the gate myself and achieved the same. What game are you playing?'

Rheas chuckled. 'Couldn't miss an opportunity to teach you a lesson, boy.'

'*What lesson?*'

Rheas sighed. 'Apparently it failed.'

'And how in the blazes is it possible to open a gate from here right into my kitchen?' Sorcs couldn't simply pick a location to gate to, that he knew. A gate opening in the Uppers would appear in the corresponding location in the adjacent realm. That meant... 'You've been living practically on top of our house all these years? And you never said anything? Never even told me you were *alive?*'

'We've discussed all this.' Rheas didn't look at his son.

Aysun struggled to keep his temper in check. He could beat his father senseless, and he felt so sorely tempted, but he wouldn't be able to live with himself afterwards.

The old man wasn't worth it.

'Something's wrong,' he said instead. 'I have to get home.'

'You were planning to tell us, weren't you Ays? Not thinking of ditching your old buddies again, surely?' Rufin wandered in, slouching as if he didn't know the meaning of the word *urgency*.

'Someone's got to stay with that kid.' Aysun jerked his thumb at the door, beyond which Orillin still frolicked with Graaf.

'I'm not a nursery maid,' Rufin growled. 'I'm perishing with boredom up here. What did you need me for anyway?'

'You're a crack shot, Ruf.'

'Sure,' he grinned. 'Soon as I have anything to fire at, that is.'

'Fine,' Aysun snapped. 'I don't have time for this. Eyas will stay. You and me are going back.'

Rufin touched two fingers to his forehead in a facetious salute. 'Cap'n.'

Minchu. Do you remember how you reached out to Isand, when she was still in her grave? I need you to do that now. Look for your mother.

Llandry obeyed Pensould's instruction without hesitation, anchoring her mind to Ynara's essence. Instantly her delicate senses were overwhelmed with the wrongness in this fragile body. Bones were broken throughout her mother's frame; her beautiful skin was torn and ruptured and bleeding. There was so much blood, seeping away as Mamma lay white and still.

She was really dying, her life seeping out as Llandry watched. She could feel the life-energy fading second by second. The realisation smote her hard, closing her throat and filling her eyes with blinding tears.

Pensould, she's almost gone! Hurry, faster, please...

You must stay calm. Above all, you must remain rational. We are going to use our own life-energy to restore hers, do you understand me? She is draykoni in large part; it will work. But you must not go too far. If you allow your emotions to rule you, your father may have to bury you both. Do you understand?

Llandry nodded frantically, consumed by her urgency. *Yes, yes. Now please, help her.*

Then follow my lead. Llandry watched in her mind's eye as Pensould cocooned Ynara in a soft blanket of his own energy. He steadily increased the flow until the life-force surrounded Ynara in a ceaseless, whirling current.

And yours, heart-of-mine.

Llandry gulped down her panic and obeyed, letting her own energy stream out of her to join the river that supported her mother. Soon the flow grew so bright that she could hardly focus her mind on it.

Good. Pensould's thoughts shifted as he redirected the current. It streamed into Ynara, mingling with her fading energy, reinforcing her life. Pensould directed the healing force first at Ynara's heart, stabilising its slow, irregular rhythm. Next he turned his attention to the lungs filling with blood and water; he purged

329

them, searing away the choking fluids. Ynara's breathing cleared.

But Llandry was beginning to feel the pressure. It started as a crushing tiredness that hit her all at once, draining her strength. Holding herself upright became too much; she dropped to the floor.

Hold on! There is much yet to be done.

The blood that seeped away internally, drop by drop, slowed as Pensould strove to rebuild Ynara's broken internal functions. He too was flagging now, his own life-energy burning lower the longer the healing went on.

Llandry's world shrank down to the simple task of drawing breath. One after another, in and out... even drawing in air came to seem almost impossible, but she hung on, grimly determined to last as long as her mother needed.

Pensould's voice broke in on her suffering, his words weak and hard to hear. *I can't—stop the bleeding, entirely. The damage is too much. We are spent. Time to withdraw.*

No! Finish it.

I dare not—

Llandry gritted her teeth and reached deeper, finding new stores of energy inside herself. She didn't question where they came from; she merely thrust them at Pensould, willing him to continue.

Please!

With a cry of anguish, Pensould did as she directed. Her mother's wounds began to close, bones began to knit, but so slowly, not fast enough...

Llandry hung on until she truly couldn't breathe. Her exhausted body lacked the energy to operate itself. The last thing she heard as her eyes closed was the sound of Pensould cursing.

Aysun had never run so fast in his life. The distance from his home to the city's main infirmary was not inconsiderable, but he never hesitated. Ignoring Rufin's gasped protests stuttering on from behind him, he powered on.

It had taken no time at all to learn what had happened. The minute he emerged from his house, a neighbour had descended on him in a flurry of wings and excitement. She had badly garbled the recent events in her haste, but he had understood enough.

It took twenty minutes of hard running to reach the infirmary's gates. He didn't pause to explain his errand to the desk clerk; he merely gasped his wife's name.

The clerk's eyes widened. 'Second floor. Room thirty-two.'

Aysun ran on. He skipped the new-built elevator in favour of the stairs. At last he burst into room thirty-two, limbs burning and chest heaving, with Rufin not far behind.

He found two beds, both containing a wan and still occupant. One of them was Ynara, her normally vibrant skin drained of colour and her eyes closed.

In the other bed lay his daughter, her state alarmingly similar.

Pensould sat in a chair beside Llandry's bed, holding one of her limp hands in his own. He too looked drained, dark circles staining the stark white skin beneath eyes that stood out harshly in his exhausted face.

'What happened?' The words came out louder than Aysun intended.

'We did a healing,' Pensould said. His voice was weak and he struggled to breathe properly. 'She went too far. I warned her, but...' He shook his head. He was gripping Llandry's hand hard, Aysun noticed, his knuckles white with effort. It was as if he intended to hold Llandry to life by sheer force of will.

Perhaps that was exactly what he was doing.

'Are they...?' Aysun couldn't say the words.

'They're both alive. But their—our—life-energy was used up in fixing, and mending, and—and—' He paused to breathe, slow, laboured breaths drawn with a struggle. 'They—have not enough left for consciousness. Maybe not enough to live.'

For a moment Aysun said nothing, merely gulped in air. For once, Rufin had no facetious comment to make. He stared at the two still forms, mute.

'What can I do?' Aysun said, when he had breath enough for speech.

'Nothing,' Pensould returned dully. Then his eyes sharpened and he gazed keenly at Aysun. 'Or perhaps...' His gaze flicked to Rufin. 'Him I cannot use, but you! Yes, it makes sense. Draykoni at heart, both of you. Of course you would be, it is why she is one of us...'

The man rambled, his utterances incoherent and nonsensical to Aysun. Frustration flooded him. His wife and daughter needed help; Pensould merely sounded insane.

'Pensould. If you have a way to help them, then please. *Get on with it.*'

'It might be enough.' The words were rasped, spoken by a soul pushed almost beyond endurance. Pensould lunged at him suddenly, and Aysun jumped as the man's free hand fastened around his wrist, hard.

'What—' Aysun had no time to say anything else. He felt *pulled,* all his strength and vitality suddenly sucked out of him with a force that drove him to his knees. Pensould's grip on his arm *hurt,* so much he feared the man might break the bone, but Aysun hadn't the breath to object. Now he understood how Pensould had felt moments before. Breathing was enough of a challenge; talking could wait.

He didn't understand what was happening. He heard Rufin curse behind him and then the gunman's hands were pulling at him, dragging him away from Pensould.

'*Stop it,'* he managed. 'Leave me—be—' Rufin swore again and backed away. Whatever Pensould was doing escaped him, but that he meant to help Ynara and Llandry was sufficient. Aysun endured.

'Enough,' gasped Pensould at last. The dragging sensation stopped and the terrible grip on his wrist eased. Aysun tried to get to his feet, but his legs gave way and he dropped.

Rufin caught him and hauled him up. 'There there, old man. You're all right.'

Was he? It was hard to tell. He was still breathing, at any rate. That was a good start.

Pensould, however, looked ready to die where he sat. If he had been exhausted before, he now looked... there wasn't a word for it. For an instant Aysun feared he *was* dead, but his chest still rose and fell.

Then his eyes opened and he actually smiled.

'Look,' he said, his eyes moving to Llandry's face.

Aysun looked. She still lay unmoving. He tried to convince himself that her face held more colour, but he couldn't really see any difference. And Ynara was the same.

'What?'

'They're stabilising. Energy regenerating... faster.'

'You're using yourself up,' Aysun said bluntly. 'You'd better stop. It's not helping.'

'My fault,' whispered Pensould. 'I woke them up. Never meant for her to be hurt. Either of them. I have to... fix it...' His eyes glazed over and his body swayed.

'You might want to lie down—' Aysun made a lunge for him, or tried to, but his weakened body didn't react. Pensould slithered out of his chair onto the floor and passed out.

Rufin swore, using all his best curse-words. 'Something wrong with the air in here or what?' He laid Aysun on the floor and stuffed a jacket under his head. 'Sorry, man. I'm getting out of here before I, too, pull a pansy fainting routine.' Aysun distantly heard the door open and shut and Rufin's heavy booted tread faded down the corridor.

Sleeping was such a wonderful idea. He couldn't think of a better one just then, so he slept.

Avane Desandry's house was small and unimpressive. Limbane hastened up to her front door, feeling harried and grouchy. It had taken far too long to find his way through this realm's muddle of bureaucracy to learn her address. He didn't know how Krays had discovered the identities of the other two draykoni hereditaries, but the rogue Lokant had been ahead of Limbane every step of the way so far. Limbane had worked fast, but he feared he hadn't been fast enough.

He looked for a doorbell but there wasn't one, only a simple doorknocker. He lifted it and tapped sharply on the door, waited some minutes then tapped again. No sounds of life reached his ears, and he could sense no movement from within.

Curse you, Krays. He traipsed to the back of the house, secreting himself in an out-of-sight corner. Then he translocated himself past the walls.

Nobody was inside the house, as he expected. Nor had anybody been home in a while. The house held that hush that descends after days of inactivity. Worse, there were signs that Avane's departure hadn't been planned.

So: both the hereditaries besides Llandry were taken. He'd made a guess at Krays's intentions for them, but the rogue Lokant's ruthlessness could still surprise him. What might the man do with two—or three—draykoni shape shifters?

And this one had a child, presumably taken along with its mother.

Leaving the house by the same means, he crossed to the neighbouring property and knocked on the door. It was quickly answered by a middle-aged woman who stared at Limbane suspiciously.

'I'm so sorry to bother you,' he said, adopting his most urbane manner. 'I'm looking for Avane Desandry, but I find she isn't at home. Do you know where she is?'

'Haven't you heard? Avane's gone. No one knows where.' She made to shut the door but he stopped her.

'When did she go?'

'Two days back.' She shoved him out of the way and slammed the door. He understood. When people fell to vanishing without trace, neighbours got wary.

He strolled back through the garden, thinking. Then, without bothering to conceal himself, he translocated back to the Library.

Andraly was waiting for him in his reading room. She read the look on his face and smirked.

'Life giving you trouble, Baney?'

'Specifically, *Krays* is giving me trouble. What do you want?'

'I thought you'd want to hear the news about your latest favourite, little Llandry Sanfaer.'

Limbane's heart suddenly contracted. Had Llandry been taken while he conducted his futile hunt for Vanse and Desandry?

'Tell me quickly.' He crossed to his cabinet and poured himself a drink. A strong one.

The tale Andraly related had nothing to do with Krays, he was relieved to learn. But it was bad enough. He sat, sipping his liquor, his free hand gripping his aching head.

'Right,' he sighed when she'd finished. He pondered her information silently for some minutes. Andraly, used to his reveries, did not interrupt him.

'Do you think that's the end of it?'

'Andraly shook her head. 'That red beast had the air of fanaticism about her. She'll be back, with more draykoni in tow I'd wager.'

'Knowing the draykoni nature as we do, I'm sure you're right.' He put his empty glass down and sank deeper into his chair, feeling weary and incredibly old.

Which he was.

'You think you've put a stop to a problem...'

Andraly rolled her eyes. 'I *know*. It's like humans just can't be sensible.'

Limbane narrowed his eyes at her. 'You were one, once.'

'Not a whole one. Only a bit.' She smiled winsomely at him. Andraly was, technically, a partial. She'd been born in Glour, many centuries ago, to a human mother. But her father had been a full Lokant, and she had taken after him in every way. As a Librarian, she wasn't far short of Limbane's own strength.

'What to do.' Limbane tapped his fingers against his knee, thinking.

'Why do anything? Leave them to it. We gave up on this Cluster long ago, and for good reason.'

'Can you mean that? This is *your* world we're speaking of, Andraly.'

She shrugged one shoulder. 'Not really. I happened to be born there, but that was a long time ago. I'm a Librarian.'

The woman was relentlessly cold. It made her a good Lokant, if he was honest with himself. It was him who was weak.

'What troubles me about all this is Krays. If not for him, I could agree with you: leave the humans and

337

draykoni to fight it out all over again, if they wish. But the fact that Krays is taking such an interest bothers me.'

Andraly considered that. 'Fair point,' she conceded.

'He's throwing a lot of resources into whatever he's doing. It certainly seems to have captured his full attention. That makes me nervous. He'll only work that hard on something that promises to put him ahead in some way.'

'Ahead? Of what?'

'Of *us*. And specifically, of me.'

Andraly grinned. 'You're really not that scary, Baney. I can't think what Krays is bothered about.'

'Thanks.'

'Jace agrees with you.'

'Oh? Why?'

'Same reason. He hates Krays even more than you do. I think he would like to eat his liver, if he got the chance.'

'I'll be happy to save him the liver.'

Andraly leaned forward. 'So we're taking him on?'

'Hm. It might come to that, yes. For a start, we're scaling up our efforts to find out what he's up to. Any word from our new agents yet?'

'Not yet. I checked in on them a while back. Her haughty ladyship said they had a man working on it.'

Limbane's brows lifted. 'You don't like Lady Glostrum?'

Andraly gave a cruel smile. 'She's competition.'

'Ah.' He dismissed that problem. Andraly could take care of her own personal business.

'All right. I'm loathe to do this, but I think we

have to consider it. Krays has taken two people I'm interested in. They're probably stashed at the pitiful little island he's audacious enough to call a Library. We're going to get them out.'

'Which two people?'

'Our other two draykoni hereditaries.'

Andraly whistled. 'Got there first, did he? That must gall you.'

'Somewhat,' Limbane snapped. 'Gather everyone, get everything. Krays may be an idiot but he keeps his "Library" well defended.'

Andraly jumped up, looking like a child with a present to open. 'Yes, sir!' She saluted, her face wreathed in a beaming smile, then left the room.

Limbane sighed. Somebody really needed to rein that woman in.

CHAPTER TWENTY-FIVE

Eva's one fear about using Recender was his cunning. If he thought he could delay her departure by taking longer over her request, he would certainly do it. She had stressed the importance of her schedule as strongly as she knew how; after that there was nothing to do but wait.

Two days passed and Recender produced nothing useful. Eva, chafing at the delay, spent many hours with the ambassador, intent on keeping him on track. But she was careful to reserve some hours to herself and Tren's company as well. Having little else to do, the two of them spent most of their time in their private parlour at Wirllen's best quality inn, both trying to read.

On the second day, Eva and Tren were sitting on opposite sides of their parlour, both pretending to read and neither feeling in any way comfortable, when Andraly appeared. Eva's mind had been more on Recender and the problem of Iro Byllant than on her book; these reflections were frustrating and unproductive and she welcomed the interruption.

Tren on the other hand took one look at Andraly and slouched deeper in his chair, holding his book in such a way as to cover most of his face. He did his best to look utterly absorbed in the book he wasn't reading.

Odd.

Andraly's manner towards Eva herself wasn't as it had formerly been either. Her smile held a cruel edge and even a hint of a challenge, one that Eva didn't understand. She dropped a mocking curtsey, grinning.

'Any news?'

'None.'

'None at all? How disappointing. But I can see you two are working hard.' She stared at Tren, who refused to look up.

'We got nothing out of our lead. Warehouse empty. But I have somebody on it.'

'Somebody?'

'A friend.'

'*Oh,* ' said Andraly with exaggerated relief. 'That's all right then.'

She vanished.

'What a pleasant visit.' Eva kept her eyes on Tren until he finally looked up, peeking at her over the top of his book.

'Is she gone?'

'Do you want to explain what that was about?'

He coughed. 'Er. Not really, no.'

'And you call me secretive.' She muttered the words under her breath, knowing Tren could hear them anyway. He contributed nothing but a crooked smile by way of answer.

'All right, keep your secrets.'

'You're becoming a grumpy old woman. It's being cooped up in here with me that does it. How about a walk?'

'*Old?* An *old* woman?'

'I, um, didn't mean that.'

She turned her back on him. 'We can't walk. Recender might send word.'

Tren heaved a sigh. 'In that case, do you have anything more interesting to read?'

'More interesting than what?'

Tren tossed her the book. The title read *A History of the Royal Family of Orstwych, 1652 - 1745.*

The book was six inches thick.

Eva sorted through the scanty pile of volumes that lay on the table beside her. 'I've got a trashy romance novel or a trashy romance novel.'

'Ooh. Are they steamy?'

Eva glanced with distaste at the pages of her own volume. 'This one is sadly lacking in racier content.'

'Ah.' Tren's face fell. 'Ah well. It's got to be better than the exploits of Old Orstwych's ninth monarch at boarding school.'

Eva threw him a book.

Sometime later, the very same green clothbound volume went sailing past her head to strike the wall.

'Not a success, I take it.' Eva spoke without looking up.

'I made it to page fifty-three. The heroine has wept on *every single page.* '

She laughed. 'Of course she has. It shows her extraordinary sensitivity.'

'And the hero? He falls for it *every time*. Like he has nothing better to do than comfort wailing women.' Tren groaned. 'Preserve me from ever being saddled with such a watering-pot, I beg you.'

Eva let her eyes grow big and mournful. 'You're saying you couldn't love a sensitive woman?'

'No!'

'Oh.' She spoke the word in a very small voice, her eyes filling with tears. 'I had no idea you were so— so—unfeeling.'

Tren glared at her, suspicion written all over his hard stare.

Eva's eyes spilled over. She let one tear roll slowly down her cheek.

Tren folded his arms. 'Come on. You're not really crying.'

'I never imagined you were so stone-hearted,' Eva sobbed, groping for a handkerchief.

'Stop it! This is silly. You're a strong woman. I doubt you've *really* cried since you were about ten.'

'*Silly?*' Eva managed a creditable wail and began to weep in earnest, using the handkerchief to hide her face.

'Okay, I'm sorry. I didn't mean silly.'

Eva cried on.

'Oh, for...' Tren left his chair and crossed to her, bending to peer into her face. 'Is this real? Because, uh, I didn't mean to upset you. And it does *look* real. Sounds it too. Eva? Are you all right?'

Eva collapsed into laughter. The giggling fit was of considerable length, leaving her short of breath when at last she stopped howling with mirth.

'So... *easy,*' she gasped.

Tren straightened with tremendous dignity. 'You,' he said with emphasis, 'are horrible.'

'I know.'

A tap came at the door. She was instantly alert, smoothing the laughter out of her face and mopping up the tears. Tren picked up the discarded volume and hid it as the door opened, revealing one of the downstairs servants.

'A note for my lady,' the man said with a respectful bow.

'Thank you.' Eva accepted it with trepidation, dreading the contents. Did Recender have information for her, or was this an announcement of failure? She felt as though her standing with the Lokants depended on success in this venture, leaving her terribly afraid of failure.

The servant bowed again and left, closing the door.

'Are you going to read it, or shall I?'

Eva scowled at him. Tearing open the seal, she quickly scanned the contents.

Ana Breyre, graduated from Ullarn's Academy of Summoning in 1897.

Griel Ruart, graduated from Ullarn's Academy of Sorcery in 1898.

The above married 1901. Disappeared from our records 1903.

No birth, education, marriage or death records exist for the one known as Iro Byllant. Conclude it is an assumed name.

One address on file. See me for more information.

- B. R.

She handed the note to Tren and took up pacing the parlour, torn between relief, elation and disappointment.

She wasn't vastly surprised to find that Byllant's was an assumed name, but it was a blow. He could be anybody. She also wanted to throttle Recender for sending her an incomplete report. *See me for more information?* Why couldn't he just send the address with the rest? Now she would have to waste more time on him.

On the other hand, it was something to have Ana and Griel's identities confirmed. She'd been right that they were Ullarni. That thought gave her a little glow of satisfaction: she always enjoyed being right.

Tren looked up from reading with a frown. 'So, back to Recender's?

'I suppose so.'

He coughed. 'Will this be another all-night visit?'

'*No.*'

Eva strode into Recender's drawing-room, struggling to keep her irritation hidden. The ambassador reclined in his silly dressing-gown once again, smoking something from a pipe. The stuff smelled disgusting.

'Brun,' she purred. 'You've done a fantastic job, but there seems to be a little bit missing in the note I received.'

The ambassador said nothing. He removed his pipe from his mouth and put it aside. Then he patted his lap.

Eva didn't move.

Recender's eyes glinted. 'I see.' He stood up and sauntered across the room, letting his hand brush across Eva's hip as he passed. She turned quickly, keeping a close eye on him.

He opened a locked cabinet. Eva tensed: here would be the final clue she needed, something she could use to chase down Byllant.

But the sound of pouring liquid reached her ears. Disbelieving, she edged around him until she could see the contents of the cabinet.

He had set out two small glasses and was filling them with dark red liquor.

'Brun. I came here for the address.'

'And you shall have it,' he said, turning. 'Later.' He offered her one of the glasses. When she didn't move to take it, he picked up her hand and curled her fingers around the stem. She was obliged to grip it before it fell to the floor.

Not that she cared for the fate of Recender's carpet, but the splash might get on her pale golden silk dress. And this was a marvellous gown.

'I don't have time for this. I believe I warned you that my stay would be brief.'

'Why so fleeting a visit, my lady?' Recender sipped from his own glass, moving to stand closer to her than she appreciated.

'The matter is urgent.'

'It can wait another hour, I'm sure.' His eyes ran up and down her body. 'Perhaps two?'

'Not another ten minutes.'

'Ah.' He set down his glass and slipped a hand into one of his pockets. Eva's heart rose with hope; perhaps this time he would give her what she had come for.

Instead he retrieved a small velvet box. Flipping open the top, he showed her the contents.

An enormous blood-red ruby ring nestled inside on sleek satin. The stone glimmered darkly in the low light of the drawing-room.

'What's that for?'

'It is for you to wear, my lady.' His hand suddenly lashed out and grabbed her wrist. Forcing her closer, he extracted the ring and shoved it onto her finger.

He specifically selected the left ring finger. As soon as his grip loosened, Eva yanked back her hand and tugged off the ring.

'This is nonsense. Give me the address.'

'You won't be leaving, my lady. At least not this evening.'

'Oh?' She kept her tone mild, but inside she was seething.

'Marry me. We make an excellent team; you've said it yourself.'

Eva swallowed. Perhaps she had overdone her mental persuasion just a little bit.

'A tempting offer, but one I'll have to refuse.' He was coming at her again; she backed away until she hit the drawing-room wall. She tried to sidle sideways but his arms shot out, blocking her escape. She took a deep breath. Here was a fine test of her new abilities; one she wasn't sure she was ready for.

'I am not nearly so much fun when I am *unwilling*,

my lord ambassador.' She met his eyes, willing him to let the matter go.

He struggled. His was a strong will, almost a match for her.

'I've never made a proposal of marriage before,' he hissed. 'Your refusal humiliates me.'

'Nobody needs to know, Brun.'

He thought about that. For a horrible instant she thought he would overthrow her efforts to influence him and proceed with his absurd proposal. Then what? Physically, he was much stronger. If he truly wished to detain her, he could do it.

To her relief he nodded, slowly, his black eyes registering regret.

'True. Though I wish you would reconsider.' He kissed her briefly. 'I've a lot to give. Power, wealth, status. Influence.' He began nibbling at her neck.

'I have all those things already.'

He groaned. 'An unbribable woman. Such a thing should be an impossibility.'

She had to grin at that.

'All right,' he sighed. 'Go, then.' He stepped back. Relieved, she put a few feet of space between them at once. The change from attractive to threatening had been unsettlingly swift in him.

'The address first, my lord.'

He rolled his eyes. 'Relentless female. Here. *Now* go away.'

She took the folded piece of paper he thrust at her, tucking it into the pocket of her skirt. With a curtsey and a mischievous smile for the ambassador, she followed his command most willingly.

As she pulled the door shut behind her, she heard

the distinctive sound of a glass object hitting the wall.

Tren was waiting for her downstairs. He took one look at her and was on his feet immediately.

'Trouble?'

She shook her head. 'All's well, but I think we should leave without delay.'

'Right.' He took her arm and led her to the front door. As they stepped through it, Eva felt a sudden conviction that Recender was watching their departure. But when she glanced behind her at the darkened staircase, she saw nobody.

Eva opened Recender's note with some trepidation. Two possibilities occurred to her worried mind. One, that the ambassador had been bluffing, and the paper would be blank. Or two, that the address written there would be for the same warehouse she and Tren had already explored, with so little success.

She was relieved to find that neither was the case. The property listed was almost on the opposite side of Wirllen, and it didn't look like it denoted any kind of warehouse. She sent a brief, private note of thanks to Brun. He might have been a pain in the rear in the end, but he had resolved her problem anyway.

She wondered briefly whether he had seriously wished to marry her. That thought made her snort with involuntary laughter. There were reasons the man had never proposed to anybody before. He was far too committed to his roving bachelor existence to consider such a thing. Aside from being absolutely unweddable.

What the experience did suggest, however, was

that she needed a little more practice at controlling her ability to influence the will of others. While there were dangers with applying too little willpower to the target, there were certainly dangers attached to applying too much also.

'What are you laughing at?' Tren craned his neck around, trying to see what was written on the paper.

'Nothing, really. Recender said some, uhm, amusing things. Here.' She handed the note across. Tren read it in silence.

'Well?' she said after a moment.

'Oh, great I suppose. But how are we planning to do this?'

She frowned. 'What do you mean?'

'We're not just going to march in there, are we? I mean, we aren't particularly well equipped to handle much of a threat between the two of us. Supposing we encounter anything dangerous.'

She shrugged. 'We'll be fine. Byllant appears to be an enterprising engineer, not a criminal.'

'Have to disagree there. He's distributing draykon bone technologies, which according to recent rulings by all the governments of the Seven—including Ullarn's—is illegal. Those draykon bones should have been turned in for research and safekeeping, not sold for profit.'

'You weren't concerned about that when we went to the warehouse.'

'Well, I should have been. I wasn't thinking too clearly at the time.'

'All right, I suppose you have a point. Do you have any ideas?'

'Er. I was thinking, maybe, we could hire

someone?'

'Someone who?'

'Someone with a nice, sizeable sharp object. Or possibly a firearm.'

She grinned at that. 'Lovely thinking, but I don't happen to know any of those. Do you?'

He shifted uncomfortably. 'I thought you might have some brilliant idea about where to go for that.'

'Not in Ullarn, I'm afraid. We'll be careful, all right? Anyway, we are not entirely defenceless. We have a quick and oh-so-handy escape route.' She pointed to herself.

Tren merely grunted, unimpressed.

Eva gave the instructions to her hired coachman and allowed herself to be handed into the carriage by Tren.

'It'll be a bit of a drive,' she said, settling back against the cushions. 'Perfect opportunity for a nap.' With that, she closed her eyes.

She heard Tren sigh as he slumped into the seat opposite her.

When the carriage finally pulled up, Eva's first thought was that they'd been brought to the wrong place.

The street in which they stopped was obviously a residential area. The houses were small, even cramped; many of them were only one-storey. She couldn't imagine there were more than three or four rooms inside.

Tren shrugged at her questioning look. 'Might be Byllant's home address?'

'True. I suppose I just assumed that it would be a factory or an office.' She shook out her crumpled skirts, glancing up and down the street. It was late, already well into the middle of the evening, and the street was quiet. 'How do you suppose we should proceed?'

'Knocking on the door is usually considered a good start.' Tren shrugged back into his jacket, his long fingers making short work of the buttons.

'Just knock on the door?'

'Why not? We're planning to ask him some questions, I thought, not arrest him. And the encounter's more likely to be civilised if we start by being polite.'

'All right.' She took the arm that he offered and they crossed the street. All the shutters in Byllant's house were closed, and no gleam of light suggested the presence of an inhabitant.

After all the trouble it had taken to find this place, it would be terribly inconvenient if the man wasn't even home.

A light tap on the door brought no answer. She knocked again, more loudly. Nothing.

'Let's try the back,' said Tren. Eva followed him down the side of the house to the small walled yard at the back. To her extreme distaste, Byllant's garden was full of mud.

'Next time, remind me to change my gown first.'

Tren chuckled. 'I thought we were in a terrible hurry?'

'That may be true,' she said with dignity, 'but there is very little in this world that is worth the sacrifice of a favourite gown.'

'Your faithful factotum ought to have been prepared for that.'

'Yes, he should have been. Why weren't you, Tren?'

He swept her a deep bow of apology. 'I can only beg your forgiveness, my lady. I am unworthy.'

She sniffed. 'Amends to be made later. You can do the knocking this time.'

Tren obliged, pounding on the door loudly enough to wake the dead.

'That might have been excessive.'

'One merely does as her ladyship commands.'

Nothing moved within. Eva noticed Tren eyeing the door speculatively.

'Forget it. You are not kicking it in.'

'Why not?'

'Because you'd bring the whole neighbourhood down on us.'

'Then I cede the floor to your ladyship. Any other ideas?'

'One. Keep close to me.' She reached out to find Tren's arm in the darkness. Instead of taking his wrist, she took his hand and laced her fingers through his.

'Er, what—'

She was getting faster at translocation. Within seconds they stood on the other side of the little house's rear door.

Tren stared at her. 'I still think that's creepy.'

'Quiet.' She stood for a moment, listening. If Byllant was home, he was a master at keeping silent.

Or maybe he was just sleeping.

'We're exploring,' she said in a low voice. 'Stay close.'

'I can't go anywhere anyway.' On her giving him a questioning look he added, 'You still have hold of my hand.'

'So I do.' She quickly disentangled her fingers from his.

'That wasn't an invitation to go away.'

'Shhh.' Some slight sound had reached her ears. From Tren's sudden tension she guessed he'd heard it too. Maybe somebody was home after all.

A light-globe went on in the next room.

'Who's there?' The voice was deep and rich, definitely male.

'Mr Byllant?' Eva made to step forward, but Tren put out an arm to hold her back. He took the lead, advancing warily into the small living room.

A tall figure stood in the middle of the room with the light at his back, leaving him largely in shadow. He wore dark clothes to help that effect along, and his face was partially covered.

'Who are you?' he demanded.

'No danger to you,' she assured him. 'At least, not yet. We must ask you some questions.'

'How did you get in?'

'We knocked. When there was no reply, we took a more direct method.' The man had made no move to attack; Eva stepped out from behind Tren, gently pushing his arm out of her way.

Byllant's eyes were black in the darkness and shadowed, but she could see that he studied her. His gaze was fixed on her hair. Then he stepped into the light, pushing back the scarf that hid his features. He had Darklander-pale skin, hazel eyes and chestnut hair tied back. His smile was confident and charming.

Eva knew that face. Last time she'd seen him he had been in a state of very ill health, his face wan and dark shadows marking his skin. But it was unmistakeably the same man.

'*Devary Kant?*'

Tren looked sharply at her. 'What? You know him?'

'We've met, once. At Ynara Sanfaer's house.' Eva stared at Yna's friend, completely confused. 'Are you Byllant?'

'I don't know who you mean,' Devary replied with another of his charming smiles. 'Perhaps you've come to the wrong place?'

'I doubt that. Getting Byllant's address wasn't easy. Finding *you* here, Mr Kant, is a pretty big coincidence, don't you think?'

'Coincidences happen sometimes.'

Eva shook her head. She didn't want to believe that a friend of Yna's would betray her this way, but Kant's protests made no sense. How could he possibly just *happen* to be here, in a house registered to Byllant?

'I'm sorry you've come all this way for nothing,' Kant continued. 'Can I offer you some refreshment before you leave?'

Eva's brow contracted. She hadn't had much conversation with Devary Kant before, but she remembered that he spoke with a hint of a Nimdren accent. It had been attractive. He was speaking her own language now, but without any trace of Nimdren inflection. Had he merely adopted the accent before, or was he disguising it now? If anything, his new intonation was Ullarni.

She nudged Rikbeek with her thoughts, surreptitiously shaking him out of the folds of her skirt. Silently, ignoring his protests, she directed his attention towards the man who claimed to be Devary Kant. The gwaystrel applied his unique senses to the task, building an image of the man that had nothing to do with his physical appearance.

'Thanks, but we can't stay,' she said in the meantime, praying that Devary wouldn't notice the black-winged gwaystrel in the darkness. 'Perhaps you can help us, though. Have you ever heard the name Iro Byllant before?'

She wanted him to speak again, but he merely shook his head.

'Never? He isn't a neighbour, perhaps, or a previous tenant of this property?'

'I'm so sorry to disappoint you, but I've never heard of him. Now, if we've finished?' He moved towards the door.

Eva sucked in a breath. She knew that voice. Rich and mellow, like honey. Where had she heard it?

Rikbeek was filling in a new image of the man. Taller than he appeared, bigger across the shoulders, his nose, ears and hands a different shape... his hair pale.

Pale. The words of the Lawch & Son clerk came back to her. *Your hair colour, ma'am.*

Tren figured it out first. 'I don't know a Devary Kant, but you sound a lot like Griel Ruart to me.'

Griel! Of course. His was a distinctive voice, and in her mind's eye she recognised the partial image Rikbeek was building. This was Ana's sorcerer husband, no doubt about it. But that made no sense.

Last time she had seen him, he'd almost been bitten in two by the draykon she now knew as Pensould. His wife had taken his corpse away, but she would never have expected that he could be healed. Not even by Lokants.

Kant's face twisted in disgust. 'I can never get the voices right.' The handsome face of Devary Kant faded, revealing the flatter features, broader figure and white hair of Griel Ruart.

'So. You two keep turning up. You were not much use last time. What do you want now?'

Eva shook her head in disbelief. '*Last* time, you were somewhat more polite. How are you not dead?'

'That's none of your business. Are you here from *him*? Perhaps you were working for him from the beginning.' Griel's manner was hostile, his posture tense, ready to attack. Eva recognised fear in his eyes.

'Him? You mean Krays, I suppose.'

The fear sharpened. 'Then you are working for him. What do you want?'

Eva decided not to undeceive him just yet. 'You remember the name of Lawch & Son, I imagine?'

'What?'

'A light-globe manufacturer in Orstwych. You supplied them with a new design utilising draykon bone.'

Griel lifted his chin, defiant. 'And?'

'By that I conclude that you are indeed Iro Byllant. Lawch & Son aren't your only customers, are they?'

He laughed. 'Course not. I have dozens of designs out there. It's lucrative.'

Tren cut in. 'Where are you getting the bone?'

'Ah, well. Somewhere I shouldn't. Hence my

dismay at finding a white-hair at my door. Though I can't figure out what your part in all this is. Krays doesn't usually pair partials with humans.'

'We're not part of Krays's organisation.'

'Is that the truth?'

'If we were sent by Krays, I've a feeling we wouldn't be standing here holding a civilised conversation with you.'

'Horribly true.' Some of the tension went out of the sorcerer's body, and the suspicion in his face relaxed a little. 'But then, what are you here for?'

Eva smiled. 'Actually we're trying to find out what Krays is up to.'

His head tilted. 'Why?'

She exchanged a brief look with Tren. How much to tell him? She read caution in his eyes and she silently agreed. Best to keep it simple.

'You remember Llandry Sanfaer,' she replied. 'Krays has been after her. We want to know why.'

'Oh, he would be.' He stepped closer suddenly, his dark eyes intense. 'Make sure he *never* finds her.'

'We're doing our best.' She took a breath and gambled, risking everything on the pure hatred she read in Griel's eyes when Krays was mentioned. 'Can you help us? What can you tell us about him?'

Griel said nothing. He turned and paced away to the other side of the room, apparently thinking. Her eyes narrowed as she watched him. She saw what Ocherly had meant: his movement was off in some subtle way. Not as if he was injured, exactly, just not quite natural.

'You want to know what he's up to? I'll show you.' Griel stood before them again. His hand moved, fast;

he held a long knife, the blade glinting in the half-light.

Tren gave a startled cry and pulled her back, out of reach of the weapon. But Griel made no move to threaten either of them. He pulled off his heavy black coat and rolled up one sleeve of his dark shirt.

The knife slashed downwards. A long wound opened in his arm, the flesh cleaved to the bone.

'What—*what*—' She could only gasp the word, too shocked to think clearly.

'Here,' Griel said through gritted teeth, holding out his bleeding limb. The light-globe brightened, drifting down to hover just over the man's arm.

Eva steeled herself and looked closer, expecting to see the white gleam of bone.

A flash of silvered indigo caught her eye instead.

Tren uttered a choked curse. 'Is that... that can't be.'

'Draykon bone? That's exactly what it is. I almost lost this arm. I *did* lose it. When I woke up, I felt changed. *Wrong*. This arm, my leg—' he slapped his left leg as he spoke '—some of my ribs, my hand. All rebuilt. My bones replaced, my flesh regrown... I'm part of a wider programme.'

Eva swallowed. 'What programme?'

'Krays is looking for the limits of the draykon bone's advantages. So far he hasn't found any. He's building devices, crossing technology with magic, creating terrifyingly powerful things. And he's playing with biology, building animals and *humans* with machine parts, with draykon parts. Like he's trying to build his own hybrids. The next step must be to combine everything. Imagine machines with all the biological advantages of the strongest animals and the cleverest humans, and wielding draykon magic. Krays did this to me to find out if it would *take*. Whether an intelligent being could be made to function this way.'

A shudder ran down Eva's back as she listened. What kind of madness was this?

'Why did he do that to you?' she asked. 'Weren't you one of his top agents?'

'*Was,*' Griel spat. 'Not that he would feel restrained by that if it suited his purposes, but for me this is a punishment. I—we—disobeyed him. If I'd known what the price would be...'

'Is that why you're telling us this?'

Griel looked at her with so much pain that she felt her heart contract. She was actually feeling *sorry* for him. She had to remind herself that this man was responsible for the deaths of several innocent Glour citizens, including her closest friend and Tren's.

'You've no idea what it's like, the isolation. Working for a man like Krays, with no hope of help, not even any companionship. He's made sure of that. It's part of my punishment.'

Eva wondered how Krays had contrived to keep Ana away from her husband, but she didn't dare ask about that.

'Why the light-globes?' she asked instead. 'And the rest?'

'I get my revenge as I can,' he replied. 'I've been careful, finding hidden ways of getting my devices out. Frittering away his hard-won draykon bone. Someday I may be rich enough to find a way out of this slavery.'

Eva sighed inwardly. Much as she wanted to, she

couldn't find it in herself to condemn him for that. She probably would have done the same in his position.

'Griel,' she said, trying to ignore the fact that his arm was still pouring blood on the floor. He didn't seem to notice or care about it himself. 'Why is Krays doing all of this? What's the purpose of it?'

Griel shrugged. 'Just because he can? I don't know. He doesn't exactly share his private thoughts with me. Didn't even before I was disgraced. But you don't build super-machines for any good purpose, and that man—if he is a man—hasn't a decent bone in his body. Whatever he's planning, it's bad news.'

CHAPTER TWENTY-SIX

Krays was undoubtedly dangerous.

It was his inventiveness that made him formidable. Lokant he may be, but his mind worked in some unique ways. Long ago, before he'd defected from the Library, he had been one of its most brilliant inventors.

But Krays could also be delightfully, conveniently predictable. Wandering through the hallways of the Sulayn Phay Library, Limbane enjoyed a pleasing glow of superiority. As an architect, the rogue Lokant wholly lacked imagination. When Krays had founded his splinter group, he'd made no secret of the fact that he intended it to rival Limbane's Library someday. To that end, he had slavishly imitated almost every feature of the original design, albeit on a smaller scale.

Krays had deviated only in extending the levels below the book rooms and turning the lower halls into a kind of prison complex. His methods always had been more direct than Limbane's.

It did make infiltration so gloriously easy. Especially since his one attempt at misdirection was so pitiful. Like Limbane's Library, Sulayn Phay was built on an island. The smaller one had the advantage of being more easily moved and more easily concealed; it rarely stayed in the same place for very long.

But Limbane never had any difficulty locating his rival's headquarters. He'd found Krays's island floating a few miles off the coast of Ullarn, concealed within a shroud of mist. Attractive, but ineffectual.

Krays would have to work harder to outwit him.

Limbane's good feelings lasted right up until he reached the outer door of Krays's little prison project. Patrolling the corridor beyond it was something... other.

Five full Lokants were assembled behind Limbane, brought to deal with just these sorts of problems. Krays was, after all, predictable. He always left toys in the same places: machines, quite sophisticated ones, stationed to keep people like Limbane out.

And Limbane's teams always succeeded in disabling them. It was a game that had gone on for some centuries.

Until now, at least. Limbane inspected the ambulatory device that guarded the door today, using both his eyes and his mental senses to ascertain the nature of the thing. It wasn't as large as some of Krays's earlier creations: this one stood only as high as Limbane's waist. Previous machines had usually been fully robotic, equipped with knife-blades, guns and shields, that type of thing.

This one was undoubtedly a work of machinery, but it looked like an animal. If it resembled any particular beast in nature, it was the whurthag: it featured the same night-black colour, though its hide was not strictly biological in substance. It had the same lean, steel-muscled build and heavy jaws. Those jaws featured metal teeth—of an alloy stronger than the original calcium-built fangs might have been—and claws of similar construction.

Despite these mechanical curiosities, there was undoubtedly biological matter inside the thing. That frame looked so convincing because it was built over real muscle.

Worse, while the thing lacked a consciousness it definitely possessed some kind of awareness. Not a manufactured one, with limitations frequently outnumbering the strengths. It was alert for intruders. It knew what it was expected to do if it encountered any. It had desires, of a sort.

The thing had some few of the advantages of a real whurthag, but being still essentially a construct it was considerably more biddable. This one was wholly under Krays's control.

'What in the name of...' That soft exclamation came from behind him; at least one of his Lokants was as shocked as he.

'All right, let's deal with it,' Limbane said. Time enough later to speculate about how or why Krays had done it. 'Egren, Rael—take its measure. I want to know everything about it, quick as you can. Yora, Melle—you're going to need to modify those tools. Iwa, you're with me. I need you to immobilise its consciousness, such as it is, so I can reverse its instructions.' The whurthag-thing had finished its patrol at the other end of the long corridor; now it prowled back towards them. Horror, for there was definitely some kind of mind at work behind those icy glass eyes; Limbane could feel it assessing them.

Categorising them as a threat, the whurthag-machine threw itself at the door. A sturdy construction of metal it might be, but it shook hard under the impact of that heavy body.

'Yes. Hmm. I wouldn't get too close to the door.'

His team worked quickly and efficiently to execute the tasks they'd been given. Iwa moved up beside Limbane, getting as close to the door and those thrashing jaws as she dared. Her disciplined mind seized the whurthag-thing's peculiar awareness and grappled with it, forcing it into submission. The approach she took was direct: there was no room for subtlety, persuasion of any kind. The creature may be aware, but it lacked the mental flexibility for friendship.

It did possess considerable bite, however. It fought Iwa's efforts violently. Limbane perceived that Krays had instilled in it an instinctive fear of any mental intrusions save his own.

He heard the low voices of Egren and Rael behind him, speaking their observations and findings to the voice recorder.

'...height approximately four spans at the shoulder. Body weight estimated at three hundred to three hundred-twenty standard measures. Creature is of mixed biological and mechanical construction: jaws, teeth and claws are of a steel-tracium alloy; hide of an unknown substance but signs suggest it is to some

CHARLOTTE E. ENGLISH

extent biological in nature...'

Iwa was finished. The whurthag's struggles had ceased; it waited, quiescent, for Limbane's interference.

'Take your time,' Iwa said placidly. 'I've got it.'

He nodded. Reaching out to the beast, he was momentarily distracted by the sheer strangeness of it. Mechanical creations he could handle, and biological constructs were equally familiar to him. But this kind of hybrid was virtually unique in his experience. There was only one other occasion when he had come across something similar, and Krays had not been involved in that.

He shook the thought away. For the moment, to work. Browsing through the beast's flickering impressions—not accurate to call them thoughts—he found the source of Krays's control over the beast. He had installed himself as the whurthag's pack leader, to be obeyed without question.

It was the work of a mere few minutes to overwrite Krays's image with his own. Limbane withdrew with a satisfied smile. He was now this beast-machine's unquestioned superior.

'All right, we're ready to approach. Egren, Rael, are you finished with your assessment? You'll get chance to create a more detailed profile later.'

'Yes, Lokantor,' was the reply.

'Excellent. Yora, Melle. Get the door open, then deactivate the thing, but carefully. I want it taken back with us, in a study-worthy state. Iwa, keep back for now.'

Limbane waited, humming a soft tune, as Yora and Melle worked at the door. Krays may have pulled a surprise or two this time, but he was still essentially no match for the Library.

'Door's open, Lokantor.' Yora was one of his youngest Lokants, but that didn't prevent her from being one of his best engineers and inventors.

'Good work! Now then. Iwa, you're with me. Advance, but take some care. If there are more, it's down to us to take control of them as quickly as possible. Egren, Rael. Are you armed?'

Both of them pulled their guns and held them at the ready.

'Good. You're in first. You see any more of these, you shoot. I don't know if they can be killed, but perhaps they can be maimed. The goal is to find Avane and Orillin as quickly as possible and get out. All clear?'

A chorus of 'Yes, Lokantor,' followed his question and he nodded.

'All right, go ahead.'

Egren and Rael swung the door open and advanced, approaching the whurthag-machine warily. The thing stood quiet; it hadn't moved for several minutes. Nonetheless its gleaming metal teeth and powerful body were thoroughly intimidating.

Four Lokants filed past the creature and it didn't move. Yora and Melle fell to work disabling the thing as the others fanned out to check the prison cells that lined up along the corridor.

'Empty,' came three voices in report. Limbane glanced through the tiny window of a fourth cell and found it empty too.

'And onward,' Limbane ordered.

A scream of pain slashed the air from behind him.

Whirling, he saw the whurthag-machine had moved; its wicked teeth were sunk in Melle's side. The older woman was down, her blood rapidly spreading across the floor.

'Back-up intelligence system,' she panted. 'On a timer. Activated when you overrode previous instructions.'

Limbane cursed. Krays was a devious bastard. How like him to put a timer on the thing; it would strike just when Limbane's team thought they had vanquished it.

Egren and Rael had come running back at the sound of Melle's scream.

'Stand back, Yora,' came Rael's terse voice. He fired. The sound reverberated around the cold and empty corridor, sending up a terrific echo.

The bullet bounced harmlessly off the whurthag-thing's hide.

Egren dropped her gun and drew a knife. Rushing the creature, she stabbed repeatedly, targeting those areas that would be soft points on any normal beast. Her blade glanced off its glassy eyes and clattered uselessly against its metallic jaws. She achieved better when she attacked its hide; the knife penetrated, but poorly, sinking in only an inch or so. She tried to pull it out for a second strike, and couldn't. The knife stuck in the strange black material.

'Hammer,' Rael said grimly. He took one from his belt, a tool designed for engineering rather than combat. But when he swung it at the creature, he succeeded in raising a howl of pain. That muscle mass was vulnerable, then.

Egren grabbed her own hammer and joined Rael,

the two of them taking it in turns to strike while the other danced out of reach of the thing's attacks. The beast whirled in confusion, distracted by each new strike. It may be aware, but it certainly wasn't intelligent. Each time the Lokants hit, the beast howled again.

Hurry it up, Limbane thought in irritation. The amount of noise they were making was sure to attract some unwanted attention soon.

At last the creature gave a final whimper of pain and collapsed, its legs twisted beyond use. It tried to pull itself along the floor, still intent on rending Rael and Egren for their offences, but its body was too broken.

Sounds from further down the corridor attracted Limbane's attention. Was that a child crying?

'Right. Yora, pull yourself together. I'm going to need you. Egren, get Melle back to the Library and get her entered for healing. Rael, keep that hammer handy. Let's go.'

He set off in search of the childish cries, trusting to his team's loyalty to bring them after him as necessary. Eight doors down he stopped, listening. The child had been quieted, but it whimpered still in the room beyond.

'Yora.'

The woman nodded stiffly. Her face was pale with shock and her hands covered in Melle's blood, but she obeyed him, setting to work on the complicated door mechanism.

It wasn't an ordinary kind of lock, he could see that for himself.

'It's a biolock, sir, new kind. I'm going to have to

reprogramme it.'

'Move it along, Yora,' he said testily. Gunfire interrupted him as bullets ricocheted off the walls, coming from the far end of the corridor. He and Rael dived to the floor, the latter letting out a grunt of pain.

'Are you hit?'

'In the leg,' Rael replied. 'Bastards.' Then his gun was in his hands and he returned fire. A dying cry reached Limbane's ears: Rael had found his target.

One foe down. How many more would there be?

'*Yora!* '

'Almost there, sir,' the girl panted. Then the lock clicked open. Limbane didn't wait to congratulate her. He flung himself into the cell, dragging Rael and Iwa behind him.

A black-haired woman in her thirties huddled at the far end of the room, her arms wrapped protectively around a child of perhaps two years old. Her eyes were frightened; they widened further when she saw him.

'You're like *him,* ' she said. 'Another one. What do you want with us now?'

Limbane scowled. He and Krays looked *nothing* alike. 'Avane Desandry?'

She nodded.

'Get up. We're taking you out of here.'

The woman actually tried to back away, despite the obvious lack of anywhere to go.

Limbane's temper snapped.

'Do you want to be helped or not? I've a woman down and another shot; my team's down to three and we've another prisoner still to find. There isn't time for this. You have five seconds to make up your mind.'

Avane hesitated.

'Three seconds,' he said. 'Two.' Rael's leg was bleeding profusely. It would be a miracle if the man could walk.

'All right,' she said, standing up slowly.

'*Move,*' he bellowed.

She moved.

Devary was lying on his bed, again. He was thinking, daydreaming, anything it was reasonable to call this state of near insensibility. He'd lain in a half-dream for an indeterminate time, waiting with steadily decreasing hopes for some event to break up the monotony of these none-days.

Nothing had come. He'd given up trying to mark the passage of time; nothing changed in here. It was as if time had nothing to do with the place at all. His attempts to break himself free had failed one and all. This place was shrouded, muffled in some dampening enchantment and not a chink could he now find in that enclosing force. Opening a gate was out of the question: it was like trying to rip a hole in granite. And the door had some kind of lock that he couldn't pick, no matter how hard he tried.

Nobody ever came. Sometimes he would sleep; while he was unconscious food and water would appear, by some means he couldn't detect. For a while he had mercilessly denied himself sleep, determined to see and speak to the person who delivered the food. All he had achieved was starvation as well as sleep deprivation. Nobody ever came.

So, at last, he'd given up, letting himself fall out of consciousness as his only defence against the stupefying boredom.

When the gunshot came, the incredible volume of the sound jolted him out of his stupor so suddenly that he feared his heart would fail him. The excitable organ skipped a beat or two, then settled, and he breathed again.

He pushed himself off the bed and stood up. For some moments his head swam with dizziness as his long-inactive body swayed, his vision blurred. He moved closer to the door and waited.

The sound was not repeated for some time. He was about to give up, putting the interruption down as a product of his own bored mind, when several loud gunshots fired in a burst. Hope surged in his heart: gunfire proved the presence of intruders, and based on the logic of enemies of one's enemies those intruders might prove to be his friends.

He heard cries of pain and another couple of shots. His door bore only a tiny piece of glass, almost too high for him to see out of. He pressed his face to this miniature window but he could see nothing but the usual, merely a glimpse of the door opposite to him. He wished he could tell who was winning the conflict; had that dying cry been one of his kidnappers or their attackers?

When everything fell silent once again, he began to worry. He certainly could not be rescued if nobody knew that he was here. He began banging on the door and calling out, kicking with his feet, creating as much noise as he could.

Nothing happened. No further sounds reached him. His heart sank; dullness closed in on his fogged brain once more. Whoever they were, they weren't coming for him.

But then: footsteps. A voice, actual words spoken. 'Is this him?'

A face appeared briefly at the glass.

'No. Too old. Next one.'

The face disappeared. Then another was pressed against his window, somebody white-haired.

'There's someone in here?' a different voice said. Then came a hissed intake of breath. 'I know this person.'

'We breaking him out, sir?' That was the first voice again, young and female.

'Be quick about it,' said the man. Devary frowned. If he imagined those words spoken in gentler tones and decorated with somewhat more in the way of courtesy, then he knew the speaker.

It sounded very much like the strange fellow he'd met at the university. He'd last seen the man in Indren's private reading room. He had known about the tracer Devary wore; he'd even indicated that he might be able to help him.

Hope flared anew. Devary stepped back, moving out of the path of the door. He waited, unconsciously holding his breath as the unseen girl worked on the other side of it. His straining ears caught every slight scraping sound as she worked. It seemed to take forever.

At length the door swung inwards. He could almost have cried with relief.

'Thank you,' he said, filling the word with all the

sincere gratitude he hadn't time to express at length.

The girl smiled at him. She was a slight figure, wearing her white hair closely braided. She was dressed in loose overalls. Shockingly, her clothes and hands were splashed with blood.

Beside her stood the man who'd spoken. It was indeed Limbane, though his formerly mild face was taut with tension and irritation. He made an impatient gesture at Devary, who hastened to obey.

'Keep up,' Limbane said tersely. 'We've three more cells to check.'

Devary fell into step behind Limbane's group as they surged down the dim hallway outside his cell. There was another white-haired woman; she barely glanced at him and said nothing. A second man, apparently younger than Limbane, had no attention to spare for the newest addition to their group. He was limping badly, his leg pouring blood.

Behind all walked a woman nearer his own age, raven-haired and almost incandescent with fear. In her arms she carried a tiny little boy.

Devary instantly gave up trying to decipher this curious collection of people. He moved instead to the side of the limping man. The fellow was obviously suffering great pain, but he clutched a gun in both hands, aiming it unwaveringly down the hallway ahead of them.

'Can I help?' Devary offered.

The man's only response was to draw another weapon from a holster on his belt. It was a mere pistol, but Devary felt better having it in his hands.

'Shoot when I say,' the man gritted.

Ahead of them, Limbane and the blood-stained

girl were checking the final few doors. The corridor terminated in a dead end; Limbane reached it with a snarl of frustration.

'*Where's the boy?*' He paced back a few steps. 'There must be more cells.'

The girl shook her head. 'Not on the layout plan, sir.'

'Then where in the—'

'Who are we looking for?' Measured footsteps approached from behind Devary. He whirled round, heart thumping. That voice was too familiar.

Krays stood blocking the exit.

Limbane strode past Devary, shouldering him out of the way. 'Krays,' he said coldly. 'You're a devious bastard, you know that?'

Krays looked annoyed. 'How in the blazes did you find us this time?'

Limbane chuckled. 'Two can play the tracer game, Kraysie.'

'You've killed a couple of my men.'

'You've shot two of mine, possibly killed one,' Limbane replied with a shrug. 'We're even.'

Krays's cold eyes flicked to the dark-haired woman and her child, then moved to Devary. 'Rescue party? I can't imagine what kind of an interest would be sufficient to get *you* personally involved, Limbane.'

'The fact that you find these people so very interesting is enough for me, Kraysie. Though I'm puzzled. What have you done with the other one?'

'What other one?'

Devary thought Limbane would say something else, but instead his fist lashed out and connected with Krays's face. The other man crumpled, his expression a picture of surprise.

'Unusually direct, but effective,' murmured one of the women.

'Lacked finesse, sir,' panted the wounded man.

'Grab him,' Limbane directed. But Krays wasn't entirely unconscious. As Limbane's team went to secure him, he muttered something and vanished.

'Crap,' said the wounded man.

Limbane shrugged. 'He's slippery. Right, we're out of time. We'll have to come back for the boy. For now, let's get out of here.'

CHAPTER TWENTY-SEVEN

Watching Griel heal his own arm was almost as chilling as watching him slash it open in the first place. He had all the ability that Eva lacked, conducting the operation with the careless lack of concern that came with supreme confidence. He gritted his teeth as his muscles slowly knitted themselves closed and the torn edges of his skin merged into a whole once more. It took some time, and by the end of it Griel sagged in his chair, exhausted.

He noticed Eva's close scrutiny. He looked again at her white hair, the same as his own. Questions formed in his eyes, but he didn't speak them. He remained grimly silent.

Eva wasn't willing to let him close up, not yet. They needed to know more.

'How long has this been going on?'

No answer.

'If you weren't meant to be waking the draykon,

what were you supposed to be doing?'

Still nothing. Griel had descended into a morose, stubborn silence from which he refused to rouse himself.

Eva spoke more gently. 'Griel, please. There are some very wrong things occurring and I need more information in order to make them right.'

He looked up at that. 'You? What can you do against Krays's organisation?'

'Not just us. We have help.'

'Oh?' Griel straightened, the suspicious look back in his eyes.

'I'll gladly share, but first I need more from you.'

Griel let out a sigh. 'We were tasked with retrieving all the bone from the Glinnery source. It was to be conveyed to Krays's factory, here.'

Tren interrupted him. 'Here? In this city?'

Griel shook his head. 'Not in Wirllen. Out in the sticks. Krays spent most of his time at the factory, I believe. He was building his machines already, and he thought that the bone could revolutionise the design. In that, he was right.

'My wife disliked being kept on the edges of Krays's project. She had other ideas and resented being used as a lackey. She conceived a different plan. I knew it couldn't end well, but what could I do? She was always so headstrong. I supported her in it because I had no other option. I certainly couldn't betray her to Krays.

'I was right, of course. Even with your fortuitous arrival and interference, nothing could dissuade or stop her. Nothing could control that draykon, either. I took the creature's bite for her. When I woke up, I was like this.' His face darkened. 'The first thing Krays told me was that my wife was dead. She was killed for her complete betrayal of her orders. And me, I was put in charge of a new workshop. It's been difficult, finding ways to undermine that bastard, but I've done it. I give him false reports on the workshop's useage of the bone, and I find unobtrusive ways to distribute the surplus.' He smiled savagely. 'It's pitiful, as rebellion goes, but it feels good.'

Eva mulled that over. 'This workshop. Where was it? Wynn Street, Wirllen South?'

Griel's brows rose. 'How did you... oh, the light-globe manufactory. Yes, that was the last one. They're only kept open for a moon or so, then they're moved to new sites. I suppose he's afraid of prying eyes making inconvenient discoveries.'

'But you aren't.'

Griel gave a half-smile. 'Certainly not. I kept hoping somebody would investigate; I didn't dare directly contact the authorities but I spread the addresses around. Can't say I expected it to be you who would find us, though.'

'You don't know where he's getting the bone from?'

Griel shrugged. 'He's pulling it out of the Off-Worlds but I don't know how he's finding it. I might guess he's using someone like Llandry Sanfaer—someone who's sensitive to the stuff. Or maybe he's invented something to do the same job by now.'

Eva made a decision. 'I think you should come with us, Griel. Your knowledge will be useful.'

He laughed. 'Where to? There's nowhere I can go

that he won't find me.'

'There's one place.'

He shook his head, vehement. 'No. I'm marked; tracered, they call it. Everywhere I go, he can find me. He can be upon me in seconds.'

Eva met his gaze and held it, applying a touch of her will to force him to consent. She didn't know if it would work on a fellow partial, but it was worth the attempt.

'Please, Griel. Trust us. There's someone you ought to meet, someone who can help. And you're wrong about Ana. Krays lied to you.'

His reaction was unexpected. He paled abruptly, staring at her as if he'd never seen her before.

'You've been trained. You're one of *them*, aren't you? All along, you've been leading me to betray myself. I should've known.' He was on his feet, the knife back in his hand.

'*No*, Griel. I've been trained, but not by Krays. Please, calm down.'

Her efforts were useless. Fear and paranoia had taken him; he was losing rationality, becoming a creature of blind instinct. The knife he carried glinted wickedly in the low light.

'Eva, forget it. We need to get out of here.' Tren took hold of her arm.

She made one last effort to reach him. 'Your wife is alive. She was seen recently, by—'

Griel snarled with pure rage and lunged for her. The knife flashed down; a body barrelled into hers, knocking her to the floor. She waited, breathless, for the pain to start, but nothing happened.

Heavy steps lumbered past her as Griel ran for the

door. She watched him go, mildly surprised. Why didn't he translocate? But he was a powerful healer; perhaps, like her, he lacked the full spectrum of abilities and hadn't mastered the PsiMap. That certainly explained his dedicated use of stationary gates last time they had encountered him.

Her reflections were interrupted by a groan from Tren. It was his body that had knocked her down, and he still lay on top of her.

'Thank you for that, Tren, but you're heavy,' she managed, gasping for breath under his weight. 'Please. Get off.'

He didn't move, so she gave him an unceremonious shove. He toppled onto the ground and lay still.

'Tren?'

'You couldn't possibly be—a bit more—*gentle* with me, I suppose?' Tren's speech was strained and punctuated with pained gasps. A stab of fear lanced through her, and she crawled to his side.

'What did you do... oh, no.' Griel had aimed—if such a wild slash could have a specific target—at Eva's middle. Tren had taken it instead, high on his side. An ugly gash was laid open in his flesh; his shirt was soaking through with blood.

'You *idiot.* '

'Wha...? I save your life and you—*insult* me?'

'Yes,' she said brutally. 'You're the most impossible, absurd, air-brained *idiot* of my acquaintance.' Her hands were busy as she spoke; she'd taken a cushion from a nearby chair and was pressing it into the wound, trying to stem the flow of blood.

'Sorry,' Tren replied weakly.

'What did you do that for?' Tears blurred her vision. She blinked them back ferociously. Now was no time to be feeble.

'Stupid question isn't it? That—hurts, by the way.'

'I know it hurts, dolt. Stay still. I'm going to heal you.'

'No you aren't.'

'Wha—I'm not?'

He shook his head minutely. 'You're rubbish at healing, remember?'

She stiffened at that. '*Rubbish?*'

'Take me—back to the library,' he gasped.

She reached for the PsiMap in her mind, but then she paused. Translocation may be fast, but it placed heavy demands on the body. What would that do to Tren? Had he strength enough to survive the pressure of the journey?

'No good.'

'Take me—'

'You might *die,* Tren.'

'I see you're—determined—to—kill me yourself.' He was struggling to breathe by now, his breath coming in harsh gasps.

'Stop talking and just breathe, idiot.' She removed the cushion and peeled back his shirt. The wound was not large, but it was deep, and blood flowed undiminished. She knew what she had to do, in theory: she must bind the flesh by force of will, mastering Tren's physical functions herself.

It couldn't be that different from mastery of the will over beast kind or other intelligent minds. This was something she could do.

'Depends. Have I—persuaded you?'

'Shut up.'

'And you—tick me off for—playing the hero.'

With a small, inarticulate sound of frustration, Eva stopped his wayward mouth by applying her own to it.

'Now shut up,' she whispered against his lips.

He was silent for three seconds.

'Wish I'd—known that before. If I wanted to— win the lady's favour I just had to—to—'

'Be quiet and let me get on with this?'

'—impale myself on something sharp,' he finished.

She swallowed a despairing laugh. He was right: he probably had saved her life. She would save his in return.

Working tentatively, she made a mental survey of the wound. The shape and extent of it was easy to grasp; she saw what needed to be done. But the means evaded her. She brought her will to bear upon it, alternately trying to coax and then order the body to re-knit the flesh, mend the muscle and skin and renew itself. It was like trying to relay information to someone who stood fifty feet away, with a howling gale in between. Her communications failed; Tren's body would not react.

Perhaps she had misunderstood the process and was going about it in the wrong way. Frantic now, she tried to think her way back through the task fast and efficiently. Tren had finally stopped talking, but that was probably because he now lacked the energy: his eyes had closed and his breathing was shallow and thin.

Panic destroyed all her attempts at clarity.

'All right, you win,' she muttered. Gathering him close, she accessed the PsiMap and found Limbane's reading room. Calling Rikbeek back, she barely waited for him to grab on to her clothes before she made the jump, back through the aether to the Library.

Limbane was thinking.

It was always a long and involved process, when he did it properly. *Thinking* involved not just musings or idly putting a few things together. *Thinking* meant locking his door, settling into his chair, closing his eyes and committing himself to a prolonged examination of the relevant sequences of facts, circumstances, events and occurrences until he began to see the patterns that lay behind them.

He had a considerable mess to deal with. Facts and events crowded upon one another, tangled up with occurrences that may be mere happenstance or may be significant. Too many characters now littered the gaming board; he was beginning to lose track. They must be set straight so that all may proceed in order.

The biggest problem, as usual, was Krays. That man had been trouble since before he'd betrayed the Library and set up a rival organisation. His band had always been too small to truly challenge the power of the Library, but he had been a persistent irritation ever since Limbane had become the Lokantor, the Library's director and leader.

What was Krays up to? Limbane reviewed the facts. He knew that his so-called fellow Lokantor had gone to some trouble to find, recruit and train some of the partial Lokants of this Cluster of worlds. Not all of them, but apparently enough to serve his purposes. From Devary Kant, he knew that Krays had taken control of at least one information agency, the one that lay concealed behind the university of magical history in Draetre. He may well have taken over others besides. That meant he was looking for information, presumably magical in nature.

Then there was the whurthag device he himself had encountered at Sulayn Phay. The purpose of that machine evaded his understanding. Was it really a more effective guard than any of his earlier creations? It would be a fearsome defence against human intruders, but that was precisely what the island was without. None but Lokants had any real chance of infiltrating that place, and they had disabled the thing (albeit with a little trouble. Melle would survive, and Rael's leg had been saved, but he was still toweringly angry with Krays for those injuries).

If he had built one unnatural hybrid of a device, what else might he be building? And why? Certainly not just to guard a few captives.

And so to consider the matter of the prisoners. Krays had gone to considerable trouble to find out who the hereditary draykoni were, and had subsequently abducted two out of the three. He had tried hard to get hold of the third as well. Why? He didn't buy the idea that they were to be used to locate draykon graves. Krays was inventive; if he sought more bone, he or his associates would long since have developed some device to do that for him.

Mr Kant's presence at the island had surprised him. According to the agent's own account, he had been confined there as punishment for snooping.

385

That made sense, as far as it went. The absence of Orillin Vanse was more troubling. Kant's presence of mind in petitioning Ynara Sanfaer may have saved the boy much, but where then was he? Kant didn't know, and by Andraly's account Ynara herself lay in a coma in Waeverleyne. Had she got to Vanse in time, or had Krays taken him?

And he had no report from his own personal complications, Mr Warvel and her ladyship. It was many long years since he had consented to the training of a partial; as yet he was unsure whether it would prove a benefit or a liability. He'd been reluctant to confer full Library access upon Evastany Glostrum until he had taken her measure. Was she an asset or a dead weight? That remained to be seen. He hoped she would have something useful to report when she returned.

Limbane was well used to the workings of his Library. Time passed here, but so slowly it was almost the same as a complete severance from the time flow. He was used to waiting in the Library while worlds rushed through their cycles outside. But for the first time in his life he was becoming impatient. He had the foreboding sense that Krays's antics meant more, now, than they often had in the past. Ordinary rivalry he was used to, but all of this amounted to something worse, he was sure of it. Why hadn't his rival made more effort to stop them when he'd found them at Sulayn Phay?

That prompted the seed of an idea. He waited, on the edge of a realisation, as his aged and deeply knowledgeable brain worked its way through this mass of information.

The air trembled, breaking his concentration. That whisper of disturbance meant one thing: somebody was translocating. Not a breach of security, this: it was a normal translocation procedure, which meant the traveller was someone whose implanted translocator device contained fully updated access codes.

All his Lokants knew never to translocate into his personal reading room except with explicit permission granted. This, then, must be their new recruit.

It was about time.

Another instant, and she appeared. But not as he expected. A mass of tangled limbs fell onto the floor of his reading-room, two bodies clinging to one another. One was his new partial. The other, he swiftly realised, was Warvel. He saw red, smelt blood on the air.

He was on his feet immediately.

'Tell me what happened,' he barked. 'Quickly.'

'Griel happened,' replied her ladyship. 'I'll tell you everything, but first, *fix him.*'

Limbane dropped to his knees beside Warvel's inert body.

'Get Andraly in here.'

Some time and a deal of mess later, Limbane was restored to his reading-room, though he was obliged to invite her ladyship to join him. His newest recruit sat slumped in a chair opposite, her face white with exhaustion and worry. Her clothes were stained with blood now dried to an ominous dark red colour.

In spite of her drawn, dishevelled state, the woman

was still exquisite. His race in general were blessed with fine symmetry of feature, and many would have been called beautiful by human standards. But this lady's mixed heritage gave her an unusual softness that elevated her looks still higher.

No wonder the foolish young sorcerer was transfixed by her.

'You may talk,' he informed her. 'You promised to tell me everything, mind.'

She nodded, but she did not commence speaking. He waited somewhat impatiently. This was information he needed *now*. He sympathised with her over the boy's fate, but this was important.

He had given her a cup of cayluch, a drink she professed to enjoy. The steaming mug sat by her side, untouched, as she stared somewhere into the middle distance and said nothing.

'Evastany,' he said. 'Now, please.'

Her eyes snapped back to focus on his face. 'Sorry,' she said with a slight cough. After clearing her throat a second time, she began.

Her narration took some time and was given with considerable detail, in spite of her distracted state. He did not interrupt, letting her relate all of her findings and experiences in whatever manner she chose. When she fell silent at last, he fell into a brief meditation.

Rousing himself after some minutes, he said, 'The use of the partial, Griel.'

She started a little, as if she'd fallen into a daze herself. 'What of it?'

'The substitution of original parts for draykoni matter is interesting. It is a pity Krays did not share his intentions with Mr Ruart.'

'I have a theory,' replied the lady in the dull tone of tiredness.

'Oh?'

'Have you ever held or worn any draykon bone yourself?'

His lips twitched. Gracious, what a question. She clearly had no idea. 'Yes,' was all he said in reply.

'How does it make you feel?'

Limbane shrugged. 'I recall no special experiences.'

She smiled briefly. 'Thought so. That is not true for humans. Those with draykon blood are benefited by wearing a piece of bone, as it will amplify their natural magical capabilities. But even those without draykon blood can feel some effects—can make some use, even if minimal, of latent draykon energies contained in draykon matter. You said that yourself. They went to war over it.'

'Yes, yes,' he agreed. 'All this I know.'

'Yes, well. I notice that draykoni magics and Lokant abilities bear some similarities. Draykoni may regenerate themselves or others, as Lokants may heal. The methods are different but the effects are almost the same. Likewise summoning and domination via the will: on beasts the outcome is similar.' Her ladyship leaned forward, apparently woken from her semi-stupor. 'In a few cases the two can be combined. Ana, for example, wields both the power of summoning *and* that of domination. It makes her very formidable when it comes to beast mastery. I am the same myself. If you can combine the two types of magics, then, the results can be powerful indeed.

'But so far the only way to do that is via inter-breeding. I believe your friend Krays is looking for another way.'

Limbane froze. He saw it all in an instant. Krays had always sought power, always more and more power. He sought to escalate his organisation's rivalry with the original Library into serious competition. If an opportunity such as this was offered him, he would grab it with both hands.

A sickening thought occurred to him. 'That's why he has been looking for the likes of Llandry Sanfaer. From what you have said, I collect that Griel's bone implants were clumsy. They were taken from a draykon grave, that's why, and refashioned as best as possible to fit a human frame. If he wishes to leech draykoni magics by literally *embedding* draykoni matter within himself, he would need to find a better source, wouldn't he?'

If possible, her ladyship paled even further. 'Hideous thought. When Llandry took on her draykon form, how much of her biology changed? Was she altered down to the very bone? If she's draykoni in human form—'

'—then her bones are human but probably brimming with the same energies Krays seeks to usurp,' Limbane finished.

She shuddered. He felt a sense of true horror himself. That woman he had taken from Sulayn Phay had not been there merely to locate draykon bone: she had been expected to provide it. Krays would aim to force the change on her in some way, then harvest her bones for installation in himself.

Though a female's anatomy would not be the best fit. Krays thought it through again. The boy, Orillin Vanse: it was his physique that would be the better match with Krays. He, then, was intended for the transformation of Krays himself; and Limbane would be willing to bet that the man had two loyal female Lokants lined up to receive the benefit of Llandry's and Avane's bones.

'That explains some of it,' he said out loud. 'But his machinery: what of that.'

He fell back into his thinking haze. The key lay in Krays's motivation. He might be testing the procedures before he applied them to himself, but it was still risky. His goal, then, must be a high one.

The one thing Krays had always wanted, yet never been able to achieve, was mastery over the true and original Library itself. Always unpopular, he had lost the election to Limbane; soon afterwards he had quit the Library and formed his rival group. But it was not enough for him, of course. A mere offshoot of the glorious original was Sulayn Phay; poorly populated, weak, absolutely inferior.

Limbane had always assumed that Krays's goal was to build up Sulayn Phay's strength and significance until it equalled, and subsequently exceeded, the importance of the real Library. What if he was wrong?

What if Krays was aiming to take mastery of the Library itself?

Limbane shot to his feet. Lady Glostrum stared up at him in surprise.

'Things to be done,' he said energetically. 'Llandry Sanfaer must be brought here. She must never fall into Krays's hands. Krays's workshops must be infiltrated and his projects uncovered. And finally, I *must* find that boy.'

'Which boy?' He had evidently lost her ladyship;

she blinked at him in a befuddled state.

'Vanse,' he snapped. 'I'll be needing your help in Ullarn. But for now, rest. I'll return.'

He left, translocating away without waiting for her reply.

CHAPTER TWENTY-EIGHT

Two pale, composed faces, framed in night-black hair spread out over white pillows. Eyes shut, breathing steady and slow. One lay alone in her narrow infirmary bed; upon the torso of the other rested a small bundle of grey fur, curled into a sleeping ball.

Aysun had scarcely looked on any other image in days. He had placed a chair between the two beds in which lay his wife and his daughter. Hour after hour he sat there, gazing first upon Ynara's face and then upon Llandry, so like her mother and yet so different also. The signs he craved never came: no quickening breath announced a wakening from slumber, no flutter of the eyelashes, no slight movement of hands or fingers. They remained still as statues, white as marble.

Pensould sat on the other side of the room, by Llandry's side. He and Aysun hardly spoke; both maintained their dejected vigils in near silence, unable to find anything to say. Pensould had been optimistic for a time, after whatever feat he had pulled using Aysun's own vitality. But when Llandry still didn't wake, his spirits had steadily sunk further and further.

Aysun still found the draykon-man unnerving, and he certainly didn't know what to make of his relationship with Llandry (of whatever nature it was). But his devoted guardianship over her warmed Aysun's heart. Whatever he might be, his affection for little Llan was obviously sincere.

Aysun shifted in his chair, his muscles cramping with inaction. He was neglecting his duties, he knew. In the aftermath of the draykon attack, there had been calls for new weapons to be developed, for Glinnery possessed nothing with which to respond to the attacks of those vast, airborne beasts. As a leading engineer of the realm, he had a clear duty to participate in the project.

He did try. Every day he left the infirmary for a few hours and turned his thoughts to the problem of city defence. But it was hard; all he could see was those two still faces, their beloved features as much dead as alive. Who could think of war machines under such circumstances? Not him. He was not equal to it.

Sigwide woke and stood up, stretching his short legs. Seeing Aysun, he gave the tiniest wag of his stubby tail, then wobbled over to install himself in the big man's lap. Aysun petted him abstractedly. The orting's fur was dense and matted; he hadn't been grooming himself properly. He hadn't been eating properly either, though he was regularly provided with food. Sigwide had always been so in tune with Llan; Aysun was afraid that this listlessness was the product of that bond. Was Sigwide already mourning?

The door clattered open and Rufin almost fell through it, his enormous feet tripping over the mat. He cursed loudly, barely managing to catch himself before he fell headlong to the floor. A mug he'd been carrying dropped and shattered.

Aysun sighed. If even Rufin's regular clumsiness couldn't wake his ladies, they were heavily asleep indeed.

'Still moping?' Rufin thrust the surviving mug at Aysun, scowling. The cup contained strong-smelling soup, the scent of which turned Aysun's stomach immediately.

'I am keeping them company,' he replied stiffly. 'Any moment there could be a change. Someone should stay with them.'

Rufin snorted. 'Has it escaped your notice that we're under attack? You're needed out there. Those creatures aren't done yet.'

Aysun shrugged. 'I'm not the only engineer in Glinnery.'

'Luckily for us, you're the only useless one.'

Aysun said nothing. Rufin couldn't rile him, not now.

'You going to drink that?'

'Can't. Sorry.'

Rufin held out his hand. 'Give it back then.' The gunman reclaimed the mug. He offered it perfunctorily to Pensould, who mutely shook his head. With a shrug, Rufin drained the contents in two gulps.

'Feels like a mausoleum in here,' he muttered. He turned to leave.

Blocking his exit was a tall gentleman, elderly, with

a full head of white hair and a commanding air. Aysun frowned, puzzled. He hadn't heard the man come in.

'Llandry Sanfaer,' said the newcomer. 'Which one is her?'

Aysun stood up and advanced. 'Who are you? What do you want with her?'

The man merely brushed him aside. 'Never mind that. She must be removed from here, with the utmost haste. Her well-being depends on it. Which one is Miss Sanfaer?' He stared into both sleeping faces for an instant or two in turn, then pointed to Llandry. 'This one, I conclude?'

'Back off,' Aysun said, his fits clenching in anger. 'You're not taking her anywhere.'

Pensould spoke, for the first time in some hours. 'It's all right. I know this man. He intends no harm.'

Aysun's brows snapped together. 'What? Then who is he?'

A small, hopeless smile crossed Pensould's strange face. 'It would take far too long to explain.'

'And I decline to make any more explanations at present; there's been enough of that,' said the impatient and autocratic old man. 'Pensould, you'll help me.'

'You will not!' Aysun cried as Pensould rose from his chair. 'Llandry is safe here, with her family. She stays.'

The old man rounded on him. 'She isn't safe anywhere, you fool. Do you think you can protect her? You are far out of your depth, whoever you are. The only way she has a chance is if I take her. She must not be left in this Cluster of worlds.'

Aysun stared, dumbfounded, as the man turned

his back on him and, with Pensould's help, picked up Llandry's sleeping form. Sigwide whimpered at his feet: Pensould stooped to collect him, too.

'Drop the young lady,' came Rufin's command. He had drawn a pistol—where he had hidden it Aysun couldn't guess, as his weapons were always stripped from him in the infirmary. The pistol was aimed at the old man's head.

'Gently,' Aysun amended.

The old man rolled his eyes and let out a sigh of pure exasperation. 'Don't be ridiculous. *You* drop it. Now.' He stared the gunman down, his blue eyes cold as winter.

To Aysun's complete amazement, Rufin let the pistol fall.

'Good. Any other objections?' His cold stare turned on Aysun, whose indignation and anger melted away like butter in the sun. He had tensed himself, ready to rush the man. Now his muscles relaxed, all desire to attack withering away.

'I gather you have some interest in this young lady's condition, so Pensould shall keep you informed,' the man continued, relentless. 'But with me she must indeed go. I assure you, it is the only way to preserve her life.'

Aysun's lips fought to form words, some silent command working to keep him quiet. 'Wh-where are you taking her?'

'Somewhere Other,' was all the reply he received.

'Then I go as well.'

'That is not acceptable.'

'Just try to leave without me,' Aysun growled.

The man simply ignored him.

'Pensould?' Aysun turned to the draykon-man, placing all his hopes of an explanation in the goodwill of his daughter's admirer.

'All will be well, I swear it,' Pensould replied.

Aysun grunted. Remembering the voice-box, he groped in his pocket for it and tossed it to Pensould.

'You *will* keep me informed,' he growled. 'If anything happens to her, it's you I'm coming after.'

Pensould merely nodded, storing the device in his own garments.

'If that's everything, it's past time to go,' said the white-haired man, his tone dripping impatience. On Pensould's nod, he secured his grip on Llandry and clamped a hand around Pensould's arm.

Released from the old man's stare, Aysun regained his will. He prepared himself, standing ready to follow the group as they left. He couldn't be kept from accompanying Llandry: he refused to be left behind.

But then they vanished.

Aysun stood dumb with shock. It was a true vanishment: there one instant, gone the next, while he had been watching them closely enough to detect any trickery.

'Huh?' Rufin rushed past him to stand where the three had been only moments before. He walked in circles, sweeping his hands through the air, as if to discover by that means some manner of trickery.

Finding nothing, he stared incredulously at Aysun.

Unease spread rapidly through Aysun's body, choking his breath and sending his stomach clenching with trepidation.

Whatever his Llandry had got herself into, it was clearly far beyond his power to comprehend.

'You'd better keep her safe,' he muttered to the empty air, trying desperately to trust in Pensould's confident endorsement of the man.

Taking up his seat by Ynara's side, Aysun took his wife's hand. Still cold; still senseless.

Cold metal touched his temple, startling him. Rufin stood over him, his pistol retrieved and once more in his hand. The barrel of it was pointed at Aysun's head.

Aysun slowly lifted his brows at his friend.

'Can't let you waste any more time sitting here like a gormless idiot,' Rufin explained. 'I mean, yeah, that was freaky beyond all reason, but you're needed.'

'Ynara needs me,' he replied.

Rufin waved the pistol at her. 'How? She doesn't even know you're there. And what are you going to do to protect her when the next attack comes?'

'Put it down, Ruf. You're not going to shoot me.'

Rufin hesitated, then lowered the weapon. 'Reckon you're right, though you deserve it.'

His old friend was right, of course. Much as it pained him to be torn from Ynara's side, he ought to do more. He must do more.

But he wouldn't leave Ynara unattended either.

'One hour, Rufin. Give me one more hour and I'll join you.'

Rufin grinned. 'I'll be back if you don't.' He swaggered off.

Leaving a final kiss on his wife's brow, Aysun stood and left the infirmary room. He needed to find Nyra. If his father's house in the Uppers was safe enough for Orillin Vanse, it was safe enough for Ynara, too. He would ask Nyra to take them both up to Rheas's house. He knew he could rely on her and Mags to tend to his wife and keep her company, and his father and Eyas would protect them all.

Or they'd better.

If the attack came as Rufin predicted, he could bear it better knowing that his wife—and, he hoped, his daughter—were out of harm's way.

Eva paced outside the door to Tren's room, afraid to go inside. He was alive, so Limbane had said, but his condition was not good. It had not been easy to save him. He had lost a great deal of blood, and while Limbane's healing skills were beyond anything seen in her own world, that was one problem he could not resolve.

It was her fault that Tren had been so severely weakened. She should have listened to him to begin with, for he'd been right, entirely right. She was incapable of healing him. The journey to the Library had been hard on him, but if she had done it right away, he would probably have been in better shape for it.

Now she feared the worst. Tren's wound had been closed and healed, but he was still desperately weak, and he would have to rely largely on his own strength to recover. How strong was he? He was young and fit, true, but would it be enough?

Steeling herself, she quietly opened the door and went in. The room was almost completely dark, though enough faint light was present to allow her sensitive night-eyes to make out the details of Tren's form, lying still in a large bed in the centre of the room. Approaching with care—she didn't wish to wake him if he was sleeping—she surveyed his face.

So pale, and his eyes smudged with shadows. But he breathed still, and his face lacked the pallor of death.

'You're too late,' he murmured without opening his eyes. 'For I am dead and gone, slain by wayward pride.'

Eva flinched and stepped back. She knew she deserved some recrimination, but it still hurt to hear it.

'Tren, I'm sorry. I feared for the journey—'

He opened his eyes and looked at her gravely. 'That might be true, but is it also fair to say you were competing with yourself? I know how you dislike to fail.'

She took a pained breath. 'Yes,' she said shakily. 'I really thought that I could make it work, somehow. I was determined.'

He gazed at her for a moment longer with that detestable gravity. Then, suddenly, he grinned.

'You did it because you care. Aren't I right? Admit it.'

Relief weakened her knees. She pulled up a chair and sat at his side.

'Perfectly true: it cannot be denied.' She took his hand and folded it in her own.

'You'll have to make it up to me,' he said, returning the pressure of her fingers.

'How would you like me to atone?'

He made a show of thinking it over.

'I think I have earned a kiss,' he decided. 'I wasn't in a position to properly enjoy the last one.'

Eva complied, thoroughly and without hesitation.

'Curse my weakness,' he said somewhat later. 'Now would be the perfect time to—well, to—'

She opened her eyes very wide. 'To what?'

'Uh. Never mind,' he said lamely.

'Later,' she promised. 'You'd better work on getting well, as fast as you can.'

His eyes widened. 'I wasn't—I mean I *was* serious but not—I didn't think you'd—um.' He blinked a few times. 'Why the change of heart?'

She countered that with another question. 'Why did you get yourself stabbed?'

He tried to shrug but it obviously hurt somewhere, for he winced in pain. 'If one of us is going to get stabbed, it had better be me.'

'Why?'

'Because your being hurt is not an option.'

She smiled at that. 'I find it hard to believe that even I could mesmerise someone into risking their life for me. It occurred to me that maybe you weren't talking complete nonsense after all.'

'Hey. I know my own mind, *my lady*. You're insulting.'

'Of course you do.' She adopted the soothing tone that adults use to reassure children.

Tren scowled at her. 'I can't think *why* I love you. You're perfectly horrible.'

'I know,' she said placidly. Abandoning her chair, she lay down next to him. They lay in silence for a while as Tren gathered his strength and regained his breath.

'So,' he murmured eventually. 'What are we doing next?'

'You're getting well,' she replied. 'Then we're going with Limbane to Ullarn. He's after Krays's workshops.'

'Right. Excellent. But what I actually meant was, what are *we* doing next? Is it too soon to think about children? Because I think our babies would be too gorgeous for this world.'

She laughed at that and kissed him. 'Ask me again when you're well.'

EPILOGUE

A week or so after the removal of his wife from Glinnery, Aysun Sanfaer stood at the top of the tallest glissenwol tree in Waeverleyne. A structure had been hastily erected, large and sturdy enough to accommodate the considerable bulk and weight of his new war machines.

The monstrous contraptions were wrought from steel and pale tayn wood brought from Irbel. It was the hardest, strongest wood available and it needed to be, for these machines were built to hurl the heaviest of missiles at intruders from the air.

One was equipped to hurl rocks. Ammunition was being brought up by pulley; a stack of at least thirty waited to be loaded into the machine.

The other was fitted to hurl something more deadly. Globes of hide rested, seemingly innocuous, in a great container at the base of the machine. They were designed to break on impact: inside was a chemical concoction that would burst into flame when disturbed, engulfing the enemy in a conflagration.

Or so he hoped.

Similar towers had been erected all over Glinnery. Every major settlement had at least three towers, and many of the smaller ones now had one at their defence. But they were not working fast enough. Aysun knew that the delay was far from promising. While they worked feverishly to prepare their defences, the draykoni were doubtless working to improve their numbers. It was impossible to guess how many would eventually come at them: the best they could do was work fast and hard and hope for the best.

It wasn't Aysun's favourite approach.

This tower was almost complete. Two machines stood ready, with full complements of ammunition. More would be delivered when they became available; since the Council of Elders had converted many of the realm's businesses to the production of weapons, war machines and ammo, Aysun hoped those deliveries would be arriving soon.

In the meantime, there were more towers to be built. He began, wearily, to clamber down the side of the tree. He hoped to be able to construct elevators at each of these defence points, but at present the engineers lacked either time or resources. A mere ladder had been built instead, wide enough for two to ascend or descend at once but shockingly vulnerable to attack. It was yet another important item on his agenda.

'Ah, sir?' a voice said, halting his progress. He looked up at the man questioningly, but the engineer wasn't looking at him. He was staring out beyond the borders of Waeverleyne, the height of this tree allowing a long view over the horizon.

The younger man jabbed a finger at the skies. 'What does that look like to you?'

Aysun climbed back up the ladder and hauled himself onto the platform. Taking his station by the young engineer's side, he squinted into the sun.

Dark patches of colour blotted the serene beauty of the horizon, rapidly growing in size. As he watched, the foremost of them began to resolve into a definite shape: he saw outstretched wings and long necks and tails.

'Looks like they're here,' he replied, quiet and grim. 'Sound the warning, Ven.'

Every tower had been given an alarm, each fairly simplistic in nature but effective. Ven pulled a lever sharply down and sound blasted out of the clumsy device, shrieking a splitting warning across the buildings of Waeverleyne. Moments later another alarm was sounded, and another. The noise was deafening.

The first draykons were now in clear view. Aysun recognised the dark red beast of whom he'd heard—the one who had led the previous attack. The one who had injured, maybe destroyed, his wife.

She didn't seem to be the leader now. She flew at the side of another draykon, an impossibly large creature with scales of deep green hue flecked with white. This one bore itself with the pride and fury of a monarch.

Behind these two flew draykon after draykon. Aysun estimated that at least twenty were so far visible; more may yet be concealed in the sun's glare.

As the draykon's shrieks competed with the din of the alarms and rocks and fire began to fly, Aysun had barely a moment to feel relief that his wife and daughter were not in the realm.

Then he strode to the nearest of his new war machines. Ven took up a position at the other as soldiers and engineers swarmed up the ladder, ready to man the tower.

'Well,' he said to no one in particular. 'Here we go.'

BY THE SAME AUTHOR

The Draykon Series:

Draykon
Lokant
Orlind

The Malykant Mysteries:

The Rostikov Legacy
The Ivanov Diamond

Made in the
USA
Middletown, DE